THE WILDELINGS

BY THE SAME AUTHOR

Harvesting
Bright Burning Things

THE WILDELINGS

LISA HARDING

BLOOMSBURY PUBLISHING
LONDON • OXFORD • NEW YORK • NEW DELHI • SYDNEY

BLOOMSBURY PUBLISHING
Bloomsbury Publishing Plc
50 Bedford Square, London, WC1B 3DP, UK
Bloomsbury Publishing Ireland Limited,
29 Earlsfort Terrace, Dublin 2, D02 AY28 Ireland

First published in Great Britain 2025

A catalogue record for this book is available from the British Library

ISBN: HB: 978-1-5266-7291-9; TPB: 978-1-5266-7290-2;
EBOOK: 978-1-5266-7289-6; EPDF: 978-1-5266-7288-9

2 4 6 8 10 9 7 5 3 1

Typeset by Integra Software Services Pvt. Ltd.
Printed and bound in Great Britain by Clays Ltd, Elcograf S.p.A

FSC www.fsc.org MIX Paper | Supporting responsible forestry FSC® C018072

LORENZO: Descend, for you must be my torchbearer.
JESSICA: What, must I hold a candle to my shames?
They in themselves, good sooth, are too too light.
Why, 'tis an office of discovery, love.
And I should be obscured.

William Shakespeare, *Merchant of Venice*

Things without all remedy should be without regard: what's done is done.

William Shakespeare, *Macbeth*

PROLOGUE

'What brings you here, Jessica?'

I regard the woman opposite. There is a stillness in her that feeds my need to fidget. I take my sunglasses off my head, twirling them. Cheap Gucci rip-offs. The lie is obvious, to anyone who could bother to look closely.

The woman coughs. I shift in my seat, sit on my hands, and look around me. Disappointing: this sterile room with its monochrome palette and chrome fixtures – but then, everything is disappointing to me these days. I arrange my face into the same neutral mask she wears. *Why have I come…?* I am joyless, incapable of an orgasm, of any pleasure. 'Dead inside,' my husband said of me, more than once. He was right. Except for that one sharp stab of emotion last week, as the curtain fell on the latest Mark Whitman play, and the audience was on its feet. Then there was a violent jolt and a flooding of jumbled, jarring feelings, and memories.

'My husband left me.'

It seems the logical thing to say, a reasonable explanation for why I've come now, decades after the event that shaped me, shaped us all.

'That must be very hard,' she says.

I look out the window. Not much of a view: a brick wall almost touches the windowpane, suffocated by lichen or mould. I imagine there are insects hidden in there, shiny and indestructible, the kind that thrive in the dark.

'But not surprising,' I answer, deadpan. I am used to people cutting out on me, and me on them. I am my father's daughter after all.

Dr Collins – 'call me Sophie' – continues looking at me, this time with a flicker of curiosity that she cannot hide. 'Perhaps you are feeling numb? Detachment is often a response to emotional flooding…'

Disappointing. What did I expect by coming here today? I am too long shaped by my history and replaying of said history to be able to transform into something new. Do I think that I deserve another outcome, that I *deserve* happiness, a fresh start? My eyes take in the high cornicing, the only feature of the building's Georgian past that hasn't been erased, and I am transported to those grand rooms, whispering their seductive promises. Wilde College.

I am back there in my first year, those nine defining months, my gestation, *our* gestation. The Unholy Quintet: Mark, Linda, Jonathan, Jacques and me. I can hear Mark's voice, beguiling us, snide and scathing and seductive all at once. He would have scoffed at all that alliteration. Overkill. But he inspired it. Just as he inspired viciousness: 'Writer, director and creator of small, crazed worlds of fierce people taking their pain out on each other' is how one critic described his body of work. The accuracy of this was breathtaking.

I have often wondered what kind of frequency Mark vibrated at, and whether there was any choice involved in the fact that we stayed in his orbit. Was there a sensor on our young, febrile bodies that only we could sense, signalling to each other, triggering an unconscious, irresistible charge?

Dr Collins's voice intrudes: 'Where have you gone to, Jessica?'

I look at this woman opposite me and think that her bland demeanour, and no doubt bland life, means she could not even conceive of the depth of my depravity.

'Perhaps you could try writing about your marriage?'

How can I tell her I have no interest in dissecting the failure of my relationship? I feel only respect for my husband that he finally left, and relief that I can go back to being alone. Finally, he saw the actress that I am. I am not built for intimacy, or love. Or friendship.

I think of Linda and my throat closes in. Will she see the play? The thought of that is accompanied by a series of clicks inside, the sound of internal doors locking. And the others? Will they go? Will his rendition of that night chime with theirs?

The good doctor asks me questions: mother, father, children, career, mood on a scale of one to ten. Dead, no contact, none, none to speak of, and minus figures. Negative, negative, negative. Time passes to no good effect. My mind keeps looping back to the play, and to the past.

Alack what heinous sin is it in me. To be ashamed to be my father's child! I hear Mark's affected voice, coaching me in my namesake's role in his new 'tantalisingly modern and sexy take on *The Merchant of Venice*' (an early sycophantic critic's response).

As he simultaneously stole any vestige of goodness left in me, he swore that I would forever be his leading lady. And he professed to live by the truth. *Without honesty what is there?* Fiction.

Dr Collins's voice brings me back to the now. 'Start by jotting any memories down.'

To dare is to lose one's footing momentarily. I see my friend's dazed face, distorted in a kind of ecstatic fear as she swayed on the tightrope branch before her flight of peril.

This was Mark Whitman's style: surreal and horrifying, heart-stopping in its execution. His trademark: never make it easy on the audience. Let them suffer on. Just like his creations.

No one has spoken out. So far.

'Start at the beginning.' Dr Collins's voice trails after me as I leave the room.

The Beginning

1

My heart – it was hijacked. The first time I met her. I desperately wanted to yank her scrawny ponytail as much as I wanted to hug her to the point of suffocation. Her breath was sweet and sour. The teacher with the extra chin was looking at me, her neck pouch wobbling as if in warning. I sat on my hands.

'You are the prettiest girl here,' the new girl said, as she sat at the desk next to mine, fastidiously arranging her stubby pencils in order. She had a small pale face, splotched with freckles. Her clothes smelled of damp and antiseptic. Her eyes were grey or green, depending on the way the light hit them, and the weather within her. The rubbers at the tops of her pencils were gnawed away.

'And you are the most *pathetic*,' I said back to her, a word I did not fully understand, but had heard at home often and liked to say. All those hard consonants, plosives.

She smiled in response to my insult, as if the sun itself were shining down on her, only her. I shifted my chair away and angled my body so that she got my back. I was used to being a lone cat. She moved her table closer to me, metal legs dragging on the concrete floor. I felt her affix herself to me.

'What's your name?'

'Jessica,' I said, still facing away from her.

'You look like a Jessica.'

I thought that was really stupid, since I'd never met another Jessica and I could bet she hadn't either. It was an actress's name, a blonde

American one who won all the awards. I was the only Irish girl I knew who ever really fitted the name. My mother had a vivid imagination, and aspirations, ideas above her station, apparently. I imagined her as queenly, beautiful.

'I wish I were adopted,' Linda said.

The teacher put her finger to her lips. 'Ciúnas.'

'Who would adopt you?' I whispered, twisting my neck to look at her.

She nodded, as if she expected it of me: the retort.

'My name is Linda.' She sighed. 'I would like a different one.'

'I don't blame you. It's common.'

She was inviting meanness, goading me.

'Your eyes are the colour of the sea,' she said, leaning in to stare at me. 'On a sunshiny day.'

'Yours are murky.' Her eyes looked mottled, washed out, in the harsh glare of the fluorescent strip lighting above our heads. They looked as if they had dimmed, having seen too much already.

I followed her gaze out the window. We both watched the fat rain drops slide down the glass.

'The sky is crying again,' she said. 'God's own tears.'

'Well, duh, this is Dublin,' I said, being clever in the way my step-mother was with my father when she was feeling insecure, which was most of the time before he left.

Dad used to tell me every day how smart I was, how beautiful, how special. I was his number one girl, his little princess with the golden skin and hair. *So, how could he have left?*

'Where do you come from that you don't know that it always rains here?' I said to the new girl, attempting to sharpen my tongue on her – as I was doing daily at home with my stepmother. *Imitation is the sincerest form of flattery, Father.*

'I come from outer space,' she said. Her face was deadly serious, then she stuck her tongue out at me, its tip narrowed, pointed like an arrow. My heart skipped a beat. She *was* a peculiar little alien.

The teacher, who was scratching something unintelligible in chalk on the blackboard, shook her head at us, her pelican pouch flapping. I grinned, a wide, practised, dazzling smile, emphasising my one sweet, delicious dimple that my father had adored. After we practised our times tables, for which I had no natural aptitude – though I had what it took to be top of the class, stubbornness and a pathologically competitive streak – it was time for lunch.

When I opened my lunchbox, it was bursting with goodies: a freshly baked fairy cake, a mini Mars bar, a packet of Rancheros (smoky bacon flavour), a crunchy green apple and a cheddar mayo sandwich. Linda had a plastic bag with white bread sandwiches, which looked dry and stale. I offered her half my fairy bun. She shook her head in mortification, her cheeks flaming.

That evening I went home to my stepmother, threw my arms around her neck and said, 'Thank you, thank you, you're the best', which made her suspicious and delighted in equal measure.

'I have a new best friend.'

'That's nice, dear,' she said, looking away, and in her tone I detected a note of jealousy. Something I had felt from her when Dad had been around, giving me too much attention. Since he left, I was her only focus.

Poor old Sue. A sweet-nothing I had inherited from my father.

2

'Want to come back to my house after school?' Linda asked a week after we first met. I saw a flicker of fear cross her face as soon as the words left her mouth, which made me determined to go. I had never been invited to anyone else's house, except to Jimmy O'Mahony's birthday party the previous year, but that didn't count as his mother insisted on inviting the whole class. Mrs O'Mahony remembered the *wound* of being rejected in school as if it were yesterday and she would not leave one child off the list, she confided in my stepmother at the school gates. Sue went cross-eyed when she told me this. *My God, someone should tell that woman to get over herself. Some of us have real problems.*

'I have to ask my stepmother,' I said to Linda.

'Are *you* adopted?'

I sighed, exaggeratedly, as I'd heard Sue do many times when my father said something she deemed to be stupid.

'Are you that dumb?' I was quite the little impersonator.

Linda's house was in the same suburban estate as mine, within walking distance of school and each other's homes. I told Sue that Linda's mother would be bringing us home, even though Linda had already told me she wouldn't be. Her mother wasn't well; she was never well. We pretended to follow one of the other mothers out through the school gates, blending in with the other kids. Linda told me she did this every day. She rose in my estimation, momentarily.

On the walk we threw shiny conkers at each other. Well, I threw them, and Linda ducked and laughed. When we arrived at her front gate she froze for a minute. Her awkwardness delighted and provoked me, even as I told myself she was my first and only best friend.

At first glance our houses looked the same: identikit white boxes, cheap brown shiny door dead centre, single-paned aluminium windows either side. But outside ours there were stray cats luxuriating on sun-warmed patches of gravel and window boxes with cheerful flowers, no matter the season. Sue swore that any day now she would paint our front door a fiery shade of fuchsia. We would mark ourselves out as different from these other suburban, stifled lives. (Didn't she know we were already *marked*?) I regarded Linda's home, huddled in its own shade, with cracked and peeling paint, and scraggy weeds pushing through the gravel driveway. I watched her tip up onto the balls of her feet to be able to put the key in the lock. Her movements were stiff and slow, as if she were fighting against an invisible force.

Inside, the thick brown curtains were drawn. It was colder in here than outside. 'Hi Mam,' Linda called to a figure lying in the half-dark. I followed her into the front room, with its swirling-patterned dun carpet, where her mother lay on the couch, brittle, beaky, bundled in a tartan blanket, staring at a TV, artificial light flickering across her grey face, sudden bursts of it animating her briefly. She barely noticed us, except to flick us away with her wrist if we crossed her field of vision. We were irritating flies. You could smell something rank underneath the stench of Dettol disinfectant, which, Linda said, her mother liked to use in her baths. Linda held her breath as she tiptoed past her into the kitchen, where she prepared a snack of cream crackers and cream cheese. The cheese had a layer of green mulch on top, which she scraped off without comment. She shouted into the living room, 'Mam. Do you want crackers and cheese?' She arranged the food in a neat circle around the edges of the plate and walked carefully back into the living room. I watched from the door as her mother accepted the food and bit into a cracker without breaking her trance with the TV. She spat it out, said nothing. Linda came back into the kitchen, put her arms around me and hugged me tight against her bony body. We felt conjoined. I thought my heart might fly out of my ribcage.

An unspoken pact was made that day. I would be her sister, her protector, her saviour.

The TV volume increased, and mumbling, sighing, shouting, crying leaked into the air around us.

The following day we went back to my house, which, though marked by my father's absence, was filled with my stepmother's high laughter and her penchant for pink, for scented vanilla candles, fluffed-up Laura Ashley cushions and sunshine pop or high sentimental music: opera, rhythm and blues, maudlin musical numbers. When she was in an up-mood she'd play Abba, her favourite, 'Waterloo', over and over on a loop. Linda's eyes were round and shining, taking it all in, as if she had fallen into a world of technicolour having known only leached shades of brown until now. Sue took her on, as one of her stray cats.

'Whatever you like, little ones,' she said, as she fed us an after-school snack of 'Nutella on toast, or ketchup on pizza, or peanut butter on Weetabix, or anything at all that takes your fancy'. Linda was overwhelmed by all the choice and couldn't decide. Sue handed her warm toast dripping with nutty chocolate spread.

'Here, eat up, sweet-cheeks. You are starved… Of it all.'

Linda chewed slowly, watching Sue as if she were a character in one of her mother's soap operas. I reached under the table and pinched her for the first time. *Mine.* It made her squirm and smile.

'Won't your mother worry where you are?' Sue asked when Linda came to our house for the fourth time in a row.

Linda shook her head, terrified that she might be told she couldn't come any more. 'She's happy that I'm here.'

'Happy to be rid of you,' I said.

'That's a terrible thing to say to your friend,' Sue said.

'It's true,' Linda said.

'Linda's mother doesn't like being a mother,' I said.

Sue rubbed her heart in a circular motion, as if it hurt to look at Linda. 'Did she say that to you?'

Linda started to babble, saying that her mother had told her she was a mistake and once it happened, she was stuck with a screaming baby in suburbia with a man she couldn't stand. The way she said 'suburbia' suggested she didn't know what it meant exactly – she overemphasised its evilness making it sound like a kind of purgatory, or hell.

'I was a hole in a condom.' She sounded even more puzzled.

'Jesus, someone should report that woman,' Sue said. 'You know that means you are a miracle.' She left the room, as if on a mission.

'What's a condom?' Linda asked me.

'Something *filthy*,' I said, having no clue.

*

'Did your stepmother report Linda's mother?' Dr Collins asks.

I have come back to this monochrome room.

I snort rudely, not meaning to. 'And say what, exactly? This was a time when women were prescribed Valium instead of contraception, and risky affairs with next-door neighbours were embarked on to feel alive. A time of high-risk trips to England for unlicensed abortions, or equally high-risk shotgun weddings; a time of cheap table wine at lunchtime, of two homegrown channels and golf on a Sunday, and page-three pneumatic bare-breasted models in the Sunday newspaper; a time before the drug of social media could reorganise the deadly present into a bright shiny package of reconstructed truths. We were the middle classes, in suburbia, in Dublin, in the seventies; in place of flower power and free love, we were controlled and suffocated.'

'By the church?' Dr Collins asks, although she knows the answer.

I am surprised by my soliloquy. I hadn't known I'd felt this strongly, about any of it. I hadn't known I had any empathy with my parents' predicament, their poor thwarted lives.

Perhaps this is why I never wanted children of my own.

Or perhaps it's because I knew what I was capable of.

'What about your own home?' Dr Collins asks.
'Great gas,' I say.

*

A favourite game of Sue's was to dress us up in Dad's suits – which she had left hanging in their shared wardrobe and which she would never remove – us tiny, swimming in all that space inside his jacket sleeves and trouser legs. She missed the wild parties they used to throw, where she was 'the Hostess with the Mostess' – Dad's pet name that would have her charging around, doing all the work, basking in his rare approval. He knew what he was doing. Now she was reduced to partying with two little girls, all of Dad's friends having deserted her (she didn't seem to have any of her own). 'You are the cutest little man-dollies,' she'd say, rolling up the trouser cuffs, the sleeves, cinching us in at the waist with her patent belts, smearing pearly pink lipstick on our already pink cheeks and lips. We loved it, this weird, wired expression of her grief. She'd play one of Dad's retro Motown records: the Miracles, the Supremes, the Temptations, Martha and the Vandellas… Our favourite was 'Papa was a Rollin' Stone'. We'd dance wildly, bottoms bobbing, hips gyrating, in syncopation.

We used to make up words like 'boobadazzle' and 'bumdalicious' which would have us falling around the place laughing. Sue told me after Dad had left – 'Good riddance, Mr Pricky Pittance' – that he was a classic victim-martyr-manipulator who played the widow card to get into her heart and her pants. When I asked her about his family, she said, 'Best not know that lot.' I never asked about my dead mother's – I knew enough not to. I didn't miss my mother; I had never known her. I had grandparents of sorts: Sue's mum and dad who visited rarely – but when they did, they made an impression, with their permanently replenished, tinkling glasses with clinking ice cubes and their filthy mouths. 'Look at those tweeny tight-asses,' Grandma said one day as Linda and I turned to leave the room. Even for Sue this was out of bounds. 'They are only children for Chrissakes. You're being obscene.' She didn't want them around us after that.

'What is *obscene*?' Linda asked me in my bedroom that evening.

'Dirty stuff,' I said.

'We are not dirty.'

'Granny and Grandad are.' Then I crinkled my nose. 'You should have a bath.'

'Let's have one together.' Linda loved the soft soapy perfumed bubble baths Sue would prepare for us, which didn't make her skin sting.

'Now you're being obscene,' I said, even though we had bathed many times together before. I liked to be inconsistent.

That night Sue prepared a bath of rose-scented bubbles, singing some nonsense, 'Oh I'm Dame Washalot, dumdedumdedum, shoobee-dooda...' swirling her hand in the water before allowing us to step in and sink down, one at each end of the bathtub. 'Once ... upon ... a ... time ... there were three children, Joe, Beth and Frannie...' she began with a flourish. I rolled my eyes, not *The Magic Faraway Tree* again, she was *obsessed*. I was, at seven, far too old. I entertained myself by scooping handfuls of suds and blowing them at Linda, who didn't reciprocate. 'Now now, none of that, my little angry pixie,' Sue said to me in her most annoying children's TV presenter voice. 'Leave Silky the Fairy alone.' She gestured at Linda, whose pupils had dilated as if she'd entered another realm. I tried to engage her in a game of footsies, but she was lost to me, in enchantment. I kicked her hard on her shins and she barely noticed, but Sue said, 'Now be careful, naughty pixie, or I'll get Dame Slap on to you.' She held her hand in the air as if threatening to hit me, but I knew she never would.

I went cross-eyed and stuck my tongue out and Sue laughed, then continued in her affected sing-song voice: 'It's a really enormous tree... Its top goes right up to the clouds – and, oh Rick, at the top of it is always some strange land...'

Linda looked like she might faint from longing and terror. 'How far up does the tree go?'

'Very, very high up,' I said, studying her face for how deep her fear went.

She wrapped her arms around her body, looking up, up, to some faraway realm.

'A looong way down from the top,' I said. And then, quoting from the book directly: 'Oh Rick...'

Linda picked up on the cue, her voice and body shaking as she said: 'What lands are these...?'

Sue went into full improvisation mode: 'The Land of Birthdays, the Land of Goodies, the Land of Take-What-You-Want and the Land of Do-As-You-Please, the Roundabout Land...'

By the time Linda climbed out of the bath she had blue nails and was covered in goose pimples. Sue leaned in and kissed her on her forehead, saying 'My little Silky', and I thought Linda might dissolve with longing. I had a strange foreboding looking at my shivering friend wrapped in an oversized towel, staring at my stepmother with so much love it was as if there was nothing left inside. She had vacated herself. Sue was right – Linda was *starving* ... for it all. One of Dad's gems came to mind: 'Lethal to go shopping when you're hungry.' I observed my friend with her jutting bones and thought that sometimes my father spoke sense, but I wouldn't allow myself to think of him – he didn't deserve to be thought of.

I pressed on a sore spot on my throat and a different pain replaced that of missing him.

3

Linda and I transitioned from childhood to adolescence together, not seamlessly, but intact. In first class I was cast as Winnie the Pooh, Linda was a tree swaying in the background; in third class I was Alice in Wonderland, she was a wobbling toadstool; in sixth class I was Annie, she was a nameless orphan. And on this went, culminating in me playing Anna in *The King and I* in secondary school while she was one of my servants. After that she opted out of being in the school play, choosing instead to be backstage, from where she actively handed me my props as I stepped into the spotlight, playing Ibsen's disenchanted Hedda Gabler aged sixteen to unanimous acclaim, while she remained watching me from the wings.

For the longest time I thought of her as an appendage and there was never a question in my mind that she wouldn't continue to be.

As I morphed into a moody, mouthy thirteen-year-old, Sue became a menopausal tyrant, jealous of our blossoming beauty and bitter about her waning youth – or this was how I interpreted it through my warped teenage lens. It was as if I were drunk on the rushing hormones that made my body distort itself and bleed. A fury came upon our house, an entity that made things happen: doors slamming, shouting, cursing, eye-rolling, stomping and worse, and most devastating of all, seething silences.

'Fuck off,' I'd say to anyone who would listen, but most especially to Sue.

'How dare you… Have some respect,' she'd reply.

'*Respect* … for *you*, the woman Dad *left*?' I'd snigger, though my chest hurt.

'You ungrateful little –'

'Go on, say it…' I would try to goad her.

She would walk away then.

And then stonewalling.

Linda shrank back into herself. She had that ability to shapeshift, to disappear. I didn't think how difficult that loss of a safe space must have been for her.

I developed intense antipathy towards life and those closest to me. Everything about Linda irritated me, yet I couldn't shake her off, nor did I want to – I did not exist without her. For a while I blamed Sue for everything: my father's desertion, my cramps, my black moods, and most especially for the way she made me feel responsible for her sadness. I can't pinpoint the precise moment I started to feel allergic to her, but that exact pattern has repeated in every intimate relationship since – a period of high adoration, and then a sudden turn, a disgust, ending with an abandoning of the relationship, of each other. It is testament to Sue that she didn't walk out on me; it is testament to her that we are still in each other's lives, however tenuous, however awkward, however much I try to stay away.

*

Dr Collins, Sophie, leans forward a little. 'I am not sure that is the whole picture.'

'Is it ever?' I am channelling my inner teenager.

'I think it would help to find some compassion for your younger self.'

I can find it for Linda but not for me.

'Climb inside that young girl and inhabit her without judgement.'

I have to battle an epic eyeroll.

'As you write, do so with love for everyone, especially yourself.'

'Or?'

'Or you will stay stuck in your frozen present.'

Frozen present. Ms Frigid. He never said it, but he wanted to.

'You need to redress the view you hold of yourself.'

As irredeemably *bad*, I want to say but don't.

'You need to hold the possibility for broadening your perspective.'

'Sometimes I don't know what's real and unreal,' I say.

'Perfectly natural. Go for specific memories. In the details lie the truth…'

*

Some moments stand out more than others, of course. I remember how Sue's evening entertainment swiftly changed from playing dress-up to drinking white wine from the box, the year I turned fourteen, the year my breasts started to show. Blue Nun, I think it was, something loaded with sugar anyway, lethal. One evening, three glasses in, she said, 'If your father could see you now… How ashamed he'd be.' This was a surprisingly cruel thing for Sue to say. She was referring to my new outfit: a green suede mini skirt and crop top that I'd bought in a vintage store in town earlier that day, with pocket money she supplied, which she could barely afford. As I strutted around the kitchen that evening, relishing in my winning-in-the-looks stakes, Sue looked at me as if she were heartbroken. I took Linda's hand and kissed the back of it over and over theatrically – she was in my camp. Sue's face was a picture of dejection. I hated the guilt she made me feel.

*

'Do you see a pattern of triangulation?' Dr Collins interrupts my flow. 'First your dad, Sue and you. Then Linda, Sue and you?'

She is onto something.

'How is that helpful?' I say.

'Insights bring awareness, bring change,' she says.

'I have no intention of being in another relationship.'

'Patterns can change, even deeply entrenched ones.'

I nod along, even though I do not for a moment believe her. But despite my ambivalence, I have to admit there is some power to this jotting-down-words-on-paper stuff.

*

As I tried on my new short, short skirt in the vintage store earlier that day, the shop assistant said I was 'the bomb' and Linda said I was '*dreamydelicious*'. I basked in their approval as I pirouetted in front of a mirror that seemed to sing an ode to my reflection. Alan White, a nondescript boy from our class, nearly fainted when he saw me on the bus on our way home. I locked eyes with this nonentity, this *boy*, who until then had only had eyes for Maeve Whelan. Maeve had at one time tried to befriend Linda, tried to take her away from me. I'd show her.

The details as far as I can remember: his tiny box-room bedroom with its peeling-at-the-corners posters of motorbikes and racing cars and the band Take That, which was so uncool I couldn't believe he hadn't raced upstairs to pull them down before I entered his lair. It stank, of course, of boy sweat and something metallic. I asked him to open the window. I couldn't breathe. He winked and said best not let the neighbours hear. I should've run out the door at that moment, but I had made my mind up and I was obtuse: get rid of the thing. I wasn't wet and his fingers didn't excite me, his tongue even less so. I pulled his head up to mine and said, just stick it in, which he thought was the sexiest thing he had ever heard, apparently, and he thrust inside me and made stupid noises and I was mortified. I remember thinking I couldn't tell the difference between his finger and his dick.

I had no one to talk to about it after as Linda hadn't let any boy near her in that way, and the other girls in our class had, with relish, turned against me since I had become a 'slut, a boyfriend stealer … you'd want to look out for that one'. Prior to this happening I had been someone to admire – from a distance. Being best in class and prettiest and the only one to come from a single *step-parent* family branded me as an oddity, and no one, bar Linda, wanted to associate with that level of weirdness. The rest of my class were all just suburban clones of suburban clones, boring, boring, boring. I didn't tell Sue about losing my virginity because I had discovered she was reading my diaries, and she didn't deserve my secrets. I knew Linda thought

I was awful to do what I had done, although she never directly challenged me on it, or anything else.

Sometimes I really wished she would have. I could have done with something to kick against.

*

Dr Collins, Sophie, talks a lot about 'boundaries' and the lack of them at home. OK, so I should not have been allowed to have peanut butter on Weetabix for supper whenever I liked. And my stepmother should not have raided my diary. But then, Poor Sue. Having met her creepy parents, I can't imagine her home was a safe place for her to express herself and be heard, and say 'NO' when she felt like it.

*

Linda didn't have sex until she was sixteen and by then she'd had a 'boyfriend' for a year, who she'd let hold her hand, *Stupid Stu.* I found everything about him irritating, especially his fake politeness, his kindness with her, his restraint with me. I was in jealous freefall. No matter how much I pressed her she wouldn't talk to me about whether they'd had sex – she walled herself off, went all prudish. 'Come on, I'm your best friend, you can tell me anything, you *should* tell me everything.' She only blushed and shrugged and didn't react when I grabbed her by the wrist and twisted hard, burning her skin, leaving my mark on her.

'You deserve so much more than that pathetic eejit,' I said to her on a day when she was particularly quiet and distant from me. I laughed. She joined in, forcing herself. All I had to do was enact a whispering campaign against Stupid Stu: on his manner of speech, which was faltering and indistinct, particularly in my presence, his dreadful spelling, his pimples, his mouldy breath. She dumped him, despite his protests and declarations of love, and the fact that she genuinely missed him once she did.

After our first failed attempts at relationships, or sex, we both decided to put our studies first – well, I decided for us. Even through my first tumultuous years of menstruating, I managed to find a kind of release through focusing on my schoolwork. My need to be number one was so strong that I couldn't let anyone else steal my place, my very identity as the best student in class.

So, Linda and I agreed, in the short term, that boys were pathetic losers and we needed to focus on our futures – the course of which would be dictated by me.

Sue was humming along to the Supremes' 'You Can't Hurry Love' – she was having a good day. Linda and I were preparing a supper of tuna mayo on toast and cheap white (yellow) wine, a Tesco special offer, in our now faded buttercup yellow kitchen with its Formica surfaces and shiny linoleum flooring, which Sue lamented daily, saying how much she resented my father for abandoning us, to live in poverty like *peasants*. She knew exactly how the kitchen should be: Shaker style with a modern twist. She had cut-outs from *Woman's Way* magazine of her ideal home on the fridge, which I thought was a cruelty to herself. 'One day,' she'd say, 'I'll meet a man who recognises my worth.' I didn't say that that time had passed and perhaps now she should get a job, as I'd be leaving the house soon. But what could she do? She was too old to work as a shop assistant or a receptionist or a waitress and she had no money to retrain. I vowed never to find myself in that position.

Linda and I were in sixth year, close to leaving school, and an equilibrium of sorts had been restored in our home. Sue had adjusted to the changes in us and, to a degree, in her – although I do remember her wrinkles disappearing around this time, her smooth, shiny forehead making her look older. I think it was the contrast with her neck. I wonder now where she got the means to pay for her frozen forehead when she couldn't afford new paint in the kitchen. Back in the day she liked to tell us – in full-on cliché mode – she'd been a raving beauty and she could have had any man. 'But look what I got saddled with,' she'd say, if her mood was bitter. 'Girls, do not give yourselves away too cheaply, or too easily. Always rate yourselves highly. You are prizes worth fighting for.'

That sort of message was not something many girls would have heard from their mothers then, and certainly not something Linda heard from hers. Mrs Cabbott used to tell Linda to 'cover herself up' around her own father. Was she trying to excite him, to incite him, to *inflame* him? Tags such as 'slut', 'whore', 'easy' were tossed about loosely then, attributed by older women to girls who were prone to getting attention – especially if they were seen to be 'flaunting it'. I was determined to prize myself highly, to erase my bargain-basement, tawdry first sexual experience, and replace it with something mind-blowingly beautiful.

'So girls, have you made up your minds where you're going to study yet?' Sue asked.

My hostility towards her had transformed into grudging respect, or maybe even a giddy love, fuelled by our shared taste for the booze.

'We're going to Wilde.'

Linda looked at me. This was the first she'd heard of it. You'd want to have *notions* to go to a place like that. My mind was made up the instant Maeve Whelan (who was back with Alan White, *pathetic*) announced – one lunchtime when we were all buzzing with possibilities – 'Only people who think they're something special would want to go to that Wilde poncey place. It's full of pretentious arty types.'

There was no way I wouldn't be going there.

Sue clapped her hands ecstatically. She couldn't help her love for me, despite my campaign of teenage terror.

'Oh, yes, you must go there, the glamour, the romance of it. I will live vicariously through you girls.'

She did not deserve me – my father's awful daughter.

'It's insanely expensive,' Linda said.

'There are grants available, and some full scholarships.' I had done my research.

'You should go for a scholarship in French. I won't get in there.'

She was right. My grasp of all things *ooh la la* was exemplary.

'I'm not going without you,' I said.

Linda bit down hard on her lower lip, her eyes shining. She was loved.

I wanted to hug her and pinch her in the same instant, but I had stopped branding her the day of our 'joint' sixteenth birthday party, which Sue organised for just the three of us (even though our birthdays were four months apart). In a moment of drunken sentimentality and startling insight, Sue made me promise never to hurt my 'sister' again. *Have you any idea how vulnerable, how damaged…?*

I reached out for Linda and pulled her into a tight embrace. I felt her heart knocking wildly against mine. 'You can always get the points for sociology, or something,' I said.

Sociology was at the time notoriously low in demand.

Sue chimed in, 'I'll help you get that government grant, Linda. I'm excellent at filling in forms and getting free money.' She took the cheap wine, poured it down the sink with a flourish, and went to the long cupboard where she hid her stash of special-occasion booze, opened a bottle of Prosecco, followed by two others, one each. 'Here's to you,' she said, air-kissing in our direction. 'And fuck your father, the narrccisssisttt…' She made it sound viciously sexy. We all clinked.

4

Fresher's week: the world experienced at a heightened level of intensity, everything filtered through a hormonally charged lens. I moved through the college grounds as if I were a star in my own movie, and Wilde – with its fairy-tale cobblestones, Gothic buildings, giant trees, its metropolitan location in the centre of town, its romantic reputation as educator to luminaries such as Beckett, Bram Stoker and Oscar (its most famous playwright namesake) – was the perfect setting for any number of narratives to play out. A rarefied, insular world, its ancient quadrants facing inwards, in stark contrast to the haphazard, depressed city outside its walls.

I imagined a camera was trained on me as 'leading lady' and Linda in her supporting role as 'best friend', a percussive rousing score following us as we walked about, drunk on all that beauty, twitching our tail feathers.

I was chosen as *number one* of the 'ten top fillies' on the list of appetising freshers that first week of college. The all-male-staffed magazine named *HUP!* rated fresh intake according to their fuckability and I made the grade – Linda, surprisingly, made it onto the list too, just about, at number ten, repeating a pattern we had established in school: number one and number ten. Top of the list: 'Pert but slappable.'

As part of the scholarship which I had been awarded – one offered by the French department for a student of promise and limited means (thanks, Deserter Dad) – I was given a room on campus, which was 'absolutely deserved', according to Linda. Her place was dark and dank and about a thirty-minute walk in the wrong direction. She moved in with me in my fully paid-for, functional room in a modern block – a gruesome addition to the original eighteenth-century splendour – for a few short weeks, until there was no room for her.

Something about landing in that place that was so alien to us and finding ourselves the objects of so much attention made us indescribably horny. Linda too felt the charge. That the two of us were ranked in the top ten newcomers deemed worthy by the *HUP!* boys seemed extraordinary in the face of all the other long-legged, shaggy, sophisticated stunners walking about. 'See?' I said to her on our first night, lying on my single bed in my tiny room, 'We are something *special*.' We almost tongue-kissed we were so overcome with emotion. I stroked her baby-fine hair, with its auburn streaks, and battled a desire to yank it.

We spent the whole of that first week scoping out new talent and the opportunities for meeting said talent. The males here were a different *species* to the ones in school. Linda and I already had each other, but Wilde offered the possibility of expanding our sacred duo; here were people I 'deemed worthy'– exceptional people.

The old Front Square was a riot of societies all vying for the newbies' attention. Stalls were set up shakily on the cobblestones, all lopsided, all at skewed angles, adding to the general air of rakishness. We lingered at the rowing society table, even though we had no intention of joining, but the guy behind the desk was exotic (a perfectly acceptable term then) and beautiful – not a word we would ever have associated with a boy before. Dublin in the early nineties was still teeming with the white and pink variety, yet here there were heavenly creatures, sophisticates from other worlds. We had fallen into another dimension. This boy was called Rico, imagine? I pictured the girls in our school *dying*. Rico invited us along to the rowing soc's first social gathering in two days' time. We would 'be there, or be square', I heard myself saying, so *suburban*, before my cheeks flared red, which was not something that usually happened to me. I could feel Linda studying me with interest. 'Fuck off,' I whispered to her. She just smiled back, as if the whole thing were the loveliest dream ever.

We passed by the debating society table, where students were espousing their opinions in shrill, earnest voices. 'Corduroy-wearing, self-important, patronising, ugly posturers,' I said to Linda, after we were out of earshot, feeling strangely provoked. She thought this was hilarious. I think I felt diminished. By their confidence and their certainty.

The array of choice was dizzying: the science fiction society, the jazz society, the historical society, shooting, diving, fencing, swimming, theology, expressive dance, judo, aikido, musical society, mime, fencing, a cappella, bel canto, contemporary dance, and other, more obscure ones including the 'toy train' society which I told Linda she had to join. There was a notable lack of anything to do with sexuality or gender, not even a nod to feminism, let alone identifying oneself as non-binary, or fluid or trans, or anything other than straight. But then, back then, it was thrilling to be a number on a list, ranked by your body parts.

There were, of course, undercurrents at play that we had no language for, and there was experimentation, but hidden, unless it was of the hetero type that could be bragged about: two girls and one guy. No doubt it was this prevailing macho culture that fostered the emergence of a character such as Mark, who was, on the face of it, so different to the *HUP!* crew – an 'enlightened male' who modelled himself in direct contrast to them, as well as to his own chauvinistic 'prick' (his words) of a father.

*

'Perhaps that was part of your attraction to him too? Your father-anger?' Dr Collins seems enlivened, her voice more animated than normal.

'Well, of course. Daddy issues played a part for all of us.'

'Did your father make an effort to stay in touch?'

'Sue wouldn't let him.'

'And you don't feel anger towards her for that?'

'The man sent me birthday and Christmas cards. He didn't send money, which we needed.'

I sit in silence for a moment. 'Money has always been an issue.'

'And is it still?'

I ponder that. My divorce will leave me secure; I chose my husband well. I had made a vow to never find myself as broke as Sue was after Dad skipped out on her.

*

The next table over had a sign: The Wilde Players – the louche, dope-smoking, dark, glamorous-in-a-boho-kind-of-way thespians. This was where I desperately wanted to be. There were three smoky-eyed girls and four highly attentive guys chatting animatedly, all skinny, all smoking, all variety of skin tones, all dressed in a shabby-chic style, patches at elbows, cigarette tips arcing in the air. I felt vaguely intimidated, but then I looked at Linda in her neat cardigan, Converse and one good summer dress from a high-street store. I contrasted her non-style with my own inimitable charity-shop vintage one: my short suede mini and fake sable fur coat and Doc Martens. I had such an eye – Linda used to say I could wear a plastic bag and still look good in it. Sue said it too, in quite a different tone. A tone that made me know it was true. Hugo or Hughie, I couldn't quite tell because of his overcooked accent, all very actorly, *dahling*, decided I had a great 'look' and signed me up for an introductory evening. Linda hung back, wisely. I wondered, briefly, where she might fit in. Perhaps she could fulfil her stage manager duties here too.

Two nights later we turned up for the first of our social gatherings with the rowing crew, in a sanitised, overlit room in the new modern wing, just the odd tinny passed around, in contrast to the stoned Wilde Players get-together the following evening in a dingy, smoke-choked basement in the old part of campus. The rowers were fit, serious young men, conformists who liked to be part of a team, who responded well to focus, discipline, training – or so I had them pegged. I was surprised to see Linda come alive in this room, particularly when she set eyes on a well-groomed, well-muscled, well-fed, well-bred guy from south County Dublin. I knew the minute he opened his mouth where he came from: nothing distinguishable about him, nothing to rub up against, no struggles, all so easy-peasy, 'Mr Big House'.

'Jonathan,' he said as he extended his hand with its neat, buffed nails to Linda. He nodded absently in my direction.

'Linda.' Her voice was high and girly.

If I'd had bubblegum in my mouth, I'd have blown a large one and let it pop rudely. I settled for running the tip of my tongue over my lips, in a less-than-subtle ploy for attention from the guys around me who all looked homogenously dull: too healthy and wholesome and *expected* with their square jaws and triangular bodies. Jonathan had sun-kissed hair and skin, and walnut-brown eyes – which, on close inspection, seemed a little sad, giving him, OK, a sort of allure. Linda seemed quickly at ease in his company, as if she had known him a long time. I was craving attention, excitement, an edgier shade of glamour.

Later in my room, when Linda told me that Jonathan had invited her out to lunch the following day, I found myself pinching her, which shocked me more than it did her. Her fault. I had been provoked beyond rational, mature thought. 'You deserve so much better than that *jock*,' I said, as if it were the worst insult you could throw at someone. 'Imagine if he knew what kind of a house you come from … think he'd like you then?' I could see the physical impact of my words on her: she was transported back to that terrible house; her body became hard, contracted, and for one shocking moment I could see her mother in her, as if I had conjured her. She was all shame. I wanted to bundle her into my arms and kick her. I would not let her turn into that woman.

I tucked a stray hair behind her ear, whispered into it (poor thing, starved of affection): 'No silly boy will ever come between us … our bond is deeper than sisters … we have chosen each other, life has singled us out for one another … we are destined to be together.' My speech was overly heightened for effect. She looked at me with such a lack of guile and so much *gratitude* that I felt frightened for her.

5

The first time I met Jacques, autumn was in full golden swing and the sky was blue, or I think it was – there was a sense of warmth and expansiveness to our meeting, anyway. I am trying to write it all down and be as specific with the memories as I can, which sometimes involves an element of inventiveness. So, let's say the sun was high and bright, like my mood, when Jacques strolled into my life and onto my pages. It was week three of first term and Sue and our home of grief and fantasy seemed far away. I had not even called her, although Linda had. Apparently, she missed me and was worried about me. I didn't want her worry; I didn't want to be burdened with duty or guilt; I didn't want any reminders of my abandoning father, or her overwhelming need. I was proving adept at reinvention.

I found myself taking up space in tutorials, even when pitted against the same 'self-assured, shrill, self-opinionated posturers' I had overheard at the debating society stall, who diminished me on first impression. My dextrous tongue and faculty for language gave me an edge in those confined, competitive spaces where the spotlight would shine intensely on whoever was speaking. The actress would always dazzle over the debater! No more 'be there or be square' inanities would fall out of my mouth. I grew in stature whereas Linda shrank. She told me she would stammer, get all choked up and break out in a rash on her neck and chest any time she had to speak.

'Just imagine them naked. They all have body parts they're ashamed of,' I told her. 'The best leveller going.'

'You are not me,' she said, wrapping her arms protectively around her bony body.

*

Dr Collins, Sophie, interjects.

'And Jacques? What happened next?'

She wants to steer me back to our first meeting.

'Write your memories in sequence; that way you can live and breathe the beats more.'

Sometimes I see impatience on her face. Sometimes I think she is controlling the course of *my* history, in a too tightly directed way.

*

Here's what I remember of our first meeting: a silhouette of impressive height against a wide blue domed sky, large reassuring hands, sandpaper stubble which made me want to reach out and stroke it, wide dependable shoulders. The wind was hurling leaves about and whipping my hair and messing with my fringe. I experienced a jolt in my body that felt like an electric shock; everything tingled. My breath came hard and fast, my vision was blurred, everything outside of his form lost focus. I felt the edges of things sliding away. Jacques immediately filled all the space in front of me and inside me. I don't recollect our first shared words – you know when people say they know? Well. We created static.

Linda said when she saw us together, she got the *shakes*, but in a good way. She was there but I have no memory of her being there. I had been on my way to a lecture on French absurdism when I found myself derailed by this magnetic stranger with his dark, soft, animal eyes, like something out of an Artaud play. Next thing I recall, we were sitting in La Cave, an underground wine bar in the centre of town, drinking deep burgundy wine. It had the sophisticated air of a speakeasy in Paris, or so I imagined. Our knees were touching in the near dark. I was trembling. Where was my best friend? I didn't have the capacity to think.

Here's what I gleaned from that conversation, when my mind stopped buzzing enough to allow me to hear: that he was half-French, which was beyond perfect in my world, that he was in second year, fourteen months older than me, undeniably sexy, that he was studying Russian. I felt as if I were in my very own Chagall painting: disembodied and fantastical. The alcohol and the dim moody lighting, the red velvet upholstery and dark wood panelling intensified the hyper-romance of the moment. I had to wrap my leg around the table to keep me from flying away. Everything about him was sensual: battered leather trousers, tangle of hair on chest and arms, visible muscles straining against his clothes, a gorgeous mouth so wide he could almost fit my whole face inside. He could certainly fit other parts of me in there. Devouring. Wolfish. So far so expected, but also, he was kind and gentle, and I felt loved by him within moments of meeting him.

I brought him back to my room that night, forcing Linda back to her dank digs. I had never had sex before. Whatever had happened with that guy in school was not this. This was transcendent: a channel to something outside my life experience so far. The beginning of it all, perhaps. I was present in a way I had never been, focused in the moment of experiencing all this newness. I was buzzed on skin-on-skin friction. 'If I could put you in a blender and suck you up through a straw,' he said. I hoovered that stuff up, that kind of Betty Blue obsessive thing. Sue would have been proud.

He christened my vagina, newly discovered to me, 'Puddle Wonderful' from an E. E. Cummings poem – one of my favourites, and his too: freewheeling, electric, *mad*, we agreed. Could we be any more perfect for each other? The first time these things are spoken aloud they are illicit, thrilling. I couldn't believe anyone else could possibly feel the way we did, do the things we did, speak the way we spoke.

I wonder what that bizarre, slightly creepy pet name revealed about us – if anything? I don't need Dr Collins's prompt to ask the question of myself: how could I have laid myself bare like this to a complete stranger? I had a high threshold for risk, having grown up in the house I did, but the sexual charge Jacques and I generated was more potent even than any of that. That first night, in my tiny, narrow bed in my tiny, narrow room on campus, I knew that I had finally come *home*. This home still had an edge to it, but also it was sweet and delicious and moreish.

Jessica, Jessie, Jess. I can hear him caressing my name as he caressed all of me. How he loved my name, the name I shared with the actress *du jour*, the one who won an Oscar for flailing about girlishly in a giant gorilla's paw. (Did the beast make her fall in love with him? Probably.)

The morning after our first night together Linda barged into my bedroom at dawn, dishevelled, unslept. She'd been terrified for me, she explained, almost apologetically when she saw that she'd woken us up, naked and comfortable in our nakedness, bodies splayed and sprawled over each other. Jacques sat up and covered the two of us solicitously. 'You're lucky to have a friend who cares so much about you,' he said to me, including her in the exchange. Linda was close to tears and so I patted the outside of the quilt, and she climbed up and lay herself down the length of the bed beside me, Jacques the other side. I felt as if we were nursing our child.

The three of us lay there for some time until Jacques said, 'I'd better get up and have a shower.' Linda rolled off the bed and stood, feet planted, her face to the wall. She wasn't going anywhere. 'Do your worst,' she said. Jacques stood on the mattress, wrapping himself in the sheet, settling the quilt back over me, not before rolling me over and landing a ticklish kiss on my left 'bun'. He climbed down off the bed and asked where the shower room was. 'Second on the right,' I said. 'Towels in the wardrobe.'

As soon as he left, Linda spluttered, 'Was that a man or a GOD?' She pulled the quilt back and looked down at my body as if seeing it for the first time, even though we had shared many naked moments in those baths that Sue had lovingly prepared for us. I pushed thoughts of my stepmother out of my mind.

'You are luminous,' Linda said. And I was: my skin was glowing, radiant.

'You're creeping me out,' I said, but didn't mean it. Being admired was my drug. 'It'll happen to you too, Lindy.'

She bit the top of her finger. 'I don't think Jonathan's into me in that way.'

I cuddled her into me. 'How could he not be madly in love with you? You're my number one gal and I have impeccable taste.'

6

The Mamas & the Papas' 'California Dreamin'' – one of Sue's sunshine-pop favourites – played in my head as I strolled in a hazy daze through Fellows' Square, which was bordered by such astonishing buildings they seemed to exist on a film set. A stunning clash of brutalist and ancient: the shiny state-of-the-art arts block, heralded a 1970s 'architectural masterpiece'; the 1937 stately Reading Room; the sixteenth-century ivy-covered Hamilton Library, housing historic, leather-bound manuscripts that seemed to whisper spells or invocations. *Open all ye who dare and enter my worlds within worlds.* This place. Intoxicating to the eye, wherever you looked.

Having skipped an afternoon tutorial on French grammar and grammatical analysis (I was incapable of focusing on anything other than *sensations*), I spotted Linda and Jonathan lying on the grass outside the arts block, their bodies close together. I threw myself down beside them, and the three of us lay there for a while, Linda sandwiched in the middle, staring at the unusually clear September sky, streaked only with a few wispy clouds.

'What a gorgeous day,' I trilled.

'Good night?' Jonathan asked, which might have been over-familiar, but I was flying.

'I told him all about your escapade,' Linda said, delightedly.

Had these two become this close without me realising? Where there should have been jealousy, I felt only expansive and magnanimous.

I rolled onto my tummy, plucked a blade of grass and stuck it between my lips. 'You did, did you? And what exactly do you know, pray tell, about said "escapade"?' I was being deliberately arch and actressy.

'You were love-drugged this morning!'

'And...' I said, prompting her.

'And that can only mean one thing...'

She blushed as she looked with longing at Jonathan. He seemed oblivious.

'It was mind-blowing,' I said.

'Go on...' Linda said. 'Details, please.'

'I don't know that I want to,' I said, surprising myself.

Linda's expression hovered between hurt and bewilderment. I had never not told her everything. This was a strange reversal.

Jonathan spoke lightly. 'Fair enough. I guess it feels private right now.'

I nodded, sucking at the blade of grass. I was genuinely incapable of putting into words what had happened. And I felt that by gossiping about it, it would make it less sacred. That was the word: *sacred*. We had had sacred sex.

'Sometimes things are better left unspoken about,' Jonathan mused.

I noted he didn't say the standard: 'Sometimes things are better left unsaid.' Was there a point to this choice of semantics? *Better left unspoken about.*

I leaned on my elbow and studied him. He was certainly not what I had imagined when I pictured our expanded tribe of *exceptional* people (Jacques fitted neatly into that category). But then, Jonathan defied categorisation. Those walnut-coloured eyes, verging on yellow in this light – fox's eyes – hinted at a secret world, a wariness, a wildness repressed. The 'handsome jock' exterior didn't tie in with the whole picture. Perhaps not surprising considering he was drawn to my best friend.

I watched them for a moment, lying so close together, and concluded that Linda was right: he was not into her in that way. Their body language was too relaxed, too cosy. There was no explosive chemistry. And I now knew what *that* looked like.

'Linda was telling me about her panic attacks,' Jonathan said, his tone kind and in no way belittling.

Was he referring to her shortness of breath and blushing when she was in a tutorial? I used to see this happen in school too, any time she was put on the spot. I remembered my attempts to minimise these reactions: 'No one else cares what you say or do. You're not that important. They're too wrapped up in their own heads.' Something I had heard my father say to Sue on occasion.

'I wouldn't quite call it that,' I said, laughing, desperately wanting to keep this day Just. Perfect. 'Lindy sometimes gets a little self-conscious.'

'It's more serious than that,' Jonathan said, sitting up. 'I know. I used to get them too.'

'I told her all she needs to do is picture the rest of her classmates naked.'

He and Linda exchanged looks that held an unspoken, *she hasn't a clue*.

'That might be a bit simplistic,' I said. I attempted to laugh again.

Neither of them joined in.

'What did you do about it?' I asked Jonathan, my bubble of loved-up self-absorption punctured for a moment.

'My mother sent me to a counsellor when I was at school.'

This was a radical thing to do back in the 1980s in Ireland. We were not exactly known for talking about ourselves to strangers, except to confess our sins in the confessional box.

'Wow. Must have been bad then,' I said, sitting up. 'What did you learn?'

'Grounding techniques, breathing techniques, present moment awareness…' He angled his body towards Linda's. 'I can teach you, Linda, if you like?'

Her face – as if she were a flower opening up to the sun.

Someone else was responsible for making Lindy happy, and I didn't experience the usual 'fuck off' urge. Jonathan felt unthreatening, cosy, in a brotherly kind of way. Linda and I both could have done with a brother.

'That'd be great,' I said, speaking for my friend. 'All the help she can get!'

Linda looked at me, her eyes brimming.

'I'm thrilled for you, Jess,' she said, her face all lit up. 'I think this guy from last night might be The One.'

I thought of how I had derided and destroyed her first love. But Stupid Stu was not worthy of her.

'What's his name, by the way?' she said, giggling. 'Or did you get that far?'

'His name is Jjjjacqqqques,' I said, overemphasising the Gallic pronunciation.

'Cool name,' Jonathan said. 'He French?'

'Half and half,' I said.

'A delicious mongrel,' Linda said, and the three of us fell about the place laughing.

7

Jacques was a brilliant cook: especially fish and shellfish and steak, which was beyond glamorous in the shared student kitchen where the only culinary offerings were ready-made noodles and cup-a-soups. He never took me back to his place, which I pushed and whined about sometimes, but also secretly revelled in. The mystery! He said that the digs he shared with four other guys were repulsive. I chose to believe him. In the beginning.

Four or five nights a week we slept, well, had sex, then slept sometimes, limbs intertwined, sweaty and sated. Actually, I wonder looking back if I was ever really sated. He could sleep, I rarely, full of a jittery kind of angst that became turbo-charged around him. What if I were to lose him? What if he were to lose interest? Just the thought of that created a hole so huge in me that I felt I might be enveloped by it, drown in it, until he opened his eyes to find me staring at him, and he'd smile, in his wolf-mouthed, devouring way. *I am a sink-hole.*

*

'Do you think it was a secure attachment, Jessica?'

Today there is a sliver of sun in the corner of the room. Dust mites are dancing.

This 'attachment' stuff is something I am going to get used to hearing a lot about.

'*Secure?* We were only kids.'

'Did you feel safe with him?'

'Yes, I suppose. None of what happened was his fault.'

'As you say, you were only kids.'

'I knew what I was doing.'

Dr Collins leans towards me in that way I interpret to mean: Is that true? Her silence fosters this self-enquiry. Which, I suppose, is the point.

*

Jacques used to say that anything that made me happy made him happy. He said he knew from the moment of meeting Linda how important she was to me and that she would always be a part of our equation. This kindness was something I really liked about him – apart from his other obvious assets. I used to joke that Linda should come to bed with us, although I wasn't made for threesomes.

'Are you mine, now?' I said to Jacques while lying on top of him, naked, one morning a few weeks after we first met.

'Say that again!' he said, laughing.

'MINE,' I said, kissing his face all over.

'YOURS,' he said, taking my face in his hands.

We kissed deeply until he started to tickle me. 'Are *you* mine, now?'

'Forever and ever,' I said, meaning it in that moment.

'Jessie, *je t'aime*,' he said.

'Jacques, *je t'adore*,' I said.

'JJJesssieee, Jessssss, Jessssiiiccca,' he crooned in a strongly flavoured French accent.

My name. How he stroked it, as if he owned it, and me.

I imagined that Linda would've loved to be adored like this, but then her name didn't exactly sing out to be caressed. She had the supporting-act name too, always playing second fiddle to my starring role. She didn't seem to mind. 'Your electrifying beauty, your *funshine* is contagious,' she used to say – or some version of this.

Pity she didn't realise then that everything else about me was contagious too.

8

I was proving to be quite the hit with the Wilde Players, having first been cast as Lesley, the actress in Alan Bennett's *Her Big Chance* and now the fiery French maid in Ionesco's *The Bald Prima Donna.* My portrayal of Lesley was perfectly 'hysterical' and even 'historical' according to some reviews. I had a special talent for this kind of performative, break-down-the-fourth-wall type of theatre, apparently, a gift for speaking directly to the audience, for bringing them into my orbit. 'Mesmerising,' claimed Drew, the director *du moment*.

'You were such a shining star up there,' Linda said, after I came off stage on the opening night of *The Bald Prima Donna*. We were in the foyer of the New Theatre – designed to ape the Globe in London, but more like a wonky garden shed, set up in the round, a recent addition to the Wilde Players' usual premises (pop-ups in dark, dingy rooms) – drinking Guinness, pints for the lads and glasses for the girls.

'Hardly,' I said. 'I'm playing a saucy French maid.'

Jacques's fingers had found their way to my bottom, and he was pinching, pleasurably.

'You really are,' Jonathan said. 'Transporting.'

I could see he had been transported with high spots of colour on his cheeks and a burning in his eyes. The theatre was a revelation to him, he said, as he waxed lyrical about the 'power of transformation', his hands gesticulating, as if he were conducting an orchestra only he could see. Having watched and witnessed a play for the first time, his language, his aura, his very being was changed. It was, in itself, an act of theatre.

'You should audition some time. You have the looks,' I said, observing his ability to shapeshift. He was not comfortable with the skin he was in.

'Christ, no. I couldn't trust myself not to have a major panic attack. All those eyes on me.'

Linda looked at him with a protective, almost maternal love. Her ability to care for others was uncanny, especially as it didn't, couldn't, extend to herself.

'Genuinely, though, Jess is onto something,' Jacques said, studying Jonathan. 'I reckon you'd be brilliant.'

This sparked a flash of unreasonable jealousy in me – I wanted to be the only 'brilliant' one in Jacques's eyes. Although the two had only met casually a few times, they made an immediate connection, despite their very different outward appearances. An unspoken language flowed between them, a vibrational frequency that the four of us shared.

'Nope. Not for me,' Jonathan said, his voice betraying his longing. He looked at me, as if I were a projection of something glamorous and elusive that he had been starved of, something that might have offered him a way to connect with a part of himself he was forced to deny. I imagined his walls would have been adorned with Rita Hayworth or Audrey Hepburn (or impossibly, Rock Hudson) as a child growing up, had he been allowed. I imagined him dancing around his bedroom in a tutu with his stocky athlete's body.

'You absolutely must audition,' Linda said. 'You can use all those tips you taught me: the grounding, the deep breathing, the present-moment stuff.'

Jacques laughed. 'You might just also throw a tequila down your neck, for Dutch courage.'

Jonathan joined in. 'What a fucking fabulous idea! Four tequilas coming up!'

He went to the bar and returned a few moments later, crestfallen. 'They don't serve the hard stuff here.'

'I have some in my room,' I said. 'Who's coming?'

'Are you sure we have enough left?' Jacques said, referring to the fact that we were both knocking the booze back of late, to intensify our *sacred* sex experiences.

'There was at least a third of the bottle left, last time I checked.' I grabbed Linda by the hand. 'Right, let's go…'

'Aren't you forgetting something?' Jacques said.

'Huh?'

'Your little costume.'

Linda blushed as I dropped her hand.

'Back in a sec. Don't go anywhere!' I was delighted with this new development.

'We are your slaves,' Jonathan said, bowing deeply.

Backstage, I bumped into Drew, who drowned me in flattery: 'Truly, you are a star of the future, Jessica… There's a light in you that is so rare, a precious diamond. We need to keep it polished and shining… I can give you private lessons if you like…'

'Thanks, Drew. I'll think on your very fine offer. For now, I need to get my French maid costume. Boyfriend's orders.' I blew him a kiss, enjoying being provocative, high on the attention.

He mumbled that he didn't think it was a good idea to take my character home with me, and that the costume department wouldn't be happy.

'On the contrary,' I said. 'I believe in absolute immersion. And for this costume? Wellll, the dirtier the better…'

He flushed an angry shade of purple and said that he'd see me tomorrow evening and he hoped I wouldn't have diminished any of my 'light'. I laughed and reassured him that I would only be deepening my understanding of my role. 'Method acting,' I said, as I skipped away. I could feel his gaze burning my back.

Jonathan and Linda clapped deliriously and Jacques wolf-whistled when I returned in the maid's outfit. 'Where's your saucy feather duster?' he said.

'I think Drew hid it. He was none too pleased.'

'He'd want to watch himself,' Jacques said, possessively. I loved this part of him; I understood it implicitly. I loved the power of it.

'Why don't you challenge him to a duel?' Jonathan said.

‘Because I’d beat the little dweeb’s ass in a nanosecond,’ Jacques said.

We all laughed and linked arms and went back to my room and drank the rest of the tequila and played charades and, true enough, Jonathan was brilliant, especially when he was acting out *Tootsie*.

I watched Linda who, though shy in her charade-ing, appeared to glow when watching her friends take up space. Her generosity was gorgeous. I loved her so fiercely in that moment I felt as though my heart might jump out of its skin. She had found a sense of belonging by my side, first with Sue, and now with our new-found family of friends. I had always been, and still was, firmly at the centre of her world.

But I underestimated my best friend and her fathomless need. Her need to be touched. Her need to be loved, to be someone’s *Special One.*

9

Those first three months in Wilde passed in a near-euphoric state that could be broken down into units of Jacques: tactile sensations, heightened sense perceptions – who knew there was that much pleasure in my fingertips? There was so much to replace my guilt around not seeing Sue: the drug of skin-on-skin contact, the musky smell of our sex, the intense intimacy of kissing, handholding, possessive displays of cuddling, golden autumnal days, sweaty nights and prolonged orgasms that would leave my body jangling the whole of the next day. There were lectures, tutorials, rehearsals, first nights, week-long runs, although, as with any addict, my span of attention didn't extend much beyond the object of my obsession – which also meant that I overlooked Linda's ever-diminishing frame. I told myself Jonathan had her back. Although I could see her hip bones jutting through her skirts, I chose to look away, like everyone else in her life. Even Sue – though she had recognised that Linda was 'starving for love' – used to also say approvingly that she was 'gamine'.

Linda and Sue spoke a few times a week, and I told myself I was glad that they could satisfy a lack in each other that didn't involve me. During one of these phone calls, Sue *insisted*, according to Linda, on meeting her in town for a glass of Chardonnay, which triggered conflicting feelings in me, too convoluted to unravel then. In a show of strident 'independence' I told Linda that if she was coerced into meeting Sue, she was not to bring her onto campus – I would not have my new environment polluted (demonstrating my dramatic flair). Linda, as usual, said nothing. I made her promise to come straight to my room after. As soon as she left, my throat closed in, and my chest constricted, making it difficult to take in more than shallow sips of air.

'How did it go? Did she ask about me?' The words tumbled out of my mouth in a gush, with my breath, the moment Linda walked back in my door, some hours later. I had spent the preceding hours staring vacantly at my face in the mirror, trying on new 'looks' – electric blue eyeshadow and mascara, which only registered in the glass as a blur. Jacques had gone back to his mystery digs to get a change of clothes, or so he said.

Linda looked at me as if she were trying to work out a mathematical equation that she'd never solve. It was the first time I'd witnessed anything like detachment in her expression and I experienced a fleeting moment of fear that I'd lose her. I patted the space beside me on the bed for her to sit next to me as I stroked her arm. This touch was all it took – I felt her leaning her whole self into me.

'So, how was she?'

'In fine fettle. After downing her second glass in record time, she announced that Jonathan was a "dish but rather dull" in front of him. Loudly.'

We both laughed, even though I wasn't sure how I felt about Jonathan going in my place. I imagined hearing Sue's spiky voice and was filled with a sharp longing, but quickly overrode any feelings of sentimentality. I had my new identity to focus on: Number One Filly, Serious Student with Serious Opinions and a Bright, Dazzling Future, and Girlfriend to Hottest Guy in College.

'Actually,' Linda's tone changed. 'She seemed a bit unhinged.'

'What's new?' I said, attempting to sound casual.

'She's missing you badly, like really badly. She looked dreadful: her mascara had streaked down her cheeks, clumps of it under eyes, and her breath stank.'

'What has that got to do with me? I am not responsible for her. She's not my child.'

Linda gave me an appraising look that meant I was no longer on the pedestal she had constructed for me. Something about the disappointment in her eyes made me say: 'What names did she call me?' It gave me a strange power to know I had the same capacity for cruelty as my father had.

'She only reiterated how much she loved you, said she couldn't understand your pulling away. She didn't know what she had done. And could I ask you –'

'Oh for fuck's sake.'

'I don't think she's OK.' Linda's voice cracked. 'I think she might do something to herself.'

I had had enough. I got out of bed, wrapped myself in a towel and excused myself to go for a shower. 'Not my problem,' I threw over my shoulder on the way out the door.

*

'That was a lot to expect you to carry,' Dr Collins says softly.

'I didn't carry it, though.'

'You were trying to individuate yourself.'

'With an axe.'

'You were overburdened.'

'I was cruel.'

'Perhaps you had to be.'

It is raining outside. A magnified raindrop is stuck to the window, slug-like. I am wet and irritated.

'I was a little bitch,' I say.

Dr Collins flinches. 'I don't know why the harshness with yourself, Jessica. Can you expand on that?'

'I don't need to. My actions speak for themselves.'

'Your journey here is towards finding perspective, the bigger picture. The view that holds space for compassion, for self-love.'

Now I do roll my eyes. And sigh.

She doesn't know my end game.

*

'Your mother is a ticket,' Jonathan said to me in the arts block café the next morning.

'She's not my mother,' I said.

Jonathan looked in Linda's direction, confused.

'As good as...' Linda said, defensively. 'Better than –'

I interrupted her. 'She's not yours either.'

Linda bit down on her lower lip so it bled. I found myself torn between wanting to kiss her hurt mouth and wanting to do the same thing to myself. I turned my back. I had shown great resolve in my commitment to 'moving on'.

10

By mid-December, the weather had turned, the dark sky was a cold threat, and the black cloud of Christmas – or 'mass-psychosis' as Linda and I termed it – was coming. Even here, in my new life, the outside world invaded with jingle-jangle tunes and hocus ads on TV and the sight of hacked pine trees in places they shouldn't be, the smell of the dying woods inside. I was catapulted back to our less-than-harmonious holidays in our family home, pre- and post-Dad leaving. The excessive booze, the awful weather forcing us inside, the food and TV-bingeing, the whingeing, the disappointment, the trapped 'everyone together' false jollity. It was as if every resentment Sue had stored up towards my father – who had destroyed her life, stifled it, *stolen* it – was vented on that day.

Before Dad left, Sue got drunk to deal with Dad's presence. After he left, she got drunk to deal with his absence.

The man in the red suit never got it right for me. Instead of Tiny Tears, I got whatever cheap knock-off was on special at the time: a plastic doll with garish lipstick, stuck on the crying setting.

'A mother's lot,' Sue said, slurring, cupping her hands over her ears.

I whispered under my breath, 'You are not my mother.'

From the age of twelve, Linda and I would meet on Saint Stephen's day in the local park and drink bizarre concoctions of whatever alcohol was to hand in our respective homes, warm beakers of the stuff. It felt good to get wasted with someone who got it – the relief it was over, the pent-up emotions which needed to be numbed.

'How about you do Christmas dinner this year, Jacques?'

We were sitting in my room, on the bed, fully clothed, which was unusual. Not even the intoxication of Jacques's perfect body could insulate me against the sense of impending doom.

He pretended not to hear. I elbowed him. 'Pretty please! I can't face going home to my stepmother's antics.'

He stood, stretched and bent to touch his toes. 'You are such a bad influence. Haven't been to the gym in forever.'

'Did you hear me?'

He continued his stretching, bending towards the floor, then back up, arms overhead, fingertips almost reaching the ceiling. 'I don't do Christmas,' he said.

'What about your family?'

'What about them?' he snapped. It was the first time I had experienced any abrasiveness from him.

'Don't you need to be with them?'

He got down on his hands and knees and stretched his body in a plank.

'Watch this: full-body push-ups!'

'Impressive,' I said, and I couldn't help but feel turned on. We shoved our books aside.

After, lying snuggled in each other's arms, Jacques relented and said he'd serve up smoked salmon and crab claws and pavlova. Anything but turkey and the trimmings.

'Let's invite Linda and Jonathan,' I said. 'OK, chef extraordinaire?'

'Whatever madam wants… Tell me again how talented I am!' he said, before his head disappeared beneath the quilt and my mind was stilled, and I was one with the Divine (and his dextrous tongue).

Later that day, after the last of our lectures, the four of us met in my room, which was becoming standard, all of us piled on the small single bed, Jacques's leg pinning me in a casual display of possession.

'Jacques and I would like to invite you both for Christmas dinner,' I announced, feeling very grown-up.

Linda clapped her hands in delight.

'Not a chance,' Jonathan said. 'You've no idea how hard I had to fight to be allowed to live out. My mother lives in fear I'm going to top myself… So emasculating,' he said, plucking at his cashmere sweater, which was pilling and unravelling at the sleeves.

I thought that was an interesting word for him to alight on: *emasculating*.

'And it would break my mother's heart. Christmas dinner with her and the pater would be a bleak affair without her precious son and our secrets,' Jonathan continued.

'You're being manipulated,' I said, my new favourite concept to justify my own selfishness.

He studied me a moment, then looked at Linda. 'I've an idea! Linda, would you come with me on Saint Stephen's Day? Nothing would make my mother happier than to think I have at long last got myself a girlfriend. I can say I'm spending Christmas day with you and your family.'

'You are!' she said.

Jonathan gave her a huge bear hug. 'You're the best!' He had no idea the kind of desperation and compulsive desire that touch could spark in Linda. I saw it. The way she leaned in and caught her breath.

'As the chef, I am setting down some ground rules,' Jacques said. 'No carols, no crackers, no presents, OK?'

'Yay, OK,' we all answered, almost in unison.

'Have you asked Sue yet?' Linda asked.

'Of course not!' I said and laughed theatrically.

'You're not leaving her on her own, surely?'

I felt three pairs of eyes on me in the silence that followed.

I would not be guilted; none of the rest of them were concerned about leaving their families. And yet. My windpipe started to close in. I felt as trapped as I had in those boozy dark Christmases in that house.

'She didn't have to stay, you know. She could have left too,' Linda said, her words blindsiding me.

'She'll be delighted not to have to cook a fucking turkey,' I said, conceding without meaning to.

'Right, that's settled then,' Jacques said. 'I ain't cooking no fucking turkey neither!'

11

Sue arrived seriously dressed up in a short spangly skirt and silvery eye shadow, and a low-cut top revealing more bone than breast. She had overdone it on the perfume front, something chemical and cloying. 'Nice to finally see your world. How cool!' She was looking around with affected approval at the definitely-not-cool modern annexe. I fake-hugged her, our chests never touching, making sure my heart could not get too close to hers. I brought her through to the stark kitchen, all stainless-steel functionality, devoid of any decorations. 'Happy Christmas one and all!' She was making a big show of being *happy*, overcompensating and fawning. 'Thanks for having me!' She had brought tinsel, which she draped around Jacques's shoulders. 'Want to come live on the top of my tree?'

Jacques laughed like I'd never seen him laugh before. I was horrified – here was my history in all its technicolour gore. My shame and my guilt and my fierce, conflicted love.

In defiance of the day, the Beach Boys' 'Good Vibrations' was blasting from the portable cassette player Jonathan had brought with him. It was perfectly incongruous: tinsel on the beach.

'Hello, darling.' Sue moved towards Linda with outstretched arms and hugged her tightly. My chest constricted. She released Linda and looked around the room at us all. Her gaze blurred as her eyes passed over me.

'OK, time to sit, everyone,' I said loudly, asserting my position as head of *this* family.

'Well, look at you. Ms Hostess with the Mostess! Your father would be proud.'

Jonathan pulled a chair out for Sue, which made her light up and smile mawkishly, a southern belle with a rare gentleman caller, like a sad, faded Tennessee Williams character. She handed Linda and me gift-wrapped boxes, the exact same shape and size.

'You shouldn't have,' I said.

Linda opened her present, saying how embarrassed she was that she hadn't got one for Sue, but she'd thought that we had agreed: no spending money on gifts. Sue countered this by saying, whoever heard of a Christmas without presents? Linda was thrilled with her Boots finest collection of cherry blossom shower gel, body scrub and cream. I was determined not to humiliate myself by opening mine in public.

'Well, this is just gorgeous!' Sue said, looking down at the starter Jacques had prepared for us: prawn cocktail with Marie Rose sauce. Her voice was high, her cheeks red, and she drank too fast. Jonathan kept filling her glass, delighting in her inappropriate comments and ever wilder gesticulations – *such a character*! 'He pushed you up against a wall yet?' she asked Linda, who giggled – though uncomfortably. She looked at Jacques and said, 'That one definitely does… My lucky little Jess.' She winked at us both and Jacques beamed, while I scowled. What was wrong with me that I felt so hostile? She was only being funny, in her distinctive way.

In truth, I didn't want Jacques knowing her; I didn't want this part of my life here. I felt ashamed for feeling ashamed. Undercurrents were floating between us, invisible tentacles that flowed from her to me, gathering me in, smothering me. I had failed in my duty as loyal daughter substitute. All that guilt. All that misplaced, desperate love.

Jacques brought a pasta dish with smoked salmon a la crème to the table, which Sue pronounced 'deeeeelisssh'. She seemed perfectly on board with our anti-Christmas theme for the day. The dessert was spectacular, a pavlova, chewy in the middle and crumbly to the touch, piled high with cream and strawberries. 'Seriously, this man is a dream,' Sue said. I could sense her loneliness, saw through her loud, leery, cheery act. How pathetic that she had agreed to come.

Had she no friends of her own? Jacques was watering down her wine glasses without her noticing, a manoeuvre he seemed practised at, which made me wonder.

As the evening wore on, Sue's defences towards me softened. 'It's good to see you this happy,' she said, coming towards me for a hug, which I both did and didn't want. As her arms encircled me, I felt a familiar squeeze of sadness, something I hadn't felt since coming to Wilde three months ago. I was immediately tangled up in her arms, and her emotions.

Sue was a star at charades, out-performing even me. The others clapped and whooped as she acted out *The Cook, The Thief, His Wife & Her Lover*. She minced, she pranced, coquettish and sensual. I realised that maybe she wasn't as 'past it' as I had previously thought – she was perhaps only touching forty then. I was shocked. My father *had* stolen the best part of her life. But then, no one had forced her to stay. I touched the sore spot on my neck and pressed hard as a realisation hit that she would never have left me. I swallowed, opened another bottle of Pinot, and swallowed easier. I felt Jacques's eyes on me as I knocked back yet another glass.

'Hey, take it easy,' he whispered in my ear. 'You OK?'

'Perfectly fucking fine,' I hissed back.

He threw his hands in the air, backed away.

Linda was stupendously drunk, unbeknownst to us all. Her tiny frame meant that one whiff of alcohol undid her. I watched her dance in an uncharacteristically sexy way to Sue's playlist of Abba and Motown classics, made for her on a cassette by my father back when they were 'in love'. Sue insisted on having their music play, our family home invading this new life I was trying to build. Linda held her hands out for Jonathan and swayed in front of him, then leaned in and held him close, dancing cheek to cheek. As she moved her mouth to his, Jonathan froze, and then abruptly moved away from her. She looked stricken, my sweet, foolish, desperate friend.

I went to her and slid my arms around her back, encasing her concave tummy in a hug, crooning into her ear, making out to

Jonathan that this was something we did with each other regularly: made fake passes at each other. Her pronounced ribcage moved against my arms as she inhaled deeply, before she gently disentangled herself from my embrace and went to Sue, who hugged her tightly. The two of them whispered into each other's ears, sharing a private joke, I felt, at my expense. A paranoia took hold of me that night, in a flavour I'd never tasted before.

'Right, I guess it's time to call this night quits,' Sue said suddenly in a sober-sounding voice, which surprised me. 'Thank you all for a gorgeous time,' she said graciously. 'And five stars to the chef extraordinaire.'

I hated that she used my expression for Jacques, realising that her cadences had influenced my own.

'I'll walk you to your taxi,' Jacques said.

'Such a gentleman… Jessie, don't mess this up. He's a keeper, this one.' She blew me a kiss. I blew her one back, feeling like I had to.

'Hey Sue, don't forget your tape,' Jonathan said.

'It's fine. Enjoy it some more, Jess can give it to me another time.' She waved at us all as she turned to leave.

In her wake: an absence, a void, both a relief and a loss.

Linda moved to the cassette recorder and turned the music up full volume. She danced madly, body swaying salaciously, completely uninhibited.

Jonathan looked away. I was entranced. Who *was* this girl?

12

It was a ghastly, bone-wet January evening and Linda and I were in the starkly lit, fluorescent loos in the arts block for the third time that day, fixing our damp, frizzy hair and reapplying streaky non-waterproof, blue-black mascara – which we both decided was just the right side of flashy without being 'cheap'. A guy walked in, seemingly unaware he was in the ladies, glanced at us both, mumbled something incoherent and backed out.

When we exited, he was waiting, lurking. He was all decked out in shades of beige: light brown corduroy trousers, a caramel-coloured full-length parka, tan suede cowboy boots. His sandy hair was mussed, streaked with premature grey, his complexion pasty, bookish beneath his salt-and-pepper stubble. He wore wire-rimmed round glasses, à la John Lennon, which no one wore then. His look was either studiously practised to look like he didn't give a shit, or he really didn't give a shit. The mishmash style was bizarre, and confident. He walked towards us with purpose, not the hint of a smile, or shyness. My first thought was, *You wish, weirdo*. I was used to these kinds of overtures. However, his gaze was fixed on my usually invisible friend. He stopped directly in front of her, blocking her way.

'Come on, Lindy, we've got to meet Jacques in five,' I said, grabbing on to her sleeve.

'Mark Whitman,' the guy said, ignoring me, offering his hand to Linda, his voice a deep baritone, at odds with his skinny frame.

Mark Whitman, a fiction unto himself, even then.

Linda didn't move. She seemed mesmerised. He pushed his glasses on top of his head and looked at her – with a bald pin-you stare beneath his blonde almost-not-there-lashes – as if he already possessed her. She seemed sort of floppy, like she might not have wanted to put up much of a fight.

'Linda,' she said, taking his hand. Once contact was made, he squeezed too hard and for too long, the two of them locked into each other. I'm pretty sure Linda was willing this to be her Jacques moment. I didn't say anything, but I laughed out loud, which elicited no response from either of them. I decided to teach her a lesson and just leave her there. She was not used to being anywhere without me. The guy held her in his thrall, as I walked away, feeling slightly winded.

My worry for her translated into my own sense of woundedness. Linda had that effect – everything became about everyone else around her.

Jacques was waiting for me in my room, sitting at the desk, reading a copy of Camus's *The Stranger*. He looked up frowning, read aloud: 'But, I reminded myself, it's common knowledge that life isn't worth living anyhow –'

I interrupted him: 'And … it makes little difference whether one dies at the age of thirty or threescore and ten…'

'Impressive,' he said. 'What's next?'

'Can't remember exactly… Something to do with the world will go on as before…?'

'Pretty depressing.'

'I find it the complete opposite.'

'That is so strange,' he said.

'I *am* strange.'

'Are you OK, Jess?'

'Perfectly fucking fine,' I said.

'I really don't like the way you say that.'

'Sorry,' I said, sounding anything but.

'You've been off since Christmas…'

The small window above the bed allowed in a slit of watery grey light which landed on his neck. I went to him and kissed him on the spot, liking how the light moved, escaping my mouth.

He gathered me on his knee, kissing me all over. 'Today you taste like something bittersweet: a lemon tart.' He grabbed me by my skirt waistband, his other hand creeping inside my panties.

'Eat me,' I said, and so he did.

A couple of hours later there was a knock at the door.

'Enter,' Jacques said.

Linda walked in, looking dazed.

'Where the hell were you?' I said.

She sort of gestured at the bed, where we were now sprawled. Her eyes were glassy, her cheeks flushed.

'Seriously? Fuck, already…?'

'Wait up, what, who?' Jacques said, sitting up and arranging the pillows behind our backs.

'Jesus, you weren't even pissed or high or anything,' I said, faking a sort of high moral stance, aware of my own hypocrisy.

'So, when are we going to get to meet him?' Jacques said.

'I already met him.'

'Well?' Jacques turned to me. 'I can't believe you didn't tell me.'

'Nothing *to* tell. Right, Linda?'

Linda sat at the end of the bed, ignoring me, lost in her own world.

'That was totally spacey. Never did anything like that before. I didn't even fancy him.'

'Bet you fancy him now, though,' Jacques said. 'The guy's got you hooked.' He looked at me as he said this, his hands slipping between my legs beneath the sheets.

'No he hasn't. Just a once-off. Right, Lindy?' I pushed Jacques's hand away.

'You'll really like him, you guys, I know it… He's … dazzling,' Linda said dreamily, as if Puck himself had sprinkled her in love juice. Blind intoxication, derangement.

'What's *Mr Dazzling's* name?' Jacques said.

'Mark,' she said, and I laughed.

'Not exactly a Bobby Dazzler's name.'

Linda looked away out the window and put her fingers to her mouth, inhaling.

She turned back to me, drew herself to her full height and said, 'I wonder why you can never be happy for me.'

He had already managed where no one else could.

13

Linda disappeared – for days. Unheard of. It hurt. So, I orchestrated that we 'bump' into each other in the arts block, by positioning myself outside her midweek tutorial. As I waited, I wondered had she found her voice without flushing crimson. When she emerged, she looked different: she seemed firmly ensconced in her own skin, not squirming to get out of it. I had always experienced Linda as flowing outwards, towards me, but this time when she saw me, her body contracted, and she waved at me, cheerily, as if I were an acquaintance. *Fuck you, Lindy, where would you be without me?*

We went to the coffee dock where I bought her a milky coffee, even though she said she was off dairy. We moved outside into the dank, damp air and sat on a rotting wooden bench in the gloaming.

Linda stood, then sat back down on her bag so as not to get her coat wet. The Linda I knew would never even bother putting up an umbrella, even when it was lashing, as if she were not worth protecting from the elements.

'So, how are you getting on?' I asked, studying her.

'It's freezing, what are we doing out here?'

'I wanted to talk to you in private. You OK?'

'Why wouldn't I be?'

'I haven't seen you in a while.'

'All of three days, Jess! Are *you* OK?'

'Bit worried about you.'

'Don't patronise me.'

'I'm *not*… How's it going with the guy?'

She looked at me sideways to see if I was being genuine, or whether there was some design on my part.

'Are you enjoying hanging out with him?' I went on, my voice modulated to come across as reasonable, inviting her into my confidence.

Her body softened. 'He's fascinating, you'll see…'

I was intensely relieved that she still wanted my approval.

She picked up a yellowing leaf and studied it.

'Nice leaf,' I said. 'Going to put it in your scrapbook?' My voice was a feather, intended to tickle and to stroke.

She nodded, her eyes round and shining, as she put it in her coat pocket.

'He's in fourth year,' she said, as if that were the most romantic thing you could ever say about anyone.

'What's he doing cradle-snatching?' I said.

She didn't react, insulated by her new-found obsession. 'He's studying philosophy.'

'Only for fools who can't get the points for anything else,' I said.

'He wants to be a writer.'

'Oh please…'

'I can tell he's talented … He's deep.'

'Is he published?'

'I've never met anyone like him.'

'Well, someone who pairs cowboy boots with a parka is surely an original!' I said. 'What does he write about?'

'The human condition,' she said, in all seriousness.

'How wretched us lot are…?' I laughed. 'Is he published?' I was not letting it go.

'He doesn't fit the mould.'

'Is that what he told you? A bit of a Joyce, is he?'

'Yes, I think he is… And he writes plays.'

I looked at my best friend and wondered at her naivety. How had we, objectively speaking, come from the same place? I answered my own question by conjuring a picture of her mother in that cold, brown house – all beaky, brittle bitterness. The smell of Dettol disinfectant filled my nostrils.

'Have you read any of his work?'

'It's stunning.'

'I see…'

'And brutal. But beautiful.'

I bit down on the inside of my cheek to stop myself saying anything further – I could see the level of her infatuation and it was severe. Sue calling her 'starving' came to mind, and I imagined her in a supermarket, gorging on rich food as she went, replenishing her trolley with fresh supplies, even as she'd discreetly vomit into her handkerchief.

'How's Jonathan?' I said, wilfully changing tack. 'We haven't seen much of him since Christmas.'

'Fine.' She brushed some fluff off her coat impatiently.

'You haven't told me about Saint Stephen's Day. What were his parents like?'

'His father was off playing golf,' she said.

She started to pick at a rotted shard of wet wood on the bench.

'What was his house like?' I asked.

'Huge. All interior-designed, like a hotel. Greys and lilacs.'

'Sounds appalling! What was his mum like?'

'Desperate,' she said, and stopped.

I waited for more.

She winced and brought a finger to her mouth, where a splinter was embedded. She sucked her fingertip.

'Well, that was bound to happen,' I said as I gestured at her to let me see her hand.

She refused and continued to suck.

'I don't mean to be cruel, but it's like Jonathan's mother is in love with him. She was so gushing,' she said.

'Is she pretty?'

'In a manicured way, I guess…'

'Did something happen, L?'

'Nothing happened. It was all very polite. But it wasn't real.'

‘I think you should introduce Jonathan to this Mark guy, if you insist on seeing him.’

‘I don’t feel that’s a good idea.’

‘Why not? Jonathan’s a good friend to you.’

‘No such thing as being “just friends” with the opposite sex.’

‘What nonsense has Mr Wannabe-Writer-Philosopher-Weirdo been filling your head with?’

‘Don’t do that.’ She looked directly at me.

I raised my hand in the air. ‘I’m just saying there’s something off about this guy, and to be careful.’

‘Right, and you met him for like ... what? One minute?’

‘I didn’t get a great impression.’

She smiled, a sly, knowing smile, blocking me out. ‘He said the same thing about you.’

A sudden gust of wind blew a few shrivelled leaves off the branches. One landed on my nose. ‘Cute,’ Linda said, as she brushed it off. She looked directly at me. ‘He makes me feel good about myself. Does that count for nothing with you?’

‘How long is it now? A week?’ I said.

‘Well, you knew with Jacques straight away.’

I didn’t point out that Jacques was sex on legs, and he would never speak badly about my best friend.

‘He said he’d like to meet my friends...’

‘Good plan. Pints in the Stag’s?’

‘I’d rather not have Jonathan there,’ she said. ‘It would be a better dynamic with just you, me, Jacques and Mark, don’t you think?’

‘A double date?’ I said.

I could see the depth of her longing laid bare in her eyes, watery grey in the gathering darkness, even as she was battling her desire for my approval.

She stood suddenly. ‘Gotta go.’

‘Where?’

‘Just...’

‘Are you not drinking your coffee?’ I gestured at the untouched drink on the bench beside her.

‘I don’t do milk.’

'Since when?'

'I told you earlier, and you chose not to hear.'

She turned to go and threw over her shoulder, 'You have it, though!'

'Make sure you get that splinter out,' I shouted at her back. 'Otherwise, it could go septic.'

14

Jacques and I were sitting in a snug in the Stag's Hunt: a buzzing, smoky, off-campus bar in the centre of Dublin city, all wrought-iron Victorian facade – a stab at ye-olde-worlde charm situated up a cobblestoned alley, which stank of piss. Inside, it was all stuffed animals' heads, red leather seating, oversized mirrors, dim lighting. It was loud with young, opinionated voices, the odd low laugh, bright flirty 'Oh my Gawd, you're unreal!'s. The air was rank with sweat, disguised by citrusy Eau de Cologne for the boys and musky Opium for the girls.

'I mean, the guy *seems* beige…' I said.

Jacques smiled indulgently at me. 'You don't approve of his clothes, I take it.'

'It's not just that.'

'He didn't fall for your charms?'

I kicked him hard in the shins. He didn't flinch, demonstrating a self-control that I so lacked. Linda walked in at that moment, Mark's arm draped around her shoulder, his hand dangling at her throat, seeming to press against her trachea. I hadn't registered his height the last time, how he towered over her, even as he stooped. They were ill-matching in style: Linda prim and neat, and Mark self-consciously louche and dishevelled. Both were strikingly angular, with enviable cheekbones, but where there was something sparrow-like about Linda's delicate features, his were hawkish.

I called out to Linda, waved them over.

Jacques stood. 'Hey! Let me get you both a drink.'

'Cheers,' Linda said. 'A glass of Guinness for me.'

An expression of disapproval flitted across Mark's face. 'A lemonade, please,' he said. Which was so strange it felt like an affront. No one didn't drink alcohol in college then.

'You don't imbibe?' I asked him.

He didn't respond, though I was sure he had heard me. They slid onto the banquette seating across from me, Linda crossing her legs, her foot jigging, as was her habit. Mark placed his hand on her knee, and she stopped instantly.

'So,' Jacques said, as he returned with the drinks. 'This is the man of the moment!'

'Yup,' Mark said. 'Lucky guy, huh?'

Jacques looked at me. 'We happen to think so!'

I found the whole exchange sickening. A male display of proprietorship.

'You must be Jessica,' Mark said, his tongue flicking to his taut upper lip. He had disconcertingly perfect 1940s starlet's lips, with a deeply etched cupid's bow. He glanced at himself in an oversized, mildewed mirror, the reflection from his glasses throwing back a distorted image he seemed to approve of.

'I guess I must be!'

He held his own gaze. 'Well, at last,' he said, speaking to me without looking away from the mirror.

I wondered at his choice of words: *at last*. Was I really that invisible to him?

'Jacques,' Mark said, turning to face my boyfriend. 'You're studying Russian, right?'

Jacques nodded, used to the fact that everyone had prior knowledge of him as one half of the coolest, cutest couple in college – it was a truth universally acknowledged.

'And yourself?' Jacques asked.

'Philosophy,' I answered for him, with a slight sneer.

'Philosophy,' he said to Jacques, acting as if I hadn't said what I'd said.

'Are you French in origin?' He asked Jacques.

'*In origin?*' I snorted.

No one picked up on it. 'My parents are French, yes,' Jacques said. 'But I grew up here.'

More than he had ever told me, I realised.

'And you?' Jacques asked him.

'Dublin through and through. My father was a publican. Good working-class stock. Pure prick though.'

I noticed as he said this that his accent shifted from a mid-Atlantic twang to a thick inner-city Dublin.

'And you?' Mark asked me. 'Where do you hail from?'

'Same place as your girlfriend. We were neighbours!'

'Ah yes, she may have mentioned it… *Suburban girls go Wilde*!' he drawled. 'You'd want to watch that kind!'

Linda and Jacques laughed. My cheeks burned.

'Did Linda tell me you were studying French?' Mark went on.

'I guess she must have!'

'Well, you chose well,' he said, referring to Jacques.

'Yes, it's the only reason I'm with him. To practise my French!' I said, trying to be ironic but instead sounding like it might have been true.

'You were awarded a bursary, right?'

'A scholarship,' I corrected him.

'I don't think so,' he said. 'But hey, just semantics. Bottom line: everything's paid for.'

Usually when I referred to myself as a scholarship student I felt a burst of pride, but this time I just felt like a freeloader.

'My father left us without a penny,' I said.

'Fair fucks,' he said, and I didn't know if he was referring to my father having the guts to leave, or to me for getting funding.

'And you act, right?' He continued his drilling.

'Jeez, Linda, what haven't you told him?' I tried to joke with my friend.

'I imagine you're good at it,' he said, and his tone made this sound like an insult and a compliment at the same time.

'Mark directs,' Linda piped up.

'Oh, I thought you said he was a writer?'

'Both,' he said, removing his glasses and placing them on the top of his head. For a moment I was blinded. His eyes: pools of electric blue, creating their own static in the dim pub light, as if a spotlight were shining from behind them, from the inside.

'What year are you?' I asked when I had recovered my composure.

'Fourth,' he said.

'And you're going out with a first year?'

His hand squeezed Linda's knee in answer.

'No girlfriend before now?' I pressed him.

'Who's asking?' he said, looking directly at Linda, who smiled.

'What kind of acting do you do?' he asked me.

'She's very funny!' Linda said. 'Alan Bennett, Ionesco…'

'How about something meatier?'

'I've just been cast as the stepdaughter in *Six Characters in Search of an Author*.'

'Of course you have!'

I didn't know what to make of this. All I knew so far was that she was 'impudent and beautiful'.

'I really admire Pirandello's work,' he declared. 'All that meta self-conscious irony.'

He could have been speaking about himself. *Mr Conscious Contrivance of Disorientation.*

'Did you say that your friend had a stepmother?' he said to Linda while staring at me. 'Interesting casting… Art imitating life…'

I realised I needed to swot up on Pirandello. I also realised that I was feeling as if I were in a spotlight on a stage, the way his attention lasered in on me, and there was nowhere in life I'd rather be.

'I have a new play I'm working on. Well, it's an adaptation of an old one. And I think you could be perfect casting…' He broke his trance with me and turned his attention to Jacques. 'That is, of course, if you agree to lending me your girlfriend!'

Seriously?

Jacques laughed. 'She's a free agent.'

I looked at him, shocked.

'I mean in the professional sense, baby,' he said as he kissed me on the tip of my nose.

'What's the play?' I asked.

'I don't like to speak about a project until it's finished,' he said, making a show of tucking a stray strand of Linda's hair behind her ear. He looked at Jacques and me. 'You two are gorgeous together.'

'Aren't they?' Linda said breathlessly. 'I told you so!'

What else had she told him? I had the feeling that she had already attached herself as ferociously to Mark as she had to me.

'Lindy…? Will we go to the loo?' I stood, determined to claim her back.

'Oh.' She looked in my direction, then back down at Mark's hand, still sitting on her knee. 'I don't need to.'

'Maybe later then?' I said, my voice childlike to my own ears.

'Is "going to the loo" a code then, for something other than needing to use the toilet?' Mark asked. I imagined him jotting this down in his writerly notebook: notes on *the female sex* and their *bathroom etiquette*.

'Of course it is. They're girls!' Jacques said, laughing.

Linda and I caught each other's eyes, and she poked her tongue at me, its tip an arrow.

'Jeez, I wonder how our president would react to that comment,' I said, referring to the fact that Ireland had our very first female president in Mary Robinson.

'Quite the liberalist feminist groover, that one,' Mark said.

'*Groover?*' I said, looking at Linda as we both laughed, aghast.

'What do you think of our new Taoiseach?' He aimed this question at Jacques.

I answered: 'I like his name – Albert Reynolds. Sounds like an old-fashioned movie star.'

'Doesn't look like one, though. He has such an Irish face, those thin lips,' Linda said.

'How about that Roscommon farmer's accent?' I said.

'How about his politics? *Girls?*' Mark said, thoroughly enjoying himself. 'Are you a Fianna Fáil-er, then Jessica?'

I couldn't admit I really didn't have a clue about my country's politics, bar the fact there were two main opposing parties: Fianna Fáil and Fine Gael. One was more 'progressive liberal' and the other more nationalistic, but I was never sure which was which. My world was wholly myopic then: me, me, me. Still is, if I'm honest. Perhaps my particular brand of narcissism, resulting from my abandonment wound? (I am not in the mood for pathologising myself, so I don't bring this 'insight' to Dr Collins.)

'Do you have a strong sense of your Irishness?' Mark asked me.

I didn't.

'Do you speak Gaeilge then?'

'As much as the next person,' I said. Studying the Irish language was still part of the compulsory curriculum. I liked it in as much as I was good at all languages, and it seemed quite romantic, all those idioms.

'Ar nós na gaoithe!' I said, which roughly translated into 'as fast as the wind'.

'Nach breá an lá é?' Linda said. (Isn't it a lovely day?)

'Is breá, buíochas le Dia,' I said. (It is, thanks be to God.)

'Dia duit,' Jacques said. (God be with you.)

'Did you have to learn it, being French?' Mark asked him.

'I was born here, so yes!' Jacques said.

'Dia is Muire duit!' I said back. (God and Mary be with you.)

'I detest that religious bent to our heritage,' Mark said. 'Though the language is beautiful – layered and unique, with its thirty-two words for "field". No wonder those marauding pricks tried to wipe it out.'

'Who, darling? The English?' Linda said, sounding spectacularly stupid.

He acted as if he hadn't heard her, as he went on: 'They needed to eradicate all that wildness, to control us…'

'Póg mo thóin!' I said. (Kiss my arse!)

'Do you like him then?' Mark asked me.

'Who?'

'Pogue Mahone.'

I was lost.

'You know, the lead singer of the Pogues?'

Jacques started singing 'Dirty Old Town' and Linda joined in.

'I love them,' she said dreamily. 'All that Celtic Punk attitude.'

'Except he's English,' Mark said.

'Really?' Linda said. 'He seems more Irish than any other Irishman.'

'Why's that, pet? Because he drinks and swears?'

Pet.

'He's more than that: his whole rebellious stance, his whole shtick.'

I hadn't known she listened to music other than what Sue introduced her to.

'Sinéad O'Connor is the real deal,' Jacques said.

'No arguing with that,' Mark said. As if everything should be an argument.

'She's a goddess!' I said. 'With her bald beauty, literally and figuratively.'

'I'd love to work with her someday. That combination of rage and vulnerability – so pure.'

'Well, dream on…' I said.

No one laughed. It seemed possible, in that moment.

'I'd like to write a part for her,' Mark went on.

I said nothing. It stunned me that I desperately wanted to hear him say the same thing about me.

15

Jacques and I were cuddling in bed, snuggled deep under the quilt, thick socks on, after a vigorous round of tension-releasing sex that left a sheen of cold sweat on our bodies. He pretended to gobble me up. 'Where are you under all these layers?' I burrowed further under the quilt, pulling it over my head. After a few moments I had to come up for air.

'What a dick!' I said.

'Why thank you, darling!'

'You know who I mean… *If you agree to lending me your girlfriend*,' I said, aping as best as I could Mark's hybrid American/Dublin accent. 'What a pretentious douchebag.'

'I didn't see you refusing. Anything for a part!' Jacques said, tickling me.

I pushed him off me and said in an affected French accent: 'Zis is ze man of ze moment… And zey are *girls*…! You pig!'

'Hey. But only girls use the code "going to the loo". You told me that yourself.'

'Not so you could throw it back in my face and publicly humiliate me.'

'Being a tad dramatic there, Jess.'

'Calling our president *a liberalist, feminist groover*. You don't think that's off?'

Jacques laughed, wiping his eyes with the back of his hand, tears streaming down his face.

I leant in and licked them off his cheeks.

'Did you notice how he was interrogating me?'

'I thought he was just interested.'

'Not over-interested?' I said, provocatively.

'No,' Jacques said baldly, which wasn't the answer I had been hoping for. He reached for his jumper, which was crumpled in a heap on the floor where he had left it the night before.

'How about the way he kept his hand on Linda's knee the whole time?'

'What's wrong with that?' he said as he pulled his jumper over his head.

'You didn't think it was a display of ownership?'

Jacques leaned in and tongue-kissed me deeply. 'Now, that's what I call ownership!'

'But this is our own private act,' I said, 'we're not putting on a show for anyone.'

'Would you like us to?' Jacques asked.

'I think Mark would like us to. *You two are gorgeous together!*' I said making a pretend-gagging face.

'But we are, darling!' Jonathan cocked his head to one side and pouted. I went in for a kiss.

'And what about the way he called Linda *pet*?'

'Bit ick, alright.'

'He's all over her,' I said. 'Handsy.'

'No more than I am with you.' He pulled me up beside him, wrapped me in his jumper.

I pushed him off me. 'Really, you really think he's the same as you are with me?'

'What is it about him that has you so riled up?' He studied my face in an exaggerated way.

'Did you see the way he stopped her going to the loo?' I forged on.

'No he didn't. She herself said she didn't need to.'

'His hand pressed down on her knee. I saw it.'

'Are you jealous, Jessie Messy?' He kissed my bellybutton.

I didn't like that nickname, wherever it had sprung from.

'Now that's pathetic,' I said, referring to both the nickname and his lack of observational powers.

'Just tell me you sensed something was off?'

'I don't think it'll last, if that makes you feel better.'

'Why?'

'I sense she's just his latest project.'

Project. That seemed chillingly on point.

'I hope he doesn't use her and then leave her. I don't think Linda would survive that.'

'Of course she would. She's a big girl.'

I chose not to expose my friend's painful history and insecurities further.

'Did you hear the way he spoke about my scholarship?'

'I don't think he meant anything by it.'

'Seriously? Did you not see that he was being deliberately insulting, calling it a *bursary*?'

'I mean, it is, in the strictest sense, isn't it? You didn't have to sit an exam…'

'That's not the point,' I said. 'He *corrected* me publicly.'

'I think his communication style is just overly direct. He might be somewhere on the spectrum.'

'What do you mean: *on the spectrum*?' I asked. (Nineties Dublin wasn't exactly known for its PC categorisations in this way; there were just a lot of 'oddballs' or 'headbangers' or 'head-the-balls' walking around.)

'Oh, nothing. It's just something that was said about my brother.'

I held my breath. The first time he had willingly offered up anything about his family. He brought his jumper sleeve to his mouth and started to suck. I watched him in silence, before he looked at me, grinned, then pulled me to him, and started to nibble my earlobe.

'Where's your brother now?' I asked gently.

He stood on the bed and climbed over me.

'Where are you going?'

'Jesus, now who's being controlling! To the loo, that OK?' He turned and grinned at me. 'You really don't like this guy, I get it. But as I say, Jealous Jessie, he won't be around for long.' He blew me a kiss before he left, then he poked his head around the door. 'Unlike me. You won't get rid of me that easily.'

I sat on the bed and wondered at my boyfriend, who was so detached from his own family, yet so invested in me. Who was this brother that his mother had said was 'on the spectrum', and where were they? Why had he insisted on erasing them so fully from his new life?

*

'Don't you think it's normal to pull away from parents at that stage in your development?' Dr Collins asks.

I look out the window and see only the wall.

'In order to forge new bonds?' she continues.

'Well, yes there's a certain amount of individuating that goes on, of course … but here's what I think…'

I imagine I can hear the insects on the wall scurrying and whispering to each other, busy in their pointless existence.

Dr Collins is waiting patiently, although I notice her right thumb is twitching.

'Those college kids who needed to maintain the most distant attitude, the greatest fuck-you attitude, were the ones who had the strongest ties, the strongest psychic connections with their families…'

I am becoming adept at making connections now. Or making things up.

'Did you feel that way?'

'Well, I needed space from Sue, yes, but not on the level that Mark declared was necessary.'

'*Necessary?*'

'*Breaking free requires a sort of severing.*' I am parroting him now.

'Like how your father did it.'

'He probably had to.' I shrug, pointless.

'Is that how you're approaching your divorce now?'

'No,' I say. 'I don't care enough to have to do that.'

'Is that true?'

'It's how I feel … or don't feel.'

'Is that what Mark encouraged you to do? Sever attachments?'

I ponder that for a moment, thinking of the complications of our respective home lives. 'How did he know?'

'Know what?'

'To alight on us?'

Dr Collins does that leaning-in thing and the ensuing silence thing. And my mind is in full flight.

*

When I try to describe Mark now and commit him to paper, the main thing I remember is a bizarre state of attuned attention that I experienced around him. How the air seemed to shift and rearrange itself around his presence, and how hard I had to work not to look into his eyes.

He was not handsome in the way that Jacques and Jonathan were – his shoulders were too narrow, mouth drawn too tightly, hair leached of pigment, hands and feet too large, his skin milky, as if he had spent his early childhood in dark rooms. Yet, those blue, blue lenses through which he viewed the world were electric portals to other realms. He carried himself with an air of *fuck you* – it wasn't charisma in the normal sense of the word, but something sort of dark-sexy. He made us, his inner circle, feel permanently horny, turned on, tuned in. Which is irresistible when you are eighteen and unmoored. He could sense the stuff pulsing beneath the veneer of 'cool'. He could smell it and he fed off it and he fed it back to us, until we were gorging on the undercurrents of hurt we hadn't even been aware we were carrying.

*

'Jessica?' Dr Collins's voice cuts through.

I look directly at her. 'I'm not sure I can trust my memories.'

'And yet you are still here, trying to untangle your past.'

'It feels as if I'm concocting a story.'

Dr Collins contains a sigh, looks down at her hands, which are now perfectly still, resting on her neat pencil skirt. I look at mine, jittery, too much life pulsing through them, the stubby nails, ragged cuticles, once slender and expressive, now veined and twig-like. I am still only in my forties. What will they look like in a decade or two? How will time distort and mar them further, and how will my memories appear to me then?

16

My eyes blurred as my finger moved beneath the lines. I was in the Lecky, the arts block library, a starkly modern, overlit, overheated place, dry air blasting from vents at my feet. My concentration was sketchy, my sleep and daylight hours having been invaded by a new anxiety. How long would the *auteur* stick around? I forced my itching eyes back to the page. 'The parasol of dove-grey iridescent silk, with the sun shining through it … cast moving glimmers of sun over the white skin of her face… She was smiling beneath it in the mild warmth … and they could hear the drops of water, one by one, falling on the taut moiré…' *Oh please.* Jacques told me I'd adore this one, and that I was sure to relate to the main character: a vain, shallow, bored, love-addicted, capricious, fatuous woman. Emma Bovary was given the male treatment, and I was pissed at Jacques. And so much unnecessary, overblown description.

'Boo,' a voice whispered in my ear from behind.

'Jesus, fuck!' I screamed.

'No fear of you going into the freeze reaction,' the voice said. 'Have you been avoiding me?' Jonathan slid into the chair opposite me.

A guy at the desk next to mine looked up. 'Would you mind shutting the hell up?' he said.

I smiled at the guy, aggressively coquettish, then turned my attention to Jonathan: his handsome symmetrical features and rigorously worked-out body in contrast with his unruly hair, and nature. I liked this at-oddness in him.

'Coffee?' he stage-whispered, for effect.

I followed him to the coffee dock, anything for distraction.

'How are you getting on with *Madame Bovary*?' he said as we joined the queue.

I fake-yawned.

'I love that book.'

'Hardly on your economics reading list, is it?'

'My mother read a lot.'

So perhaps not quite as 'manicured' as Linda had surmised.

'Don't you find her a bit overwrought?' I paraphrased: 'Tremulous, hopeful, vulnerable, reckless, ecstatic, breathless, oh, of course beautiful, and spirited, and smelling like a spring morning … her dewy skirts, her pounding heart, tumultuous, modest lips and shining face … hardly *scrupulous* literary realism, as the male critics attest.'

'Oh my God, someone should cast you as her, you'd be brilliant!'

We were at the top of the queue and Jonathan ordered two cappuccinos, which was deliciously sophisticated.

'He was a fat, spoiled man, you know, Flaubert, who loved to visit whore houses. Apparently, he lived his life in fear of contracting syphilis.'

'So? I wouldn't have thought of you as giving a shit about morals!' Jonathan handed me the souped-up coffee and I went to the counter and pulled open two sachets of sugar and emptied them, stirring vigorously. I had never put sugar in my coffee before, but now I needed to feel the rush and the tang.

'I just feel the male gaze all over her. He scorns her even as he indulges her.' I sipped, grimaced. My teeth sang from the sugar overload. I quoted, speaking exaggeratedly: 'For her, life was as cold as an attic with a window looking north, and ennui, like a spider, was silently spinning its shadowy web in every cranny of her heart.' I put a finger in my mouth and pretend-puked.

He laughed as he led me to one of the plastic seats, where I slid in beside him. 'I think that's kind of brilliant.'

'The ultimate Sleeping Beauty…'

'Well, at least he didn't write her as happily ever after, finding her prince.'

'There is that! But it's creepy, how he writes about her.'

'I guess so… I never thought of it that way,' Jonathan said.

'What else did your mother read?'

'She had a stash of Jilly Cooper.'

'So horny.'

'*Riders* was my favourite!'

'Me too!'

'Would you feel that way if a man had written it?'

'Probably not…' I concede.

'How's Jacques?'

'Speaking of hot stable hands?'

Jonathan plucked at his jumper, rolled up a tiny wool ball between thumb and forefinger and flicked it at me. I threw my hands up in a gesture of mock surrender.

'He's great. You should have a pint with us later. He was only asking for you.'

'I'd like that. I feel like Linda's avoiding me.'

'This new guy has quite a hold over her,' I said. 'But Jacques doesn't think it'll last.'

'Do you?'

'Too early to tell, but you know, she loves the attention. She needs it.'

He shuffled a little, went red around the tips of his ears. 'I was a bit cruel at Christmas, I know that, but I didn't want to lead her on.' He lifted his cup, cradled it.

'She was just pissed.'

'Well, look, I'm happy for her, if she's found someone to love her. She deserves that.'

I studied him. 'Doesn't everyone?'

'I think it might be more extreme with Linda…'

'Why do you say that?'

'My mum said Linda seemed unloved. She intimated that it wouldn't be good for me to be around someone so damaged.'

'God. That's harsh. So, unloved equals unlovable?'

'That's typical of my mother. Her capacity for empathy is limited: it only extends as far as herself – and me, as an extension of her.'

We both fell silent. He exhaled too hard into his cup and hot liquid splashed into his face. 'Fuuuck.'

'You OK?'

He wiped his cheeks with his sleeve.

'Here.' I handed him a bottle of water from my bag.

'Cheers.' He tipped some into his palms and patted them onto his face. 'Will you organise a drink or something?'

'Sure,' I said, feeling a strange trepidation.

'I miss her, you know. I have dreams about her … not in the Jilly Cooper kind of way, obviously.'

'Obviously… Maybe you two vibrate at an unconscious level you're unaware of. Maybe it's the sadness your mother spoke about?'

'God, that's terrible,' he said. 'Counselling for Dummies!'

He laughed; I didn't.

She was that type. The vulnerable who inveigle their way into your subconscious. When Linda attached to you, you felt as if you were the only one. And then I thought of invisible webs and invisible spinners. And of Linda's cold, north-facing home, nurturing no living thing. And of her having to get up on her tiptoes to reach her front door. I blamed Flaubert.

17

'You look great, Linda,' Jacques said. And she did. She was lovely in a new lemon-yellow cardigan and below-the-knee full skirt, which should have been twee, but instead looked retro-sweet, sort of fifties housewifey. Her skinny frame gave her a wistful *Revolutionary Road* April Wheeler quality. Mark smiled, as if the compliment were aimed at him, suggesting that he was the architect of this new look.

We were in the Dungeon, a dark, windowless bar on campus, thick with smoke and a palpable whiff of cheap toilet-cleaning fluid choking the airwaves – the place where the arty crew, the thespians, the dope-heads went. I had organised that we have a drink there, thinking that Mark would look ridiculously affected set against the boho laid-back vibe of the place, and Linda would see him for the imposter he was. Except that Mark could blend in or stand out at will, it seemed – even the surroundings organised themselves to accommodate him. Suddenly his parka and cowboy boots looked outré, not farcical. There was no denying the stares he got, but they had nothing to do with ridicule.

'Jonathan's coming in a bit,' I said to Linda.

She immediately looked anxious. 'Didn't you think to tell me?'

'Well, I'm telling you now!'

'Loo?' It sounded code red.

I got up, followed her, Mark's delighted voice trailing us: 'I wonder what urgent business those two have to discuss.'

'Actually, I just need to pee,' I said, determined to have the last word on the discourse of female loo-going politics.

The lights in the ladies were blue fluorescent, making both of us seem ghoul-like. 'What are you doing?' Linda said.

'What do you mean? Jonathan misses you, so I invited him.'

Linda turned the tap on and watched the stream of water, saying nothing.

'What has you so worried, Lindy?'

She continued staring, trance-like, down the sink.

I turned it off, clapped in front of her face. 'Come on, if you're that freaked about your boyfriend meeting your handsome friend, then perhaps you should re-think your boyfriend?'

'Oh, fuck off, Jess.'

I was stunned. Linda had never said those words to me before; she had never uttered those words. Full stop. They were my domain.

'Do you really think I'm not attractive enough to have a man who fancies only me?'

'I did not mean it like that.'

'Yes, you did.'

A silence fell between us. I remembered with shame our early days.

'You know I love you, Lindy.'

She looked at me with suspicion, and longing. We locked eyes, the blue strip lighting overhead casting shadows that made our eyes look deeply grooved.

I spoke in a softer tone. 'What has you so worried?'

She was searching carefully, as if anything she said might sound ridiculous. 'I don't know. I just wish you hadn't invited him. I'm not ready.'

Not ready. Was she more hurt than I had realised about Christmas? I found myself saying something I rarely said, to Linda, or anyone: 'Sorry.' It diminished me, instantly. It felt fawning. Was I sorry, or was I just being tactical, attempting to inveigle my way back into her affections?

'Forget about it,' she said huffily. 'It's done now.' I was surprised my apology did not have the intended effect; I doubt anyone had ever said sorry to Linda before. She looked at herself in the mirror and it was as if her mother's eyes were staring back at her: the depth of her self-hatred was breathtaking. I put my arms around her from behind and regarded us both in the mirror, making sure to catch her eyes, which were grey and misty in this light. 'You look really beautiful tonight, Lindy.'

'Right,' she said, as she pushed me off her and turned away.

I wondered why she felt more worried about Jonathan meeting her boyfriend than she had me. Surely I posed a greater threat? I looked at my reflection and saw only an outline occupying empty space, as if I were a hastily drawn sketch.

Jonathan was already sitting on a bar stool, deep in conversation with Mark and Jacques by the time we returned. His sporty jock get-up looked more incongruous than Mark's eclectic designed-to-disorient ensemble. Linda stiffened, pulled her shoulders back and affected a saunter in their direction. Jonathan stood when he saw us. 'Hey, stranger.'

'Hi Jonathan.' She sounded far away, and muffled, as if underwater.

'It's been a while... Mum was asking for you,' Jonathan went on.

I wondered why he was lying. Linda smiled in that new tight way she had, not giving eye contact to anyone. She sat quietly beside Mark who put his hand on her knee. She seemed soothed by this, also trapped, but willingly, as she placed her hand over his. A bird bred in captivity would only ever feel comfortable in confined spaces. I scoffed at my own attempt at doing a nineteenth-century man of letters on her. But Linda *did* put me in mind of a caged bird: tiny, yet full of power and potential that had been stolen from her. And at that time, there was still a possibility that she might have found her way out.

*

Dr Collins makes effective use of silence here.

'I should have done more.'

A flash from that night. *To dare is to lose one's footing momentarily* – I hear my wild voice quoting Kierkegaard – or was it Mark's voice? The memories are shadowy, flitting. The night continues its distorted echoes.

She leans in.

'I shouldn't have let him play her that way.'

'Or you.'

'Or any of us, yes.'

'You were young and impressionable.'

'But I was into it: the competition for Linda, the games he engineered.'

'Can you understand why?'

'I was a selfish, adrenaline-addicted, spotlight-seeking fiend.'

Which is aligning with Mark's version of me in his new play: a seductive, exhibitionistic, damaged stepdaughter, masquerading as 'best friend'. How had I not seen the parallels before now?

'*Fiend?*' Dr Collins repeats my word back to me.

I shrug.

'Not helpful, Jessica. Locking yourself down like that.'

A favourite of Mark's: stay open to surprising yourself, stretching your limits. In life, as in art.

Is that what this is? Just another attempt at 'refashioning', 'reorganising' the self into a different shape? Well, fuck that, I know how this goes. The potential for harm is too extreme.

I look at my phone. Five minutes to go. 'Forgot I have to be somewhere,' I say, standing.

Dr Collins says nothing, nods.

'Thank you, for everything,' I say, and I mean it.

I turn and leave the room. From now on this story is mine.

*

'Drinks?' Jonathan asked. I said I'd get them, then Jacques said he'd like to get them, then Mark said he'd get them, and his tone of voice meant we let him. After we gave our orders, Jacques turned to Jonathan and sort of slapped him on the back. The two of them play-wrestled a bit, as Linda sat stiffly on a bright orange plastic seat – a retro nod to primary school and an ironic nod to the stoners of the future. I sat beside her and placed my hand on her jigging knee, but she brushed it away. Mark returned, his pianist's hands – elegant and long-fingered – easily holding the five drinks. As soon as he placed them on the table, we all reached for them and drank deeply and quickly, except for Mark himself who sipped his lemonade with restraint. I could feel him studying us: our collective thirst.

'Great to meet you, finally,' he said, taking Jonathan in.

'Yeah, good to meet you too.' Jonathan was more interested in trying to get Linda to engage, but she wouldn't look in his direction.

'Weird how resistant this one was to our meeting,' Mark went on as he squeezed just above Linda's knee. Her leg involuntarily shot out. He laughed, as if he were laughing *at*, not with, a cute toddler. She buttoned up her cardigan, but not before I could see the beginnings of a flush on her chest.

'I guess she was just busy with other stuff,' Jonathan said.

'Not her studies, certainly…' Mark said as he tucked her hair behind her ear.

'Well, plenty of time for that. Exams are a way off,' Jonathan said.

'How's your studying going? I saw you and Jessica bunking off earlier.'

That observation felt distinctly stalkerish, and yet it was entirely possible he had just seen us in passing…

'We were having a coffee, discussing *Madame Bovary*.'

'How are you getting on with her, Jess?' Jacques asked me.

'She's nothing like me.'

'There you go, bringing it all back to you again, Jessica,' Mark said, knocking the wind out of me. The fucking audacity of it.

I looked to Jacques for backup, but he seemed not to have heard; Linda was still preoccupied by her blushing; only Jonathan seemed to notice as he flinched.

'What are you studying?' Mark asked him, deflecting expertly.

'Business, economics and social studies … for my sins,' Jonathan said. 'Deathly dull.'

'I'm really enjoying the calibre of the teaching here,' Mark said. He sounded so formal and old-fashioned, as if he were play-acting at being a Victorian-era scribe.

'What do you study?' Jonathan asked him.

'Pure philosophy.'

'Cool. I didn't think that was a thing. I didn't have a choice. My father wouldn't pay the fees if I didn't study BESS. I'm to take on the family business, apparently. His way to alleviate his guilt for being an absent prick.'

'No fear of mine needing to appease his guilt.' I laughed too brightly.

'*Appease*…' Mark seemed to ponder the meaning of that word. 'How about you, Jacques?'

'All paid for.' His face shut down. I studied him, determined to grill him later.

'And yours?' Mark said to Linda. 'Your father isn't the worst, is he? Paying for everything.'

'He owed her so much more than just fucking money,' I said. 'That man knew what was going on at home and he just left her there.'

Her body contracted, as though she thought maybe if she shrank enough, she might disappear. I shouldn't have exposed her – her expression reminded me of the moment when she told Sue that her mother hadn't wanted her. The fact of it being witnessed making it real, the public humiliation of it.

Jonathan stood suddenly, scraped back his chair, the legs screeching against the concrete floor. 'Hey Linda, can we go outside for a moment? I'd really like to talk to you.'

'I don't feel like it now,' she said.

'Good,' Mark said. 'That's good. You're getting better at voicing yourself.'

I wanted to tell him to fuck off, but it was as if my throat was stoppered.

'Linda, you're grand as you are.' Jonathan sounded exasperated.

'I'm just trying to help her be the best version of herself.' Mark said, looking at me. 'No one taught her to take up space and speak up for herself.' Then he spoke directly to Linda: '*Be that self which one truly is.*'

I sniggered.

'Something funny?' Mark asked.

'You are! *Be that self which one truly is!*'

I felt that schoolgirl edge again, that sharpness that enabled me to survive my father leaving.

'Ridiculous posturer.' This guy was stoking my mean-girl.

'Jessica!' Jacques sounded shocked. He didn't know this side to me. The 'fuck off' version who appeared anytime my friendship was under threat.

'Not now, Jessie,' Linda said.

'Those words belong to a famous philosopher,' Mark said, seemingly delighted.

'Who? Nietzsche?' I said, scoffing.

'Do they sound like the words of a nihilist?' Mark said.

I really didn't have a clue and should have acknowledged as much to myself instead of launching into an ill-formed argument: 'Aren't they all the same…? In some form or another. This world is a big black hole, and it will devour you.'

'Wow. Limited,' Mark said. 'Kierkegaard was, in fact, an existentialist and a Christian who believed in the power of love.'

'Is that a fact, *in fact*?' I said.

'A Christian who believes in love?' Jonathan said.

'Holding the paradox,' Mark said.

To which there could be no retort, or none that could satisfy anyone. I was riled. His presence, the very *essence* of him, inspired a scrappy excitement in me.

'You don't deserve my friend.'

'I'm not sure you deserve your friend either,' Mark replied.

'You're talking about her as if she's *property*,' Jonathan said.

Linda laughed, as if perhaps she liked that notion. Two people fighting over her.

My next shot was suitably schoolgirlish: 'Those glasses are poncey. That parka is pricky, as in only a prick would wear one!'

'I take your point,' he said, easy in himself. 'And I raise it.'

'Go on then,' I said, goading him.

'Jacques?' he said.

'Are you asking my boyfriend permission to insult me?'

'Permission for some home-truths,' he said.

'Jess?' Jacques said, looking at me perplexed. He was no match for our games.

'Your accent is fake,' I said, lobbing another one at him. 'Everything about you is an act.'

'Ever the provocateur,' he said. 'I'm beyond excited to see you play the stepdaughter. Pirandello himself would be hard with excitement at the thought of it.'

'Why, thank you,' I said, curtsying theatrically.

Jacques, Jonathan and Linda all looked various shades of appalled, though equally transfixed by the unfolding duet.

'A word of truth, Jessica?'

'Go for it,' I said.

'That red top really doesn't suit you. It clashes with your complexion, and everyone knows red doesn't go with blonde hair, it makes it look brassy.'

Jonathan stood. 'Fuck's sake.'

'Pathetic.' A harsh laugh escaped me.

Jacques joined in nervously, taking his lead from me.

'All in the spirit of truth-telling among friends!' Mark said.

'Is that the best you can do?'

'I'll save that for another day!' he said.

I felt unconscionably excited.

He stroked Linda's hair, as he said, '*Love does not seek its own, for there are no mine or yours in love.*' She seemed to dissolve into him.

'I should hope those words are your existentialist fellow's and not yours,' I said.

'They are,' he said as he kissed Linda on the lips. 'And I share his belief.'

'Handy for a controller!' I said.

'Telling – that you'd interpret it that way.'

He scored that point. I pinched my palm.

'I feel we're being quite rude, Jessica. There are three other people here, in case you hadn't noticed.'

Masterful: how he managed to lay the responsibility for our performance at my feet. And how he suddenly appeared reasonable. And how the tone of his voice changed from combative to conciliatory in a second.

He turned to Jacques. 'Hope you don't mind. I was in fact testing Jessica for a part I'm writing.'

'How did she do?' Jacques said, getting drawn in

'Smashed it!' Mark said.

A smile played at the edges of Jacques's lips; he was struggling to keep himself in check. A part of him was enjoying witnessing our vicious sparring. What did that say about how he viewed me…?

Mark trailed his fingertips over Linda's right cheek, and lightly pinched. Uncanny, the similarities with how he was treating my friend and how I used to be with her. He then kissed her pink cheek.

Was it my imagination, or did Linda look at me smugly, as if to say, *you're not the only one who is desired like this*?

The two of them stood, hands intertwined, and turned to leave.

'Don't drink too much,' was Mark's parting shot. Nothing from Linda.

As soon as the two of them were out of range, Jonathan said, 'What the fuck? You were like Burton and Taylor, going at each other like that.'

'I should hope not!' Jacques said.

'In *Who's Afraid of Virginia Woolf*?' I said. 'God, yes. He's just like George!'

'And you were a perfect Martha,' Jonathan said.

'Mais, merci!' I genuflected graciously.

'I didn't mean it as a compliment.'

'Drinks?' Jacques asked, standing to go to the bar.

'Mais, oui!' I said, feeling jangled.

'Definitely,' Jonathan said.

'I hope she's OK,' I said, quietly. 'I hope she knows who she's dealing with.'

Jonathan looked at me sideways, not a trace of humour between us, a silent acknowledgement.

Jacques returned with three pints.

'*Don't drink too much*,' Jonathan said, aping Mark.

'Cheers to that,' I said.

'Amen,' Jacques said.

And we drank. And we drank. And we drank. The three of us. Not quite to oblivion, but to the edge. The laughter vanquished, drowned by the booze.

18

The next morning I woke up hungover, raw, oversensitive. I cried after Jacques came inside me, making sure not to let him see. Something to do with feeling like a receptacle, an object, my body a place of physical release for him; something to do with making strange, where before having him inside me felt like a homecoming. (Later on, sex became associated with a feeling of being invaded, but not then – there was no aggression in Jacques.)

I got up early, leaving Jacques in my bed without waking him for the first time ever, and headed to the coffee dock. I ordered a strong black coffee heaped with sugar – my need for manufactured sweetness had fast become a habit – and waited outside Linda's lecture hall. She appeared, talking animatedly to someone I'd never met before: a nondescript, mousy-looking girl, brown hair, washed-out blue eyes, with a sharp, fast-speaking voice. Ratatatatat. Her arm was resting possessively on Linda's.

'Lindy?' I said, loudly.

'Oh hey… What are you doing up so early?' Then she turned to the mouse and giggled with her, at me. 'Jessie doesn't usually surface before midday. With a hottie like *Jacques Cousteau* in her bed, who can blame her.'

The girl sniggered back, squeak, squeak.

'I need to speak to you.'

'Sorry,' Linda said. 'I'm going for a coffee with Mairin.'

'Well, I'm sorry, but I really need to speak to you, now. I'm sure *Mairin*'ll understand.'

Linda stared at me. I tried to signal 'code red'. She looked at her new sidekick. 'Sorry about this. Jess is known to be quite dramatic!'

I linked arms with Linda in a show of female camaraderie and friendly fuck-you.

'See you tomorrow?' Mousey said.

'Sure,' Linda said, then turned to me. 'What's this all about?'

I steered her through the automatic doors that opened onto the square in front of the arts block. She was wearing the same outfit from the night before.

'Someone didn't go home last night,' I said.

She looked up at the sky. 'Bit spitty,' she said dubiously.

'It's just a bit of drizzle.' I was craving space and sky and fresh air.

'What's with this new obsession of yours with the great outdoors?' she said. 'You were never exactly the nature type.'

She was, though. I thought of how, as a child, she noticed beauty and magic everywhere: the lone ladybird on a blade of grass would move her to tears, the bees buzzing in early summer would have her literally spinning with delight. I recalled her rapture as Sue would read one of her many renditions of *The Faraway Tree*.

The rain intensified as I led us in the direction of the playing fields. Linda wrapped her arms around her thin body, clad only in a light blouse and cardigan. I manoeuvred us both under the canopy of a huge evergreen tree on the edge of the cricket pitch, its leafy branches providing some shelter. A large drop fell on her neck, and she pulled her collar high, shivering.

'Here.' I took off my jacket, put it over her shoulders. 'You need to dress more appropriately.'

'Yes, Mam.' She looked up at the branches above our head. 'I think this is an oak, an evergreen. Unusual … I've seen it from afar but never this close up. It's majestic.'

She leaned her back against the tree, closed her eyes and inhaled deeply.

'Aren't you going to hug it?' I asked.

Her eyes snapped open. 'What did you want to speak to me about?'

I put my ear against the tree's trunk. 'Shhhhh. It's talking to me…'

'What's it saying?' she whispered, unable to resist the lure of enchantment.

'It's called the Wise One, did you know that?'

'Not very original.' She laughed.

'It's saying: be careful of that man,' I went on.

She stopped laughing. 'You seemed to be enjoying his company last night.'

I wasn't sure what her tone was suggesting.

'Lindy, I'm worried about you.'

'Not this again,' she said.

'I saw what he did to you,' I said, referring to the pinch.

She stared at me. It was a revolt of a stare. She had a right to hold that mirror up to me.

'If Mark acts like that in public, what's he like in private?' I said, carefully.

'I think you might know the answer to that better than anyone, Jess.'

It was as if she'd punched me in my windpipe, such was the force of the shock.

'He's actually very sweet when you get to know him,' she continued.

'*Sweet?* He insulted me, your best friend, in front of everyone.'

'Hey, he was just being honest: that red top *is* terrible on you!' She grimaced as if amused and apologetic at the same time. 'He doesn't beat about the bush. I like that: his directness. He tells the truth. It's refreshing.'

'Does he use that expression with you – "a word of truth" – before he launches into an insult?'

'No, just with you,' she said. 'He doesn't spar with me like that. He could see you got off on it.'

I wondered if she was feeling jealous, but nothing in her bearing suggested this.

'You met your match, at last!' She grinned widely, something I'd never witnessed before. Her smile had always been tight, as if she was afraid to give expression to pleasure, for fear that it might be snatched away from her.

She ploughed on: 'Actually, he might have outsmarted you.'

For now. I didn't say anything.

'You know I think you should go for that part in his new play. It'd challenge you as an actress.'

'What's it about?' I said, getting sucked in, despite telling myself the whole reason I needed to see her was to warn her off him.

'Top secret,' she said, tapping the tip of her nose with her finger, a ridiculous affectation, and something I'd never seen her do before. 'He has an interesting way of working with his actors. He only allows them to read their part. The rest of it is discovered in the moment, in rehearsal.'

'A way for him to retain ultimate control,' I said.

'Actually, I think it may be a way for the actor to lose control,' she said. 'Ironically.'

'You wouldn't mind?'

'Why would I mind?' She studied me, then burst out laughing. 'Oh Jess, he really doesn't fancy you. Not everyone does.'

I smarted, felt my cheeks get hot.

'He told me you're categorically not his type.'

'I wonder why he felt the need to tell you that,' I said. 'Jacques would never say anything like that about you.'

'Oh come off it. Don't pretend you don't know that I've never come out on top, in any man's eyes, where you and I are concerned, before now.'

'What about Stuart?'

'Stupid Stu, the halitosis goon?' She shook her head. 'Man, you were mean… He couldn't even speak in front of you. Mark, on the other hand… He could wipe the floor with you!'

'Lindy?'

'Huh?'

'Are you sure you can trust him?'

She started humming some obscure tune to block me out.

'OK,' I said. 'OK, I get the point…'

She stopped, looked directly at me. 'He told me last night that I was the best thing that has ever happened to him.'

'Of course you are. You're the best thing that ever happened to me too.'

This didn't seem to have any impact on her.

'I'm in love, Jess for the first time ever.'

'Love?' I said, startled. 'Bit early for that word.'

'You know when you know,' she said.

My heart started to race. Excitement? Worry? Revulsion? Its opposite? This was not a thought I would give space to.

'Hey J,' she said. 'I'll always adore you. No man will ever come between us, right?' Then she lightly pinched my forearm. A first. It felt right. 'I get that you're concerned. But don't be, OK? Give me that respect this time.'

I kissed her on her cheek. 'OK,' I said, knowing as I said it that I shouldn't have.

'Now can we go back inside? It's feckin' freezing.'

'Fine, but before we go…' I rested my hand on the trunk of the tree and looked up. I put on my best Enid Blyton voice: '*Its top goes right up to the clouds – and, oh Rick, at the top of it is always some strange land…*'

She was doing her best to supress a smile. 'Oh Rick.' She sighed and shivered, as if she were seven again, hearing the story for the first time in the lukewarm bath.

'Have you been talking to Sue recently?' I asked.

'Been too busy,' she said.

'Well, when you do, will you tell her I was asking for her?'

'Tell her yourself,' she said as she turned on her heel and walked away. '*Strange lands*,' I thought I heard from behind me.

'Where did you disappear to this morning?' Jacques wrapped me in a bear hug as I came into the student kitchen, where he was preparing a lunch of pasta puttanesca.

'I just needed to talk to Linda,' I said. 'I'm worried about her.'

'Are you? Funny way of showing it last night…'

'Ah, I was just pissed.'

'Were you?'

'Yes, I was. That guy gets to me.'

'You don't say!' He ladled a bowl of pasta for me. 'You were pretty rude!'

'*I* was? He insulted me from the get-go, and you didn't defend me.'

He studied me, bit his bottom lip. 'You really didn't seem to need defending, Jess.'

'Did you enjoy watching him humiliating me?'

A girl walked into the kitchen, stared too long at my boyfriend.

'What the fuck are you looking at?' I said.

'Jesus, cool the head,' she said before walking back out.

'Are you PMS-ing?' Jacques asked. Which pissed me off even more.

'If I am *moody* as you are suggesting, it's because I am pumping my body full of synthetic hormones so you can have free and easy sex on tap.'

He laughed lightly. 'It's not just me who wants it free and easy… Or on demand, for that matter.'

I thought of Sue. She had suggested I go on the pill when I was sixteen because of my terrible periods. And a by-product of that, she told me, was that I wouldn't get pregnant. Not a word about the dangers of STDs. I missed her.

'You know the way you met Sue?'

'Not likely to forget!' he said, shovelling a spoonful of pasta into his mouth.

'Well, I'd like to meet someone from your camp.'

He seemed to have difficulty swallowing.

'Did you hear me? I'd like to meet your parents.'

'Well, you can't. I told you already.'

'Why not?'

'They're in France.'

'Are they together?'

'Of course not. They're French.'

His flippancy was off-putting.

'Where do you live?'

'With you most of the time.'

'And the rest of the time?'

'What is this?'

'Where is your brother?'

He drank slowly from a glass of water. 'My brother is the only member of my family who lives in Dublin.'

'I want to meet him, I insist…'

'I don't think that's a good idea, Jess.'

'Well, for your information, I refuse to continue with this charade of ours unless you introduce me to your brother.'

Jacques stood and scraped the remainder of his half-full pasta dish into the foul, overflowing bin, and in a cold voice I had never heard before said, 'I do not respond well to threats.' And he left.

19

'Good morning!' Their two voices a cacophony: his low and sonorous, hers high and chirpy. The greeting was so upbeat and jazzy, it sounded like a taunt. I had just come out of my Monday morning grammar and comprehension tutorial and was on my way to the canteen to get something to cut through the fog in my brain.

'Good morning to you too!' I said, dragging up reserves of fake politeness. I was unslept and aggravated after my first night apart from Jacques since I had met him four months ago. 'Where are you two coming from?'

'Mark's rooms in Front Square.'

'The *Schol* rooms?' I asked.

'The very same,' Linda said proudly.

I turned to Mark. 'Why didn't you tell me you were on a full scholarship before?' I was appalled. He was obviously in a league far above me. The Foundation Scholarships were highly prestigious, only granted to the very top first-class honours students.

'I guess I didn't feel the need to!' Mark said breezily, landing a jab.

'You OK, Jess?' Linda asked. 'You look a bit rough.'

'Fine.'

'You know what that acronym stands for?' Mark said. 'Fucked up, insecure, neurotic, erotic.'

'That is bullshit. The "e" actually refers to "emotional".'

'Same thing.'

'Look at you two go!' Linda said. I thought she might clap.

Mark smiled warmly. 'You know, Jess, I think it would be good for us to get to know each other better, seeing as this one is so important in both our lives…' He kissed Linda sensuously on the lips, and I felt that something that I couldn't name, or wouldn't allow myself to.

'There's a Lebanese cafe in the Herbert Arcade. Meet you there at one thirty for a quick bite?'

'You coming, Linda?' I asked.

'No, you go,' she said. 'You can talk about the play.'

'And about you!' Mark said as he kissed her again.

'I'm meeting Mairin anyway.'

'Good, spread your wings a bit,' Mark said.

The prick.

The Lebanese cafe, George's Place, was situated in an arcade that sold antique silver trinkets, heavy amber jewellery and incense, with more of a hippy vibe than I'd have thought Mark would be into, but then Mr Mercurial was just that: slippery and uncategorisable. He knew all the staff by name, was seated in his 'usual' spot by the grubby window, which looked out onto the alley, thronged with art-student types.

'So, are you getting on any better with *Madame Bovary*?' he asked, turning the full force of his electric gaze on me. The female staff were overly curious, buzzing around us.

'She's a male creation.'

'In what way?'

'Self-absorbed, flighty, full of uncontrollable feeling.'

'Someone should cast you as her.'

'That's what Jonathan said. Not sure how I'm meant to feel about that!' I was trying to be flippant, just the right side of flirty, hoping he'd say you're beautiful enough, and complex enough, to play her. Instead, he switched his attention away from me and towards a waitress, and it was as if I was immediately plunged into a cold shadow. I found myself desperately wishing that he had seen me on-stage – particularly in my French maid's outfit in Ionesco's *The Bald Prima Donna*. *HUP!* gave me a five-star review for that performance.

'Hey Marky!' The waitress came over to us, all lit up, her pen between her plump lips.

'Hey Celine. How are we today?' He tangled her up in his stare.

She sucked on the lid of the pen.

'I'll have a falafel. You want one?' he said to me.

'Why not?' I said, not knowing what I had ordered, but feeling as if it were a dare – and I could never resist one of those. The girl smirked at me before she walked away. I noticed Mark noticing me noticing her behind. I felt pathetic.

'So, Linda tells me you're a really good actress.'

'That's nice of her.'

'Are you?'

'What makes a great actress?'

'A combination of self-obsession, fearlessness and vulnerability.' He looked at me, his eyes glittering with a greedy intelligence. 'Though not sure you possess the latter quality.'

'That's a total contradiction, what you just said: self-obsession *and* vulnerability.'

'Is it?' he said, pinioning me with his stare. 'I'd say they're two sides of the same coin.'

I was flummoxed, momentarily. I looked around me at the dodgy decor, which didn't seem to know what part of the world it was in – Mexican tapestries on the walls and Moroccan tealights on the tables – straining at the edges of the eclectic boho look. I laughed at the questionable taste of George, whoever he might be.

'Not everything has to follow strict logic,' he said. 'It's a big melting pot of a world out there.'

It was as if he could see the stultifying suburban housing estate where I grew up; as if he knew the extent of the parameters of my world.

Celine delivered our falafels. 'Enjoy!' she said, sounding naughty.

I looked down at my plate. Dry balls of rabbit food, or bird seed. I pushed them apart with my fork.

'Don't like the look of them, huh? Your face! So see-through!'

He smiled, looking pleased with me, then wiped his mouth with the back of his hand, looked out the scummy window, then back at me.

'A vital ingredient for an actress: transparency … though they have to be a consummate liar too…' He was musing. 'Everything worth anything in this life holds a paradox.'

'Indeed.' I looked down at my plate. 'Can I get anything edible here?'

'I don't think anything that will suit your limited, bland Irish palate.'

'What are you on about? You're as Irish as they come… Is there a paradox in there I'm missing?'

He laughed a full-throttled, delighted sound, then waved at Celine who was hovering near our table and ordered a house special mezze platter.

'Have you brought Linda here?'

'No. I don't think Linda would like this place.'

Or Celine in it, I thought. The new food when it came was delicious, oozy and wet, distinctly new sensations to my *bland Irish palate*.

'I'm a convert!' I said, my tongue dancing.

'You like new things,' he said, looking directly at me. 'That's a good sign.'

'Of what?'

'Of someone who's willing to stretch themselves, to reach new heights…' He yawned insolently and stretched his arms over his head, as if to emphasise his point. His shirt rose up to reveal a line of dark hair from his navel to the top button of his corduroys. I had imagined him hairless – I felt giddy.

'So, what will you tell Linda? That I'm not such a bitch after all?'

He laughed again, in an easy offhand manner.

I hadn't surmised that he had much of a sense of humour – maybe it was my presence that made him light up in this way. I liked that idea.

'Some appetite you've got there,' he said.

I was soaking up the last of the dips with the pitta bread and shoving pieces in my mouth.

'Insatiable!' He continued.

I wiped a slick of sauce from my lips and felt my cheeks flare red.

'You blush easily.'

I folded my napkin, started shredding it. I could feel him studying me.

'That navy top suits you. A good choice for a blue-eyed blonde prone to high colouring.'

His eyes were shimmering, voltaic, and I was existing in his spotlight.

'I think we can tell Linda we have a truce, don't you?'

The way he said it made me feel like I was colluding in an illicit secret. I must have smiled.

'That's some dimple,' he said, referring to my father's favourite feature of mine.

'What else did Linda tell you about me?'

'Honestly?' He leaned in as if about to share intimacies, then sat back and smiled. 'You're not that fascinating to us.'

I looked away out the window, gathering my reserves when he spoke again: 'She told me about you and her at school.'

Heat coursed through me.

'I imagine you had her best interests at heart. That's something we both share.'

He folded his napkin and neatly dabbed at the corners of his mouth.

'Sometimes it takes shock tactics to get a person to change.'

Suddenly my body was icy cold, my emotional thermostat haywire.

'How are you and Jacques getting on?' He swerved.

'Fine,' I said, before I had time to think.

'You're quite fond of that inane word.'

I was surprised by how inarticulate I became in his presence. It seemed I needed an audience to give back as good as I got. In silence, I rolled the shredded napkin pieces into tiny balls as he continued watching me. Abruptly, he stood. 'Finished?' I nodded. He went to the cash desk, paid for himself, and stood waiting while I fumbled in my purse. After I paid, he turned away into the alleyway.

'Are you going to audition me?' I asked his back.

'You already have the part!' He walked away.

I steadied myself against the table of a jewellery stall. My eye caught the light of a tiger eye pendant, and before I knew what I was doing it found its way into my pocket. The guy who ran the stall turned to me. 'Can I help you with anything?'

‘I don’t think you can,’ I said, sweetly, my finger rubbing the pendant in my pocket. I imagined it was pulsating, winking in the darkness.

I went straight back to my room, my whole being tingling, and lay on my front, my fingers finding their way to my clitoris, and then inside me. Everything felt raw and painful, yet intensely necessary. I came, relaxed a moment before the charge built in me again. I hadn’t noticed Jacques walking into the room until I had finished and turned around.

He was standing at the door, looking embarrassed and excited. ‘You want some help?’

I pulled my jeans back on, zipped them up without looking at him.

‘Where were you last night?’ I could hear the wheedling tone in my voice that Sue used with my father when he’d go away and reappear without a word of explanation.

Jacques sat on the bed beside me and gently put his hand on my thigh. I felt unaccountably sad and mad at my young body which was getting turned on by his touch. I smacked his hand away.

‘I’m going to take a shower. I’d really like you not to be here when I get back.’

‘You don’t mean that.’

This was a remark that Sue used to make when I’d blow up at her over some preposterous behaviour that she was indulging in with dear Dad – usually something to do with throwing him out of the house with all his belongings in the middle of the night. I’d say, ‘Oh *you* just go, will you. Do us all a favour. You go, and he will stay.’ Her voice would be shaky and small as she’d respond, ‘You don’t mean that.’

‘I mean it,’ I’d say, before slamming the door.

Imagine if she’d taken me seriously?

Dad would still have left, and where would I have been then?

Again, I couldn’t help myself; again, the words flew out of my mouth: ‘I mean it,’ and again, the door clanged heavily in my wake.

In the shared bathroom along the hall, I ran a scalding shower, stood under it for as long as my skin would allow, hot angry tears joining the cascade. A heady mixture of feeling righteously victimised and abandoned, although I was the one doing the pushing away. I held my breath until black dots appeared in front of my eyes. Dizzy and scalded.

Someone was banging on the bathroom door, and they weren't going to give up. 'That's not allowed, you know. You've had way more than your allocated ten minutes.' They kept at it. I stepped out, dried myself roughly, wrapped the towel around me and walked by a guy I'd never seen before.

'Niiiice!' he said.

I rounded on him. 'Do you dicks think of nothing else?'

He threw his hands in the air. 'Oh, OK, not so nice front on!'

Bloody hilarious.

'Nice buns, though!'

Jacques was lying on my bed when I returned to my room, which made me so relieved I could feel tears threatening. He tugged at my towel playfully.

'Get your hands off me.' The opposite to how I really felt.

He withdrew and sat up. 'What's wrong, Jess?'

'It's not OK for you to leave when I bring up something you don't like … and then waltz back in here and expect sex.'

'Jess, it's not OK for you to make demands of me or make threats either.'

He had a point.

'And I'm not demanding sex. I'd never do that. I just thought you were in the mood.'

Again, he had a point. I hated that he was so reasonable, it made my erratic behaviour seem even more pronounced. I opened the door to the wardrobe and got dressed behind it, blocking his view, making a show of hiding my naked body from him.

'I need to know where you were last night. I need to know about your family, your history. You're hiding stuff from me,' I said.

He struggled to find the right words. 'Jess, I don't want to hide from you … but I don't want to destroy what we have… What we have is precious… A bubble of you and me, and I don't want to burst that.'

I was quite moved by his use of the words 'precious' and 'bubble'. I appeared from behind the wardrobe door and winked at him.

'Hey, I risked introducing you to Sue, and it didn't destroy us!'

'My family's different: a whole other level of dysfunction.'

'Try me.'

'My brother is the reason both my parents left: Mum as soon as she legally could, Dad years before, the minute things got difficult.'

Jacques was no stranger to abandonment either. Strange how this didn't surprise me.

'What's wrong with your brother?' I spoke softly.

'He could never do life. And now he spends his time blotting out his days, drinking.' A muscle in his jaw twitched.

I put my arms around him, whispered into his ear: 'Hey, I love you more knowing that about you.'

It was the first time either of us had said 'I love you' to each other, in any context.

'You never have to keep anything from me, you know,' I said as I snuggled into him. This was the only time we had cuddled that wasn't a precursor to sex. We held each other for a few moments before I couldn't help bursting out: 'Jacques – I want to meet your brother.'

He sighed, and spoke so quietly I could hardly hear him, 'You don't say.'

'I *do* say, I insist.'

'You don't have to do that, Jess,' he said. 'I am asking you to please not do that.'

'OK. But you agree? From now on no hiding stuff from each other.'

He said nothing, just hugged me closer, kissing me on the top of my head.

I chose not to tell him about my lunch with Mark.

20

We got the number 6 bus outside the college gates and sat on it for about twenty minutes before disembarking in a leafy suburb with fine Georgian houses. I thought of the suburban semi-d where I grew up, in the estate with hundreds of exact replicas, and felt that usual stab of mortification. Why had I been born into such *ordinariness*? I followed Jacques up the pathway to a three-storey house, which on closer inspection was not all that salubrious, with weeds between the paving stones, filthy communal bins outside, and nine bells: three for each floor. He turned the key and climbed ahead of me, up a narrow, brown-carpeted hallway that stank of bacon and cheap Brut after-shave. The seediness shocked and excited me.

The flat was tiny and dark, every curtain drawn, the air rank with something mouldering. Jacques stayed silent as he walked into the front room: TV on low, a man asleep on a corduroy beanbag with cans of Heineken strewn about the floor. Jacques turned the TV off, drew back the curtains to reveal a leafy sycamore tree, its branches touching the window, as if gently probing. He opened the window and the man grumbled. Jacques could barely look at him as he went into the kitchen, a brown and orange throwback-to-the-seventies affair, lino on the floor and worktops. He ran hot water, started to methodically wash and stack dirty dishes that were on every surface, then scoured a burned pot with a Brillo pad.

'What are you doing?' he said.

I was opening various cupboards. 'Looking for coffee.'

'Sit down,' he said. 'I'll do it.'

He filled a cafetiere with real coffee and allowed it to brew as he continued cleaning every surface with disinfectant. Neither of us said a word. He poured a coffee, heaped it with sugar and took it back into the living room. I followed, although I felt I shouldn't.

'Louis?' He spoke the man's name aloud, shook his shoulder, not all that gently. The man stirred, rubbed his bleary eyes. They were so like Jacques's: pools of liquid, kind, Labrador eyes – except that the whites were yellowed and latticed with red criss-cross lines. He took the cup, closed his eyes, inhaled the smell of the coffee but didn't drink it. Jacques bent and picked up all the cans. 'At least I've made him graduate from the Polish variety,' he said, trying an ironic tone which came out bitter and biting. He looked like a combination of an old man and a very young child as he walked back into the kitchen, where I could hear him depositing the cans in the bin loudly, venting. I stayed where I was, hoping that if I didn't breathe I might not be noticed. I wasn't. Jacques's brother was a hologram of a man.

I traipsed after Jacques into the kitchen, where he was busy removing a frozen pizza from its wrapping.

'Not your usual Cordon Bleu fare,' I said.

'It's all he'll eat,' he said, as he bent to put it into the oven. How had Jacques modelled a version of himself that was so far from this?

'Who taught you to cook?'

'My mother.'

'Is she also responsible for the shitty decor?'

'We didn't live here with her.'

I hated his absent, abstract mother with a vengeance. 'How could she desert you both?'

His face closed down.

'He needs to find something to want to make him live. A girl, a hobby…' I said, grasping. I was experiencing that same terrible, yet thrilling, rescuer high as when I witnessed Linda in her dreadful home for the first time.

'Fuck's sake, Jess. It's never that simple.' He looked exhausted.

'But no one should be alone like that…'

'I'm going to feed him and then we're leaving.'

I sat at the table and watched Jacques arrange the pizza on a plate. He poured a glass of water, walked away. I knew enough not to follow. He was gone a few minutes, low rumbles coming from the next room.

His face when he returned was ashen. 'Right, time to go.'

'We can't leave him like that. He needs a brisk walk in the fresh air.'

'Look, this is exactly why I didn't want you coming here.' He sounded so alone. 'You think a brisk fucking walk is going to change anything?'

'But we have to *do* something.'

He turned to me, his eyes glimmering with sadness or anger, or both. 'He doesn't want to go outside.'

He took his coat from the back of the chair and forced his arm into the sleeve, the lining ripping in the process. 'Do you think I haven't tried? The addict needs to want to get sober. I can't do anything. God knows I've tried…'

I placed my hand lightly on his arm and he shrugged me off. For once I was able not to take it personally; I could see he had to steel himself to leave. I looked at his stiff back as he turned to go, and thought about what it cost him every time he came to see his brother.

21

'I need a pint,' Jacques said, an unusual statement for him at any time, but particularly in this set of circumstances. We were almost back at campus, having spent most of the bus journey in silence. So much for truth-telling leading to a greater intimacy. I knew from similar situations with Linda to leave him be, though everything inside me screamed for closeness. I was struggling to reconcile this new troubled version of Jacques with that which I had constructed: the competent, gorgeous man who existed only to love and serve me.

When we got off the bus he headed straight for the Dungeon. He pushed the door open and without waiting for me, forged on ahead through clouds of smoke. I lost him to an underscore of Shakespears Sister's 'Stay', the plaintive chorus 'Stay with me...' fuelling my sense of rejection and melodrama. I allowed myself wallow for a few moments in those familiar emotions before I took hold of myself and went looking for him. *Not about me.* I found him perched on a bar stool, a full pint in front of him. 'I'll have what you're having,' I said brightly. He ordered for me, and we drank together, even though I didn't want alcohol just then.

'Hey, you two!' a voice shouted from a dark corner of the bar. 'Over here.' It was Linda, sounding unusually buoyant and directive. Jacques stood and walked towards her, relieved not to be alone with me, I presumed. 'Hi you gorgeous creatures!' She smiled up at us, her body twisted into a pretzel shape against Mark's – as if she were grafted on to him or growing out of him. *There are no yours or mine in love.* I felt the separation between me and Jacques even more keenly (not that I wanted to be a symbiotic leech).

'Hi Lindy,' I said. 'Want to come outside for a cig?' I desperately needed to confide in her.

'No,' she said. 'I've given up. And it's miserable out there.'

Mark rubbed her knee. 'Getting so much better at being direct,' he said.

I stifled a fuck you.

'Here, squeeze in,' Mark said, as he and Linda slid as one to the far side of the cigarette-scorched fake leather banquette.

Jacques sat down as I remained standing.

'Aren't you going outside?' Mark asked me.

'Actually, I've changed my mind.'

'Something you girls seem to do a lot of,' he said as he patted Linda's knee. She didn't react even as I eye-balled her.

'All good?' he said to Jacques and me.

'Absofuckinglutely,' Jacques said, loudly. His second pint glass was empty.

Mark stood. 'Another?'

'I think he's had enough,' I said.

'I think I can speak for myself,' Jacques said. 'Don't mind if I do!' He nodded at Mark, who slid out of the opposite side of the booth, leaving Linda alone. I thought she might crumple, having his body removed from hers, but if anything, she seemed stronger, as if she had been fortified by his close proximity, as if she had fed on him. Something about Mark's close attention was bolstering her. I think I preferred seeing her in the outright victim role – it suited my narrative better.

Mark returned with drinks for everyone except himself.

'Are you a teetotaller?' I asked.

'Alcohol is the drug of choice for dummies.'

'Cheers,' I said as I held my glass up to him.

'Much better ways to experience an enhanced reality,' he said.

'I thought the booze was about taking the edge off, not sharpening it up,' I said.

'Dulls the instrument, yes,' he said.

I looked at Jacques, who mimed inhaling a cigarette and flicking a lighter at a girl at the next table. The pack and the lighter flew across at him. I didn't like the way she was looking at him.

'What better ways are there to experience this *enhanced reality* then?' I said.

Mark and Linda exchanged a glance and there was something about it that suggested a covert, superior way of being, as if they had all the answers to questions we didn't even know we should be asking.

'Another time, Jessica,' Linda said, delighting in her new-found number one position.

Jacques lit the cigarette, and threw the packet back at the girl, making a fatuous thumbs-up sign at her. She waved friskily back. I plucked the thing out of his hand and took a deep drag, in what I imagined was a sensuous way.

'Have you guys seen Jonathan lately?' Mark asked.

'Not since the other night, why?' I said.

'I just don't want him to think he's not welcome around Linda, or me. Tell him that, yeah?'

'I'm sure he'll be delighted to be granted permission by you to see his friend!'

'Congratulations, by the way!' Linda said.

'About what?'

'The part.'

'What part?' Jacques asked.

'Oh didn't Jess tell you? Mark cast her as his lead.'

'No, she didn't tell me…' Jacques said, looking at me.

'I was going to tell you later.'

'When did you audition?'

'She didn't have to,' Linda said. 'Mark took her for lunch, and he came back and said he just knew. The MADDEST thing of all is that the character is called Jessica too.'

'I didn't know that,' I said.

'I didn't know you had lunch with Mark,' Jacques said.

'Did you not tell your boyfriend?' Mark asked provocatively.

'What's this about the character being called Jessica?' I asked Linda. 'Bit fucking weird.'

'Not so,' Mark said. 'It's an adaptation of *The Merchant of Venice*.'

'But Portia's the lead in that,' I said.

'I am more interested in Jessica, Shylock's daughter. *Alack what heinous sin is it in me/ To be ashamed to be my father's child...* The thief, the rebel, the one who throws off the shackles of her past.'

'She sounds amazing,' Linda said, looking meaningfully at Mark.

'I don't even remember her,' I said.

'Well, soon you won't be able to forget her,' Mark said.

'When do rehearsals start?' Linda asked.

'In a few weeks. I have to get my thesis in first.'

'On the Christian philosopher?' I asked, snidely.

'Kierkegaard, yes.'

'I looked him up in in the library. Strange little man, with his religiosity, his spindly legs and sticky-up hair.'

Mark laughed. 'Was that the extent of your research?'

'Not fully. I also read that he had a tyrant of a father.'

Mark quoted him verbatim, making it sound as if he had written the words: '"He made my childhood an unparalleled torture, and yet he was the most loving father."'

'Something very dark there,' I said.

'You think so? Or just honest?' He looked at Linda in a way that suggested he knew things about her that no one else did.

'Do you have a title?'

'A working one: *The Truth Seeker*.'

'Ah yes, that explains your preoccupation with truth-telling,' I said.

'Neat,' he said.

'But actually, I meant do you have a title for your play?'

'Not yet.'

Jacques sucked noisily on the dregs of pint number three. I had never seen him drink this much before. He stood, unsteady on his feet, and swayed towards the bar, shouting back at us: 'Who wants what?' He dropped the burning cigarette on the ground. No one replied.

'Everything OK between you?' Mark asked.

'Perfect,' I said. 'You two?'

'Not perfect, but we're working on it. Communication is key. Honesty above all else.'

A girl walked towards us, sporting a just fallen-out-of-bed look with her tousled, dirty-blonde hair and a slouchy, oversized men's shirt paired with a very short mini skirt. I could feel myself stiffen.

'Hey Honor.' Mark called her over.

It was Honor Cave-Tempest-Stuart, *HUP!*'s 'top filly' the year ahead of me: a legendary blonde, hailing from a crumbling pile, in line to be a lady or duchess or countess or something entitled, her laugh filthy, her voice gravelly and perfectly articulated. She had a pouty potty mouth, according to the rumour mill, and knew exactly where to put it.

'This is Honor,' Mark said.

'I know who she is,' I said, taking in her translucent skin and cornflower-blue eyes, accentuated by a black slick of eyeliner that made them seem impossibly huge.

She smiled, as if of course everyone knew who she was.

'How've you been?' Mark asked her, patting the seat beside him. She slid seductively onto the banquette and folded one shapely leg clad in sheer black tights over the other.

'Well, look who it is.' Mark looked up as Jacques approached. 'It's the sexy Frenchman!'

Linda started crooning 'Joe le Taxi,' in a terrible imitation of Vanessa Paradis.

Jacques seemed to love the attention. He was smiling rather foolishly at Honor, his eyes shining in a way I had only ever seen them shine for me.

'Honor, this is the golden couple, Jessica and Jacques.'

The duchess glanced at me dismissively before her gaze roamed all over my boyfriend, settling uncomfortably close to his crotch, or so I decided.

'Nice to finally meet you,' Honor said. 'I've noticed you around.'

Jacques's smile stretched and brightened.

'Sit down, why don't you?' Mark said.

Jacques did his bidding, and slid in beside Honor, while I remained standing. Their thighs touched and Honor giggled. I felt it catch in my chest.

'Jacques, we've had a long day, time to go…' My voice was high-pitched and whiney.

Jacques looked up, as if in a trance. 'I have a full pint here, Jess. You go and I'll follow you later.'

I leaned over, reached my hand up Jacques's sleeve and pinched viciously.

He pretended not to notice, or he really didn't notice. Was he drunk or enamoured?

I could feel Mark's eyes on me. I looked up and he winked.

'Jessie?' Linda said. 'Loo?'

'No, I don't need to… That direct enough for you?' I aimed this at Mark.

'I doubt you've ever had a problem stating your needs or taking up space.' He laughed. 'I'd encourage you to go in a different direction, to be less me-centric. My first acting note for you…'

I looked at Jacques. He hadn't heard; he was so wrapped up in his intimate duet with Madame Tempest.

'Right, I'm away,' I said, trying hard to appear cool. I wasn't going to give any energy to Mark's games right now. There were too many pieces being played against me on too many fronts.

Linda stood. 'Want me to come with you?'

Mark's hand landed on her forearm, lightly restraining her.

'No, you're grand. See you tomorrow,' I said breezily. I bent down to Jacques and planted a wet kiss on his lips. 'Don't be too long,' I said. 'I'll be waiting up for you, baby.'

He looked up and smiled hazily. I didn't even glance at the duchess as I turned on my heel and stalked away. I imagined I could hear Mark clapping behind me as I made a perfectly executed dramatic exit.

Jacques stumbled in about an hour later, fell into bed beside me.

'You'd want to watch your drinking,' I said. He turned his back, curled away from me, and was snoring within seconds, as I lay staring at a serrated crack in the ceiling above my head, its edges bleeding.

The next morning, he woke me by stroking my cheek, which was wet from tears.

'What's wrong, baby? he said.

'Please don't ever treat me like that again.' I was furious to have been caught in such a vulnerable state.

'Sorry,' he said. 'Though I'm not sure exactly what I am supposed to be sorry for.'

'Right,' I said. I got up and climbed over him.

He grabbed me by the ankle. 'Where are you going?'

'Anywhere but here.'

'Stay, Jess. I'm sorry. I drank too much.'

I shook his hand off my ankle and got down off the bed. 'Don't ever treat another woman like that in my presence again.'

'What?' he said.

'You heard me.'

'That is ridiculous,' he said.

'No you don't get to do that to me,' I said. I was reminded of my father minimising and ridiculing Sue's jealous outbursts following a party where he'd given some woman all his attention and withdrawn it completely from her. I saw him in action; I knew how he made her feel, and then how demeaning her actions would be. There was no winning by admitting to jealousy.

'Is that why you were crying?' He looked appalled. 'What did I do, Jess? I wasn't that drunk.'

The power dynamic had shifted too much. 'I don't know what you're talking about,' I said. 'I wasn't crying.'

'You know I only love you, Jessica.'

'I'm going for a shower.'

'Can I join you?' he said.

'Why not?' I threw over my shoulder flippantly. I desperately needed to feel close to him again.

I let myself dissolve into him as the hot shower pummelled us both.

'Baby. I'm sorry. I never meant to hurt you. I'd never hurt you.'

He meant it but he had no idea what he was up against with Honor Cave-Tempest-Stuart. But I did. And so did Mark. I wondered how he could have orchestrated proceedings last night so perfectly.

'Forgive me?'

'Your poor brother,' I said, as the two of us melded into each other's skins.

22

'So, you decided to come back, Jessica?'

It's February, the same dank, depressing month I have just been describing at Wilde.

I debate making pleasantries, decide against it.

'Mark is in the news.'

Dr Collins remains silent.

'Someone has outed him as a bully, a misogynist. And then the inevitable deluge. It's all over social media.'

'You did say that you felt this was bound to happen, someday.' Dr Collins's tone is careful. 'Do you know who might be behind it?'

'Not me, if that's what you're inferring … though, obviously I've thought about it over the years…'

'And how does reading these allegations make you feel now?'

'The same way I always felt in his presence: as if I've been injected with a shot of adrenaline.'

Dr Collins studies me, then says calmly, 'Now there's the possibility that your version of the man will be believed.'

'I'm not sure that I have settled on any one "version" of Mark though.'

'You need to trust the veracity of your recollections.'

'But they constantly shift and change.'

'Will you add your voice, Jessica?'

'Not in that way, no. I wouldn't expose myself publicly, but perhaps I could publish my account under a pseudonym.'

'Where would the satisfaction be in that?' she asks.

I am surprised by this stance.

'You are onto something with this story,' she continues.

Interesting that she should use that word: *story*. The act of writing has taken on a life of its own and is gaining in momentum and scale. Whether real or unreal, remembered or imagined, a whole world is building that is beyond my control.

'I'm curious,' she says.

'Yes?'

'Why did you feel the need to tell me?'

Because you are guiding my pen, I almost say but don't.

'I guess because I felt you might want to know.'

There's a brief pause when I hear her inhaling sharply then: 'How are you doing yourself, Jessica?'

How do I tell her that I do not feel there is a 'myself' any more? That I exist fully in service to my memories and my characters. That Mark would finally be proud of me: the *artiste*, cleared of ego, of limitations, of conditioning, has finally emerged.

'I'm good, I think. Curious to see where this new development in Mark's life will lead.'

'And how about your own life?'

'I am in it,' I say.

'Are you?' Dr Collins says. 'Really?'

23

First year, term two. Permanent mulchy skies overhead, too much indoor activity, too much alcohol, too much intensity, too much dope, too many hormones, too much sex, too much introspection. Linda was moving further away from me, which Jacques said was only natural, a stage in her 'individuation' – a word that Mark would later alight on under the banner of *Project Linda* and her 'improvement', her 'liberation' from her past. Jacques said it was good for Linda to be less reliant on me, which would have been fine had she not replaced one dependency, or obsession, with another.

Jacques and I skirted the subject of his brother. It only took a mention of Louis's name for him to harden and disappear. Our sex life became even more intense; in the darkness our hands and mouths could say what words could not. I have never been so familiar with the contours of anyone's body since, not my husband's, certainly not my own.

Jonathan often joined us for dinner, replacing Linda in our triangle. He was a generous friend, supplying booze and hash and jokes, and lately, brilliant, funny impersonations. 'Becoming quite the performer,' I said one evening, prompting him to launch into a meticulous imitation of me: the slight tilt of the head, the upward inflection at the end of my sentences, as if everything was a sort of question – do you love me? There was no cruelty to him, just a keen and observational wit. He captured an uncanny likeness of Mark too. He pushed imaginary glasses on top of his head, pitched forward and stared at us, his gaze a spear, his accent shifting between inner-city Dublin and Americana, his voice lowering an octave, as he intoned: '*Be that self which one truly is*.' We fell around the place laughing, though the absence of Linda was acutely felt.

The possibility of a threesome between Jonathan, Jacques and I was ever-present: we were too gorgeous not to – the rumours went. In truth, there was something passive and asexual about Jonathan, as if whatever he wished for himself would always remain out of reach.

Linda and Mark withdrew for that dreary, spiteful month into their own gated world and when they did appear, Linda seemed fortified, as if she'd had love spells whispered into her, in the same way she used to with the daisies in the back field in our estate; in the same way she wished her own mother would have done. She was undeniably blossoming under the hothouse stare of her extraordinary boyfriend. When she emerged into an early spring, her body flowed with grace and ease, in stark contrast with her previous angular, brittle self.

I tried to let her go and trust that she would come back 'in her own good time', as both Jacques and Jonathan asserted. But the sight of her walking arm in arm with Mairin one day punctured any good intentions I held in that regard.

'Lindy,' I hollered, my voice bouncing from one end of the arts block to the other.

'Oh hey,' she said, as I came closer.

'Where've you been hiding?'

She looked embarrassed for me. 'Just busy, you know.'

'Busy, busy, busy bee,' I said, sounding pathetic.

'I hear you're in rehearsals for the Pirandello play. Jacques told Mark it's going really well. Delighted for you!'

When had Jacques been in touch with Mark? I wracked my brains to see if he had mentioned having a conversation with Mark at any stage.

'The two of them seem to be getting on great,' she said, further intensifying my unease. I didn't like the thought of my boyfriend and Mark alone together, ever.

I was tempted to ask more but couldn't expose myself in front of Mousey. I turned to her. 'How are things, Mairin? Enjoying *sociology*?' I asked.

'Going great,' she said. 'I look forward to seeing you in the play. Linda tells me you're a fine actress.' Her tone was perfection: polite but unmistakably patronising. *Actress.*

'Are you coming to opening night, Lindy? I have two comps for you. One of them is for Mark,' I said pointedly.

'We can go together another night,' Linda said to Mairin. 'We might gather a gang of *sociology* students, for an outing.'

The two of them giggled and I found it hard to breathe.

'Mark has cast Jess as the lead in his new play,' Linda continued.

'Good for you,' the mouse said to me.

I couldn't get a handle on their dynamics.

'Jonathan is always asking for you,' I said to Linda, trying to bring her back into my orbit.

'Jeepers, it's not been that long.'

'A few weeks,' I said.

'Exactly,' she said, laughing, easy in herself, in a way I hadn't seen before.

'Well, you'll see him on opening night,' I said.

'Can't wait,' she said, her tone ambivalent.

I looked at my friend and wondered. Was she that blinded by her sense of rejection that she couldn't see that Jonathan's turndown at Christmas wasn't personal? Or was it that she was avoiding putting Jonathan and Mark together? No doubt Mark generated an anxiety that led to secrecy and withholding between friends, and lovers. What did she fear might happen?

'I'm looking forward to being directed by Mark,' I said.

'I hope you'll be up to it. He demands a lot from his actors.'

Said the woman who effectively pushed me into working with him.

'I know you fully believe in his talent. Generous of you to share him with me in that way.'

I could see a flicker of unease flit across her face. Perfection. Just enough. I had to proceed with a tactician's dexterity to unpick his finely woven web. Oh fuck you, Flaubert!

24

'So cunning,' Jonathan said. 'The way the playwright made it seem as if it were the despotic director who was pulling all the strings – a character he had himself written.' He was puzzling it all out, flushed in the face with excitement.

We were in the Players' bar following the opening-night performance of *Six Characters in Search of an Author*. I was humming with nerves and elation.

'You were magic, Jess. Truly,' Jacques said. And I believed him. I felt inspired up there, possessed, as if I were fully embodying my character, not a moment of self-consciousness or awkwardness. I had *become* the volatile stepdaughter.

'Prosecco?' Mark appeared in front of us with a bottle of bubbles and four glasses. 'Congratulations, Jessica,' he said. 'You really were made to play that part.'

I felt a rush of excitement and adulation.

'So provocative, performative, seductive.'

My mood was teetering, up, down, conducted by his words.

'You were especially "in the moment" in the scene with your uncle.'

The scene where the uncle makes a move on the stepdaughter as she plays with him.

Jacques coughed. 'Parched. Let's have those drinks.'

Mark unscrewed the bottle and poured the Prosecco with a flourish.

'Fizz for the ladies,' he said, as he handed me and Linda a glass. Linda's measure was much smaller than mine.

'Bit mean,' I said, referring to Linda's glass.

'She knows her limits,' he said. 'If alcohol were put on the market now it'd most likely be a prescription drug.' He looked pointedly at Jacques as he said this. 'Some of us know the havoc it can wreak on loved ones' lives.'

My body stiffened.

Jonathan downed his glass in one and held it out. 'I have no limits.'

I clinked my glass against his. 'Me neither!'

I looked at Linda who was sipping from her glass in tight, tiny sips. 'Did you enjoy the play?' I asked, fishing for a compliment.

'Strange affair,' she said. 'Seemed a bit try-hardy. All that meta *now you're an actress, now you're not* stuff.'

Mark laughed. 'It was all deliberate on the part of the playwright. You do know that?'

'Of course I know that!' she said.

He regarded her proudly, as if she were his prize pony showing off a trick he had taught her in the paddock. 'Good to see you voicing your opinions so clearly.' His voice like a pat on the head.

'So great to see you, Linda,' Jonathan said. The second glass of bubbly already making his tongue loose: 'I've missed you, my friend.'

She regarded him with surprise tinged with disdain. Jonathan's ears flushed crimson. How the power dynamic had changed between these two since Christmas, only two months previously. That wantonly drunken dancing girl came to mind, the first time I had seen that side to Linda: sensuous and reckless. I regarded her now – her skin had a permanent rosy glow, where before she had been chalky white (almost entirely, were it not for her freckles). There was also an energy to her: she *crackled* as I stood beside her. I was meant to be the one who was electric.

'To Jessica,' Mark said. 'Our talented supremo!' I was so easy to hook, and he knew it. Later it would become impossible to untangle without tearing off bits of myself.

'To my best friend!' Linda said. As she raised her glass, I thought I saw a red mark encircling her wrist: a welt, a fresh scar, or the mark of a Chinese burn …? I looked into her eyes, and she smiled, welcoming my discovery. Did she miss what I used to do to her?

'Tell me,' Mark said to me. 'Did you enjoy yourself up there?'

I cheers-ed him. 'Very much!' I said.

'A bit too much, I'd say.'

Jonathan coughed. 'I think she pitched it perfectly. The play demanded a certain dramatic quality.'

'Never artifice, though,' Mark said portentously. 'Never at the cost of the truth.'

I felt as if I had been stabbed in my ribcage by the tip of a very sharp spear.

'I thought she was brilliant,' Jonathan said.

'She's a total star,' Jacques pitched in.

'No one is denying that,' Mark said. 'She could just perhaps tone it down a bit.'

'Actually I agree with Jonathan,' Linda said. 'I think she pitched it perfectly. It's meant to be overcooked.'

Overcooked, tone it down, artifice, at the cost of the truth. These words were like poisoned arrows to an actress's heart.

'I can't wait to get you into rehearsal,' Mark said. 'With some calibration you'll be a remarkable actress.'

The room spun, whether from the alcohol, or the sudden shift in tone from praise to denigration. I was unsteady on my feet – and in myself. I looked at Jacques and Jonathan, both of whom were regarding each other with an expression of bewildered amusement. I wanted more: I wanted Jacques to be furious and to defend my honour; I wanted Jonathan to belittle Mark with a clever impersonation; and yet, I wanted more than anything to be in a rehearsal room with Mark. Linda poured the remnants of the bottle into my glass. 'Drink up, Jessie. The night is but young!' Her speech was becoming infected by her boyfriend's pretentious mannerisms.

I drank fast, craving more of the spinning feeling. 'I'd like more,' I said to Jacques.

'Now who needs to watch their drinking?' he said.

So, he had heard me that night after he came back from flirting with Honor. I had thought he was unconscious.

'This is MY night,' I said becoming a parody of the actress I was.

'Yes, it is, my darling,' Jacques said, as he kissed me on the mouth.

'Will we go on somewhere?' Linda said. 'The bar is closing here.'

'I've some tequila in my place!'

'I'm on,' Jonathan said. He seemed as crazy for obliteration as I was.

'Do you want to go?' Linda asked Mark.

'What do you want to do, my sweet?' he asked her.

'I'd like to go if you'd like to.'

I desperately wanted to pinch her, to shock her back into some semblance of herself.

'OK, but no more alcohol for you,' he said.

'Do that one!' I said to Jonathan, who picked up on it immediately.

He shifted his register and launched into an uncanny impersonation of Mark: 'No more alccohhhhhol for you my sweeeeet,' he said in a priest-like, or creepy child-catcher voice.

Mark laughed and clapped. 'Talented… Do you want to try out for my play too?'

'No thanks!' Jonathan said. 'Come on Jess.' He grabbed me by the arm and the two of us skipped out of the bar into the night air, improvising a song: 'In Dublin's mangy city where the streets are so shitty…'

Mark shouted, 'Dreadful dross, my dears.'

I sang even louder and in a broad Dublin accent, caricaturing Mark at his rawest: 'In this filthy city where nothing is pretty—'

Jonathan cut in: 'Except for you, my sweet.'

I rolled my eyes and shouted: 'Dirty old Dub/Dirty old town…' to a melody that I only I could hear.

25

The minute we walked into my room I realised it had been a mistake to invite everyone back. It was filthy: the bed unmade, bowls of half-finished cereal on the floor, congealed coffee cups on the bedside table, dust particles swirling in the dim light from the window. Mark sat down in the one swivel chair by the desk, his eyes scanning the space. Jacques, Jonathan and I sprawled on the single bed, as Linda perched on the edge. Jonathan lit a joint and Jacques and I sucked on it greedily. I offered Linda a pull, but she refused, looking towards Mark who swallowed her up in his stare. I wanted to cartwheel or clap or sing or strip, anything to draw their attention away from each other, and back to me.

'Do you two do tantric?' I asked, to which everyone laughed uproariously.

Mark gestured at Linda to sit on his lap. She did, pushing her body against his, burrowing into him. He smelled the top of her head, then kissed it. He swivelled them both 360 degrees in the chair. Bizarre and strangely endearing.

'What did you think of your friend up there tonight, my sweet? Genuinely?'

'I genuinely thought she was on fire,' she said.

Now I wanted to smell and kiss her pretty head too.

'Your generosity is such a beautiful part of you,' he said.

I happened to agree, though I wouldn't give him the satisfaction.

'You two are sweet,' Jacques said lazily, his voice already blurred at the edges by the dope.

Jonathan looked at me and crossed his eyes, evidently not sharing this view.

Mark positioned the chair so that it faced the one tiny window above the bed. 'Due north,' he said. 'I'd never take a room facing north.'

'I didn't exactly have a choice.'

'Not true.' He was talking to himself in the window's grimy reflection. 'We always have a choice.' He kissed the top of Linda's head again, then turned the chair to face us all, Linda still snuggled on his lap. 'Do you ever do housework, Jessica?'

'Maaark,' Linda said, giggling. 'Not nice.'

My cheeks became hot as I looked at the crumbs and dust on the carpet.

'I love hoovering,' he said. 'It's one of the strange pleasures in my life.'

Along with another of his *strange pleasures*. I wanted to lift Linda's sleeve and expose their sordid secret. I could imagine him orchestrating the exact pitch of her pain.

'Well, feel free to come here and hoover anytime!' Jacques was laughing hysterically, tears spilling on his cheeks.

I wanted to slap him.

'Anyone on the horizon, Jonathan?' Mark asked, smiling. 'You're not a bad-looking guy.'

The sudden swerves in his conversation were disorientating and no doubt designed as such. 'Jessie here your type? She's pretty much everyone's type, according to *HUP!* But then, they only see the obvious… See, had I been scoring these two,' he gestured at Linda and me, 'I'd have scored them very differently.'

I felt a giddy, almost sickening, mixture of excitement and humiliation.

'Someone should shut that publication down, don't you think? Everything filtered through the hetero male gaze. That rag reminds me of my father's stance on things. *The rigid, homophobic sexist bollix*.' This was quite the speech, even for him, and it was aimed squarely at Jonathan. His accent was full-on inner-city Dublin in that moment, scrubbed free of artifice.

Jonathan got off the bed abruptly, pulling the quilt with him, and wrapped it around him like a toga. His skin was still tanned in the depths of mid-winter, his hair still sun-streaked; only his eyes lacked light. I remember thinking he looked so beautiful and melancholy, like a Greek god. A broken one.

'I'd have marked Linda a top ten out of ten for her delicate bones, her pronounced clavicle, her slender neck,' Mark went on, his finger tracing Linda's breastbone.

I checked mine to make sure that it was equally protruding.

'How would you mark them, Jacques?'

'Ten out ten, both of them,' Jacques said, inhaling the marijuana smoke deeply, his body settling against the mattress, seeming to fall through space.

'That's nice,' Mark said. 'If not, perhaps, completely honest.'

Jacques put his hands in the air in a gesture of, you win, and I'm not going there.

'If this is not you buying into the whole "male gaze" thing, inviting "marks" for our bodies, then what is?' I said, making a decent point – though undermined by the quavering in my voice.

'Jonathan?' Mark continued. 'Is my girl your type…?'

Linda flushed crimson. Mark stood, leaving her sitting alone on the swivel chair, looking tiny, as if she'd supped of a shrinking potion from a Lewis Carroll novel.

'It's fine – I know it was before I came on the scene.' His voice was eminently reasonable. 'She told me about you making a pass at her before I came along.'

I almost laughed but didn't want to add to Linda's mortification. Mark was playing us all brilliantly. I could picture Linda telling him in secret, in the afterglow of making love, how her handsome friend had made a move on her, believing in the moment that it had happened, that she was desirable and lovable. Perhaps she could rewrite all the rejection, erase it. Years later, I understood Mark's tactic better: his grooming of Linda, his training her in her make-believe, encouraging her to fabricate these scenarios so to have the ammunition at a later point to undercut her. In the moment, though, I mostly thought she had been stupid to say what she said.

'I've got to be up early for training,' Jonathan said, avoiding looking at Linda.

'I might join you some time,' Mark said.

'Truthfully?' Jonathan said, as Mark looked up. 'I doubt you'd be able to keep up.'

He dropped the quilt from around his body and kicked it on the floor before he walked out the door. I was strangely, fiercely proud of him.

Mark made a 'tetchy' expression at us, suggesting that Jonathan was being hyper-sensitive. 'I think we should set him up with someone. He seems lonely. Poor guy.'

He moved towards Linda and bent his head to hers and kissed her movie-style on the lips. It was preposterous. 'Now this is what *special* looks like: someone who doesn't see themselves that way.'

He took Linda by the hand, drawing her onto her feet and patted her on her bottom as they left. She didn't look back at me and I felt bereft.

'The *HUP!* crew got one thing right. You *are* a ten out of ten, Jessica … from behind.' His parting shot.

Jacques laughed, wanting to make light of it all – or else he genuinely found it funny, he was that stoned.

I remember wanting to throw Jacques out of my room, wanting to be alone, wanting to somehow process what had just happened, but instead I let him kiss me and undress me and have sex with me and I felt like crying, but I wouldn't let myself. What was it about me that made Mark target me in this way? Sure, I was a threat to certain men, who either wanted to fuck me to shut me up, or just fuck me, or just shut me up. But with Mark it was something else: a more sophisticated something else. The building me up, the putting me down, the glare of attention, followed by complete withdrawal, made me feel as if I were eight again and craving Daddy's love. '*The worst has already happened, you have already been abandoned.*' I came across this quote from Kierkegaard in my cursory research of him. It didn't seem a coincidence that Mark had chosen to do his thesis on him. He put me in touch with that part of me: the abandoned, snivelling girl. And I could find no love for her.

26

'I feel my grasp on things is slipping.'

'What does that mean, exactly?' Dr Collins looks down at her smooth, unmottled hands, flexes her fingers.

I look out the window and feel hemmed in.

'I have come to a wall.'

'In what way?'

'My memories are so vivid until a certain point and then they start to blur.'

'Perhaps you're not remembering what happened next for a reason?'

Dr Collins bites the pad of her thumb, as if she's pondering the next right thing to say.

After some moments she speaks. 'What has happened since I last saw you? Since the allegations about Mark broke?'

'Absabloodynothing,' I say.

'And this is frustrating for you?'

'Even now, the puppet master is pulling all the strings.'

'I'm sure the case is in process.'

'There is no "case". It was all anonymous, possibly spurious.'

'Jessica. You look tired,' she says. 'If you don't mind me saying so.'

'Well, I haven't slept more than a couple of hours a night since the post went out. I've been obsessively checking my phone. Last I looked, the content had been deleted from Twitter and Instagram. The thread is dead.'

'For now,' she says. 'There is no smoke without fire.'

Clichéd – but I hope she is right. That man cannot continue to evade his reckoning – or can he?

'Where are *you* now, in your life, in the present?' she asks gently.

'I'm not sure I understand. I'm here, now, with you.'

'I mean your everyday life. What do your days consist of?'

'I shower, I eat, I drink coffee, and I write, every day.'

I'm being flippant; I don't get dressed most days.

'Do you see people? Friends, family, colleagues?'

'I don't have any colleagues, and friends are avoiding me since the divorce. Family is not a place I go to for comfort.'

The truth is I haven't been to see Linda and Sue in months. The last visit was too excruciating. The how are yous?; the I'm fine thank yous; the sipping of the tea, the endless cups of the stuff; the lack of eye contact; the polite pretence; the sharks swimming beneath, circling for blood. And those handrails glinting at me, accusing me.

'Don't you need to work?'

I shake myself out of my memories, back to the present.

'I *am* working; I'm writing my version of events.'

'The act of writing is not a magic formula, nor an exclusive one.' She smooths the creases on her tasteful pencil skirt. 'Can we press the reset button here, Jessica? Can I tell you what I'm observing?'

Something that Mark used to say: *Can I tell you what I'm observing*? – in pursuit of scrupulous truth and honesty. I begin to vibrate.

Dr Collins continues, 'There is a blurring of fact and fiction that I can see.'

'Writing is a creative process. Natural, I'd have thought.'

'But you don't seem to be able to come out of that space.'

'I could if I wanted to.'

'I am concerned that you are engulfed by the past.'

She takes out a writing pad from a drawer in the table between us and starts making notes.

'Should I be worried? You never did that before,' I say.

'Standard procedure.' She looks up absently.

'I'm not hearing voices.' I smile in what I imagine is a rueful manner, but then, these days I have lost all social ability, so it's most probably a smirk. It's also not entirely true that I don't hear voices. Mark's is often stronger than my own.

She bites the top of her pen, chews on it, then catches herself, momentarily embarrassed. I stand. We regard each other. She is below my eye level, still in her chair, her mouth ink-marked.

'Can I be honest with you?' she says.

My whole body trills. It is back there, vibrating with dread and anticipation.

'Your isolation is becoming a problem.'

'I like it,' I say. 'It's a relief.'

'It's important you interact with another human being every day. Can you do that?'

I can see Mark shaking his head at this *inanity.* The rest of them: Linda, Jacques and Jonathan are snorting, eye-rolling, pushing down laughter that's threatening to explode.

'Go out for a walk, at least. See the sky above your head. Join some groups, volunteer.'

I want to say: Seriously? Is this what I pay eighty euros an hour for? But I don't. Something stops me from saying it. I expect I will need to come back.

'Will do,' I say. I am bright, jovial, or trying to be.

The sky above my head is an impenetrable wall of grey. Low, and getting lower every day.

Dr Collins takes out her diary.

'I think it might be wise to check in with me again next week, Jessica.'

She restates the importance of doing something as simple as meeting someone every day, even for a walk, or a coffee. We take our leave of each other politely, and I make sure to fix a smile on my face and make promises to return.

I can't deny as I walk home, stopping to get a cappuccino on the way, smiling at the barista, exchanging a few words, *pleasantries*, that I feel a little less blocked, a little less stuck in my head – and in my phone. I look up: the sky is piebald grey on grey, some relief in the mottled shades when you take the time to notice. I sip the coffee, *taste* it, savour the sensation of froth against my tongue, feel alive, momentarily frisky. I notice a clutch of pale daffodils in a pot outside the coffee shop. Lovely, I think, pretty, dainty, nature's bounty, but then I see with fierce clarity that they are too fragile for this world. They will no doubt be battered by all that an Irish spring will throw at them, including hailstones: the cruellest, most sharp-edged surprise of them all.

27

A few days after I'd made the mistake of inviting everyone back to my room – as I was coming out of my linguistics lecture (which had catapulted me back to trigonometry class, where the world would blur and spin, the only class I had ever failed) – I bumped into the two-headed monster of Mark and Linda in the arts block. I was jangling. '*Jessica McSwain as the stepdaughter seemed too aware of herself, too self-congratulatory. She never once fully dissolved into her character.*' The *HUP!* review for my performance on opening night wasn't the usual five-star one. Didn't they get that I was playing her archly, exactly as Pirandello had intended?

Mark studied me. 'Had a tough night?'

My hand automatically went to the back of my head and started to pluck individual strands of hair – something I hadn't done since the year my father left.

'I need some food,' I said, heading to the coffee dock.

'Hi baby.' Jacques was coming towards me, arms outstretched. 'You left before I had a chance to say goodbye this morning.'

'Hey Jacques,' Linda said.

Jacques hugged me and then Linda and greeted Mark warmly. Clueless – could he not read my body language?

'Can I get anyone anything?' he asked.

'I'll get ours,' Mark said, going to the glass case and picking an egg sandwich for Linda.

Jacques got Tayto crisps and lemonade for me. The four of us sat at high stools, Linda's and my feet dangling in the air, while the boys' long legs meant theirs were planted firmly on the ground. We sipped our drinks, the sandwich sitting unopened on the table, which was etched with graffiti: initials and love hearts and a stand-alone: *Rape doesn't exist on the moon*. I shivered; was sure I was the only one who noticed.

'Aren't you going to eat that?' Mark said to Linda. She immediately lifted it out of its packaging and bit down on it, looking like a kid whose parent has said she can't leave the table until she's eaten all her veggies.

I decided to help her out, so I reached in for the second one. It was dry and disgusting. I stuck my soggy-bread-covered tongue out at the table. 'Gross.'

'We're trying to get Linda to eat more, aren't we, sweetie?' Mark said as he nibbled her earlobe. She took a swig of her coffee and swallowed.

I should have been glad he was encouraging her to eat but I was furious.

'You hate eggs,' I said. 'You know these are from battery hens.'

'She needs more protein,' Mark said.

Linda looked like she might get sick as she took another bite. He put his hand on her forearm. 'You know what I said about the jaw clicking.' She chewed more cautiously. 'My father did that too. Loud masticating. It's revolting,' Mark said.

He had the ability to stun. Neither Jacques nor I seemed capable of a reaction.

'What about you, Jacques? Anything about Jess that irritates you?'

Jacques swallowed the last of his crisps, washed it down with a gulp of sparkling Ballygowan. 'Nope, she's pretty perfect as she is,' he said.

I blew him a kiss which he caught and pretended to eat.

'My man is exquisitely perfect,' I said, looking at Jacques.

'You two are such beautiful liars!' Mark said.

Jacques laughed and excused himself to go to the toilet. Could he never be relied on to back me up when I needed him?

'Honesty is a necessary rigour for any relationship,' Mark said, once Jacques had left.

I thought about that: how my enforced visit to see his brother, in pursuit of absolute honesty between us, had completely backfired.

'Thank you for bestowing me with your wisdom,' I said. 'Though uninvited. Again.'

He smiled. 'You're welcome.'

'He's right, Jess. Without scrupulous truth what is there?' Linda said. Little parrot.

'Have you joined a cult or something?'

Neither of them laughed.

'Being able to access honesty is the touchstone for any great actress,' Mark went on.

'Really? I thought you said we had to be consummate liars.'

'You have to be able to hold the –'

'Paradox,' I said, interrupting him, rolling my eyes.

'Expressive,' he said.

'Linda…? Could you please tell your boyfriend to kindly fuck off? I have quite the headache today.'

She laughed. 'Come on Jessie, he's only trying to help you get real.'

That felt like a veiled reference to the shitty review. My character was meant to be *performative*. I was play-acting at acting. Mark knew this but he wasn't giving me an inch.

I stood. 'I'm really not in the mood,' I said.

'But you still want to be the lead in my new play?'

'Of course she does,' Linda said.

'I encourage my actors to always speak their truth. My take on the Meisner technique.'

A notoriously brutal-in-the-wrong-hands method to get actors to stay fully present and connected with each other as they itemise the 'truth' in each other as they see it. Phase one: scene partners sit or stand across from one another. One actor makes an observation about the other. Phase two: the second actor repeats the observation back word for word with no reaction allowed. The objective: to stay impassive, to get the focus off self, to eradicate the ego. *You seem self-conscious, I seem self-conscious, your skin is blushing, my skin is blushing, you're fidgeting, I'm fidgeting, You're a ham, I'm a ham...* Stay receptive, non-reactive.

'Linda. You start. With Jessica.'

She looked at me, into me.

'You seem nervous.'

'Your turn, Jessica,' Mark said.

'You sound like an idiot,' I said.

'No. You repeat after Jessica what she said about you.'

'You're alright.'

'I hope you won't be this obstructive in rehearsal room.'

'We're not in rehearsal room right now.'

'Jessie?' Linda said. 'Look at me.'

I did. Into her grey misty eyes.

'A word of truth...? You have a "special-me" complex.'

There was nothing funny in how she delivered this.

'That's very astute, Linda,' Mark said. 'I get that. Jessica does see herself as *special*: the bursary that she calls a scholarship, the Number One Filly listing, the handsome French boyfriend, the father-abandonment complex, the always-the-lead actress... It is rather an exceptional identity.'

He was poking my latent she-wolf.

'Says Mr Pretentious Philosophy Scholar Wannabe *Auteur*, who hates his father with a dark passion, who pairs a parka with cowboy boots and who quotes a religious fanatic at anyone who will listen...'

His eyes gleamed as he looked at me – he approved.

Linda was coming over to me, her arms outstretched. 'I made that observation out of love.'

I could imagine Mark following up an honest (or cruel) 'observation' to her with these exact words.

'How exactly is that supposed to be helpful?' I said, ducking out of her reach.

'Come on, Jess. Don't fool yourself. You've always had a superiority complex.'

And this from my so-called best friend who used to call me *Ms Funshine* and swore to my face everlasting allegiance.

'What...?'

'Think of us at school.'

I was furious. 'I did not set out to make your feel bad about yourself; you excelled at doing that already.'

Linda looked down at her scuffed Converse. She was quiet and pale.

'You know what you did,' she said.

'Sue and I only tried to help you.'

'You two!' Mark said, sounding delighted with us.

'What about us?' I said.

'Female friendships.'

'What about them?' I rounded on him.

He smiled. 'You know…' His eyes locked onto mine. 'You girls are stuck in a pattern from so long ago, neither of you even realises what you're doing to the other.'

'Except, it seems, you have made Linda aware of my awfulness.'

'No. I have made her aware of the impact of your shared past on her.'

Jacques returned at this moment and came to me, wrapping his arms around me. He kissed me passionately on the lips. Was this for show? Mark was watching. I felt intensely aroused in a way I didn't understand.

Perhaps this is why my marriage didn't stand a chance – my husband played it straight with me, never understanding what kind of a twisted dynamic I needed to feel turned on.

28

I am naked on a rotating stage with strobing lights, running, running, running, getting nowhere, Mark is shouting, *fake, you're a fake, push yourself beyond your known limits, find the Truth*, and Linda is scoring my body parts brutally and my acting ability at minus numbers, *such a ham*, and Jacques and Jonathan are pointing at me as I trip and they all laugh.

Hands reached out for me, and I screamed. Jacques was staring at me, his eyes shining and full of light. 'Bad dream, baby? Come here and I'll make it better.' He kissed me on my head and tried to gather me in his arms for our usual morning sex. I refused – a first. He looked hurt, though he did his best to hide it. 'That bad, huh?'

'I need to see Sue,' I said. I felt homesick, a gnawing hole inside.

'Why? Is everything OK?' he said.

'I don't know. I know I just need to see her.'

He kissed me, then murmured sleepily, 'OK. Tell her I'll come live on top of her tree!'

I pushed him away, tried to laugh.

On the bus, I realised I hadn't been home since I'd left for college six months ago, and I hadn't seen or spoken to Sue since Christmas. What would she make of me turning up unannounced like this, and how would I cover my guilt …? All I knew was that I was overwhelmed by a raw craving to see her. I thought of the smell of fairy buns and my always-packed lunchbox which was the envy of the whole school;

I thought of her feeding Linda and her face full of tenderness as she watched her eat; I thought of her dancing and storytelling and laughing. But there was something else in the mix too – a nameless anxiety that steered me not to call her in advance. I reserved the right to change my mind right up until the point I pressed on our front doorbell.

Her face when she opened the door was a moving picture: shock first, swiftly followed by delight, then anger. But she couldn't help herself, her love for me won the battle.

'You little divil. You should have let me know you were coming.'

'I was just passing,' I said.

There was an awkward silence before she ushered me inside. The place looked dreadful, as did she: tarnished and uncared for. I was shocked to smell stale sweat and cheap ready-made meals, the stench of microwaved plastic and overheated processed meat filling the air. I wanted to pull her into my arms and kiss her on her nose, like she used to with me, then tell her to take a shower and do her make-up and we'd both clean the place up and get baking together. Instead, I looked at her in a way that made us both cringe. Sue's body contracted, and I wore that supercilious, superior look that possessed me whenever I felt any softness in her presence. My ambivalence blindsided even me.

She started twittering: 'Honestly, you could have given me a chance to freshen up! This place doesn't see many visitors these days.'

I experienced that familiar squeeze of sadness in my chest – poor Sue – and I resented feeling it. A sort of polite stasis took hold as we stood in the hall, neither of us moving for fear of upsetting the delicate balance.

'How have you been?' she said, after some moments.

'Good! Great! Busy, you know…'

Neither of us were saying what we really wanted to say. Her: *Where have you been, you selfish ingrate?* And me: *I miss you and I need you to advise me, things are weird, Linda's met a real piece of work and I'm worried about her*, which of course was only half the story; the other half I couldn't articulate, but even if I could have, she wouldn't have had a clue what to say – she chose my father, after all.

I could see her visibly working herself up into a twist of anxiety, disguised as 'Fun'. She propelled herself into the kitchen, me following, took out the polish and squirted it into the air and put on a CD of the Temptations. 'Tea? Or wine?' she said as she moved her hips half-heartedly to 'Papa Was a Rollin' Stone'.

I realised how much I needed her to be an adult.

'Tea, please.' I said. 'It's early.'

'Party pooper,' she said as she got down two cups from the cupboards and quickly washed and dried them while waiting for the kettle to boil. 'Tea o'clock!' she sang, as she opened a pack of Jacobs Mikado, their sugary coating bringing back memories of being wired on a sweetness overload any time I wanted.

As soon as we sat at the table, she stood to get a cloth, which she used to wipe away crumbs, again apologising for the state of the place. Eventually, she settled, looked me in the eye. I noticed that hers were bloodshot, deeply grooved.

'Well, this is nice,' she said, staring at me from underneath her naked, barely-there lashes, which were usually coated in glossy mascara. I hardly recognised her without her face of make-up. Was I the reason that she had kept herself together all those years, and was I now the reason…?

'Hmmm.' I pushed half a Mikado in my mouth.

'Is everything OK?'

I nodded, my cheeks bulging, pretend-smiling.

'Linda tells me you're still with that French boyfriend.'

I swallowed, sipped some tea. 'Yup.'

'Well that's nice for you. He seems nice.'

Nice was not a word that had ever escaped her lips before.

'I really wish you'd visit more often,' she said. 'Or at least call.'

The usual conflicted feelings tripping over each other: guilt and love and irritation and yearning.

I ate another biscuit, this time making a show of removing the top with my teeth, then the bottom, to reveal the sticky sweet marshmallow inside.

'Some things never change, sweetie,' she said, smiling at me.

I hated when she called me sweetie. Poor Sue. There was no winning.

'Why don't you invite all your friends over for dinner some time? I'd like that...'

There was no way I would expose her to Mark's sharp ridicule. Even the thought of him here, in this ticky-tacky house, made me blush.

'Thanks, I'll ask them,' I said.

The hurt expression on her face meant that she knew I didn't mean it.

'I went to see you in that play,' she said.

I caught my breath. 'You did? Why didn't you come to see me after?'

'You were surrounded by admirers.'

The thought of her there, alone, was unbearable; the thought of her unwavering love for me, the fact of her not abandoning me, was unbearable. I hardened myself. 'What did you think?'

'I don't think I understood it,' she said. 'But you were incredible up there, enigmatic, no one could take their eyes off you.'

Her eyes were shining with tears held in check. Was she proud of me, or was she feeling regret about her own unlived life?

She stood, sighed, went to the sink, turned on the tap, poured water and drank it quickly. Then she turned to face me. 'I hear Linda's met a new man.' Her voice was unnaturally high. 'Have you met him?'

'Have you?' I asked.

She shook her head. This was painful for her.

'You really don't want to,' I said.

'Are you not happy for her?' she said, sitting back at the table opposite me.

'I'm not happy it's him.'

'You were the same about her boyfriend at school.'

'Stupid Stu?' I snorted.

She snorted back. 'He was a bit pathetic, alright. I remember the poor eejit standing outside our window for days after she dumped him ... or you dumped him for her.'

'There's nothing pathetic about this one.'

‘Oh well, that’s good then, isn’t it?’

How could I describe Mark’s potent, dangerous allure? But of course, she herself had been under the spell of someone similarly addictive and treacherous.

‘Have you had any dates?’ I asked, fervently hoping she might have.

She laughed, bright and tinny. ‘Who would have this old bag?’

‘Well, with that attitude, no one,’ I said, telling myself I was practising a version of tough love.

‘You haven’t a clue,’ she said, almost mournfully.

I wanted to shake her. (As I am now the same age she was then, I get it.)

‘When you see Linda, will you tell her to come visit me? I’m worried about her.’

In the mix was my usual conflict about wanting to push them together so I would be absolved of responsibility, and then stabbing jealousy that she cared for her more than me.

I stood, the metal chair legs screeching against the lino. ‘Right, I’d better be off.’

‘What, so soon? Won’t you stay for lunch?’

I went to her, pecked her on the cheek.

‘I have to get back. Afternoon lecture.’

‘Don’t leave it so long next time.’

‘Sure thing… See ya soon,’ I said breezily, as if it were true, as if I hadn’t spent the last three months ignoring her.

‘I enjoyed Christmas,’ she said, and it sounded so sad. ‘I love you.’ Those invisible tentacles were circling, closing in, close to choking me. I couldn’t say it back. Three little words that would have made her very happy, a kind untruth. I convinced myself I didn’t want to be a hypocrite. I forced myself to kiss her on her other cheek but stepped away before her arms could encircle me. I waved back at her lone figure standing in the doorway, then turned and bolted, charging through my childhood streets, past the field where Linda and I used to get pissed on beakers full of blow-your-mind mixes from our parents’ alcohol cabinets, past all the identical houses that looked even smaller and sadder now, past the scrawny trees with their sickly, peeling barks. My chest was so constricted I had to force air in somehow. I reached the bus stop but continued past it; there was no way I could sit on a bus without internally combusting. When I could run no longer, I walked, for hours. Poor, blighted Sue. She made me feel so bad and angry and sad and so full of a smothering love I didn't want to carry, or couldn't, or just wouldn't.

She made you… Is that true? I can hear Mark's voice.

*

'He made you question your version of reality. Dangerous stuff,' Dr Collins says.

'Is it? His point was that no one can make you feel anything.'

'And yet, he had the power to make you believe that what you were feeling was not true. It had to be true. It was *your* experience.'

I am unconvinced. She sees this.

'What I am saying is that Mark's influence over you was greater than you are acknowledging. He had a hold.'

'Oh, I know that.'

'But I don't think you are fully acknowledging the extent of the power he wielded over you.'

'Not yet. I am getting to that…'

'Even still, Jessica. All these decades later. He is still exerting influence over your life.'

You don't say? I roll my eyes, sigh, shrug. Every clichéd gesture in the book. I am frustrated by my knowledge that I was unduly influenced by that man; that though I thought I could play the game, and win, I too was bedazzled, bewildered, used.

Me too.

The Middle

29

As soon as I stepped back through the palazzo-style front arch of Wilde, onto the cobblestones, into my new life, I was Number One Filly and the Players' favourite actress and one part of the coolest, cutest couple in college again. I *was* special, I couldn't help it. I drank in the majesty of the ancient buildings enclosing this rarefied place, where I belonged. I felt jittery and high, Sue's face and voice receding with every step I took further into my new life. I would never get trapped like that: in smallness, in sadness and poverty. I would never saddle myself with a man like my father who had a kid he didn't want. Sue chose her man badly; she chose her life badly. *Not my fault.*

The sky was low, the grounds covered in a misty shroud, romantic in a gloomy way. I was again starring in a movie of my own making: a story of reinvention, of triumph against the odds, the odds being an unlikely escape from stultifying suburbia. *I am a person in my own right, I am free, I am me…* My body was trilling to my heightened adolescent thoughts, and the more I repeated them, the more I believed them, or the more I tried to convince myself I believed them.

'Well, this is a surprise!' a familiar voice said, coming up behind me. It was as if I had conjured him in my exalted state. 'What are you doing in my neck of the woods?'

'*Your* neck of the woods!'

He waved his arm to signify the palatial rooms behind him in Front Square.

'This pleb decided she wanted to see where the *real* scholarship folk live!'

He laughed; he approved. He walked in the direction of the campanile, gesturing at me to follow him. I froze.

He stopped, looked at me curiously. 'You don't believe any of that old superstitious nonsense, do you?'

'I'm not willing to see if it's true.'

The lore was that if you walked underneath the bell tower's arch you would fail your exams, the person you loved would suddenly hate you, you would end up childless, penniless and alone. Also, the bell would ring if you were a virgin.

He sauntered underneath its roof. 'No bells ringing,' he said, looking up.

'No surprise there,' I said, staying on the edges. I had never heard of a single student who had risked going there before.

He looked at me, his eyes shining with mirth and provocation. 'I can guarantee you I'm not failing anything.'

'Aren't you scared of any of the rest of it?' I asked.

'Linda won't suddenly wake up and hate me, will she?'

The cocky bastard. I wanted to tell Linda not to be so pliable and available.

'And no, I do not foresee that I will die penniless and alone. And I do not ever want children.'

I wondered if Linda knew this about him. Even as I had the thought, I remembered Jacques saying that Linda was just Mark's latest pet project, that he would tire of her.

'Come on,' he said. 'You're not someone who blindly follows the crowd.'

'Just not willing to try my luck.'

'Really? I'd have thought you were all about pushing the boundaries and trying your luck,' he said.

'That curse is ancient and has patience. I'm not willing to test it out.'

He found this hilarious, slapping his hand on his thigh, a parody of the gentleman-scholar he purported to be. 'You need to reclaim your narrative. You are in charge of your life, your future.'

It was uncanny how perfectly this statement fed in with what I had been thinking just before I met him. *I am free, I am me…* I looked up at him and the light in his eyes burned a hole in the centre of me.

'Go on. I dare you.'

Adrenaline coursed through my body. That word had a power over me, and he knew it. Magnetically drawn, irresistibly charged. Speed built up in me until I found I was running as fast as I could, underneath the tower, holding my breath the whole time, as if the curse's vapours contained in the clock tower's ancient walls couldn't infiltrate me if I didn't breathe them in. As I streaked underneath the campanile, the clock struck one o'clock. I was jangled, jarred, thrilled.

'Are you now going to tell me you're a virgin?' he shouted.

'Stranger things have been known to be true,' I bellowed as I charged through to the other side.

'Well done!' he said, reaching me at the far side. 'Proud of you. Stretching your limits.'

I couldn't help feeling like Daddy's little girl who had come home with yet another A-plus and a star on my copybook.

'Hey. So, you'd like to see where the *real* scholarship people live? I have an hour or so before my next tutorial.'

He walked away, without waiting for my answer.

I followed his back – of course I did – clad in its parka, which was strangely clean, leading me to wonder how many identical others there were hanging in his wardrobe. I imagined a whole army of them, standing stiffly at his beck and call. I stifled a laugh. His cowboy boots were loudly clack-clacking on the cobbles, in time to my wildly beating heart, or so it seemed.

'Where's Linda?' I asked as we reached his rooms.

He shrugged. 'I'm not her keeper.'

'Could've fooled me!'

He turned, grinning, his eyes flashing. We were back at it. He jangled his keys theatrically as if he were a gaoler, wielding unconscionable power, before he inserted the main one into the lock.

'Follow me, madam,' he said, loping ahead of me in the darkness.

At the top of the first flight of the winding staircase he stopped, and again noisily fumbled with the keys in the gloom. As soon as he opened the door the smell of incense hit me.

'I wouldn't have put you down as the hippy type,' I said.

'You should know by now that I defy categorisation.'

His rooms were huge, high-ceilinged and soft, with amber light spilling from the streetlamps outside the large sash windows, lit even in dreary daylight hours. The floor was creaky, bare floorboards, books everywhere, in stacks on the ground and teetering on tables in precarious piles. In the corner sat an old gramophone and a stack of vinyls.

'Is it antique?' I said, moving closer to it.

'How old does something need to be to be antique?'

'I don't fucking know. Retro then?'

He went into the galley kitchen, laughing.

'Want a whiskey?'

'If you insist. A secret vice of yours, is it?'

'I don't touch the stuff,' he said. 'It's purely for guests.'

Guests. He got a tumbler from a cupboard and poured a generous measure of whiskey into it.

'What are you trying to do? Get me pissed?'

'I don't like pissed,' he said, and I set the glass down. 'Alcohol is such a poor choice.'

'For what?' I said.

'For seeking alternative experiences.'

'Oh come on, it's just a way to relax.'

'I know better ways to do that,' he said.

My body danced to the promise.

He went to the tap, poured himself a glass of water and turned to me. 'Cheers.'

'Cheers back.' I found myself lifting the tumbler of whiskey to my mouth and swallowing as he held me captive with his brilliant gaze.

'How's Jacques? You're such a beautiful couple you know.'

'Why, thank you,' I said and curtsied, like a cringing fool.

'There's something about him, don't you think? So handsome but sad, as if his heart has been smashed to smithereens.'

I opened my mouth to contradict him, but nothing came out.

'Jonathan too,' he continued. 'Gorgeous but wrecked.'

I knew what he meant, but his words about Jacques were still reverberating. What did he see? What did he know?

'And you...' he said softly, studying me.

'A damaged nutter!' I said, trying to bat him away.

'They fuck you up, your mum and dad. They may not mean to, but they do...' he intoned. 'Larkin.'

'I know who it is,' I said. I swallowed more of the whiskey. 'And anyway, that's a bit reductive.'

He studied me. 'You really think so?'

I wiped my mouth with the back of my hand, liked how my lips tingled. 'We all know how you feel about your father, the poor bastard.'

He mock cheers-ed me. 'How about your parents?'

I pressed on the sore place on my throat.

'An interesting habit of yours,' he said. 'We can use that in your character work. It's a great gesture, speaks volumes.'

I removed my hand, feeling strangely teary and furious at myself.

He came close to me. 'Does that hurt?' He touched the same spot on my neck.

'Can I tell you what I'm observing, Jessica ...?'

My body was vibrating.

'Your vulnerability. The truth of who you are.'

I wanted to tell him to fuck off, but I also wanted his fingers to stay where they were.

'Your father left. You loved him. You thought he loved you, yes?'

What had Linda told him? I welled up, looked towards the ceiling, swallowed, pushing back the tears.

'A good choice. The best actresses don't cry.'

His hand remained where it was.

'Let's rewrite that story in your playing of my Jessica. Let's have you be the leaver, not the left.'

I liked that idea. Felt my body flooding with strength.

One finger lightly traced the hollow at the base of my throat.

Now my body was flooded with something else.

'This is a beautiful part of a woman,' he said.

I wanted to ask him if he really meant what he said about not scoring me top marks against Linda.

'Do you believe in God?' he asked, dropping his hand abruptly as if it were scorched, as if he had heard my crass thoughts. I was left desperately craving his touch.

'Where did that come from?' I said.

'Do you?' he went on.

'I guess I haven't given it much thought.'

'Well, you should.'

'I thought you didn't believe in Divine Providence,' I said, referring to his disregard of the campanile's curse.

'I believe in a higher power. The role of the artist is to channel this power. I look forward to getting you in touch with it.'

'How do you propose you do that? I said, thrilling to the idea that there might be drugs involved. I swallowed back the dregs of the whiskey.

'By opening you up, by emptying you of ego, by getting you in touch with your real, raw self…'

'Not pretentious or anything,' I said, trying on an ironic tone but just sounding pathetic.

'Let's knock away those harsh edges and see what pain and beauty shines beneath…'

He wasn't laughing, nor was I.

'Let's get you in touch with magic.'

I presumed he was talking about the substance that wasn't alcohol. *An enhanced reality.*

'Are you up for it?' he said. 'Pushing your boundaries to their limits?'

'I am,' escaped me in a whisper.

'*To dare is to lose one's footing momentarily*,' he said.

Before I knew what was happening his hand was pressing hard on my neck, and his other one was unzipping my jeans, then a finger, then two, then three, were inside me. I climaxed almost immediately. Appalling, shameful ecstasy.

He went to the sink immediately after, washed his hands.

I pulled my zip back up with shaking fingers.

'Let's say nothing,' I said in a small, voice.

'About what?' he said, his face impassive. He looked at his watch, a 1920s leather number. 'Gotta go. Don't want to be late for my student.'

'Nice watch,' I said, for something to say.

'Bulgari, Vestiaire… Now that is a true example of what qualifies as *vintage*.'

He walked me to his front door. 'Break a leg tonight!' he said, his tone neutral, as he ushered me through the door: 'I look forward to directing you.'

His voice in my head, deconstructing my reality, as I walked blindly in the direction of my room: *Before you knew what was happening. Is that true, Jessica?*

An hour later I was lying on my bed – paralysed, listening to the rain outside, dreading the moment when Jacques would walk through the door – when someone knocked. The door opened and there was Linda, electrified, her hair standing on end. It was as if she was shot through by light.

'Mark just told me he loved me.'

I sat up. 'When?'

'Just now. We had the best sex ever, then he told me he loved me.'

Something hard and cold settled in me, freezing me at my core, making movement impossible. Linda didn't notice, tied up as she was in her wonder. She was breathless and a tear rolled down her cheek. I wanted to brush it away and hold her close. I wanted to rage, warn her, bring her into my confidence, tell her he was a dangerous, toxic, manipulative predator but really, who did I need to warn her about?

She went on, riffing in a voice that was not her own: 'I also wanted to say sorry I've been a bit of a bitch recently. I've never been in love before. And it's scary, right? That experience of falling through the cracks of known experience…' She looked at me with pure, unfiltered love. 'But you are my best friend. Sisters, forever, right?'

I turned away, curled into the foetal position to stop my stomach from coming up through my mouth.

She sat gently on the edge of the bed. 'You OK, sweet-cheeks? Cramps? Hope you'll be well enough for your performance later.'

She reached out and brushed my hair off my forehead, stroked me as if she were soothing a child. I wished she hadn't used that expression of Sue's. I remember thinking I might crack from the weight of guilt, or the force of it, a solid concrete juggernaut hurtling my way. I had already set the thing in motion.

30

'You seem overwhelmed, Jessica. Perhaps you could bring yourself back to the present moment, connect with your breath, plant your feet on the ground?'

I am sitting on a chair that is too high for me, my feet swinging above the ground, my body is strangely torqued, my breath is caught. I push myself to standing, inhale, exhale. She counts with me. Four, four, four, four, then six, six, six, six, then eight, eight… Box breaths, which make me quite giggly and light-headed. I stretch my arms over my head, thinking of Mark's observation about my ability to reach new heights, to extend beyond my limits. I look out the streaked glass at that sad, lonely wall.

'That is the moment I should have stopped it.'

'Perhaps you couldn't…'

'Of course I could. But I didn't.'

'Would you mind if I shared what I saw as you relayed that episode?' she says.

Episode. This is where the making things up really happens. I nod at her.

'I saw a bereft child,' she says. 'Who'd do anything to please.'

I do not laugh, though I should want to.

'Abandonment for a child is an overwhelmingly painful experience.'

I remain standing, peering through the dirty looking glass, finding nothing real there.

'I was not a child then,' I say inaudibly.

Dr Collins continues: 'It's not surprising that your way of relating with people has been skewed.'

'And does that excuse my behaviour?' I sound harsh. 'Are you going to tell me now that I was looking for love in all the wrong places?'

She says nothing, leaves my cynical remark hanging until it gains substance.

'I was guilty, as charged.'

I walk to the window, huff on it, pull my sleeve down and wipe it. 'Some time since you've had a window cleaner.'

'Not much of a view,' she says.

I press my nose against the pane.

Dr Collins spends some time in silence before she says, 'Is this a familiar feeling? A pane of glass between you and the world, and you pressed against it?'

I am disappointed in her. Again. And yet I keep coming back. Why? Company, a listening ear? I rub the end of my nose, which is probably filthy.

'Back to that guilt you spoke of,' she says.

I feel the full weight of it in my chest, moving up, gathering in my throat, pushing behind my eyes. *Don't cry, don't cry.* I look up towards the ceiling. The best actresses are those who don't cry. The best writers are those who don't allow their characters easy tears.

'I am not sure that was a fully consensual sexual experience.'

I am not going down that route. I know what I felt. Overwhelmed, yes. But wanting it.

'I'd better get back.' I look at my watch exaggeratedly. *I'm late, I'm late, I'm late for a very important date.*

We both know I have nothing to get back for: no child that needs minding, no proper job that needs doing, no husband to make dinner for or talk to.

She doesn't ask when I would like my next session, which perversely makes me wish she would. I feel strangely grief-stricken at my own leave-taking.

As I turn to go, I hear her voice behind me. 'Locate that hurting child within. She needs some care.'

I roll my eyes dramatically but on the way home I think about her words. How? Buy her a never-ending supply of Smarties? I go into a newsagent, buy ten tubes and pick out the orange ones. Little me is very happy until she wants to get sick. I have never had any limits, internal or external.

I decide when I get home that the only place for me is on the page. There is nowhere else to be.

31

Jacques barrelled into my room a few minutes after Linda had left. 'Hi baby!' I was still lying fully clothed under my childhood purple polka-dot quilt (a Sue special), which was pulled up around my ears.

'Why are you hiding in there?' He reached in and placed a hand on my hot cheek. 'Are you sick?'

I smacked his hand away. 'I'm perfectly fucking fine.'

He flinched. 'What have I done?'

'Are you going to make this all about you?' I said, shocking myself. 'This has nothing to do with you.'

He went to the window, opened it, breathed in deeply. 'Well, what then? What's happened?'

'I don't feel like talking about it.'

'Since when do you not feel like talking, about anything?' He turned back to face me.

'Oh I don't know… How about … since now?'

I curled into a tight ball, pulling the quilt back high over my head, shutting myself off from him as best I could. 'Can you close that window? It's freezing.'

'You look like a sweet little caterpillar in there,' he said.

In my chrysalis of wickedness.

Jacques settled himself on the bed and patted the space beside him. I sat up, the quilt still wrapped about me as he plumped the cushions behind my back.

'Your eyes…' He was looking at me intently, searching.

Could he see what I had done?

'Have you been crying?' He kissed my eyelids gently, then fluttered his eyelashes on my cheeks.

'Sue used to do that,' I said. 'Butterfly kisses…' I felt myself flood with a nameless grief.

He continued planting eyelash-kisses all over my body and then started to undress me gently. I let him. There is no precise word to describe the betrayal and comfort of coming home to his body. I faked an orgasm for the first time. He didn't seem to notice.

'I love you,' I said, my voice scratchy, disgrace catching in my throat.

He wrapped me in his arms. 'Do you want to talk about it?'

'About what?' I whispered in the darkness.

'Whatever happened to make you cry?'

What came out of my mouth next felt divinely (or diabolically) inspired: 'I can't believe you've been talking to Mark about Louis.' In the moment my hurt was self-righteously justified. My sense of rejection temporarily erased my treachery.

He wiped my tears away with his thumb. 'I knew you wouldn't approve, so I didn't tell you.'

'Oh right, so now we just pick and choose what we tell each other?' I was gaining in momentum, shocking and thrilling myself by my duplicitousness.

'He's not that bad you know.'

'He's forever dissing me in public, and you never say anything.' I was in full-on 'victim' immersive role-play now.

'Listen, I just bumped into him one day and we got talking. He spoke about his own father who was an alcoholic and I found myself sharing my story with him. He knew what I was talking about…'

'Oh, and I don't?'

His silence said it all.

'That guy is not to be trusted,' I said. *Be careful, Jessica.*

'I'm not excluding you, just trying to protect you.'

Someone should have been trying to protect him from me.

'Strange as he is, I think he really does care for Linda,' he went on.

'What about your assertion that she's just his latest *pet project*?'

'I think I may have been wrong... I hope I was.'

'And he told you this, did he?'

'He said he knew you didn't approve of him, and it hurt him seeing as you're Linda's best friend.'

Hurt him. I held my breath to the point of dizziness. *Say nothing*. 'Something' would have destroyed us.

'He's having a small gathering on Saturday. We're invited. I think we should go, for Linda's sake.'

There was an inevitability to this; no amount of resistance was going to stop the train now it had left the station.

He kissed me on the lips, with just the right amount of pressure, lightly loving, demanding nothing of me.

'When do rehearsals start?'

'I'm not going to do it.'

'Don't let one bad review put you off acting.'

He was so way off the mark there that I felt further away from him than I ever had.

'Mark's really excited about it. He thinks you're going to be brilliant.'

'And he told you that, did he?'

'He did. Indeed.' He seemed so proud. 'I get the sense he's one talented bastard.'

Say nothing.

'I won't let you walk away from this part. It's going to be a big one for you, I can feel it.'

'And you don't mind that he puts me down?'

'You're well able, Jessie,' he said. 'No part of me worries that you don't know how to handle yourself.'

A sensation like a hand pushing its way down my windpipe, gagging me. I coughed.

He patted me on the back. 'OK, baby?'

I nodded, swallowed, inhaled deeply.

'And remember, you are made to be up there.'

I dragged myself out of bed. 'Speaking of which,' I said, 'I've got to get ready for tonight.'

'Don't let the bastards grind you down!' Well-meaning but intensely patronising. 'Only two more nights to go.'

Strange though it was, I was going to miss my *self-conscious* performance as the seductive stepdaughter. Pirandello had climbed inside me, claimed me as his. I was in his service, for now. Better that, than to be *in service* to Mark Whitman.

32

The following morning, Linda, Jonathan and I were in the coffee dock in the arts block, at Jonathan's instigation, drinking coffee none of us really wanted, perched awkwardly on high stools. The artificial strip lights above our heads felt probing, interrogative, and I had to keep blinking to keep my panic at bay. The three of us hadn't been in a room together since the opening night of *Six Characters* ten nights previously. As I looked at Linda, the outline of her was blurred, my guilt clouding my vision.

'Are we all going to Mark's do on Saturday night?' I said, trying to sound normal.

'*Do*?' Linda said. 'How suburban of you!'

'Yup! Something Sue would say!' I played this for laughs, putting my hand over my mouth. No one even smiled.

'I don't think so,' Jonathan said.

Linda looked at him sideways. 'You're invited,' she said, sounding inhospitable to the point of being hostile.

'First I heard of it,' Jonathan said.

'Mark said to tell you you're invited,' she went on flatly.

'Come … it'll be fun!' I said, which sounded imbecilic in the context of how un-fun it was the last time we were all in the same room together, when Linda's lies were laid bare. No wonder she had been so nervous about Jonathan and Mark meeting in the first place. Not that I judged her, being somewhat prone to exaggeration myself. But lying to her boyfriend that her best male friend had made a move on her was spectacularly messy. *How about not telling your best friend that her boyfriend made a move on you and you let him?* Fucking hypocrite.

'What's the party in aid of?' I said to Linda. She looked down, worrying the skin around her nails with her teeth. Not something I had ever seen her do before.

'Not sure,' she said, sounding as if she did know.

'Will there be drugs?' I asked.

Jonathan looked at me curiously.

'Don't know what you mean,' Linda said, stonewalling me.

'I came to see you last night,' Jonathan said to me.

'Again?' I asked.

'I'm your biggest fan.'

I felt a rush of gratitude towards him that was all out of proportion. I threw my arms around his neck. 'Thank you. I needed that.'

He looked at me quizzically, tilted his head: *Do you love me?* Jonathan knew exactly when I was in manipulation mode, and this was a part of our friendship that I valued. Not even Jacques could see clearly when I was playing him, lust often distorting the picture. Linda was absently circling the rim of her coffee cup with her right middle finger, until she looked down and seemingly noticed for the first time the state of her cuticles, one of which was bleeding. She put her finger in her mouth and sucked.

'Well, this is a nice surprise! Three of my favourite people all in one spot!' Mark's voice boomed at us from a distance.

I imagined this was very much *not* a surprise. My whole body started to vibrate at a disturbing frequency. I was scared of what might happen, what might fly out of my mouth.

Jonathan stood. 'Well, I'm off.'

'Good to see you, Jonathan,' Mark said.

Jonathan said nothing to Mark in response. 'Linda?'

She looked at him warily.

'I'd love to have lunch together, just you and me?'

Mark laughed. 'Hey, hey, there. Bit much. I am here, you know!'

Mark knew there was zero threat, but to play at feeling insecure was a winning move.

Jonathan wasn't biting. He walked past Mark making some excuse about being behind with his studies, and I noticed Mark brush his fingers against his arm as he passed him by.

'Tomorrow night at eight-ish? Wouldn't be the same without you. I'll have some goodies,' he said.

Jonathan mumbled something about being too busy before walking away.

Mark sauntered over to Linda, pulled her finger from her mouth and put it in his own. She looked up at him, then kissed him, her finger still in their mouths. She probed him with her tongue, which felt appalling to witness. She closed her eyes as Mark opened his and tangled me up in his stare.

My body was a discordant violin concerto, nerves jangling. I was incapable of movement or speech until he broke the trance by looking away.

I stood shakily, feeling as if I might faint.

'Make sure to persuade Jonathan to come, will you? We all need to build bridges and get over ourselves. And I know the perfect way to do that!'

I stopped myself from asking him, though somewhere in the midst of all that trauma and tumult, there was space for an excited adrenaline rush. Linda laughed, a knowing, insider's laugh, the sound tinny. Not the natural order of things. This man was an interrupter, a breaker of new circuits. I was tingling, shot through with static.

'Bye Lindy,' I said attempting to get things back on even ground.

'See you tomorrow. You're in for a treat!' She leaned in to kiss her boyfriend again, who, this time, pushed her away.

'Don't be so needy,' he said.

She looked tiny, as if someone had taken a pin to her and all the life force in her had leaked out. I wanted to hug her but instead I steeled myself and walked away.

'Knock 'em dead tonight.' Mark's voice followed me. 'I'd say you're glad that fiasco's over.'

My breath came fast and sharp and my cheeks were on fire. Is this what Linda used to feel? Was this a panic attack, or a shame attack? How had that man so upended our status quo…?

33

'You look beautiful, baby,' Jacques said. I was a replica of Honor Cave-Tempest-Stuart, in my fishnets, mini skirt and an oversized men's shirt. How conscious I was that I was copying her, I'm not sure, but I do know I thought Jacques was a fool to say what he said.

'Oh, this outfit,' I said, looking at myself in the mirror. 'Bit ridiculous.'

'Not at all,' he said as he came behind me and wrapped his arms around me, nuzzling my neck. 'It's sexy.'

Now I was furious with him. Anger seemed to be my go-to emotion to deflect the guilt I felt in his presence.

'I'm not something to be objectified,' I said.

'Oh, OK, baby.' He looked confused, though he laughed.

In the mirror I imagined I saw Mark's eyes, penetrating me. And I felt that explosion in me. *It didn't happen, it never happened* – all I had to do was think of Mark with his back to me, washing his hands at the sink. Although I had been tempted to cry off going to the party with a sick stomach, I knew that the longer I avoided being in the same room with him and Linda, the more strained my behaviour would become.

We walked through the grounds in the rain, Jacques holding his coat over my head so as not to let a drop fall on me. I did not deserve this man. I walked up to the door of Mark's rooms, careful not to look too confident this was the place. 'What number again?' I asked. 'I think three,' Jacques said as he pressed on the doorbell.

Linda met us at the door, her cheeks flushed with happiness. The exact shade of her blush was different from that of her shame – this was new: a pretty pink glow. 'Come in, come in,' and she kissed us both on our cheeks, reminding me of Sue in her role as the glittering hostess at one of Dad's long-ago parties. Linda, like Sue, believed she had found her permanent home, her permanent belonging, by her man's side, in her man's orbit. She was wearing another new dress: this one, still vintage in style with its gathered A-line skirt, had a plunging sweetheart neckline, racier than the April Wheeler number. It was moss green to offset her eyes. I had to admit that Mark had impeccable taste.

When we walked into the candlelit living room, the waft of incense floating on the air, I was struck by a stabbing sensation low down in my pelvis, painful and pleasurable. What was wrong with me? Mark was sitting on the edge of the couch, his etched profile in shadow, chatting to someone we couldn't see. As soon as he noticed us, he stood solicitously, again affecting the perfect gentleman role. The someone he had been talking to was revealed to be the duchess, her hair deliciously dishevelled, her mouth red and luscious, as if she had just been involved in a vigorous love-making session. My sight became laser sharp in her presence. Mark walked towards us and wrapped Jacques in a bear hug, play-acting at being long-lost brothers. It seemed there was more to their 'just meeting casually' than Jacques had said. He greeted me coolly by comparison; he was just my best friend's boyfriend after all.

We were ushered into the kitchen where there were a few intense-looking students, scholarship types, drinking wine from goblets, declaiming loudly on politics and poetry, as if they were scoring marks in a public debate, or so I had them pegged. I don't remember one specific thing that was said in that room, my mind full of Honor lounging on the couch in her clinging green velvet catsuit. Tonight she had plumped for the over-the-top, sex-goddess look, and it was killing me. Mark was the consummate host, introducing everyone, his manners impeccable, proffering delicious wine and canapés.

'What's the occasion?' I asked, looking at the waitress making her rounds. It was hardly a big enough crowd to warrant staff.

'Oh, didn't Linda tell you? It's my birthday…' He cleared his throat and shouted, 'Lind …ah?' accentuating the ah sound at the end of her name, sounding both amused and cruel. She appeared instantly and he spoke to her as you would a child, admonishing her. 'You know because of your oversight your two good friends here didn't know it was my birthday?'

Her voice was small as she said, 'I didn't think you *wanted* me to tell them…'

'Why on earth wouldn't I have wanted them to know?'

'Well, you didn't tell your other friends… You don't like a fuss being made of you on your birthday… You don't even *like* your birthday… Reminds you of who you were born to…' She trailed off, realising she had said too much, and by the expression on Mark's face, said entirely the wrong thing.

'Jesus, Linda is nothing sacrosanct to you?' he said, sounding really hurt. This was clever and confounding. I could see it, a reversal of one of his favourite moves: *get her to reveal stuff to you and then expose her later in public*, but Linda didn't make the connection. Also, If he really hated his birthday that much, what was he doing have a party? Even if it was one where no one knew it was his birthday.

'Sorry…' she mumbled.

He kissed her cheek gently. 'That's OK, my sweet. Just an oversight.'

She brightened instantly.

'Now, let's all go mingle, shall we?' he said, pulling Jacques towards the couch where the cat-suited siren was enticingly draped.

Linda turned to me. 'I'm certain he told me not to say anything…' She didn't sound certain.

'Don't worry about it, Lindy. I'm sure you're right.'

She shook her head. 'He's so complicated…'

Sue used to say that exact same thing about my father, day after day, year after year, trying to make sense of his behaviour that left her feeling confused and worthless, trying to make excuses, trying to make sense of the fact that she stayed.

I gulped down the goblet of red wine, said nothing.

'Here,' Linda replaced my empty glass with a full one. She hugged me. 'I'm so glad you're here.'

I hugged her back, though I wanted to hit and pinch. This time not her, but myself.

I drank too much and too fast and my feelings were intense and jumbled. My boyfriend was sitting on the couch beside the *vision*, just as I had fantasised. He was also drinking too much, intimidated – or so I tried to convince myself – by the embodiment of beauty and privilege in front of him. This was all Mark's doing, this pushing Jacques and Honor together again. *Poor you, oh dear, but don't you deserve it, you harlot?* No part of Mark was acknowledging what had happened between us. My jealousy was becoming uncontrollable. It was as if I could see it, a person, a female form, a female fury hissing at me. I decided to name her 'La Jalousie', trying to wrench back some semblance of control (I had read somewhere that naming emotions can lessen their impact.) I felt speedy and spinning and slightly sick by my own imaginings. I breathed deeply, rooted my feet into the ground, exactly as Jonathan had instructed Linda, to ward off her anxiety attacks. It didn't help.

I regarded Mark. He was surveying the room as if he were watching his actors in a play on opening night, everyone in their proper place, following the script he wrote. I went to the kitchen, drank a glass of water, then another. I was determined not to fit into the role he was expecting of me: the craven, jealous, attention-seeking girlfriend, flipping her lid. I was close. I took charge of myself and walked down the stairs, in full control of my faculties. This was not an expected exit, and the act of taking it felt disruptive.

Outside, the night air was damp, the rain had dried up, and I looked up at the stars. *What to do, oh celestial ones?* I found myself walking in the direction of Jonathan's apartment, a dreadful modern student complex about ten minutes outside campus. I wanted to be with my friend who got me in all my needy glory. I noticed almost nothing of the city on my journey there, except that the buildings were grey, people's faces were grey, and the air was damp and choked with exhaust fumes. My thoughts were circling and contradicting each other: he loves me, he loves me not, he loves … *loves…*? I trust him, I trust him not, I trust … *trust…*? I arrived outside the glass-and-steel complex, keyed in Jonathan's apartment number. 'Whoever this is, I'm busy,' he said. 'Please, it's Jessie. I need you.' I knew not to try on any drama, and it worked. He came down, looked at me straight. 'What's up?' I told him about Honor and he put his arms around me, said that Jacques wasn't that kind of guy, that he adored me and he would never do anything like that, ever.

'You haven't seen her!' I said. 'I'd do her!'

He laughed. I couldn't expound on my theories about Mark's manipulations, his machinations, his grand design – which was what? Divide and conquer? Stretch and break? To what end? – without confessing to my own part in it.

'Please come. I can't go back there alone.'

'OK, I'll escort you back and we can go in together and rescue Jacques from the vixen. Then I'm leaving, right?'

I hugged him tightly. 'You're the best!'

'Unnecessary, Jessica,' he said, calling me on my dramatics.

'No, I mean it. You really are!'

He got his coat and we left together, walking in the dark night, arms linked. He looked up, riffing on the weather like a baby poet: 'The cloud-scudded night … the velvety darkness, the weight of it.' I couldn't help thinking that he wasn't living the life he should; his was a life prescribed by his father. I regarded him: my thwarted, melancholic dreamer. Would he have the gumption to live his own life? I thought of Mark saying *reclaim your narrative*, and I shivered. Jonathan laughed and pulled me into him, wrapping me in his coat. I suddenly, desperately, wanted my friend to experience freedom, to be his own person, to live life on his own terms.

Mark's provocative, seductive logic had infiltrated my thinking.

34

'Well, look who has decided to grace us with his presence!' Mark greeted Jonathan with genuine warmth, as he glanced at me. His look said, *thank you for bringing him to me.* He acted as if he had orchestrated the whole scenario – me leaving and bringing Jonathan back. He squeezed Jonathan's upper arm and said, 'Sorry about the awkwardness last time… Wishful thinking on Linda's part, I guess.' Jonathan looked at me, threw his eyes to heaven, and flared his nostrils – a quirk I loved. Mark laughed, just as I noticed Linda lurking at the open kitchen door. She had heard, and he knew she had heard.

'Let me introduce you around…'

'You're OK. I'm just here for a moment.'

'Don't be ridiculous! The night is but young…'

Now who was being *ridiculous*?

'Linda?' Mark continued. 'Will you get your friends a drink?'

She appeared almost instantly with two goblets of red wine, viscous and purple, conjuring images of blood-sucking vampires and bacchanalian sacrifices. Jonathan shook his head at me as I took a full goblet of the bloody liquid– my imagination was in overdrive. He was right, I really shouldn't drink the stuff, and yet. My nervousness made me.

'There's someone I'd like you to meet,' Mark said, taking Jonathan by the arm and manoeuvring him in the direction of a smug, sandy-haired guy in the corner. He might have been Honor's cousin, with his air of entitlement. I was surprised Jonathan let himself be pushed around like that.

'How're you doing?' Linda asked me.

'Cool,' I said, though I felt anything but.

'Mark thinks Jonathan and Phil there might get on well.' There was unmistakably an undertone to this. *Poor lonely guy.*

I looked at Jonathan. He was hoisting up his trousers as if to give himself strength. His ears were bright red. Mark still had him by the arm; I decided he need rescuing.

'May I interrupt?' I said, walking over to them. I felt three pairs of eyes staring at me: Linda's, Mark's and the new guy's. 'I need my friend.' I kept my gaze trained on Jonathan, who seemed equal parts relieved and irritated by my intrusion.

'Sure, Jessie,' he said. 'At your service.'

Phil arched his eyebrows at Jonathan and smirked, a defiant come-on. 'See you later, yeah?'

Jonathan's flush spread onto his chest, a nervous rash. 'Yeah, maybe, yeah,' he said as I pulled him away, gripping his arm tightly, my hand now steering him in the same way Mark's had.

'Gah. What a cocky cock!' I said, sure my friend would agree. But he seemed flummoxed by the attention, and barely registered my words. I clicked my fingers in front of his eyes. 'Rescue me,' I said, my head tilted to one side.

'Oh Jessie. Ever the dramatics!'

I pouted at him, my lower lip protruding.

He laughed, coming back to the task at hand. 'So, where's the offending article?'

I pointed to where my boyfriend sat on the couch, exactly as I'd pictured it – had he not missed me, not even noticed I was gone? – his muscled thighs spread apart, one of them almost touching the duchess's knee which was angled provocatively at him. Jacques was probably thinking, in his own kindly way, that he was being polite, not that he was being played. 'She's wearing velvet,' I whispered to Jonathan, and he looked at me as if to say, 'Whoa, I know what you mean, intervention necessary.'

He plonked himself right in the middle of the couch, a human shield between my boyfriend and the sorceress, and looked into Jacques's eyes, making some quip that caused Jacques to laugh and then look up at me. He reached his arm out to me: 'Baby.' I went to him, sat on his lap, curled up there and stared rather aggressively at Honor, who batted her blue-black lashes at me sleepily, then yawned.

I looked up at Jonathan, mouthed 'thank you', then audibly said, 'Go mingle!'

'You sure?' he whispered.

'I'm sure,' I said. 'Now go have some fun … don't even think of going home!'

He kissed me on my forehead, said, 'Look after her now,' to Jacques who smiled guilelessly. 'Cool party, huh?' Jacques said.

Jonathan stood, glanced in Phil's direction. Their eyes met. He feigned nonchalance by sauntering across the room, stopping first at a table to knock back a glass of the purple Claret and then take another full one. I noticed Mark watch this with vampiric delight.

I snuggled against my boyfriend, who said, 'Honor here was just telling me about her father's castle.'

'Daddy's castle … how nice for you!' I sneered, acutely feeling my suburban-ness. She stood, stretched, didn't even bother to answer, which asserted her superiority much better than any retort. *This one isn't even worth the bother of talking to.* She scoped the room, then swayed languidly towards Mark and Linda. The three spoke briefly before Mark held out something in his hand to her. Honor smiled, her lips still sensuous and full, unlike the rest of us mere mortals, before she took the pill, drinking from a glass Linda offered her. Within minutes, the two girls were hugging and kissing, so at ease with one another that you could have mistaken them for best friends. Linda was simpering, looking at the siren in that obsequious way she had. I had to fight a desire to go to her and twist her wrist.

'Bit rude,' Jacques said, sounding amused, referring to my exchange with the princess.

'She deserved it. Obnoxious.'

'I don't think she was being obnoxious,' he said. 'Just being herself.'

We both regarded her.

'She's stunning,' I blurted out.

'Not as stunning as you!' Jacques buried his head against my then washboard stomach, pulling up my top to kiss my bellybutton. How he loved my bellybutton; said it was the prettiest one he had ever seen. It was small, sunken, and he liked to poke it with his tongue.

'I think they're doing drugs,' I said.

'Isn't everyone?'

'These are something else, though.'

'What do you mean?'

'Remember the time Mark spoke about experiencing an *enhanced reality*...?'

Jacques looked confused as I went on, 'Remember when you were drinking lots – after we went to see Louis that time, and Mark said that alcohol was a drug for dummies?'

'Not really...' Jacques said.

'Well, I guess that just proves his point!' I laughed. 'He said there was something recreational, far superior to alcohol, and Linda looked like she knew what he was talking about.'

I stood abruptly, disentangling myself from Jacques's embrace, and strode across the room, glancing at Jonathan who was still talking to Phil. Honor pretended not to notice me, Linda seemed vaguely irritated, but Mark smiled broadly. I felt that queasy excited sensation in the pit of my stomach.

'Curious?' he said.

'Not sure it's a good idea,' Linda said.

'You just gave some to her!' I gestured towards the duchess, who looked at me as if I were a worm she was about to squash underfoot. My body involuntarily felt like squirming.

'Your ego is sort of out of control already,' Linda went on in a voice that wasn't her own.

Mark laughed. 'It might mellow her out...'

'Fuck you!' I regretted it the moment I said it, the words reducing me to a tantrummy teenager. Honor regarded me through sexy, hooded eyes, before deciding, I guessed, that I was too much of a downer to engage with. As she walked away, I watched her perfect silhouette, my head flooded with unfavourable comparisons.

'Not a big fan of hers?' Mark said, amused.

My face betrayed me, as usual.

'I think the feeling is mutual,' Linda said.

'Does the drug make people mean?' I asked.

'No, it intensifies their reality, makes them speak and act in ways according to their true nature,' Mark said.

'Has it worked already?' I nodded at Linda.

'Hits the blood stream fast,' he said, sounding detached and forensic.

'Have you taken any?'

Jacques joined us, moving close to me, his hand on my lower back. I leaned against him. 'How's everyone?' He slid his arm around my waist, drawing me to him.

'Fucking weird,' I said.

Jacques tried to laugh it off, sounding nervous and conciliatory. 'Jessica!'

'No, really. Everyone is really fucking weird!' Linda's pupils were huge and there was a thin sheen of sweat at her hairline. 'How do you feel, Linda?'

She spoke without a hint of embarrassment: 'Glorious … there's a golden umbilical cord connecting me to everything…' Her eyes filled with tears as she looked in wonder at Mark, who regarded her with a possessive love. 'I feel … blessed … shining…'

I wanted to burst out laughing, but perhaps because she had spoken the words with such sincerity, even gravity, I felt I couldn't undermine her. Linda was not known to be verbose or druggy or mystical. These elements of life terrified her. She needed to feel safe and secure, and that meant small – so far, the extent of her dabbling in anything beyond the realm of the tangible was to lose herself in Blyton-land and whisper love spells at daisies. If she had been in any way herself, this outburst would have mortified her, but instead she was beaming and crying, revelling in her emotions. It was both appalling and fascinating to witness her transformation.

Jacques and I were silent, as if audience members at an absurdist play, where none of it made sense, but it was no less entrancing for that.

Linda stared at me, into me, her pupils large pools of black, as she continued: 'You are a true friend at times, but always, always on the make. Nothing is without an agenda with you.'

Not much *love* flowing between us on her 'golden umbilical cord'.

'Oh come on now,' Jacques said. Ineffectual, but at least he tried.

'Oh and the drug sees all this, does it?' I said.

'It's not the drug, but me that sees it. The drug makes it impossible not to say it.' She was swallowing rapidly, making a smacking sound with her tongue against the roof of her mouth.

'An instrument of verbal diarrhoea then, is it?'

'I would say it's much more refined than that,' Mark said. 'But look, let's leave it for now. You two have had too much to drink tonight anyway –'

Jacques cut in, looking at Linda. 'I hope she's OK...'

'She's fine,' Mark said. 'It's a lovely experience for the person taking it, just not always for the person on the receiving end... But I love it, that naked, unfiltered truth.'

'What is it?' I asked. 'Exactly?'

Mark tapped his finger on the side of his nose (a recent Linda affectation), which made him seem like a prissy schoolmarm. I stifled a giggle.

'Do you take it?' Jacques asked him.

'Look, it's really not that big of a deal,' Mark said.

'Jess?' Linda said. 'I *do* love you, my sister blister... I love you, and Jacques and Mark and Jonathan and everyone in this room and the whole world, and I *see* you, warts and all. I mean ... well ... we're all putting on masks, acting parts, parts that were ascribed to us at birth and which became more deeply etched in our childhoods and on into adulthood ... the pain of that, the pain...' She sounded dreamy, as if programmed. 'But there is a way ... to break these patterns, disassemble these masks...'

Mark leaned in and kissed her long and hard. He pulled away, patted her on her cheek. 'OK, pet, enough now. Let's get some food into you.' He rolled his eyes at us as he led her away towards the food, all the while talking close into her ear.

'She *is* his pet,' I said. 'Literally.'

'I hope he wouldn't give her anything that would mess her up,' Jacques said.

'If it serves his purpose, then yes, he would,' I said.

'What purpose? What are you talking about, funny face?' He kissed my nose.

I didn't know for sure, but I was sensing into it. Break her, then build her, mould her – to his specifications? Was I part of that 'project' too?

What had Mark given her? She didn't seem like she was tripping. There was a clarity and forthrightness in her manner that I had never seen before. Yet her limbs were loose, her body flowed like liquid, and her words were completely alien in her mouth. To be so completely laid bare like that, by someone you believed adored you, was destabilising and strangely enthralling.

I watched Mark and Linda, arms entwined, walk towards Jonathan and Phil, who had migrated to a dark corner of the room. The boys looked up, startled at the interruption, and stepped apart, allowing Linda and Mark to join them and form a circle. Pretty soon they were all laughing in Linda's direction, Phil's baying most demanding of space and attention. Linda was obviously providing much entertainment; she sparkled, even from a distance. Mark put his hand in his pocket, then offered his palm to the guys in a theatrical gesture for me to witness. Jonathan looked towards me to check I was OK with Jacques, and when I gave him an approximation of a thumbs up, he took one of the pills, following Phil's example. Shit, this was all my fault. I was sure that Jonathan was a virgin in more ways than one and I was equally sure this night would end both those realities for him.

'Everyone's on that stuff,' I said to Jacques. 'I wonder what it is.'

'Probably E,' Jacques said.

'I doubt it. Aren't people meant to be only expansive and loving on that? Knowing Mark, it's some advanced compound, designed to cause maximum havoc. All that "makes you speak your truth" stuff.'

'You are funny!' Jacques said, kissing me on my forehead. He thought about it for a moment. '…I guess it could be ketamine, or acid, or a cocktail of stuff.'

'Yes, that's it! "Candyflipping" – I read about that. Makes sense now: "goodies".'

'Dangerous stuff.'

'I'd love to try it, though, wouldn't you?'

'Why? You loon!'

'Something new, exciting, expansive. Oh come on, we'd have each other.'

'You heard what Mark said. We've drunk too much.'

'Pretty please, I want to.' I sounded like a child demanding all the orange Smarties in the tube.

'Not tonight, Josephine,' he said, his tone patronising to the point of provocation.

I stomped away from him towards the group, and he followed on my heels.

'Hey Jono!' I said, not knowing exactly what I was looking for by joining them. More humiliation?

'Hey,' Jonathan said, fuzzily.

'Feel anything yet –?'

'We decided not to give Jess any treats tonight,' Linda broke in abruptly, her voice cutting and clear as glass.

Mark smiled, slow and sly. Jonathan looked like he hadn't heard, preoccupied as he was with whatever sensation was newly arising in him. I noticed his body was jigging, energy and heat radiating off him, even as he stood on the spot.

'You know something, Jess?' Linda continued. 'You can be insufferable.' She said it in a way that made it sound like, 'I love you.'

'Yes. You mentioned something to that effect that already.'

Where was my Lindy, the girl I rescued? Her eyes, now huge and shining, made me think of her that first time she came to my home and met Sue and smelled the fairy cakes and took in the bright pink on the walls and the cushions, and the music and the laughter and the dancing and the storytelling and the tales of faraway lands, and her smiling up at me, as if I were her portal to another world, a world far from her cold brown house and her catatonic, cruel mother. She had never criticised me, ever, even when I totally deserved it, until she met Mark. She had never confronted me, or anyone, until she met Mark. She had never taken drugs, until she met Mark. She had never had an orgasm until she met Mark. And no man had ever told her 'I love you' until she met Mark.

As if he could see my thoughts, Mark's eyes, opaque in the flickering light of candles that were artfully arranged on every surface, met mine, probing me, *I dare you.*

'Hey Lindy?' I said, 'In the spirit of truth-telling, can I say something?' My voice sounded flinty, as if I was about to say something harsh, but then I saw Mark's mouth curling at the edge – and I decided not to follow that line. If I was to outwit him, then I would have to feel into his inclinations and do the opposite.

Linda looked at me, guileless, her voice open and pure: 'Yes, sweet-cheeks. Say anything, anything at all. I'm open to improvement –'

Mark broke in: '"When the heart is filled with love, then the eye is never deceived…" She needs this, Jess; as her best friend, you know she does.' Was this his justification to her any time he felt the need to improve her? How clever to quote his little spindly philosopher in this context.

Jacques mumbled something inaudible like 'fuck's sake' on an exhale.

I smiled at Linda. 'You're pretty perfect as you are,' I said.

Tears flowed freely and unselfconsciously down her smiling face. 'Happy crying!' she said, unabashed.

'That's nice, but not wholly genuine,' Mark said to me.

Don't rise to him, don't rise to him.

Jacques came to my side, placed my hand in his and squeezed it hard. 'Maybe we should go home now, Jess,' he said.

I looked at Jonathan who was whispering something in Phil's ear, their bodies so close together they were touching. There was nothing asexual or passive about him now. I didn't want to leave. I wanted to be a part of this: this elaborate puppet show. I wanted to feel that thing that made Jonathan lose his inhibitions so completely that he would risk publicly revealing his attraction to a man; I wanted to experience that heightened, blissful, uninhibited state that Linda was in, even as I knew that it was risky to the point of annihilation. To loosen my already loose tongue to that extent. And yet. Logic lost out in the battle against desire. I looked in Mark's direction and his gaze was fastened on me. I felt a stirring in the pit of my stomach, no, lower down, and a thought struck me: was I his true sparring partner, the one he had intended to get to all along? The possibility filled me with power and shame and lust and intense exhilaration.

Jacques spoke churlishly (I wondered if he had felt the undercurrents floating between us). 'Make sure Linda gets enough water.'

'Don't worry,' Mark said. 'This stuff is less dehydrating than booze. Looks like you two could do with a pint of aqua before bed...'

Jonathan and Phil turned as one – as if a kinetic force were guiding them – their hands reaching towards each other's, as they left the party together without looking back. Mark looked at me and I felt his teeth at my nipple, which hardened.

In response I kissed Jacques passionately and forced myself to turn away and leave the party.

'Shit, Jess. I hope Linda'll be OK.'

'She'll be fine. She loves it.' There was a part of me that believed that what I had witnessed tonight in my friend was sublime – she was no longer cowering or meek or controlled by her mother's hatred, which constricted her in the world. She was powerful and a little bit frightening. Maybe Mark knew what he was doing; maybe he *was* motivated by a desire to see her grow. This distorted, or perhaps wishful, thinking on my part was willed by me, to justify what I wanted to continue.

'Ah, he's just being provocative,' I said.

And there you had it: a reversal of our stances where Mark was concerned, and this would happen time and time again. Onside, offside, but always, always, in the ring.

As we walked down the stairs, I saw Jonathan and Phil in front of us and I remembered my first time with Jacques and wished I could experience all that newness again and have my mind blown. I was thrilled for my friend, yet also aware that his first sexual experience would be with a guy Mark had engineered he be with. I could have run after him and warned him off, but, conflicted as I was, the draw towards danger and excitement was too strong. Mark knew exactly what he was doing by refusing me 'the goodies' this time. He knew my desire to partake would only grow. He knew how I experienced being left out as rejection, as agony, and he knew the extent of my appetite. *Greedy girl.*

35

I hardly slept the following two nights, my nerves frayed, my mood oscillating between feeling anxiety for Linda and Jonathan, and fury that I had been denied the drugs, and in such a public, humiliating way. Jacques was even more caring and attentive than usual, not leaving me to go to Louis as he normally would on a Sunday. He had an uncanny knack for sensing what I was feeling, even when I couldn't put it into words (except where his lust was involved – there he was blind). I told him I wanted to go see Jonathan and he convinced me to leave him be, at least for the day.

'Give him his space today, Jessie. You don't want to barge in on him now, do you?'

How could I articulate that that was exactly what I wanted to do, not wanting to be left out of any of it?

On Monday morning, having spent the previous night lying immobile on my back staring at the zip-like crack on the ceiling, I slipped out of bed at dawn, my eyes scratchy and sore, as if the sandman had come and deposited bags of sand in them. Dad used to threaten me with that bogeyman when I was very small and wouldn't go to sleep. I remembered lying in bed, heart pounding, eyes squeezed tightly shut – I never slept in the wake of that threat.

I needed to breathe fresh air, so I decided to go outside, careful not to wake Jacques. I made my way towards the reassuring old oak tree, blinking painfully against the steel light of dawn. Standing underneath the tree's winter canopy, I looked up: no message to decode in the few straggling leaves that stubbornly clung on, nothing to glean in their vein-like fibres, the brown splotched patterns. *Oh Wise One, should I venture further into the lair, or withdraw now?* This time the tree whispered her answer as a stiff breeze blew, dislodging a frail branch which knocked me on the side of my head. *Wake up, dope*! I laughed wildly.

I was still unconvinced that I could walk away, even when expressly warned to. *What would you do, Sue?* I found myself beseeching the air. Sue would have gravitated towards the danger. All that possibility, all that life yet unlived, all that potential yet untapped. I revelled in the expansive sky above my head as I ambled back towards my room.

'Where were you so early?' Jacques said blearily, as I entered. He was half-asleep as he looked at the digital alarm clock by my bed which read 7 a.m.

'Out for a walk.'

His hair was mussed, the side of his face crinkled from the pillow. 'You OK?'

'I don't know if I should go to rehearsal this morning.'

'You absolutely should go.' He forced himself to sit up as I climbed onto the bed beside him.

'Really…? I didn't think you'd want me to, after Saturday night.'

'Yes, really. Just don't let him give you any of those drugs.'

'Who do you think I am?'

He grinned and kissed me on my forehead, then his brow furrowed, as he said: 'Seriously, though, he really shouldn't allow Linda take that stuff. She's too delicate.'

'*Allow* her?' I said. 'Oh come on, he's positively feeding it to her.'

'You don't think he's dealing, do you?'

'No, just *supplying*. From the goodness of his heart!'

He tickled me. 'You were gagging to try it.'

'And my boyfriend wouldn't *allow* me,' I said, wriggling under his fingers. He kissed me, featherlight, first on my forehead, then my cheeks, then lips, then breasts, then bellybutton, where he lingered, savouring. As he pulled my sweatpants off me, he rubbed his lips along my inner thighs, then his tongue was inside me. My mind was somewhere else; I wouldn't admit where. I orgasmed loudly and freely.

Jacques bundled me in his arms. 'I love when I make you do that.'

Something about that remark was so off, but I didn't even try to engage with this line of thought. I couldn't trust myself not to blurt the wrong thing. I had been struggling recently with my Big Lie, wanting to offload my guilt on Jacques in the name of 'truth-telling', but a part of me knew that this would play perfectly into Mark's plans: turn us all against each other so he could unleash chaos and then shape it to his own ends.

'Right, drama queen! Time to get you some breakfast...' Jacques climbed over me to get out of bed.

'Don't call me that.'

'OK, sweets,' he said, laughing, as he picked his clothes up off the floor and started to dress. 'But I meant it as a compliment. You are my queen. And you are –'

'Don't say it.' I put my hand up.

'A damn fine actress, is what I wanted to say.' He leaned over and kissed me on my cheek.

If only he knew just how *damn fine.*

'Stay there. I'll bring you breakfast in bed.'

Channelling a higher power to our own ends; I can't wait to get you in touch with that power. Mark's words, crackling like an irresistible curse-charm in my ear. I told myself that my decision was purely a creative choice. And one endorsed by my boyfriend.

Jacques returned some moments later with croissants and coffee.

'I love you,' I said.

'Here's to your first day of rehearsals!' he said. 'I still don't doubt that you and Mark will create magic.'

Oh fuck. What kind? Necromancy, devilry, divination, diabolism... Would there be animal sacrifices, voodoo dolls, deviant sexual exploits...? Adrenaline surged through me. In the name of my art, I would do whatever it took.

36

When I arrived at the Atrium, a subterranean cave-like space, it was illuminated only by Mark's by-now trademark candles, which were throwing frisky shadows against the walls. As my eyes adjusted to the gloom, I could make out the silhouette of his hands gesticulating theatrically, conducting the play of the flames. As I looked up, I noticed balconies on different levels, spiralling upwards from the ground floor where we were standing. Dizzy-making.

'It's perfect,' I said. 'Why does no one put plays on here?'

'Some nonsense about insurance,' he said. 'But I'll get around them. I plan on being the first.'

'All the world's a stage.' I couldn't believe that slipped out. Mark groaned.

He flicked a switch, and the room was flooded with artificial blinding light, which felt like an assault. He was revealed in his usual uniform: the cords, the parka, the cowboy boots, the circular wire-rimmed glasses. I had decided on casual and comfy: stretchy (though figure-hugging) jeans that showed my 'buns' to best effect, Jacques's oversized sweatshirt that made me look 'tiny and adorable' (according to Jacques) and my purple Converse with their pink laces, which Sue would have heartily approved of. *Sweet 'n' saucy.*

'Did you enjoy your birthday celebrations?' I asked.

'Very much,' he said.

'How's Linda…?' I stopped for dramatic effect. 'She seemed really off her head.'

'What happens out there stays out there,' he said. 'What happens in here stays in here.'

I felt a delicious shiver of fear and arousal.

'I don't want the real world polluting our rehearsal space. This is a sacred space.'

I couldn't help myself. I wanted to play this game. 'Yes, Father, sorry, Father,' I said, blessing myself.

'Five Hail Marys,' he intoned. 'Down on your knees. Now.'

Too far. I laughed, batting him away.

'Not joking,' he said.

'I don't care,' I said in my best teenage voice.

'Genuinely, Jessica. If you want to access your inner acting goddess, your sensorial superpower, you have to let go of your control and be guided by me.'

I imagine I snorted.

'I'm serious,' he said, pushing his glasses back on top of his nose.

Ridiculous posturer. And yet. I looked around me. 'Where are the others?'

'What others?'

'The other actors? It's not a monologue, is it?'

'No, it's not. But I need to rehearse with each actor in isolation.'

He removed his glasses, twirling them in his hand, throwing me off balance.

'How does that work? Don't you need us to play off each other to generate chemistry?'

He leaned in closer, to look at me. I was temporarily blinded, discombobulated.

'It'll keep it fresher if I can keep you apart for as long as possible. In the last week of rehearsals, I'll put you all together and then the alchemy will happen…'

'And in the meantime?' I was breathless.

'One-on-one time with me.'

I felt my nipples harden and my cheeks flare. I swallowed, planted my feet, breathed.

'How many actors are in this play then?'

'Jessica. Switch off that brain of yours and just go with it. I know what I'm doing.'

He put his glasses back on, the lenses obscuring the intensity of his naked stare, leaving me both relieved and aching for it. Flashbacks of that moment in his kitchen: he knew exactly what he was doing.

'Have you ever had any other play on?'

He shook his head impatiently. 'I wanted to wait for this moment. For everything to be perfect: the script, the process, the space, the cast.'

The process. His accent was all his own, a strange mix of ye olde Dublin and old-school American movie star, a blend of James Joyce and Humphrey Bogart, mannered and oh so manly.

'How can you be so sure that you know what you're doing then?'

'I. Just. Am.'

In that moment I believed him. This play was going to be HUGE. I felt it in my bones.

'Now. To your part: Jessica. The daughter born to a selfish, narcissistic father. She has agency. She is wilful, disruptive, powerful. You'll be perfect.'

He was right; I would be.

'Now let's talk about your own father. Tell me what you remember of him…'

Three hours later and I was wrung out, strung out, elated, starving, high, low, jagged. *That's it, let it all go*. Mark's 'process' was designed to empty the actor of any ego, any 'story' they were carrying so they could be a pure vessel to inhabit their character fully. He said he wanted me to be a channel, to be *possessed* by his Jessica.

To be raw, real, embodied.

To remove the tendency to 'act'.

To be in the moment and react truthfully.

To listen and respond…

It was a lot.

I needed air, so I decided to grab a sandwich and a Coke in the coffee dock and then go outside and sit on a bench. The world seemed altered. The light more intense, even though it was a low grey sky, the same as any other that March. Noises were sharper, louder, stereophonic. I felt as if I were wearing my skin inside out.

'Hey, Jessie.' Jonathan waved at me from across the quadrangle.

I waved back as he loped over the green manicured lawn that had signs all over it: 'Do not walk on the grass.'

'Rebel,' I said. He looked like he wasn't sure what I was referring to: the other night or this small transgression.

He sat beside me, squeezed me around my waist, which tickled. I slapped his hand away. I was reminded of my father's relentless funnyman prodding of me, resulting in uncontrollable giggles rendering me speechless and teary.

'Don't like that, huh?' he said.

'Nope,' I said. The powerlessness.

He smiled, unperturbed. He looked almost beatific he was so nonplussed.

'So?' I said, when I had gathered myself sufficiently.

'Sooooo?' he said, savouring the word, elongating the vowels dreamily.

'The other night?'

'You know the way you said, "some things are better left unspoken about" the morning after you were first with Jacques…?'

'Actually it was you who said that.'

He looked at me and laughed. 'Fair enough… But I do remember you saying your night was sacred and secret.'

'Wow. That good, was it?'

An energy radiated off him.

'Did you not get the comedown blues?' I was intrigued that the drug still might have had a positive after-effect on him.

'None at all, weirdly. I've felt amazing since.'

He looked amazing. He seemed to be glowing and vibrating on a higher frequency – spiritual, or sexual, or psychosexual, or druggy or…? There was a coherence to him now and he seemed completely at ease with himself. His sporty jock get-up was a little dishevelled: the cashmere jumper slung low around his waist instead of neatly arranged around his shoulders.

'Imagine if my father found out? He'd kill me,' he said with relish. 'Actually no, he'd probably kill my mother. Say it was all her fault for *namby-pambying* me.'

'Well, you don't have to say anything. This is your life. You live it as you see fit,' I said. Of course I did.

'Exactly!' he said. 'Fuck my father's rules.'

'Have you made up with Mark then?' I asked, seeing his hand all over this.

'I mean, he's still a controlling weirdo... But he throws good parties and, man, those drugs...'

'Do you think Linda's OK with him?'

'I'm not sure. We need to keep an eye on her. She's not herself.'

'She's a chameleon in his presence,' I said.

'A shapeshifter, like you,' he said.

I wasn't sure how to take this. I studied him: his new rakishness. 'What are you then? A changeling?'

He sounded delighted: 'Chameleons, shapeshifters, changelings ... a whiff of the supernatural!'

He wasn't wrong. 'I've never seen you like this,' I said.

'I guess I'm me, for the first time in my life. I'm free,' he said.

My body started to vibrate. Those exact words. My words. Mark's words.

'So? Are you going to tell me anything about Phil?'

'I think I like him,' he said shyly.

I felt a fierce desire to protect him. 'Don't give yourself away too easily,' I said, Sue's warning falling out of my mouth.

He looked at me, amused. 'Look who's talking!'

I glugged from the Coke can and Jonathan took it from me and finished it off. 'So sweet 'n' fizzy,' he said. He could have been speaking about himself. He turned his whole body to face mine. 'How was first day of rehearsal?'

'Intense.'

'What did you expect?'

'True! But there's something afoot. I think his play is going to be THE ONE this year.'

'I've no doubt. He's lucky to have you.'

I smiled, like the sun was shining on me, only me.

'Why did Mark not give you guys the drugs?' Jonathan said, after a beat. 'Seems weird. Everyone else was being offered them.'

I was immediately plunged into a cold shadow, the effects of exclusion. 'Linda stopped him. She was pretty mean. Said my ego was out of control already.'

He smiled. 'Shit! It does loosen up the tongue alright.'

'What's in it?'

'Haven't a clue,' he said brightly.

'Would you do it again?'

'Do I look like I wouldn't do it again?'

His fox's eyes in the weak sunlight seemed to glow amber. I longed to experience that wildness, that elemental power, that recklessness which could take a person to their edge and stretch them beyond it and reshape them. Neither Linda nor Jonathan were the same people they were before: they were magnificent.

37

The first week of rehearsal was relatively mild, designed to make me feel safe, I imagined. A few intense sessions of the Meisner technique by candlelight, most of them involving Mark commenting on my physical quirks. Clearing me of any attachment to my ego, apparently. I had to repeat observations about my appearance over and over, so they lost all meaning. You have such a dainty nose. I have such a dainty nose. You have such a dainty nose. I have such a dainty nose. You have such a … what did 'dainty' even mean? Or 'nose' for that matter? Your upper lip is too thin. My upper lip is too thin. Your upper lip is too thin … thinnnnnnn… Your earlobes are hanging down … hanging down? Earlobes? Fleshy, heavy things. Your earlobes are… My earlobes are fleshy, heavy things. Not what I said, Jessica. What you meant, though. No. Repeat after me, exactly what I say. My earlobes are hanging down. I burst into uncontrollable laughter. What does that even mean? Hanging down. He ignored me. Your skin is ruddy. My skin is ruddy. Your skin is ruddy. Ruddy. Man, he was mean. Your eyes are deep pools of pain. My eyes are deep pools of pain. Your eyes are midnight blue. My eyes are… Your eyes are riveting. My eyes are…

There were no goodies on the table. And no more touching. And no innuendo, or intense stares. He was the perfect professional in rehearsal room, keeping a detached distance, which, confusingly, set up an ache in me.

On our final day of the first week of rehearsals, Mark the trickster told me with a glint in his cold, clear, bluest-of-blue eye that opening night was going to be April the first. I felt giddy, wired, in anticipation of the inevitable prank – April Fool's – at whose expense?

At the start of week two, he told me we would be 'amping things up a gear'. At last. He brought in a costume. A bizarre naughty-nurse-cum-Joan-of-Arc ensemble. A toy shield, a bow and arrow and a short, short nurse's outfit with thick clunky boots.

'I want you to experience her strength, her sexuality *and* her caring nature.'

'It's a jumbled mess,' I said.

'Good. Let's lean into that,' he said, flicking on the overhead lights.

'The paradox,' I said, blinking.

'Exactly,' he said, without a trace of irony.

I was all in, drugged on his lasered attention.

'I'd like to start learning my lines,' I said. 'Can I see the script?'

'It's evolving.'

He was, he said, still in the process of developing 'a new, experimental, hybrid language incorporating Shakespearian phraseology and the working-class Dublin idiom.'

Ah, so that was what was going on with his shifting accent.

'Do you want there to be an American twang in there too?'

'*Twang?*' he said, imitating me.

'How do you want me to sound?' I couldn't get my head or tongue around it.

'*Sound?*' he said, as if I were an idiot. 'It's how I want you to *feel* that matters.'

'Oh?'

'Find your father-rage and channel that. The right accent will naturally evolve.'

'But what about the others?'

'What about them?'

'Don't you want us all to speak in the same accent?'

He sighed, a full-throttled I'm-so-disappointed-in-you sigh, as he pushed his glasses on top of his head.

'I hadn't taken you for such a *literalist*.'

I didn't say anything, though I was intrigued.

He spoke more to himself than to me: 'There's still time for a breakthrough…'

'I've an idea,' I said, smiling brightly. 'Why don't we partake of those *goodies* to help with that?

'I do not use mind-altering substances in rehearsal room,' he said, deadly serious.

'Why not…? I'm sure I'd feel free in all regards.'

'I need your conscious mind alert here, Jessica. To that point. I'd like you to look at me, really look at me, and tell me what you see.'

I see a superior, mind-fucking, withholding, controlling, sexy wizard with electric blue eyes that pierce my…

'I see blue eyes.'

'You can do better than that,' he said.

'I see insanely high cheekbones…'

He liked that one. You see high cheekbones. Yes, I see high cheekbones. You see high cheekbones. I see high cheekbones. Bones, cheeks, high. I am so high on this. *Insanely* so.

'What image do they conjure in you?'

'A Beckett or an Edgar Allen Poe,' I said.

He liked that even more.

On day three of week two, he invited me to 'lean into the anger.' He got out his Walkman disc player and hooked it up to portable speakers, then played a CD of a loud, atonal, heavy-metal band I didn't recognise. It conjured images of fat sweating men ripping tiny bats' heads off and eating them. Gross and disturbing.

He turned off all the lights, blew out the candles, and gave me a piece of paper. Your father. Write it all out. He cranked the music even louder and handed me a baseball bat and pointed towards a pillow.

'No way.'

'This is not only for your character. But for you. A necessary clearing. We need to unshackle you from your psychic ties to that man.'

'I haven't seen him since I was six. I doubt I could be less disconnected.'

'Not seeing him is not the same as freeing yourself of him.'

'Can you turn that noise off?'

'Why?'

'I hate it.'

'Good.' And he turned it up even louder. 'That prick,' he said. 'The hurt he caused you and your stepmother, the selfishness, the abandonment … release it all…'

Something came over me and overrode any feeling of embarrassment. The bat was in my hands, and as if it took on a life of its own, the bat, or my hand guided by it, started to beat the shit out of the pillow. The darkness helped. The 'music' helped. I was laughing, crying, yelping, cursing spectacularly. I was possessed and I was ecstatic.

'Good.' His disembodied voice spoke. 'Great … good girl, Jessica. *My Jessica*. You're getting closer to her…'

The rage erupted. A primal force that, once tapped into, might never end. I bashed and I bashed until I ended up lying on the ground, welts already beginning to form on my fingers, spent. *Good girl.*

'You have vanquished the psychic ghost of your prick-father,' he said, sounding too gleeful.

Truth be told, my rage seemed bigger than anything personal. It was free-floating in the ether. It was mine and it wasn't mine.

On the Friday evening at the end of week two, I was wandering about the grounds, feeling scarily emotional and explosive, when I spotted Honor and Linda sitting on *our* bench. I barrelled over to them and promptly wished I hadn't. They were both luminous, sharing a bottle of wine, sipping from its neck. Even I could see 'the golden umbilical cord of love' flowing between these two beauties.

'Hey,' I said to Linda, who was wearing her April Wheeler dress with a distressed denim jacket over it, paired with new leopard-print Converse. Very cool.

She looked up and giggled, high-pitched and coquettish. What was it about me that made her make those sounds?

'Can I join you?'

'Sorry. Under strict instructions not to give you any *substances* until the play is over.'

'Oh poo,' said Honor, as she crossed and uncrossed her lovely long legs, clad in shiny barely-there black tights underneath a suede mini skirt, very much like my own. Who was copying who?

'Can't I have some wine?' I asked, my tone petulant.

'Oh, alcohol?' Linda said. 'I think that's allowed.' I doubted it. She handed me the open bottle and I put it to my mouth and glugged.

'Maybe leave us some?' Honor said. *Rude bitch.*

I handed it back to Linda. 'I might go buy a bottle and come back and join you.'

'That's OK,' Honor said. 'We're off to a party shortly.'

A silence descended. I was not invited. Obviously.

'Oh, where?' I was desperately trying to appear casual.

'Honor's brother's castle in Wicklow,' Linda said.

Had she quite forgotten who she was, where she was from?

'How are you getting there?'

'Spencer's driving,' Honor said.

I didn't know who Spencer was but the way she said his name made it sound as if I should have.

'Cool, cool…' I said.

'Do you not have any plans for later then?' Linda said.

'I'll see Jacques for dinner.'

'Oh,' Honor said. 'Tell Jacques hi.'

I would fucking not.

'If he wants to come to the party, tell him he's welcome. With you, obviously.'

Obviously.

'Thanks. You're OK. We'll just have a cosy night in. Just *nous deux*.'

Honor smiled lazily. 'Whatever…' She stood. 'Look who it is. The delectable Philip!' She made a big show of kissing him on both cheeks.

'Even more gorgeous than ever,' he said, stepping back to admire her. 'How is that possible?'

He lifted the bottle of wine off the bench and took a long slug. 'Come on, Spence is waiting. We're going to pick up Jonathan on the way.'

My Jonathan?

Phil seemingly noticed me for the first time. 'Oh hi, you're Jonny's friend, aren't you?'

Jonny. I smiled tightly. 'I am.'

'Your name again?' he said.

Had Jonathan not been talking about me then? 'Jessica,' I said, pouting.

Just at that moment, Mark arrived. He went to Linda, kissed her performatively on the lips. 'Enough alcohol for you, sweets.' She nodded. 'I hope you didn't give Jess any substances.'

'Nope. Under maestro's orders,' she said.

'*My Jessica*,' he said.

How he loved colonising my name. I laughed.

'Something funny?'

'Not remotely,' I said.

'See you Monday at 8 a.m. Early start next week.'

The others had all stood up by this point and were walking away.

'You should mind yourself in the middle of this process, you know. It's going deep. No alcohol, sleep well, eat well.'

'Yes, sir!' I said as I saluted him.

He stared right into me, almost lifting the heart out of me, before following the others.

'Lindy?' I shouted after my friend, suddenly devastated by her departure.

She ran back to me and enfolded me in a girl-crushing hug. 'Don't worry, sweet-cheeks. You'll always be my number one! I love you I love you I love you…'

'Lind-ah!' Mark's voice.

She looked at me, tears in her beautiful green eyes – her now sparkling emerald eyes. 'See you later, alligator.'

'But not tonight, crocodile,' I said to her after she had run away from me.

I felt like a sad little child.

'How's rehearsal going?' Jacques asked me later that night after we had finished our dinner of spicy pasta puttanesca, one of my favourites.

He had been distant with me all evening, despite me sitting on his knee and wriggling my bottom on his lap – something that would usually have had him apoplectic with desire. This time, he just shifted and looked uncomfortable.

'It's bolloxology,' I said.

In a low, strangled voice he said, 'How's Patrick?'

'Who's Patrick?

'Your co-lead.'

'Haven't met him yet'.

'No need to lie to me, Jessica. Mark told me you two were dynamite together.'

'Maybe we will be,' I said. 'But as I said – we haven't met yet.'

Jacques looked at me with an expression I had never witnessed on his usually adoring face before: suspicion, distrust and something else, something colder. Detachment.

'Hey, baby?' I said.

'Huh?' he said, turning away from me and going to the sink to wash the dishes. I went to him and cuddled him tightly from behind. I crooned, 'You are my sunshine, my only sunshine ... you make me happppyyyy, beee, beee, beee, beee...' I was buzzing into his ear. Usually, he loved when I sang a stupid love song to him, but this time he froze, and said, 'Come on Jessica, it's getting late...'

I cuddled him even tighter. 'I love you and only you...'

He turned to me. 'Sometimes you are such an actress.'

I was shocked into silence.

'I think I should go check on Louis.'

'I'll go with you,' I said.

'You're OK, thanks,' he said. 'I won't be long.'

I went to my bedroom alone, opened the tiny window and positioned myself below it so that the rain fell in on me and soaked the pillow.

Rage? I'll show you my rage, Oh maestro.

38

On the first morning of week three of rehearsals, Mark looked at me intently. 'Feeling a little blue?' He sounded hopeful. 'Perfectly normal at this stage in the process to feel discombobulated, lost.' He said he presumed that I was feeling a little lost – was I? I told him I had been summoned by my French tutor to a meeting later that day and that couldn't be a good thing. I would have to rehearse less and focus more on my studies. He looked at me like I was an imbecile, that look that made me struggle not to drop to my knees in supplication, and cringe.

'You need to reclaim your vision for the future, Jessica. If you're to be an actress, and you can be, an outstanding one, then this has to come first. If you want to be a French teacher,' he sounded snide when he said this, 'then by all means, refocus your attention there.'

What about lecturer, or an academic? Why *teacher*? I pulled a strand of hair into my mouth and sucked.

'Unlikely that will be your path, though, Jessica.'

I almost curtsied.

'Only two more weeks to go until the single most important night of your life, which will surely launch a stellar career.'

He removed the hair from my mouth, an overly intimate gesture that wasn't unwelcome. And, he went on to say, reasonably, that I had a full month after the play ended to focus back on my studies. And then a full three years after that, when he wouldn't even be in college. (How I would miss him, he intimated by these words.) He would, by then, be a professional writer/director in the theatre. Mark Whitman, making a name for himself. He sounded like he was in a trance when he said this.

'What are your intentions around Linda?' I asked him.

'Have you forgotten our ground rules for the rehearsal room?'

I stared at him, baiting him.

'Our sacred space. Only you, me and our burgeoning Jessica allowed in here.'

'When do I get to meet my cast members?'

'Next week.'

'It's not enough time.'

'Trust. Me,' he said.

'Who's Patrick?'

He smiled mysteriously.

'Why did you mention him to my boyfriend?'

'To set the seed. If Jacques believes in your chemistry, then you will too…'

Bamboozling nonsense for which I could find no funny quip, or any kind of retort at all.

He handed me a script with only my lines on it.

'But how can I learn this if I don't know my cues? How will I know when someone else is supposed to speaking?'

'By the time you'll all meet, you'll be so immersed in your characters that you will know intuitively when to speak and when to listen…'

'That's ridiculous,' I snorted.

He abruptly wrenched the script from my hands. 'Actually, I've changed my mind. Today is all about active listening… For now, you say nothing. You simply react to what I feed you.'

He flicked the overhead lights on, startling and exposing me.

I nodded. This would be brutal, I felt it. And I wanted it.

Off he went about my insecurities, my self-consciousness, my 'selfdom' that needed dismantling, yes? I nodded, belittled, befuddled, and turned on. I told myself I was acting. He asked me to find a gesture that signified when I felt insecure. I was blank. He mimed plucking hairs from the back of his neck. Ah, so he had noticed that quirk. 'Another one?' he said. 'Self-conscious.' He mimed sucking a tendril of long hair. 'Rejected.' He pointed at my throat. Would he touch me in that same spot? He just watched, from a distance, inviting me to press on the spot. 'Is it sore?' I nodded. 'Good, good… And now, sadness.' I balled my hands into fists, looked towards the ceiling, swallowed. 'Excellent, excellent,' he said. 'The best actresses don't…'

'React to these words in the moment, no thought, pure impulse. Physicalise it. *Embody* it:

Unwanted.

Damaged.

Alone.

Unloved.

Abandoned.'

I performed a mime moving between my actions: plucking hair, pinching myself, biting my hand, biting my lips so hard they bled, pressing on my neck, almost choking myself. He liked my desire to hurt myself. He liked how far I was willing to push it. 'Raw, uninhibited, limitless.' My body couldn't distinguish between the acting of these emotions and the generating of them.

'Now for a shift in gear:

Empowered.

Choice.

Seeing the truth.

Leaving.

Freedom.

New life.'

I gave it everything I had. I kissed and hugged myself; I danced freely, joyfully; I zigzagged across the room, my arms outstretched; I jumped up and down and hopped and skipped and pretend-hula-hooped like a five-year-old. By the end of that afternoon, I was on the floor, lying like a starfish spreadeagled for 'New Life'. Mark was delighted with me, particularly when I ran to the top balcony and climbed to its edge and stretched my arms to their widest span, as he shouted up at me: 'FREEDOM!' I almost jumped.

The meeting with my French tutor was scheduled for 5.30 p.m., straight after rehearsal. I floated into his office, that sensation of flying in my body. I was high on disregard. Monsieur Tortue, a perennially smoking, polo-neck-wearing man in his forties, asked if I was OK. Were there any problems he should be aware of? He was being delicate, but, ahem, 'the faculty had been alerted to the latest drug craze to hit the campus.' He sucked on his cigarette, his pallor grey, as he stared out the window at the rain that I hadn't even noticed on my way over. He wondered had I got caught up in it. The drugs, he qualified. Class A: ecstasy and acid. Dangerous stuff. I was not myself, he was sorry to have to say. 'You seem disengaged, distracted and "elsewhere" in our tutorials lately.' He blew out smoke. He seemed apologetic to be calling me out on this. 'You are very wet,' he said suddenly.

'I'm fine,' I said. 'Thank you for your concern.'

I had a tickle in my throat from the smoke and my eyes were watering because of the flickering fluorescent tube lighting overhead. What a disappointing room: I had imagined at the very least a leather armchair, low-slung lighting, maybe some wood panelling, rickety, groaning bookshelves. Instead, it was a ticky-tacky plastic modern box, like the house I grew up in. No style, no soul, not at all French.

He carefully tried to articulate, ahem, that I was in danger of losing the bursary if I did not focus. He looked at me for a reaction, and when he saw that I was smirking and not in the least fazed by his words, he seemed to work himself up into righteous ire. 'This is highly sought after,' he said, his Gallic lisp becoming more pronounced. 'There are many others who would be very grateful for this opportunity, and who would benefit from the financial help.' Again, he looked to me for a reaction. Again, I failed to produce one that satisfied him. I was thinking of how exhilarated I felt having run up the spiral steps to the top of the Atrium, how the world spun as I looked down, how I almost sprouted wings. 'This is not the civil serviiiiccce,' he almost spat at me. He was furious at my lack of humility, my lack of gratitude.

I bit down on the inside of my cheek and drew on my inner acting superpower to assemble a mask of remorse. With a voice dripping with sincerity, I said: 'I am sorry, Monsieur Tortue. I will do my best from now on. I'm not doing drugs' (though I sorely wished I was). I manufactured tears, and told him that my dog, a childhood pet, my *sister*, really, seeing as I was an only child, had just died and I was feeling bereft. He said he was sorry to hear that but that he and other members of the faculty had noticed that I had not been giving my studies my full attention for quite some time now.

'That is because Wendy has been dying for quite some time,' I said. I let the tears fall. I let myself be a bad actress. He wasn't falling for it anyway.

He led me to the door, said he'd like to check in with me again in a couple of weeks.

'I'm in a play,' I said, rubbing away the tears. 'Opening night is April Fool's. Come, if you can. Should be great…' I was convinced that if he saw my brilliance up there it would more than compensate for my shoddy work of late.

'What's it called?' he said.

'Untitled, as yet. It's an adaptation of *The Merchant of Venice* by a guy called Mark Whitman. He's one to look out for,' I said proudly and possessively, weirdly. 'I'm playing the lead.'

'May I remind you, Jessica, that you are not a drama student,' he said, bursting my bubble. 'Good luck with the play but remember why you're here.'

He closed the door politely but firmly behind me.

I was dying to tell Jacques about M Tortue's dire warning about my scholarship not being the civil serviiiiccce, imaging him choking with laughter. *Jacques*. It was as if I conjured him by thinking about him. Uncanny how this was beginning to happen more and more. My imagination bringing forth reality. The line becoming blurred, which was what it was all about, Mark said. Fantasy merging with reality merging with fantasy merging with… Which was this? Certainly not something I would have wanted to will into existence, but maybe my fears had manifested this scenario. There he was: my soulmate, *mine*, deep in conversation with the duchess over a coffee. OK, it was broad daylight, and they were only talking. But why? And about what? How had she wangled this time alone with him? I watched them from a distance, unable to trust myself not to blurt out something wholly inappropriate. *La Jalousie* was stalking me, jeering me. With superhuman effort I managed to drum up enough willpower to walk away. My mood and my heart plummeted into my boots so that I felt like I might topple over. 'You're like a yo-yo,' Sue used to say, her hand exaggeratedly miming the up and down motion required for manipulating the toy. 'You need to learn to regulate your moods better.' And my retort? Usually some form of fuck-you.

Fuck you, Honor Cave-Tempest-Stuart. Fuck you from a height.

39

It was the first day of the final week of rehearsals and Jacques and I were not in a good place. I had been haranguing him since spotting him with Honor: But why? And what were you talking about? I need you to shut that down *now.* And him answering, oh so reasonably: I was just being polite. We bumped into each other. Her uncle had died. She was upset. Her *uncle*? Oh come off it. She's playing you. He didn't like this. And no amount of sex was helping. I ramped up my antics, giving thoughtful, long head. He lost himself in those moments, but he was never fully with me.

Jonathan and I had hardly seen each other, except to wave at each other from a distance across the arts block. He looked distracted, ever more dishevelled, unshaved, his hair unkempt, his limbs loose and louche – surrounded by his new friends, way cooler than when we had first met. It stung that I was not the reason for this transformation.

Linda and I had not spoken since I bumped into her and Honor on their way to Spencer's party. Where was poor old, plain old Mairin now? How I wished Linda was hanging out with the mouse, and not the queen. I told myself that everything would get back on track once this play opened. I'd have more time for my friends then. What I didn't want to admit was that it wasn't just my busyness that had caused this schism. There were other forces at work, an unseen hand.

'What's going on?' I asked Jacques over dinner, determined not to bring *Madame Jalousie* to the table.

‘I don’t know what you mean, Jessie.’ He was there, but he wasn’t there. ‘How are rehearsals going?’ he asked absently.

‘Dreadful bolloxology,’ I said, though this time I didn’t mean it.

Rehearsals were *radical*. Finally, I had been introduced to my fellow cast members: Dearbhla (Portia), Ciaran (Bassanio), Bill (Shylock) and Patrick (Lorenzo) and they were brilliant, absolute *stars*. Mark had reduced the cast to its essentials, stripped away any ‘incidentals’. We were the core of the story, he said. We were where the drama happened. And we were all equally important (although we all knew I was the lead). In his version of *The Merchant of Venice*, our characters have our names, or we have theirs. ‘You are now indistinguishable from your roles.’ His voice was dripping with self-congratulatory delight.

Back at the kitchen table, Jacques was sucking on his spaghetti sulkily.

I laughed at him, called him out on his lack of manners, then told him that I loved him no matter what, even though he was a peasant.

‘How’s Patrick?’ Jacques asked, his jaw clenched, not even the trace of a smile evident on his features.

‘He’s good. He’s a fine actor. Mark did a great job of casting…’

‘I’m sure…’ he said, wiping a slick of tomato sauce from his upper lip.

‘It’s going to be brilliant, I can feel it,’ I said, obviously striking the wrong note.

‘Good for you,’ he said, before getting up and emptying the remnants of his spaghetti into the bin, leaving me at the table. I sucked on my teeth to generate the sound of wind whistling through me. A new one.

Patrick. Lush, Byron-like, tall, leggy, long-lashed and dark-eyed. Jessica’s love, the man she (I) eloped with to escape her father, Shylock (Bill). He was soulful, he was deep, he was generous, he was giving, he was sensual. All words I attributed to him in our first Meisner session. He used ‘sensual’ too to describe me. You’re sensual. I’m sensual. You’re sensual. I’m sensual. You’re… I’m… He also said I was fairy-like, elfin, delicate with not just a hint of magic.

A sorceress, a powerful maiden. By the end of day one we were in manufactured love.

Where were our scripts? We all asked each other at 5 p.m. that day. Isn't it time?

Mark ceremoniously produced them and the poster. *The Female Avenger.* With a picture of me in my sexy nurse-cum-Joan-of-Arc ensemble. I hadn't known he was taking a photo of me wearing it.

'Bit sneaky,' I said, feeling a rush of warmth, not sure whether to attribute it to embarrassment or excitement.

'It's good though, right?' he said.

'It's perfect,' Patrick agreed.

And it was. It was. Just. Perfect.

That evening, I stayed up all night poring over the script. It was powerful, fluent, jarring. Jessica was ahead of her time: an avenging girl-woman born to smash the patriarchal system. She was highly sexualised, but on her own terms. Even her loving was a powerful act. The language was all its own: highfalutin yet base. The narrative consistently surprising: who was this girl-woman who called out the men around her and who, when she loved, did not let herself 'fall'? Mark said this was an important facet of her. She was not seduced or bedazzled by Patrick. He sounded snide when he said this, as if women who fall are pathetic. I thought of Linda and a shiver ran through me.

Patrick and I had a love-making (sex) scene, where it was suggested in the script that Jessica just wear her underwear. 'What about Patrick?' I asked. 'Just you,' Mark said. 'But it'll be tasteful. Don't worry.' I wasn't worried.

Day three of week four and the alchemy was happening. Bizarre how well we all gelled, as if we had known each other forever. Bizarre also how easy it had been to learn our lines. They felt as if they had come from inside us; they were so natural and spontaneous. We were a symbiotic unit, working off a kinetic energy, each feeding off the other for our cues. I felt no embarrassment taking off my clothes and getting into my underwear. I felt liberated, powerful. The cast was gracious and generous and kind. Mark was effusive. I was burning bright.

By day five, we were all on fire. Only two more days of rehearsals to go and Dearbhla, Ciaran, Bill, Patrick and I were like family. We were each other's *darlings*. We were each other's supporters – and foes – when the script needed us to be. Mark was humming with elation and pride. We were his creations.

Opening night: the Atrium was packed to the rafters. My heart was thrumming so loud in my chest I felt it in my ears. Never had I been given so little time to learn lines. The fact they were so new made them fresh in my mouth. I had never known such anticipation, such sweet fear. This was THE play of the year. Mark Whitman was already a phenomenon, and the play hadn't even opened. The rumour mill had been going crazy. It helped that Jessica McSwain was the lead. Could she redeem herself after the fiasco of her self-conscious last performance? (The idiots didn't get just how brilliantly *Pirandellian* she had been.)

Backstage, Patrick and I were holding hands and jumping up and down. I love you I love you I love you, he said, in character. I ADORE you, I said back, in character. Now let's shake it all out, he said. The nerves. We shook our whole bodies and jumped and swore and told each other we had each other's backs, and nothing could go wrong, nothing could go wrong, nothing could go wrong. The lights went down in the auditorium, the audience hushed, and I was pushed, by Patrick, gently onto the stage for my solo opening. I almost puked.

The play opened on me, in my underwear (unnecessarily, according to Jacques), in a spotlight, looking wistfully out of a window in my father's house. The window looked directly onto a wall. I started with an original Shakespearian line: 'But though I am daughter to his blood, I am not to his manners,' then I launched into a 'postmodern' monologue replete with colourful 'fucks' about being trapped, about being suffocated, by my father's house, my father's greed, his aberrant love, his religiosity, his fake piousness, his control. My accent was sliding between cut-glass RP and working-class Dublin, my consonants either carefully articulated or slushed over. Nothing in moderation. Specially composed contemporary music came on, a sound like cats mating, and I danced, a fierce, expressionistic dance of freedom, still in my underwear. I aced it. I was lit. The audience was eating out of the palm of my hand. What had Sue said when she'd seen me as the stepdaughter? *You are mesmeric up there.* I was. I could feel it. The power of it.

The play had a runtime of one hour fifteen minutes with no interval. A new, sexy innovation by Mark Whitman. The tension never flagged, the actors tirelessly generating the energy required of them. The language crackled. It felt explosive, inspired, touched by magic and grace, this Whitman phenomenon. Until … until … the love-making scene where … when … Patrick devolved into some other creature, a depraved demon. He whispered in my ear, Trust me, Mark and I spoke about this, as he pulled my bra down … to expose my tiny breasts to the whole audience. He then proceeded to run his hands across my bare stomach, and onto my hips. He levered me to him and dipped his head, pressed his tongue against my bellybutton. I froze. I couldn't speak I couldn't speak I couldn't speak. Even as Patrick, the devil, was feeding me my lines, I couldn't play.

This scene was the crescendo, the final big act before the lights came down. So perhaps it was fitting that I was rendered speechless – although this was a complete reversal of how I viewed my character, of how Mark had spoken about her. How could the female avenger be overpowered and rendered mute in the final moments? But then I remembered how much our *auteur* liked upending presumptions, subverting the expected.

'*An extraordinarily real, embodied performance by Jessica McSwain*,' went the *HUP!* review the following day. I was redeemed.

The moments following my exposure to the audience, to my friends, to the whole fucking world – or so it felt – were slow and treacly and cartoon-like. I felt like a little plastic figurine tinkered with and distorted and made to look like her male creators wanted her to look. Such a cutie with her little breasts. Such a talented, brave actress to go for it. So raw and unencumbered and powerful. I had never felt less powerful.

When I came off stage, Linda and Jonathan were clapping wildly, while Jacques looked stricken. I wasn't up to a confrontation, I wasn't able to comfort him, to reassure him, I was too full of need myself, so I turned from him. And then – as if I had magicked her into being (had I manifested that debacle on-stage by being overly provocative in rehearsals?) – I saw Sue standing on her own shyly at the edge of the room. I ran to her and threw myself in her arms. She almost keeled over she was so shocked by my public display of affection. 'You were incredible, Jess,' she said. And she meant it. No one else felt my shame. Except perhaps Jacques – although it wasn't mine he was feeling, it was his own.

Mark emerged from backstage to thunderous applause, Patrick trailing him. Patrick couldn't look at me. At least he had the decency not to look at me. But Mark stared straight at me and said, 'See? We tapped into the magic, in the end!' I looked around for Jacques and saw him making for the exit. I ran after him. He told me in a cold voice that he needed some air and that I should attend to my fans. He'd see me later, he said, or maybe not, I thought I heard him mumble. I felt Sue quietly come to my side and reach her hand out for mine. She squeezed it hard, whether to pass on some strength to me, or whether to appease her own awkwardness I wasn't sure. 'This is your night, sweet girl. Savour it…' She guided me back to the centre of the room. 'To your waiting fans and friends.'

I was sure Mark had seen Jacques leave, just as I was sure he had overheard Sue trying to comfort me. That delighted smirk was playing at the edges of his mouth.

'So this is the famous Sue!' His tone was patronising and cordial and ironic all at once.

'Hi Sue,' Linda said, keeping her distance. Usually, the two of them would have folded into each other's arms at first sight.

'Hi love,' Sue said shyly. 'You look great.'

'Wasn't Jessie incredible?' Linda said.

'Absolutely!'

'Hey Sue,' Jonathan greeted her warmly and kissed her on both cheeks. 'Great to see you again.'

'You too, you too…' I could see she was struggling to remember his name.

I was desperate to find Jacques, but strongly pulled to stay by Sue's side, her hand in mine.

'Patrick was inspired up there,' Linda said, I thought slyly. Had she been in on the 'twist' too?

'He was totally in the moment,' Jonathan agreed. 'Where's he gone, by the way?'

'Just enjoying his moment. And rightly so,' Mark said, nodding towards the other side of the room.

I saw him, the traitor, in a huddle with the rest of the cast, his arm resting on Dearbhla's shoulder, her face upturned to his. I tried to communicate by osmosis to Linda, Jonathan and Sue that I was in turmoil, that I had been blindsided, that I felt tarnished, used, but no one seemed to pick up on my distress.

'A definite, five-star review tomorrow all round,' Linda said, as she kissed Mark. Then she looked towards Sue. 'Oh hey, Sue, this is Mark,' she said in an offhand way.

Sue smiled. 'Yes, I gathered as much. Nice to meet you, Mark,' she said.

He took her hand and kissed the back of it. 'Enchanté!'

He then said 'excuse me' to us all as he took his leave to mingle among his many admirers. I was getting slaps on the back, exclamations of: you were brilliant, on fire, a star … wow, wow, wowee, incredible … all the words I lived to hear, but which now made me feel even more like someone else's puppet. Sue whispered in my ear, 'Do you want to go find Jacques, sweetie?' My eyes welled and Jonathan noticed, but he thought it was because I was overwhelmed by the moment. 'You deserve a good cry,' he said. 'Happy tears!' Just at this moment Phil came over to us, put his arms around Jonathan's waist and kissed his ear from behind, a flagrant display of proprietorship. Jonathan looked conflicted: delighted but also mortified, his chest flushed and mottled. He didn't introduce Sue. I noticed Honor in the corner talking to Mark before she started to make her way over to us. This night could not get any worse.

'Where's Mairin?' I asked Linda.

'Mairin?' she said, as if she didn't know who I was talking about. How shallow and capricious she had become.

'Your *friend*. The one you invited to come to opening night?'

She shrugged, just as she saw Honor coming towards us. Her face lit up as she waved.

'I have to go,' I said. I was feeling unsteady, like the ground beneath me was swaying.

'What, already?' Jonathan said.

'Jacques's not feeling well, so I'd better go look after him.' I managed to say to everyone in what I thought was a normal-sounding voice.

'Really?' Linda said. 'I was chatting to him earlier and he seemed fine.'

'It came on suddenly,' I said.

'Hi Honor!' Linda said, as the duchess arrived and planted three kisses on her cheeks. 'Did you enjoy the play?'

'I didn't see it,' she said lazily. 'Theatre's not really my thing.'

'Oh you must see it,' Linda gushed. 'Mark is a genius.'

'I heard,' she said.

'And Jessica's wonderful in it!'

'I'm sure,' she said, looking me up and down.

'Don't go, Jessie,' Linda said to me. 'The substances ban is lifted! Knowing Jacques, he'd rather you enjoyed your night,' she went on, winking at me.

Even I knew I was too off balance for any drugs this evening.

'I really better go mind my *boyfriend*,' I said, emphasising the word to Honor.

'I'll walk you back to him,' Sue jumped in. 'You must be exhausted anyway.'

'Nonsense,' boomed Mark's voice at us from the ether. How had he overheard from across the room? 'Jessica McSwain is tireless.'

'Actually, no, she's not,' I heard myself say. 'She's actually feeling quite sick herself tonight.'

'Oh noooooo,' Linda said. 'I hope it isn't something awful and deeply contagious.'

'Thank you for your concern…' My tone and face were impassive. 'You can celebrate for me,' I said to her.

'Oh we will, we will!' she said, grabbing on to Mark's arm as he came back in our direction.

Sue started to steer me towards the door, her hand on the small of my back.

'Goodnight, Jessica,' Mark said. 'And congratulations on a truly real, embodied performance. There was no posturing up there. You were scrubbed raw.'

He continued: 'I liked how you found power in submission in the final moment.'

Did he believe that? Was there…?

On our way to the exit, we passed Patrick who had his arm around Dearbhla's shoulder, while also being thronged by a flock of female fans. Sue moved in his direction, to congratulate him, I imagined. I pulled her away. She looked from me to him and something resembling a dawning recognition of what had transpired crossed her features. 'Oh, sweet-cheeks,' she said.

Outside the night air was damp and still. 'Who was that dreadful girl Linda seems friendly with?' Sue asked.

Suddenly I was struck by an onslaught of powerful, conflicting feelings which were kicking me about so I couldn't think, or barely stand. 'What is it, Jessie?' she said, intuiting some undercurrent.

I stopped us in our tracks as I said, 'Thank you for coming. Now it really is time I found my boyfriend.' I was dismissing her, pushing her away again. All I wanted in that moment was to be with me and me and me and me. And yet I despised all that was me.

'OK, Jessie, if you're sure,' she said quietly. I could hear the notes of rejection in her voice, and I recoiled. I couldn't handle her need in any form.

'I'm sure,' I said. 'Thanks for coming.'

My tone said, I didn't ask you to, anyway.

She hugged me and said, 'No matter what happened up there this evening, you were brilliant. No one can ever take that from you.'

'Cheers!' I said, flippantly, *brilliantly* playing the opposite of how I really felt.

'You have a great future,' she said. 'Never forget that.'

Then she turned to leave, and I desperately wanted to be back in her arms. I looked after her, at the slump of dejection in her shoulders, and I wondered at my capacity for cruelty. Had I deserved what happened tonight? Had I willed it into being? The weirdest part of the whole harrowing episode was that Patrick's lips and tongue had lingered on my bellybutton – as if he knew what would cause maximum distress for Jacques. Had I told Linda how much Jacques loved to kiss my bellybutton? Had she told Mark? Had he, in turn, told Patrick…?

Was I making plausible, possible connections, or was this my growing paranoia? My mind felt like a hissing, fizzing TV screen, permanently turned on, tuned to static. My body was all need, and there was no way to meet it.

40

Tiny tits, but cute, Mark was pointing at them; *You're such a chameleon*, Jonathan was laughing at me as I cried real tears; *I don't want to know*, Jacques had his hands over his ears; *You're such an actress, such an actress. No rest for the wicked*, Linda was singing in my ear as I lay staring at the ceiling, unable to move, scenes from my public humiliation playing over and over. And the guilt. That heavy weight in my chest, pushing behind my eyes. *Jacques*. I really wanted to wake up with him this morning and laugh over the 'mishap', and put it in its proper perspective and agree, that well, yes, maybe it was a powerful moment, all in the service of 'art'. I wanted to call Sue and thank her and apologise and tell her that I loved and appreciated her, but it was all beyond me.

Eventually, I managed to climb out of bed, not having had a moment of restful sleep. I stood under the shower, let it run cold, stayed there, shivering and covered in goosebumps, until a loud knocking on the door alerted me to my surroundings. I had come to the bathroom without a towel, so I had to shake myself dry and then climb back into my sweat-covered clothes from the night before. In the kitchen, I ate somebody else's stale cereal by the fistful from a Rice Krispies packet.

I had no idea of the time, so I went outside into the grey spring day and asked the first person I encountered, a preppy-looking girl, who was walking gingerly in high heels on the wet, slicked cobblestones, her arm tucked into a guy's for balance. 'Two fifteen,' the girl said, looking at her giant pink Swatch watch. The cast was due to have a note-giving session by Mark at four today. What would I do? What could I do? 'Congratulations, you were incredible last night,' the incongruously glamorous girl said. The jock-styled guy with his Brylcreemed hair said, 'Best thing I've ever seen. You and that dude were insanely brilliant.' He went to high-five me, and I staggered backwards, thinking he was about to strike me. They both looked at me as if I were drunk, or high, that look that said, *OK, so you're a cool thespian-type, but really? At this hour?* 'You alright?' the guy said. 'Fine,' I said. Fucked up, insecure, neurotic, erotic, no, not that, emotional, yes, that was it, emotional. 'Break a leg tonight,' the girl said. 'We're going to come see you again at some point in the run. I told everyone I know about it… It's a hit. You're a *hit*.' I'm a hit, yes, you're a hit, I'm a hit. Hit me. 'Thanks,' I managed, or I think I managed.

My feet took me wandering around the campus grounds, through the playing fields, to the back field, until I found myself standing underneath the oak tree. *What to do, Oh Wise One?* No guidance from above, not even a gentle leaf drop, but then, Sue's voice hovering on the wind: *You're going to continue to be your magnificent self. And you're not going to take any shit.* I'm not going to take any shit. I high-fived the air. And so, I made the decision to go to the feedback session on an empty stomach.

When I walked into the Atrium, classical music was playing, and the smell of incense and candles burning cast the space in a restful, ambient mood. Ciaran and Bill were there, deep in conversation with Mark. Dearbhla and Patrick hadn't arrived yet. I exhaled. The others looked up at my arrival. 'Beautiful work last night, Jessica. Inspired,' Bill said. No, not you too, Bill, I wanted to say, but nothing came out of my mouth.

'How's Jacques?' Mark said, sounding genuinely concerned.

'He's grand,' I said. 'Just a case of the lurgy.'

'I hope you're in tip-top shape yourself.' His eyes roamed all over me, taking in my frizzy hair scraped back into a ponytail, my face scrubbed free of make-up.

Just at that moment, Patrick and Dearbhla walked in, their body language suggesting they had been raunchily intimate the night before. So much for female solidarity.

The 'note-taking' consisted of mainly congratulatory feedback from Mark, with the odd, 'watch your blocking in that moment' to Ciaran, or 'your timing was slightly off on that line,' to Dearbhla. To me, he simply said, 'mesmeric.'

Don't take any shit. When I tried to articulate how I felt, that I hadn't given my consent for that scene, the others all rushed to tell me how inspired the moment was. Electric, they said. A moment of unplanned magic. Patrick was looking down; the tips of his ears were scarlet. I wanted to say that it had been planned, an ambush. But the consensus by Bill and the rest of the cast was that we all needed to up the ante now and allow for these improvisational moments of pure unfiltered impulse. Mark butted in to say no, he didn't think that was a good idea. The rest of the play was perfect, exactly as he had imagined it. The only scene where that kind of fluency was allowed was the one with Jessica and Patrick. 'Jessica, I throw down the gauntlet to you to do whatever you feel moved to do.'

As if I would give the boy head, or something.

That night, after the show, Jacques came back to my room very late. The relief I felt was so vast it almost swallowed me up. I was already in bed and practising my deep breathing. He sat at the edge of the mattress with a wounded, haunted look on his face. His body was all harsh angles. He didn't touch me.

'I didn't know that would happen,' I said. I was crying. Genuinely crying.

He looked at me sideways. 'If that's true, that is appalling,' he said. 'No matter what way you look at it, this is appalling. If you agreed, if you didn't agree.'

'No, Jacques,' I was shouting at him. 'What is *appalling* is if your girlfriend didn't know what was coming and she was blindsided on-stage and made to feel like a whore.'

'Actresses are glorified whores though, aren't they?'

I doubled over, a stabbing pain slicing through me.

He coughed, exhaled loudly, said in a hoarse whisper: 'Sorry, baby. That was unforgivable. I don't know what's come over me.'

I did. The green-eyed monster. Some part of me was mollified.

'Please say that you at least believe me.'

'Didn't Mark warn you there'd be some improvisation?'

'No.'

'What are you going to do then?'

'Get my own back on that prick on-stage.'

'Hurt him,' he said.

'Yes.'

We were united in our thirst for revenge. I had already started my campaign. Throughout the show that evening I hadn't lost any opportunity to pinch Patrick, on his arms, anywhere I could on his torso. My fingers were live pincers finding their mark. In the final 'lovemaking' scene I grabbed his hair and pulled a clump of it off in my hand. He yelped. I also bit him, on the neck, making it appear as if I was kissing him passionately. All very 'sensual'. As soon as he pulled my bra down, I wrenched it back up. He then tried yanking it up higher to reveal my breasts that way, but I tugged it back down, and so the pantomime went, three times, until he got the message: this wasn't happening tonight. When he manoeuvred me to face him, I was ready, and I pushed him with such force that he toppled backwards. I straddled him, lying there, on the concrete floor. I prayed he'd be covered in bruises in the coming days. 'Jessica has agency, Jessica is *free*,' I whispered in his face. This was what Mark had wanted all along: this spontaneity, this danger, this edge.

'Darling,' I said to Jacques, coming back to the present moment with my boyfriend in my bedroom. I looked deep into his eyes. *Your eyes are kind Labrador's eyes.* 'You know I love you and only you, and I'd never do anything to hurt you.'

He looked devastated. 'I am sorry I didn't show up for you there, Jessie… I'm such a disappointment to myself sometimes.'

'You could never be a disappointment to me,' I said as I held my arms out to him. He came to me and curled up against my chest like a baby. I rocked him fiercely. 'Your heart is beating wildly,' he said. Mark would not destroy this. I would not let him.

The play went on for an interminable two weeks, each night a battle for dominion between Patrick and me. We should have grouped together to vanquish our common enemy (the despotic director) and re-establish trust and rapport, but I had been so brutalised on opening night I couldn't engage with Patrick at all. I couldn't look directly at him, either offstage, or on, instead, I stared to the right of his nose, my eyes blurring in the process. I knew this was throwing him off and his performance was less assured, more erratic as a result. But still winning, apparently. A critic from a national newspaper came and wrote that Mark Whitman's 'tour de force' simply had to transfer to a professional house, and that Patrick DeLoitte and Jessica McSwain were stars in the making. Their chemistry was electric, raw, unfiltered. The real deal.

There were no more note-giving sessions with Mark. He had unleashed the forces. And now he could sit back and watch the anarchic fruits of his mindfuck wizardry play on.

On the last Friday night (our penultimate performance) in the bar after the show, Linda handed out invitations covered in glitter, inked in luminous marker with the words: 'Bring your booty to the ULTIMATE after-party!!' to everyone in the cast. Everyone except for me.

'I know what you were doing to Patrick up there,' she said. 'I saw it.'

'Lindy…? Don't you know what he did on the opening night?' I sounded desperate. I had tried to talk to her about what had happened but could never manage to get any time alone with her; she was always surrounded by Honor and her crew.

'Oh come off it,' she said. 'Mark told me it was all your idea.'

Virtuoso, maestro.

'No big deal,' I managed. 'See you around sometime so.' I turned my back to leave.

This was one of Mark's tactics in action: *Frankly, my dear, I don't give a damn.*

Instead of succumbing to this ploy, and reacting with need, she spoke in a clear, strong voice: 'I will not collude with your violent behaviour any longer.'

Violent behaviour. A bit of pinching? In response to his utter betrayal of my trust? Hardly. I turned to look at her. Her eyes were scorching. Where had those younger impulses come from? My need to brand her. I was tempted to expose her wrists and ask whether she was continuing to hurt herself, or whether she was asking her boyfriend to do it, and how much she wanted it. But now was not the time. I smiled at her, steeled myself, said, 'Sorry you see it that way,' and this time I managed to walk away, head held high.

I was developing into quite the actress, an undertow of emotions swirling beneath my words.

The final night played out as if in a dream. I was a version of myself I could not even have conceived of – I was fierce, uncompromising – the embodiment of *The Female Avenger.* I made sure that Patrick would have marks all over his body for weeks to come to attest to this.

Despite my agony at being excluded from the party, I decided to go to the bar after the show to see how the rest of the cast would react when they found out I wasn't invited. Jacques wasn't there. He didn't want to see me cavorting and dancing around in my underwear on stage ever again. I pleaded with him, so he could see how much control I had wrested back from Patrick. But he wasn't interested. 'I don't doubt you, Jessie,' he said. 'I just couldn't sit through that play again. Please don't ask me to.'

Jonathan was there, with Phil. He had, he told me that night, seen the play four times. I was surprised. He hadn't made his presence felt to me, afterwards. He hadn't congratulated me on my artistic choices, or deconstructed the minutiae of my performance, as he normally would have. And we hadn't seen each other at all during the day for a coffee, or a chat. I was surprised by the force of my missing him.

'Mark's talent is without doubt in the realm of genius,' Phil declared, as if he knew what he was talking about.

'He would be nothing without his actors,' I said.

'Aren't actors just pawns in the director's vision?' he went on, as he waved and blew a kiss at someone across the room. *Honor*. Of course.

'Good actors are both generative and interpretive,' Jonathan said.

'I guess so,' Phil said, sounding like he couldn't care less.

'Anyway, I'd have thought it was more the writer that is responsible for the artistic vision,' Jonathan went on.

'And Mark Whitman is both,' I said. 'The ultimate creator.' I was being snide, but no one picked up on it.

Mark stood, raised a glass which probably had water in it, and tapped the side of it with a spoon. 'Her ye, hear ye,' he said in a fake Shakespearean voice. 'Gather round, my friends, and let us continue the merriment of this night…' Everyone stood and started gathering their things, anticipation in the air. The invitations had said 'a secret venue' – which turned out to be none other than Mark's rooms, the site of my 'private tryst' with him (I heard stories in the days that followed).

'I'm not invited,' I said to Bill, as he stood to follow Mark and Linda.

'Of course you are, honey,' Bill said, putting his coat on. 'Don't be silly. We all are…' He linked arms with fellow cast members, Patrick, Dearbhla and Ciaran, and they all left, hugging and giggling, without a backward glance.

I hung back, curious to see if anyone would wait for me. Jonathan was next to leave with Phil and Honor (in her fake fur and hot pants) without checking in on me, which really hurt. I drank the dregs of my glass of Prosecco, holding on to the bar countertop for strength. I tried to convince myself I was fine with this, I would go home to my gorgeous man who adored me, and this whole humiliating episode would be over. No more Patrick, no more Mark. I could do this; I could make a clean cut. I would be the best girlfriend, the best stepdaughter and best friend. I would convince Linda of that man's malevolence. I would get Jonathan back on side too and we could go back to being just us four. Cosy imaginings that didn't fill me with much excitement – nor for that matter did I really believe them.

'Jessica?' Mark's voice from the doorway. The rest of the bar had emptied out. 'Aren't you coming? Where's Jacques?'

'I'm not invited,' I said, stupid tears filling my eyes.

'Don't be silly,' he said. The second time that evening. *Silly Girl.*

'That lens of rejection through which you view the world needs to be challenged,' he said.

I should have wanted to laugh, instead: 'Linda told me I wasn't welcome,' slipped out of me.

'She did, did she?' One side of his mouth lifted. 'I'll have a chat with her later… Now, come on, we can't have an after-party without our star.'

I was so flooded with gratitude that my tears betrayed me.

'Oh Jessica, being excluded hurts so much for you…' He sounded like a priest, or a psychiatrist. He reached in and wiped away the wet on my cheeks with his thumb. 'Now go on home, get your handsome man and come to the party. There'll be goodies…'

It was this fake-loving, patriarchal, creepy child-catcher tone that finally shocked me back into a cold reality. What was I doing? Of course, this was all part of the plan. *Withhold and then offer, and she is putty in your hands.* Linda had only been acting according to his instructions: 'don't invite her' – just as she had been when she refused me the drugs at the last party: 'don't give her any … her ego is too out of control already.' I could imagine those words coming out of his mouth and being planted in hers, and her putting up only a meagre fight in my defence. The power imbalance in our history was playing right into his hands.

I breathed deeply, stood my ground, thanked him, and said that Jacques had made dinner arrangements somewhere very special for just the two of us.

'What a gem your boyfriend is,' he said. He took his glasses off his head, blew on them, cleaned the lenses with his T-shirt. 'If you feel like coming along later, do. There's plenty to go around tonight.'

'Thank you. We'll think about it.' Who knew I could exhibit such restraint?

He turned to go, twirling his glasses in his hand. 'Great to have you on board, Jessica… I was right to take a gamble on you,' he threw casually over his shoulder.

I couldn't help myself. 'Was I the target of your April Fool's prank on opening night?' I said to his back.

'You know I wouldn't jeopardise my artistic integrity for something so juvenile.' He turned back to face me.

'Risky, though. To render your female protagonist mute in the final reckoning.'

'There was nothing mute about your shock and pleasure. You were beautiful in your vulnerability.'

'Your heroine was not meant to be vulnerable.'

'Says who? There is great power in vulnerability, just as there is power in rage. You expressed both.'

'Holding the paradox,' I said.

He placed his glasses on the top of his head, then held my stare for a beat too long with those naked, blazing eyes, before he bowed at me, and left.

Jacques was waiting for me in my room. 'You must be starving, baby.' He couldn't bring himself to ask me about the play. He steered me towards the kitchen, where, true to form, he had a delicious meal at the ready, the air pungent with garlic and chilli, accompanied by red wine the colour of stewed plums.

'Why don't we ever go out?' I greeted him sulkily, hating myself in the moment.

He studied me, didn't react, but said with a calm voice, 'It's over now Jessica. You don't have to continue to be an abrasive –'

'Bitch,' I said. 'An abrasive bitch.' I looked directly at him.

He came to me, wrapped his arms around me. 'I'm sorry. I feel responsible for advising you to do the play.' Sweet, in a way, that he thought he held that much sway over me. I cast my mind back to that morning when the fates and the furies had warned me off by knocking me on the head with a fallen branch, but I paid no heed. There was no way I was walking away from the potential of such a part, the potential of being in a room with such a *genius*, the potential of so much drama and kinky promise.

'There was an after-party and I wasn't invited,' I said.

'Jesus,' he said, his back to me as he filled our plates with steaming ratatouille. As he came back to the table, he bent down and kissed me. 'Probably just as well,' he said.

'Well, yes, here we are, just the two of us. Nowhere I'd rather be,' I lied, or at least tempered the truth, to be kind. Why couldn't I tell such sweet, white lies to Sue, when she desperately needed to hear them?

Jacques and I ate heartily and drank deeply and laughed wildly and we kissed, and I could feel his relief that I was no longer 'cavorting' publicly in my underwear.

'I'm all yours,' I said to him as I kissed him and kissed him and kissed him.

'Mine, mine, mine,' he said, drugged on possession, as he took me by the hand and led me back to the bedroom.

He undressed me hungrily and licked me all over. I let myself go completely as we revelled in the delight of each other's bodies. I was determined to have and give mind-blowing orgasms. No acting required. But through it all, there was a nagging whisper in the back of my mind: You're missing out, you're missing out, you're missing out. After Jacques had fallen asleep easily, I tortured myself with images of my friends at the party experiencing heightened states of bliss: 'An enhanced reality' beyond the realms of known experience, beyond anything Jacques and I could generate between us.

And the worst part of my fantasies was that no one even noticed I wasn't there.

41

I decide that now is as good a time as any to address this feeling that plagues me still: that I am not welcome, not loved, not missed, by anyone. Undeniably this was my fatal flaw in the unravelling of the final act. Mark knew exactly how to leverage my abandonment wound; he knew how far I would go to alleviate the agony of being excluded. And so, after a hiatus of six weeks from therapy, I return.

I notice that Dr Collins never asks why, where was I? She just smiles and accepts that I am here. I could have learned a thing or two from her in my relationships. My pattern of haranguing continued into my marriage: but why, why, why did you do that, look that way, say that thing?

After a polite exchange of greetings and general catching up, Dr Collins leans forwards, her customary posture of anticipation.

'How far have you got with your writing?'

I fill her in briefly on what had happened in Wilde since the last time I was here – when we discussed my (non-?) consensual sexual tryst with Mark and my subsequent guilt, which she had tried to deconstruct: the birthday party, Jonathan's sexual awakening, rehearsals, the opening-night betrayal, the subsequent revenge on stage, the estrangement from my friends – which is where I am living on the page now.

'Don't you miss it?' Dr Collins asks. 'The acting? I hadn't realised it was such a big part of who you are. You hadn't really spoken much about it before now.'

'I never became the star in the making that I was allegedly destined to be.'

'Was that difficult?

'By the time I met my husband I was reduced to doing bit parts in soaps and the odd commercial. It was a relief to give that up.'

'And now? Would you like to reconnect with that part of your life?'

'I have no desire any more. Now the only place for me is on the page.'

'Can you expand on that, Jessica?'

'I'm loving the act of writing. The agency, the power of it. I feel as if Mark threw down the gauntlet by writing that play. *Another challenge, Jessica McSwain*.'

She leans in further, her silence probing me.

'I feel as if he expects something from me. A retort.'

'What are you going to do?'

'A novel,' I say, my voice faltering. 'I'm writing a novel, I think.'

She says nothing but I intuit by her level of interest in my 'story' that I may be right.

'I want him to know it was me that wrote it.' I surprise myself.

'So you won't use a pseudonym?'

I shake my head.

'An empowering choice.'

I think of Linda and Jacques and Jonathan and Sue reading it, and my throat closes in.

'Have you decided yet how the ending goes?'

I walk to the window and rest my forehead on the cool glass. *Jessica's fault, or not Jessica's fault?* I squash my nose hard against the pane.

I turn back to her. 'Do you want to know what happened next, in sequence? I know the next chapter.'

'I imagine there was more separating you out, more creating of discord, unleashing sexual jealousies?'

'You're good at this.'

'Mark's behaviour sounds like that of an alcoholic parent: pitting the children against each other… You said he had one himself?'

‘Yes. Poor thing.’ The first time I had ever spoken of Mark with anything like compassion.

‘He was possibly a damaged narcissist as a result.’

‘*Possibly?*’ I laugh. ‘No damage to his ambition or ego, though.’

‘A falsely constructed self,’ she is musing. ‘I imagine he’d crumble if truly challenged.’

I think of the way the social media rumour had been quashed. ‘I doubt that.’

I don’t believe in the concept of a *real* self, I almost say. For all his obsession with the *truth*, Mark was, and is, a liar.

I breathe on the window, pull my sleeve down and clear the condensation. Some clarity is emerging, something real, through the looking glass.

My own reflection in startling relief.

42

April came, the cherry blossoms bloomed a delicate marshmallow pink, but my mood was distinctly grey. *It's better to get lost in the passion than to lose the passion.* I could hear Mark's voice in my head quoting Kierkegaard. I had lost the passion and I felt bereft.

Monsieur Tortue's warning was more real now that the thrill and distraction of performing was over. He had not come, nor had anyone from the French department, so I couldn't delude myself that I would be given a pass because of my considerable thespian talent. I had to recommit to my studies, the prospect of which did not fill me with much *funshine* (oh, Linda). In the days after the play ended, I saw nothing of my best friend, or Jonathan or Mark, or my fellow cast members. The void was terrible: the inevitable comedown after a play ends, intensified by my missing my friends. These attachments – were they that shallow, that fickle, simply because of our age and the lure of sex, drugs and all that went with it? Was their promise enough to sever our bonds?

I was a walking lament. I missed feeling as if I had siblings, friends, admirers, a tribe; I missed the thrill of the stage, the whipcrack sound of the applause; I missed hurting my co-star and the feeling of righteous retribution my pinching fingers gave me. At eighteen, nearly nineteen, I felt as if my best days were over. No more 'violent tendencies' being catered to, no more being the centre of everything, no more being adored by my old and my new 'friends'. Not even sex with

Jacques could alleviate the yearning, the physical ache of the withdrawal from all that irresistible drama.

'I saw Linda earlier,' Jacques said as we were walking through the grounds on our way to lunch, an uncommonly blue sky overhead, the sound of birds chirping, a gentle breeze blowing. I should have felt spring-like.

'Oh, how is she?' I said, feigning being casual, though I hadn't seen her for over two weeks, the longest time we'd been apart since we'd first met.

'She looks great.'

'In what way?' I was hooked, imagining a complete transformation, of clothes, hair, body size.

'She just seems easy in herself, carefree and happy.'

I thought of how I had observed the same changes in Jonathan the last time I saw him. 'Did she mention me?'

'Of course,' he said, his voice cracking. Jacques didn't ordinarily lie.

'Was she with Honor?'

He didn't answer, but waved at some guy I didn't know across the quadrant.

'Who's that?' I asked.

'Spencer,' he said.

Cold blasted through me.

'How do you know him?'

'Everyone knows him,' he laughed. 'I mean, I don't *know* know him, I just know who he is.'

'Have you seen Mark recently?' I asked, trying to contain myself.

'Just around.'

'And Jonathan?'

'Same.' He pulled his jumper sleeves down over his wrists.

'I wonder why I'm not seeing them around…'

'Maybe 'cause they don't want you to!' He started tickling me.

I saw red, or I was consumed by the colour red. I was gone, as gone as I had been in the dark with the baseball bat with Mark. The blood pounded in my temples, my fingers, my every extremity. Snippets of destruction unleashed: 'You don't give a fuck about me anyway/

no one does/you're all just using me/no one cares/you're the worst fucking imposter…' Jacques shrank, then stretched and loomed over me, as if he were a character who had fallen down the rabbit hole alongside me. My rage was as potent as a draught of poison.

Mark knew what he was doing in rehearsals when he first got me in touch with the force of my anger. A faulty tap can never be turned off, not fully.

'Of course I care.' Jacques's shaking voice pulled me out of my trance. He looked stricken, tucked away inside himself. This was worse than any harsh words he could have thrown at me.

I breathed deeply, ground my feet into the earth and managed to speak in a reasonable tone: 'I'm sorry, I'm so sorry, that was appalling.'

'Why would I be using you?'

'No, don't take those words seriously,' I said. 'You've heard the expression: a moment of madness?'

He breathed out, as if in relief. 'Pretty bloody mad alright!' He tried to smile.

We might just survive this.

'I felt excluded,' I whispered to him. 'Unwanted.'

How pathetic I sounded.

Instead of walking away in disgust, he came to me and wrapped his arms around me. 'I love you for being you. I just don't want to see you on stage in your underwear again.' He managed a strained laugh.

This was not the expected script. I had played the role Mark had provoked me into. But this was not the response that anyone could have predicted from Jacques. My man was consistently surprising; his kindness knew no limits. We still just might manage to thwart the *auteur*. His creations had gone off-piste.

43

One drizzling night (the sunshine hadn't lasted long), as I was walking across the front square a few days after my almost-bust-up with Jacques, I thought I saw Jonathan and Mark from a distance. I had just come out of my last lecture of the week, featuring Simone de Beauvoir's *The Second Sex*. My head was ringing with: 'a woman is not born but made' – by men. (Not wholly accurate, but it served my purposes.) As I came closer to the boys, I saw that they were indeed who I had thought they were. They were ambling close together, seemingly at ease, their strides in sync.

'Hello, you!' Mark said as they came upon me.

'Hi! Hi! I said to Jonathan, my voice high and overly bright. I was trying, and failing, to contain my delight at seeing my friend. 'Where are you off to?'

'Hey,' Jonathan greeted me warmly, utterly unaware of how devastated I'd been by his casual withdrawal from me. 'Meeting Phil in the Stag's Hunt in a bit.'

'Cool! Can I come?'

They both looked at me as if I were a funny little monkey in the zoo.

'I don't think Phil would appreciate it if I turned up with you!' Jonathan said lightly.

My ribs constricted and I felt as if I couldn't breathe. The sensation was intense and out of proportion to this brush-off from a virtual stranger, and one I didn't even like. I rearranged my face into a tight smile and said, 'No problem. See you another time so.'

'Deffo!' Jonathan said, in an offhand way. I justified his insensitivity by telling myself he was just love-drugged, and not to take it personally. I seemed to be constantly coaching myself Not To Take Thing Personally. Period.

'See you on Thursday, if not before,' he said to Mark, and there was no denying his tone. It was *friendly*. Nothing else in the mix. Not a trace of irony, or his usual distancing humour. How had Jonathan let his better instincts be so erased? (I was one to talk.)

Thursday, though. What was happening on Thursday?

He blew us both a kiss, a new affectation for him, and totally out of character, as he turned to leave.

Mark and I looked at each other, and I was stunned by the beauty of his eyes, the power in them. I wanted to stay like that forever, fixed in his spotlight stare – I couldn't even pretend any differently.

'Jessica,' he said. 'How are we?'

We are fine, fine, just F.I.N.E. 'Grand, thanks,' I said brightly, knowing enough not to utter that word.

A sardonic smile preceded the words: 'Would you like to go to the Dungeon for a drink and catch up? It's been a while.' His voice, full of seduction.

I wish I could report differently. But I followed, like a docile little lamb. As we walked, me trailing a pace behind, I oscillated between feeling revulsion and attraction and excitement, as ever. I was *alive*.

'How's life treating you and your *amour*?' Mark asked, throwing the question over his shoulder.

'Nous sommes merveilleux!'

'Really? You guys didn't seem so *merveilleux* the last time we were all together,' he said as he reached the door to the Dungeon. *Don't rise to him.* He held it open for me, as I was still a pace behind. 'Drink?'

'Why not?' I said. 'A Carlsberg.' Not knowing why. I had never drunk it before.

'That stuff will make you fat.' He threw over his shoulder as he walked towards the bar.

I inwardly winced as I pointed at one of the booths. 'I'll be in there.'

'Nice choice,' he said. 'Give us some privacy.'

That pinching pain in my pelvis. Stupid girl.

He returned with the pint for me, a glass of sparkling water for himself.

'So,' he said, as he leaned in to study me.

'So,' I said, and my voice sounded breathy.

'We're overdue a catch-up.'

I miss you, I almost said, but instead I smiled brightly, hoping to accentuate my one delicious dimple.

'Are you feeling a bit flat post the play ending?'

He was uncannily astute, as ever.

'I am,' I said, regretting it the moment I said it. I had wanted to present a front of 'I'm-doing-so-great-without-you-all.' *Come on Jessica, act, like the star you are.*

'I'm sure it won't be too long before you tread the boards again. You were born to be up there.' Exactly what I had longed to hear him say.

I almost spoke to him about opening night, the betrayal of it, convincing myself that it was Patrick who had initiated the 'turn' – but I stopped myself just in time by focusing on the upturn at the side of his taut, perfectly shaped mouth.

'I've decided not to do any more plays this year. I really need to get the focus back on my studies.' I was doing my best to act like an *adult* – though I could only have a stab at that. Sue was my example, after all.

'You're evidently missing your friends, by the way you spoke to Jonathan.'

The way he could see into me, through me… All that was *missing* in me.

'Cancer stick?' he said, offering me a cigarette from a pack of red Marlboro.

'I thought you didn't smoke.'

'I don't,' he said, thrusting the pack in front of my face.

I took one and he whipped out a lighter and offered it to me. I sucked on it deeply. I didn't even like smoking.

'So, how's Linda?' I ventured, though the plume.

'Have you not seen each other then?' He pitched forward, flapped his hand in front of his face to clear the smoke, seemingly very interested in my reaction.

'You know we haven't,' I said, taking a gulp of the beer, which was lukewarm and the colour of piss. I coughed.

'She's great. Spreading her wings, broadening her horizons, her friendship group,' he said, studying me closely.

I wanted to tell him to go fuck himself, but I was still coughing. I drank again and again, not tasting the beer, wanting only to stop the tickle in my throat, and to dilute the anger.

'It's best for her to be removed from people from her past, for the moment.'

I stabbed out the cigarette and picked at a beer mat in front of me.

He observed coolly. 'A great choreographic gesture,' he said. 'For an actress to convey turbulent wordlessness.'

The fury rose. *How's this for wordlessness?* 'Where is she getting those marks on her wrists?' I turned on him, my voice crackling and hissing. I needed to control myself better.

He didn't react. 'Change is hard, it needs to be incremental…' he was musing to himself. 'She needs a certain level of pain to feel like herself.'

I bit down on my tongue and continued my choreography with the beer mats, rolling pieces of them into tiny balls between thumb and forefinger.

'I hope she's OK,' I managed. 'I don't think those drugs are good for her.'

He stared at me, said nothing for a beat, put his hand over mine to stop me shredding the beermat. I let him. My hand tingled.

'And yet. You are dying to try them,' he said.

'I'm built of different stuff to Linda. She's delicate.'

He laughed. 'Didn't stop you hurting her when you were younger, did it?'

I pulled my hand back, feeling as if he had twisted my skin, viciously.

'I only loved her,' I said, my voice shaking. 'Sue and I looked out for her. We were her family when she had none.' I stood, trying to wrest back some power.

'That's an interesting narrative you've concocted,' he said. 'I guess there's truth in that, from a certain perspective. I'm just not sure you're seeing the bigger picture…'

'You can't justify what you're doing to her now by blaming me or pointing to "a bigger picture".'

He sat back, breathed slowly. 'And what, exactly, am I doing to do her now?'

'Controlling her,' I said, knowing as I said it that it wasn't the best response. Far too expected.

'Really?' He seemed to ponder my words, weigh them in his hands, as he looked down at his cupped palms. The he closed them together as if in a prayer position. 'I think you know that Linda is evolving, freeing herself from the shackles of her painful past. You just don't want to admit it, seeing as you were so much a part of that past.'

'I was the good part!' I blurted. 'Me and Sue.'

'I'll leave you to ponder that,' he said as he stood.

No. He wasn't going to be the first to leave, and not on that note.

'And Jessica. You need to let your friend go if you really love her. Encourage her to spread her wings.'

'Is that what you're doing?' I couldn't help it.

'I love her. Truly.' What he said next was stunning: '*He who does not know how to encircle a girl so that she loses sight of everything he does not want her to see, he who does not know how to poetise himself into a girl so that it is from her that everything proceeds as he wants it – he is and remains a bungler.*'

'That your crazy philosopher?' I said, hoping he'd laugh and deconstruct the words, say it was a nonsense, the opposite of how he felt, which was that he wanted her to feel free and empowered.

He nodded. 'I love how he thinks. I'm immersed in his teachings. So profound and they hold the paradox, beautifully.'

'You believe that's "setting her free"?'

'There is freedom in absolute love,' he said. 'And I believe in granting her that.'

Could I run away, find my friend, tell her what Mark just said? She'd probably find it romantic, that level of possessiveness. It was what she sought: being claimed, encircled.

'I do adore her, you know. I only want what's best for her,' he stated calmly.

I managed a small: 'That makes two of us then.'

'Good, glad we're on the same page there.'

I grabbed my coat from the back of the seat, determined to be the first to leave. I needed to run. To where I didn't know. I just knew the feeling of the building up of speed inside my body. As I turned to leave, he spoke to my back: 'By the way, we're moving the play to the Burning Bush Theatre next September.'

I stopped in my tracks. The best new writing venue in the country. Where stars were made.

'I'm going to have to recast it, obviously,' he said.

'Why, *obviously*?' I turned back to face him.

'You're going to have to focus on your studies. Otherwise, you might lose that bursary.'

'Is Patrick going to be in it at the Bush? I asked, unable to stop myself.

'Patrick is in fourth year, so yes, I plan on giving him the part.'

The pain was intense, a kick to the guts.

'You're upset. I'm sorry I upset you.'

He didn't sound in the least bit sorry.

'Also, we can't have you and Patrick on-stage together again,' he said thoughtfully. 'That was building to a painful crescendo. And I know who would have got the most physically injured out of the two of you.'

Ohohohoho, funny guy. I stood slowly, recalibrating.

'Right. Well, I didn't think Patrick was any good anyway. Bit bloody vanilla.'

Tears streamed down his face he was laughing so hard. 'You're quite the comedienne.'

I curtsied and turned to go.

'Come to one of our soirees,' Mark shouted at my back. 'You and Jacques. You're welcome any time…'

At least I was the first to leave. *You are devastated to be un-cast. I am devasted. You are devastated. I am devastated.* My ego was decimated. He had succeeded in that.

How about my friend? What could I do there? Not much right now, I realised. If I pressed her too hard in one direction she would only push back. Our past was playing against me. Her present was entirely seductive. She was being given all the love, all the attention, that had usually been reserved for me. She was no longer in my shadow, but – God, or the Divine, or the Diabolical – what pall was now being cast over her? I pulled my coat around me and roughly brushed away my pathetic tears. I had fully devolved into a bad actress, a bad friend. You are a bad person. I am a bad person. You are a bad person. I am. A. Bad. Person.

*

'You can't convince me otherwise,' I say to Dr Collins.

'I see that.' She doesn't even try.

'And don't say, "There is a bigger picture here".'

'I won't,' she says.

'Well, what *can* you say?' I challenge her.

'I am not sure there is anything I can say right now,' she says gently. 'I feel I am where you were, when you spoke of the powerlessness you felt over your friend.'

We both fall silent.

'I can only hope that time will allow a softening, that your position will be less entrenched the next time we meet, that you can find a chink of compassion for yourself.'

My heart – it hurts. I guess that's a good sign.

I thank her, genuinely this time. I know I'll need to come back. As much for the jogging of my memories as for the dismantling of this hateful persona I have concocted.

44

At the beginning of May, after weeks of being deprived contact with my friends, I was standing outside on the 'catwalk' – a ramp that connected the arts block to the outside, a place to preen and be seen – wittily dissecting Sartre's *No Exit*. I was dazzling a fellow student with my droll humour and sartorial taste, drinking in his attention, as a weak sun shone. 'Cool, cool,' the guy said, nodding, looking me over approvingly. Someone waved at me across the grassy quadrangle. As the figure came closer, I recognised a female form clad in an oversized khaki parka – Christ, she was literally morphing into Mark.

'People aren't damned for nothing,' I recited from *No Exit*, my classmate regarding me with something close to ecstasy. He had seen me in the Whitman play, he'd said, and it was spectacular; I was spectacular.

'Nice threads,' I said to Linda as she came up to me.

'Thanks! We got it in the army surplus store in George's Arcade.'

We?

'L'enfer, c'est les autres.' My fellow classmate took his leave, nodding dismissively at Linda, as if he were heartbroken that she had broken up our party.

'Besotted!' Linda said, after he was out of earshot.

'We were discussing Sartre,' I said, outwardly feigning nonchalance, inwardly thrilled by his attention and her apparition.

'Of course you were!' She looked me up and down. I was wearing black drainpipe jeans and a checked oversized men's shirt, top buttons open to reveal my black lacy bra and the stolen amber pendant. 'You look well.'

'Thanks, you too. Though not sure about the parka.'

She laughed unselfconsciously. 'I like it. Makes me feel more masculine, powerful.'

'I thought he liked you in 1950s housewifey gear!'

'His likes are not fixed. Anyway, it was my idea to get this.'

I doubted that. Even if she thought it was her idea, he'd have been behind it, planting notions.

'Matchy-matchy!' I said.

'I missed your caustic wit,' she said.

I didn't dare to tell her how much I missed everything about her.

'It's so nice to be out and about and feel the sun.' She tilted her face towards the milky light.

'Drink?' I asked, trying to keep desperation out of my voice.

'Why not?' she said, in an offhand fashion.

Time to play it cool, I coached myself – not very well as it turned out, as 'Where's Honor?' slipped out of my mouth.

'How would I know?' she said. 'I don't track her every movement.'

A veiled insult aimed at me, her needy friend. When had that become our dynamic?

We walked past the cricket pitch and the rugby fields at the rear of campus towards a bar that we had never frequented before, the Pavilion, which was full of rugger-bugger types with polo shirt collars turned up, the girls with twinsets and tweedy skirts, short enough to hint at slutty when rolled up at the waist, long enough for Daddy's approval when worn as they should be. 'A sociological experiment!' Linda said as we walked through the doors. She removed her parka, and many pairs of eyes fixed on her in her pleather mini skirt, fishnet tights and Doc Martens.

My fashion thief, on this occasion, outshone me. Never before had she been the focus of more attention than me, and yet all eyes were on her. Her hair was tousled on top of her head – had she put in highlights? Her eyes were smoky and lined in kohl, a light touch of foundation, enough to camouflage her freckles, or at least make them seem blended, so that her skin looked sun-kissed, not blotchy. She went to the bar and ordered us two gin and tonics, something we didn't ordinarily drink.

'Cheers!' she said brightly as she handed me my round-bottomed glass, tinkling with ice cubes, a slice of lemon floating on top.

'I thought Mark didn't approve of alcohol,' I said.

'Do you see him anywhere?' She looked around her, theatrically. 'And anyway, I am free to do as I like.'

I took a sip of my drink and stopped myself from saying anything. A shaft of sunshine crossed her face, and her grey eyes were luminous in the light.

'How is Mark?' I asked, fake-casually.

'Amazing…! And how is your gorgeous man?'

Who were we before we met our men?

'Amazing!' I said, but my echo just sounded childish and churlish.

'Jacques is a keeper,' she said, downing her gin in one.

'Whoa,' I said. 'Easy.'

She ordered another one in response, not bothering to get me one as I had barely sipped mine. She drank greedily, ordered Tayto cheese and onion crisps, ripped open the packet and ate them by the fistful, not stopping to talk, or breathe.

'Are you on a food bender?' I asked in what I hoped was a caring voice. 'You don't have to do that.'

'I'm just hungry!' she said. 'That OK with you?' She ordered another drink and another packet of Taytos.

'I'm fine, thanks for asking,' I said ironically, as she didn't offer me any.

She started feeding me one crisp at a time by hand, which was strangely seductive. I wondered who had taught her that move.

'Can I tell you something?' she said.

I nodded, my mouth full.

'You were a shit friend.'

I swallowed, took a big gulp of gin.

'I only wanted what was best for you,' I said, maintaining eye contact.

'That eye-balling trick won't work any more,' she said. Her tone was throwaway, as if she didn't really care what I thought or did any more, which hurt much more than her words.

'Just admit it. You were a bully,' she said.

These words were never meant to be uttered aloud. An unbearable mixture of guilt and humiliation and possessiveness made me do it: my hand reached over and pinched her, on her upper arm.

She didn't even wince, just continued looking at me. 'Did that make you feel better?'

I pulled up her sleeve to reveal her wrist, red-welted. 'Does *that* make you feel better?'

'Actually, yes, it does,' she said. 'And anyway, I am not hurting anyone else by my actions.'

'But you are hurting yourself,' I said. 'Let me see…'

She withdrew her arm and leaned in close to me and whispered, 'I could never hurt me as much as you hurt me.'

I drew back, knowing exactly who was behind this reasoning. I softened my tone. 'Sue and I looked out for you. All those years. You were family.'

'I didn't enjoy you hurting me.'

I wanted to say, yes, you did, you enjoyed me pinching and twisting your skin, but then I would have had to admit to my actions.

'Are you OK? Genuinely … you don't seem yourself.'

She laughed. 'And that could only be a good thing!' She reached over for my glass and drained it, then ordered another.

'Hey, slow down … where are you getting the cash, moneybags?'

'My man. What's his is mine and mine is his, except I don't have anything, so that one works very much in my favour!' She laughed freely, catching the barman's eye.

Except Mark owns everything about you, I thought. Was this getting drunk an expression of revolt, or was he encouraging her in this new behaviour?

'Seriously, Linda. This isn't good for you.'

'What do you know about what's good for me?' she said, belligerently. 'I'm done living by other people's expectations for me.' Her words were slurred.

'Come on, let's get you home,' I said.

'Home?' she said, as if she'd never heard the word before now.

'Come back to mine.'

She stood, dragged me off my stool and put her arms around me, her cheek against my chest, a helpless child.

'OK,' she said.

'You can have dinner with me and Jacques later.'

'I'd like that…' Her eyes were glassy.

She pushed me off her and went to the bar, asked the barman for a pen, then proceeded to write her number on the back of a beermat, winking at the guy. Who was this person?

'Linda, what are you doing? Mark –'

'Mark, Mark, Mark … you are obsessed,' she said.

I needed to be more careful. 'He's still your boyfriend … isn't he?'

'He is still my man, yes, and he would heartily approve of me giving my number to this eejit!' The bartender seemed to think this was cute as he grinned at her.

'What? Are you guys not monogamous any more?'

'You sound so small-minded, Jessie J.'

'What does he make you do?'

In response she leaned across the bar to the bartender and whispered something in his ear. His face burned. 'Nobody *makes* me do anything I don't want to do!' she said.

I grabbed hold of her by her upper arm and literally hauled her out of there. 'Damage limitation,' I said to the guy. 'She has a boyfriend.' He shrugged. What does that matter?

She swatted at me, drunkenly. It was now fully dark outside. As we walked back across the cricket pitch and the rugby fields a thin moon shone wanly. 'Oh look, a tiny silver slipper of a moon!' she said in a terrible southern American accent. 'Look over your left shoulder and make a wish!' I said, playing along, in my excellent Tennessee Williams voice.

She stopped, stared up at the moon. 'I wish –'

I interrupted her. 'Don't say it out loud. It's your secret!'

She whispered in my ear, 'I only wish for love.'

A chill swept through me, looking at my chameleonic friend. How far would she go for whatever she mistook for love?

When we got back to my room, Jacques was sitting in the chair under the window, reading my copy of *Les Enfants Terribles*. He looked up.

'Oh hey, you two!' He seemed delighted to see us together.

'Hey J-J-Jacques,' Linda said.

'This is freaking me out,' Jacques said, holding up the book. 'What a twisted world...'

Linda giggled.

'A Cocteau cocktail ... irresistible!' I said.

'Come here,' Jacques said and pointed at his lips, his arms wide.

Linda launched herself at him and kissed him. 'I've always wanted to do that!'

'She's pissed,' I said, trying to recover the moment.

'I can see that,' he said.

'Don't talk about me as if I wasn't here,' Linda said. 'I'm right here, look at me!' She started to undress, pulling off her skirt first, then the tights, then the top, so she was in her panties and bra. Jacques turned away and I grabbed hold of her by her arm and manoeuvred her towards the bed. She climbed in and I covered her with the quilt. She closed her eyes and within seconds was snoring, on her back. We both stood at the side of the bed, looking down on her, like she was our drunk teenage daughter. I felt old.

'Turn her on her side,' Jacques said. 'She might get sick.'

I sat on the bed beside her and gently pushed her onto her side.

'Who is that person?' Jacques said.

'I know! Complete personality transplant,' I said. 'We went to the Pav and she gave her number to a bartender with a crewcut!'

'Jesus, what did they make of you two in there?' He laughed, then looked back at her. 'I don't think Mark would be too happy to see her like that.'

'That's what I said to her, but she said he'd be thrilled, and that he'd have wanted her to give her number out to some randomer.'

'I'm sure that's not true,' Jacques said.

'Have you seen him recently?' I asked as casually as I could, feeling sure that they were meeting behind my back.

'You'd never give your number out, would you?'

I pulled his head down to me and kissed him in answer.

'I'll go make us some pasta. She'll need some soakage.' He motioned at a bottle of Ballygowan on the desk. 'If she wakes, give her lots of water.'

'I know how to be mummy!' I said.

He looked at me with adoration in his eyes. 'You'll be a lovely mummy someday.'

How had he got that so wrong? Could he not see that I'd be a terrible mother? How could I possibly be expected to know what to do? And I was selfish through and through. Linda was right: everything had an agenda with me. You don't opt to be a mother with an agenda. I didn't think I was capable of loving without conditions. Jacques fit the picture right now of the other half of the coolest couple in college, but that didn't mean I wanted marriage, babies, the whole suburban nightmare.

Thankfully, I managed to stay silent and blew him a kiss, which he caught in one hand and inhaled. Bit much. I hated when he revealed his soppy side like that. He headed for the door and left without a backward glance. And then: that pain of someone leaving.

I lay down on the bed beside Linda and spooned her back. I whispered a prayer into her hair, 'Come back to me, my darling, stupid friend, don't give it all up to that man.' I thought of Sue and her warning to us: *Don't give yourselves away too easily. You are prizes to be cherished.* I thought of how my father had diminished her, and I pressed hard on the sore spot on my neck.

45

When Linda woke, she turned towards me and snuggled into me, chest to chest. We breathed together, in unison, like we used to when we were little. After some moments, I pulled back, looked into her eyes. Her mascara had flaked onto her cheeks, and it looked as if she had black tears etched onto her face, like a Pierrot doll. She kissed me on the lips. 'I love you,' she said, and I nearly wept. 'How did I get here?' She looked around her, sounding slightly stunned. I plumped the pillows behind her so that she could sit up.

'You got pissed,' I said. 'I brought you here, rescued you from some scary cadet-like guy in the Pav bar.'

'I what…?' She giggled.

'Do you not remember any of it?' I said.

She looked at me blankly.

'You were pretty funny. Very unlike you!'

'Mark thinks I'm funny,' she said petulantly.

'Does he?' I said, surprised. I wouldn't have thought that Linda having a sense of humour would be a part of their dynamic.

She stared into my eyes so intently I had to look away. 'Something you're not telling me?' she said, and I felt sick.

'Hey, come on… Let's get you into the shower and get some grub in you.'

'You didn't answer.'

'You're talking gibberish,' I said. 'I've never seen you so off your head.'

'Oh I'm sure you have. Remember when we'd get pissed on those beakers filled with dregs from our parents' alcohol cabinets?'

'God, yes. We'd both drink to spinning and puking!'

'And blessed blackouts,' she said.

There was so much she needed to obliterate.

I bent down to pick her clothes up off the ground and lay them on the bed. 'What *were* you wearing?'

'Mark says I look extremely sexy dressed like that.'

Was he creating a clone of me?

'Did he pick out your clothes?'

'What kind of a pathetic fool do you take me for?' She pushed back the quilt. 'Honor and I went shopping. She has the best style, don't you agree?'

I felt hot and then cold and then hot. My cheeks flared bright red. 'Except that's my style,' I said weakly.

She looked at me with a cruel kind of pity. 'Can I have a towel?' she said.

I got her one from the wardrobe and directed her to the shower.

'I know where it is.' She caught my eye as she left the room and in that wordless exchange there was an acknowledgement of who I was, what I was capable of. Or perhaps my guilt made that up.

A few moments later, Jacques came in. 'I just saw Linda go into the bathroom. She looks a wreck.'

'I think she looks beautiful, wanton, with the mascara all down her face.'

He laughed awkwardly, knowing enough not to agree with me, and said that the pasta was ready, before he turned and left.

'I'm starving,' Linda said as she burst back into the room, dressed in her mini and T-shirt, bare-legged. Her milky-white legs, untouched by the sun, made her look like a porcelain figurine. She held her hand out to me and I felt as if I might burst with joy.

'Yumtious scrumptious,' she said as we entered the kitchen and smelled the carbonara simmering on the stove. I thought she was about to kiss Jacques again, and guide his hand beneath her skirt, but of course, only in my world could something like that happen.

'Delicious,' she said, as he heaped the sauce onto a full plate of pasta and pushed a glass of water in front of her. I sat on the opposite side of the table, to better observe her. She ate heartily and fast, asking for seconds before we'd even finished. Jacques got up and served her another full bowl. I groaned, but she ate every last morsel, licking the bowl at the end.

'Gross, have some manners,' I said, half-jokingly.

'You sound like my mother,' she said, not at all jokingly.

'Have a good time this evening?' Jacques asked her.

'I don't know. Why don't you ask Jessica?'

'Not like you,' Jacques said.

'There are parts of me that not even I know about.'

Was this more of Mark's deconstructing of her?

'Ah look, I just wanted to let off steam. I've been studying hard. No biggie.'

'Are you sure everything's OK?' Jacques asked her, looking old, in the way he did when he looked at his brother.

She stood abruptly. 'I'd better get back to my man. He'll be wondering where I am.'

Jacques pushed the glass of water in front of her. 'Drink that first, and I'll make you a coffee.'

'He's not my keeper,' she said to us both, sounding very much as if he were. 'Mark knows and respects that I am my own person with my own will and desires.'

Is that what he told her? Very clever.

Jacques got up to make the coffee, while I placed my hand on hers. She abruptly drew back, and I felt as if she had slapped me, although the Linda I knew wasn't capable of smacking someone – ever. I was grappling with what to say next when Jacques returned with a jug of hot milk and a steaming cafetiere. 'Café au lait,' he said. 'Do you like yours with hot milk?' She nodded.

'Oh you drink milk now? What about the terrible cruelty to the mamma cow and her calves?' I said.

'I need more protein,' she said flatly.

'Good idea,' Jacques said, and I could have killed him.

'You're lucky to have a man who cooks for you.' Linda turned to me.

'Who does the cooking with you and Mark?' I asked.

'Me usually,' she said.

'I didn't know you could cook.'

'There are many things about me you don't know,' she said, as she sipped her coffee. I looked at my half-naked, hungover friend and felt terrified for her. I wanted to tell her about my impulse to protect her, but I couldn't. It would have backfired, or so I convinced myself.

(I still try to persuade myself of this today: that I couldn't have done anything.)

'What's your favourite meal to prepare?' Jacques asked her.

'Mark likes fish, so I've learned to prepare a few dishes with salmon.'

'Do you eat fish now?' I asked, remembering her sobbing when she found out about the hooks fishermen used and how they clobbered the fish over the head, or worse, left them to suffocate, flip-flopping in the bottom of boats. Sue could never coax her to eat anything with a heartbeat, no matter how hard she tried, and she tried. She was worried about her growing bones.

'Do you?' I wasn't letting it go. 'Do you eat fish now?'

'I already answered that,' she said, smiling at Jacques as he went on: lemon butter, tinfoil, 180 degrees in the oven.

'Does she?' I rounded on Jacques. It felt imperative to find this out about my friend. How completely had she been reconfigured?

He smiled back at Linda, as if to say, she's being a bit insistent, isn't she? I was enraged by their secret smiles and had to sit on my hands and bite my cheek. I stood abruptly, the chair leg screeching against the floor. Linda took my cue and stood up alongside me, said she'd really better be getting back.

'You're not going out like that, without your undies and your tights…? What if the wind blows?'

She blushed, and not in a pretty, excited way, but in the old way that signalled her usual baseline state of shame.

'Come on, Lindy, I need to get changed too.' I held my hand out to her, which she ignored.

'You're alright,' she said. 'I'll just grab my stuff and I'll be on my way.'

She looked from Jacques to me. 'Be good to him.' And now the shame was all mine – where it rightfully belonged.

'That was a tad unnecessary,' Jacques said, as soon as she was out of earshot. 'And unkind.'

I looked after Linda's departing back. 'Ah it's just something we girls do, slag each other off. She knows that I love her,' I said, as much to convince myself as him.

I cupped Jacques's beautiful face in my hand, then I cupped his bottom. 'I need you … I love you.'

He said it back, though I wasn't entirely convinced that he wasn't just saying it because it was expected of him.

'Eat me.'

And so he did. And he went beyond what was expected of him.

But still I remained. I was not erased or obliterated, which was what I wanted.

46

A few days later I spotted Jonathan and Phil in the arts block, from a distance. Jonathan looked up and waved. I pretended to wave cheerily, friskily back. I was such a busy person with so much to do, so many people to see… I went to the coffee dock alone and tried to force a dry cheddar cheese sandwich and a cup of tea down my throat. My appetite was virtually non-existent. The guy from my tutorial who I had dazzled with my hilarious dissection of *No Exit* saw me and his face lit up. He didn't even ask could he sit beside me. I stood as he sat. I was developing a taste for being the leaver, not the left. I felt him cringe inside himself and I really didn't give a shit. *Frankly my dear I don't give a damn.*

Today was a day for the library. I had to force myself to study again, my concentration was scatty and flitting. I decided to hide out on the top floor of the Lecky in a nook, cocooned in a private space by the window, reading *The Stranger* for the fourth time. (I was doing my dissertation on 'Alienation and the Search for Self' in Camus's work.) As I tried to focus, I kept getting assaulted by images of my so-called friends who now hated me. Did they even care enough to hate me…? And then I thought of Linda in my bed, saying I love you, and how I had humiliated her, again. And Sue… Why did I continue to hurt those I loved? Had I inadvertently done something to Jonathan, too…? Nothing came to mind. The last time we were close was at Mark's 'non-birthday' birthday party. Jonathan hadn't wanted to come, but he came, for me. And then he left with that dick, and he had taken drugs and he had changed. Nothing to do with me, I assured myself, but still that niggling feeling persisted that I was the cause of all this separation and distancing. My mind was ruminating, circular, small. All of it about *moi, moi, moi*.

I sat in the nook for hours, concocting catastrophic stories that were myopically self-obsessed in scope. The light outside faded to dusk. It was peaceful in here, I told myself, though my head allowed for no peace. I thought I felt someone staring at me and when I looked up, Phil's, *the dick's*, cold eyes met mine. They were a sort of insipid pale blue – no hidden depths there. He was sitting at a desk in the centre of the brightly lit space, his legs splayed wide, studying me. 'Yo,' he said, standing and walking over to me. 'Yo,' I said back. The first time I had uttered such an inanity.

'You coming to the soiree tonight?'

I didn't know what he was talking about. *Thursday*. It was Thursday. 'Yes,' I said, on impulse.

'Great, see you later then? You bringing your handsome Frenchie?' He seemed friendly enough.

Something made me ask: 'Is Honor going to be there?'

'Shut the fuck up,' some guy at the next desk said. He was, to be fair to him, trying to study.

'Or what?' Phil countered, while I said 'Sorry' simultaneously.

'I don't like rudeness,' Phil said loudly.

I mouthed sorry again to the guy who muttered something like 'fucking entitled asshole', and moved his stuff.

Phil was studying me. 'Are you always so apologetic?' he said.

Which was ironic, given that I never apologised to those to whom I owed one. I shrugged, attempting to appear nonchalant.

'You asked about Honor?'

I tried to shrug again but it came across as an awkward one-shouldered tic.

'I guess she'll be there, yeah. Why?'

'No reason,' I said. *Little weirdo*. But I made my mind up to go alone. Just for a while. Just to see my pal, Jonathan, I reasoned. He'd be happy to see me, wouldn't he?

'Jono will be delighted to see you,' Phil said, as if he could read my thoughts. His tone was mocking. Or was it? *Get a grip, Jessica.*

'See you later then?' He grabbed all his stuff off the desk and flung it in a satchel. There was something cruelly casual to how this guy moved through the world, to how he handled things, the people around him.

I tried to get back to reading Camus, but life itself held the promise of too much drama. I decided to channel Meursault's detached aloofness as I gathered my things together, determined to just drop in at the party and be cool. Jacques had said he was going to see Louis this evening and that he'd be back by ten or so. Plenty of time for me to *casually* reconnect with my friends. I didn't even allow myself to think of the possibility of the goodies. I changed for the second time that day, dressing artfully, hinting at sex yet not overtly flaunting it, in my leggings, boots and oversized purple-and-black checked shirt, purple bra peeking out. The pendant hung just above my small breasts, to best highlight my breastbone. This was something Mark would notice: my jutting bones, my clavicle.

The night was covered in a soft rain, causing my hair to frizz. As I arrived outside Mark's rooms, I noticed that I was shaking. The first time I had not been invited to a party, and yet here I was: a gatecrasher, and a wet one at that. Phil seemed to think I'd been invited, and Mark himself had said 'You're always welcome,' the last time we met. He had said that hadn't he…? I drew myself to my full height, rolled my shoulders back and was just about to press on the buzzer as a group of other students arrived, one of whom had a key. I followed them up the stairs, my heart thumping, my face flushed. Why hadn't I had some tequila before leaving? Also, why had I arrived without my hairbrush and make-up bag? My hair was a mess; I was a mess.

The other students peeled off on the third floor as I continued up to Mark's room on the fifth. His door was ajar, the smell of incense – or was it dope? – wafting in the corridor outside. I inhaled deeply and steeled myself for my grand entrance. No one noticed me as I arrived, no one even looked in my direction. I wasn't used to this. I went straight to a side table and gulped back a goblet of red wine before I could steady myself enough to look around me and focus properly. The room was in semi-darkness, lit only by the dancing candles. A psychedelic fusion of hip hop and electronica was playing, setting a cool, druggy mood.

'Well look who it is!' Mark was upon me.

'Hi. Hope you don't mind,' I found myself saying, trying to straighten my sopping fringe with my fingers.

He laughed. 'Why would I mind? Make yourself comfortable...' He gestured at the space around him and seemed to be about to leave. It was all I could do not to hang onto his trouser leg.

'Did you come alone?'

I nodded. A sardonic expression flitted across his features, something I couldn't read.

'Great music,' I said, just for something to say.

'Massive Attack's *Blue Lines*,' he said. 'The soundtrack for our generation. I'm going to try and get the rights for the score for the Bush Theatre.'

'Brilliant idea,' I answered flatly.

'Patrick's here ... just giving you the heads up.'

'Cool,' I said, pretending not to care. 'Have Jonathan and Phil arrived yet?'

He pointed towards a dark corner. 'I think you'll find them in that general direction.' Then he walked away to do his host's duties. 'Have fun,' he said. 'But not too much!'

My heart was by now hammering loudly in my ears. I drank another glass of wine as my eyes adjusted to the gloom. Who were those two bodies sitting close together on the couch? I shook my head. Stop being paranoid, I ordered myself, even as my gut told me otherwise.

Linda barrelled over to me and enfolded me in a hug. I was flooded with gratitude, a new experience for me. She didn't hate me. She didn't seem hurt, or in the least bit diminished by what I'd said the last time we met. She was glowing and dressed in a long, flowing hippy dress – yet another incarnation.

'You look beautiful,' I said.

'Wow. That's something you've never said before!' She was electric and I was dead. I knocked back the end of the glass of wine. 'Take it easy,' she said. 'Can't mix too much booze with the goodies.'

'I won't tonight, thanks,' I said. 'I have to be home early to see Jacques.' I was willing it to be true as I said it.

'Oh maybe I can persuade you both then!' she said. 'He's here.'

A cold wind blew through me; I was empty space. I tried to laugh, to pretend that of course I was aware of my boyfriend's movements. 'Yes, I know, I meant we both had agreed together to have an early night.'

She looked at me with pity in her eyes – again.

'Well, don't you two look just adorable?' Phil said loudly, as he and Jonathan walked in our direction. I wanted to run into Jonathan's arms, ask for help, backup, look, there was my boyfriend with the duchess again, and I hadn't even known he was coming. He lied to me. But then, I had planned on doing the same to him. But not so I could flirt with someone else. Who was the bigger liar here? What had happened between Mark and I had receded, but still it remained a fact. It *had* happened. In these very rooms. In that very kitchen. Was this that bloody campanile curse playing out…? Would the person who had loved me the most no longer love me? It seemed entirely possible. My world upended in an instant.

Jonathan came to me and hugged me easily. 'Lovely to see you, Jessie. Wasn't expecting to see you here tonight.'

Why wasn't he expecting to see me? I was among friends, wasn't I?

'I invited her!' Phil's voice boomed. I shrank.

Linda looked at Phil. 'Quite the gentleman,' she said. 'Gathering up all the waifs and strays.'

Had she really just said that?

'How are things?' Jonathan said to me lightly.

I amped up my megawatt smile.

'I was surprised to see Jacques arrive earlier without you.'

'Oh yeah, I had to be somewhere… Couldn't get here till now. I told him to come ahead of me.'

Jonathan looked around him. 'And where is he now?'

I tried to signal my distress to him, but he wasn't picking up on it. Did that drug make people lose their ability to experience empathy? Jonathan had always been the most sensitive of friends and yet here now, and in all my recent interactions with him, he seemed devoid of any compassion, or insight.

'He's over there,' Phil said loudly. 'With Honor.'

Only then did Jonathan regard me with some level of concern, and with the same shade of pity that had been in Linda's eyes. This was unbearable. I lifted another goblet of wine and downed it.

'Whoa, easy, tiger,' Phil said and laughed loudly.

'Do take it easy,' Jonathan said, gently.

'I said the same thing to her earlier. She seems intent on getting pissed. And that can only end badly,' said Linda, the girl who only three nights previously had drunk to blackout. 'Oh hey, Will,' she said to someone I'd never seen before. She moved away to kiss the guy on both cheeks.

'So,' Jonathan said looking at me.

'Sssoooo,' I said, hearing myself a little slurred at the edges.

'You want rescuing?'

I did, obviously, but I couldn't believe he would expose me so publicly.

'Who me? Never!' I said, shaking myself off as I tried to laugh and walk in a straight line towards the kitchen. Jacques didn't once break his focus from his conversation with Honor. I noticed that much. In the kitchen I drank two glasses of cold water and splashed a little on my face. Someone was observing me from the doorway. I felt those eyes like lasers, burning into me. Mark walked towards me and came close enough to touch my chest bone, my clavicle, his long fingers brushing against my hot skin. He lifted up the amber stone to better observe it in the candlelight. 'What a thing of beauty,' he said. 'It has the look of a talisman, don't you think?' He dropped it back against my chest bone so it hurt. I had to fight a desire to grab his fingers and put them all in my mouth.

'I think it's time to confront your boyfriend,' he said, smiling benignly.

'I don't know what you mean,' I said.

'Oh, I think you do.'

On impulse I lifted the amber stone and placed it in my mouth, to suck.

'I see your insecurity, Jessica.'

And I raise it. I almost started into a Meisner back and forth: You see my insecurity. I see your insecurity. You see my… I see your…

'The thing that makes you such a great actress isn't so great in real life, is it? That transparency.'

You're so transparent. You're such a prick. I was rendered mute.

I watched him turn and walk away, his tall, proud, hateful back with its slight, stooped shoulders. Breathe in, out. Onetwothreefourfivesixseven, Onethreefiveseven, Twofoursixeight, Whodoyou*appreciate*? Another glass of water. Some stranger came up to me. 'Hi,' he said. 'I saw you in Mark's play. Fucking insanely brilliant!' He was staring at my tits as if he knew them intimately. I guess he did. I debated flirting with him, but I didn't have it in me. 'Thanks,' I said flatly before I turned my back to him. I liked the momentary power that gave me.

I was standing staring out the window when I felt a pair of arms encircle me from behind. 'Hi baby.' The relief was indescribable, but also the anger, the outrage. He kissed my earlobe, nibbling it. 'How lovely to see you here!'

I turned to him. 'You weren't expecting to see me, huh?'

'I just dropped by on my way to see Louis,' he started babbling, then he dug himself a hole: 'I bumped into Honor, and she told me to join just for one drink. She was upset, wanted to talk…'

Pathetic, easy-to-manipulate eejit, I thought, but thankfully didn't say.

'I'm heading to see Louis now,' he said. 'I didn't know you were planning on coming here either.'

'I wasn't planning on it,' I managed casually. 'I bumped into Mark earlier and he invited me.' I didn't know why I felt the need to lie on that front. But I wanted Jacques to pick up on our *frisson*. In this moment I wanted him to become blindly, madly jealous. I wanted *Madame Jalousie* to stalk him and claim him. But it seemed the only person she was interested in bothering this evening was me.

'How's poor Honor?' I asked, my voice vicious and mean.

'She's having a tough time…' He was into dangerous territory now, and he knew it.

'You two looked very cosy when I arrived.'

He looked into my eyes. 'Please don't start that again. You have to trust me; you know you can trust me.'

Did I *know* that? At that moment Patrick walked into the kitchen, clocked me, and promptly left.

'Your co-star!' Jacques said, sounding relieved to be able to deflect from the dangerous focus on him. 'You know that guy's mad about you. All that power-play on stage…'

I knew he wasn't. But I wasn't going to tell Jacques this.

'Lovely to see you two together again!' Mark's voice, loud and intrusive, from the doorway.

I held my hand out for Jacques. He took it and squeezed tightly. I loved him with an intensity that shocked me.

Mark moved closer to us. 'How's Louis doing?' he asked Jacques, in a low voice. 'Is he considering what I suggested?'

'He's thinking about it,' Jacques said.

I was finding it hard to breathe. 'I didn't know you met Louis?'

'I know all about alcoholism,' Mark stated, as if he were the world's expert on the topic, and as if that answered my question.

'Are you suggesting that Jacques should cut his brother out of his life the way you did your father?' My voice was shaking.

'Louis is drinking to cover the pain of his abandonment.' His tone was so *superior*. 'So, no, I don't suggest cutting him off.'

Had Jacques any idea how much he had corrupted our relationship by sharing this part of his life – that he had completely shut me out from – with this man who drew shameful secrets from people only to use it later as ammunition against them? I couldn't believe he had brought Mark into his family home, extending his sphere of influence.

I caught myself, smiled. 'So, what was your suggestion? The one that Louis is considering?'

'Rehab,' Mark said.

'Brilliant!' I said caustically. 'I wonder why Jacques hadn't thought about that before.'

‘Sometimes it takes someone neutral to reach the alcoholic.’

I wanted to laugh but couldn’t.

‘Would you two like to try some stuff tonight?’ As if we hadn’t just been discussing someone who was on the brink of death from addiction.

I was glad of Jacques’s response, which was to say, thanks, but some other time.

Mark said, ‘The Wilde ball is coming up soon. Let’s all do some that night.’

‘Including you?’ I asked, genuinely curious.

He didn’t answer, instead said that he had to go ‘look out for’ Linda. She had taken more than the usual amount of the drug and he wasn’t happy. She was becoming careless. I wondered where she had got it from, if not him.

‘Will she be OK?’ Jacques asked, concerned.

‘I’ll keep a close eye and mind her. But going forward she’ll need to follow the correct dosage.’ He sounded as if he were an exasperated parent talking about his teenage daughter. *She’ll be the end of me.* ‘See you both later! And beautiful people … be good to each other!’ He walked away.

I turned to Jacques. ‘Why didn’t you tell me that you brought Mark to see Louis?’

‘Because I knew you’d react like this.’

I was furious, and as usual, tangled up by Mark’s manipulation of us all.

‘Have you been hanging out with him much?’ I asked.

‘We just bumped into each other last week. I’d had a hard visit home, I was upset. He offered to talk to Louis, he sounded like he might know what to do.’

I knew that tone of voice, that ‘I’m-an-expert-on-everything’ voice, even an expert on the person to whom he was talking. *I know more about you than you yourself do* – I knew that one.

‘And you didn’t tell me?’ I was doing that thing again – making it all about me. We were both silent a moment. ‘Your poor brother.’

He looked devastated, spoke defensively: ‘He might just get the help he needs now.’

I selfishly, fervently, hoped and prayed that Mark wouldn't be the architect of Louis's recovery.

Even to this day, I don't know what became of him. Although I have wanted so many times to reach out to Jacques in later years, I knew I could never hurt him with the sight of me again.

*

'That's probably not an accurate summary of how Jacques felt about you,' Dr Collins says.

Today the sun outside at noon is dazzling but in here it is cold and dark. The artificial light is on, dangling overhead. I've never visited at this time of the day before. This room must face due north.

'You don't know what happened…' I think of Jacques's stricken face that night, the way he looked me – as if I were a dangerous stranger.

'Ultimately, no,' Dr Collins concedes. 'But from what you've described so far it sounds as if you were all under the sway of that man.'

'He was only twenty-two – hardly a man.'

'And you were only eighteen.'

I let that land.

'I do think you need to give some credence to the fact that you were all being controlled and manipulated.'

'You don't say?'

I look back now and think of us as participants at a mentalist's show. *And now you are chickens. Cluck cluck cluck. And we grow wings, and we waddle and we cluck and we peck at the ground for scraps. It's impossible not to.*

'Jessica?'

I look at her.

'No matter what happened next, you were not solely responsible. It is my professional opinion that you were unduly influenced.'

I stop, breathe, feel tears pricking my eyes. But then I hear my voice, wild in the wind, egging her on.

'They were my words,' I say.

She looks at me expectantly. No judgement.

'I spoke the final words Linda heard before her life was changed forever.'

'And your life, Jessica, and yours,' Dr Collins says.

47

On our way back to my room, Jacques talked non-stop, a strategy to make sure the conversation didn't curve back in a certain direction. I let him. He talked about Linda's and Mark's stance on the drugs. She was rebelling, I said, against Mark's ultimate control. Jacques laughed, said he loved my dramatic take on everything. As if by labelling everything I thought or felt as 'dramatic' he could minimise what I had witnessed between him and Honor: their easy intimacy, his kindness, his naivety being taken advantage of. Nothing more, I tried to convince myself. He was here with me now, wasn't he? Not with her, and no doubt he could be.

'She is vulnerable, though,' he said.

'Who? The duchess?' I snorted. 'Manipulative madam, more like.'

'No, Jessica.' He sounded fed up. 'Linda – your best friend – is vulnerable.'

I didn't say anything, just counted fast in my head, backwards from one hundred.

No place like home, no place like home, no place like home. Linda is clicking her heels in sparkling red slippers and Sue is showering her in confetti, or sequins, or bubbles, or glitter. I am green, ugly with jealousy and covered in warts and hair, hubble-bubbling some dark mischief in my otherworld, unseen, excluded. Sue is covering young Linda in kisses and then Mark appears, puts his arms around her and the two fuse, like a Siamese twin entity, Mark sucking all the vital nutrients from his smaller twin, until Linda shrivels and disappears. Sue is frantic, *Bring her home*, she beseeches me, tears running down her cheeks. The Sue who appears is the one Dad had loved: young, spirited, full of love and feeling, overflowing with song and dance and sweet buns. I can smell the baking.

'Home' – I thought about that word. Did Linda really have no sense of belonging except to the house she was born into?

The next morning, I felt as if I hadn't slept at all. Jacques had been kind and loving all night, cuddling me to him each time I woke, which was a lot. 'Bad dreams, baby? Tell me about them.' I shook my head; I had no intention of reliving the horrors. When I said I wanted to talk to Linda, he seemed relieved and encouraged me to go find her. 'And when you do, say hi,' he said. 'Sure,' I said, neither of us talking about the thing that needed to be talked about, which wasn't a natural stance for me; I usually dived right in.

Linda didn't seem surprised to see me waiting for her when she came out of her lecture hall. How could she still manage to turn up for her morning lecture and look this radiant after a night of taking hard drugs?

'Shit. You look rough. Everything OK with you and Jacques?'

I didn't share my night terrors with her, the sweats and the shakes. 'I'm just a bit tired. We're good… How about you and Mark?'

'I've never been happier,' she stated confidently. 'Even you have to concede that's true.'

'I don't know what's true any more.'

'And that has to be a good thing!' She linked my arm in hers. 'Let's go shopping. Mark gave me money to buy something for the ball. Will you be my stylist? Pretty please, you have such great taste!'

'What about Honor?' I couldn't help myself.

'Mark suggested that you go with me.' I felt ridiculously happy and *special*. 'He mentioned a 1920s look. What do you think?' I regarded her. He was right, she'd look stunning dressed in clothes from that era: flapper dress and feather boa, hair styled like Clara Bow. 'Have you thought about what you're going to wear?' I had. I'd seen a 1950s Marilyn Monroe ruched swimsuit and thought I'd pair it with a fake fur that I'd seen in the Herbert Arcade. We'd buck the trend of the shiny crinoline debs' dresses with the puffy shoulders, a hangover from the eighties.

'OK,' I said. 'Let's go shopping!'

The Wilde ball was in two weeks: a weird tradition, seeing as we'd have to sit our year end exams a few weeks later. The college was considering banning it because of the recent acid and ecstasy craze that had flooded the campus, meaning brains were considerably more fried in the aftermath and results were on a downward trajectory. (Our year, 1992, was the last one for over a decade.)

'I expect absolute honesty from you about what looks good on me,' Linda said, her energy high and scattered.

We walked, arms linked, across the rarefied grounds – our very own Wonderland – out the front arch into the 'real' world beyond. A world of grey skies and grey buildings and grey faces etched with stress and disappointment. This would not be the story of our lives.

Once we reached the arcade, Linda skipped from stall to stall pulling things off rails with abandon and an exuberance I didn't recognise. There seemed to be no design to the items she chose, then threw on the ground.

'Sorry, sorry,' I kept saying to the shop assistants, following in her wake of destruction.

'Stop apologising for me!' The irony was not lost on me.

'Hey,' I said. 'Have you eaten?' She danced away. 'I'm starving. Let's go to the Lebanese.'

'Mark's Lebanese?' She stopped short. 'Is there a girl called Celine who works there?'

'Why? Did Mark mention her?'

Her face closed down. 'I'd just like to see the place.'

We walked into the cafe, Linda looking obsessively around her, her energy wired. I led her to the booth by the grubby window looking out into the alley. 'This is where Mark and I sat.'

She looked at me sharply. I hadn't intended to play any games.

Celine herself glided over towards us. 'What can I get you?'

Linda seemed mesmerised by her, her eyes roving over every body part.

‘We’ll have the vegetarian mixed mezze,’ I said. ‘And two waters.’

Celine sucked on her pen nib in a sexy yet desultory way, then walked away, Linda tracking her hungrily. ‘Is that her?’

I nodded. We sat for a few minutes, making comments about the dodgy decor, Linda’s knee jigging at a ferocious intensity. I put my hand on it, but she slapped it away. (This version of Linda *was* capable.)

When Celine returned with our food, Linda stared at her in an openly hostile way, though she was trying so hard to be cool. ‘I see what he sees in you.’ Her voice cracked as she said harshly: ‘What does he like to do to you?’

Interesting that she worded it that way – I thought back on my encounter with Mark, when all of it was done *to* me. Was that Linda’s experience too?

Celine studied her as if she were weighing up whether she was worth the effort to engage. ‘I don’t know what you mean.’ She turned away. Not worth it.

‘What was that?’ I asked.

‘I don’t know what you mean.’

I could read her tight expression and body language, *don’t push it*, so I veered off topic, spearing a forkful of food and helicoptering it towards her mouth. ‘Open wide!’

She pushed my hand away. ‘Little cunt.’ She put a crumb of the falafel into her mouth chewing methodically, being careful not to make any sound.

‘Me or her?’

She didn’t respond.

‘Does Mark compare you to other girls?’

‘Where you’re concerned, I come out on top.’

‘How about her?’

Linda stood. ‘Fuck off, Jessica.’ And she stalked out of the cafe without eating another morsel. I sat there, stunned – who was this spiky, mercurial girl? As soon as I could gather myself together, I went to the counter, not giving anyone eye contact, paid quickly, and walked out into the arcade. On my way through, I passed Linda, who was standing in a stall in a long, cream satin 1920s dress. The assistant was telling her how stunning she looked, just as her eyes met mine. 'Ah, here's my bestie! What do you think, Jessie?' She turned around to reveal a low-slung back, her skin translucent and lightly freckled, her shoulder blades delicate and defined, two porcelain wings at rest. I stopped, caught my breath.

'Sorry for being a bitch,' she said. 'That girl really pissed me off.'

'That dress is made for you,' I said, astounded by how beautiful she looked, the silk clinging to her angular body made her appear, in Sue's words, 'gamine'.

The assistant handed her a string of pearls and long satin gloves, and then draped a fur stole around her shoulders. She froze. 'Take that thing off my back.'

'It's not real fur,' I said.

'Actually it is,' the guy said, proudly.

'Take it off, take it off,' Linda incanted under her breath. She looked like she might faint as I removed the article from her body.

'Have you any imitation ones?' I asked.

'Sure, but why have fake when you can have the real thing?'

'We have an animal lover here,' I said.

He looked at us as if we were mad but returned a few moments later with a fake stole. 'Bit cheap looking,' he said.

'It's perfect,' Linda said. 'What do you think, Jessie? Is this it?'

Although I felt cheated that I hadn't been the one to spot the outfit first, I had to concede that yes, it was perfect. I even liked the rat's tails nature of the wrap, it added to the decadence of the look. Linda flashed Mark's card and bounced out of there, me following on her heels. As soon as we hit the fresh air, she fumbled in her pocket for cigarettes and a lighter and lit up with shaking hands. Did Mark encourage her in sucking on 'cancer sticks'? She inhaled deeply.

'That was a dead animal around my shoulders.'

'Well, it's not suffering now.' I studied her. 'But you are.'

She exhaled smoke through her nose, like a dragon queen.

'Can we start again with our girls' day out?' she said, as she took another drag, held it in her mouth for a moment before she pulled me to her, and blew smoke into mine. She handed me the cigarette and I took a puff, then threw it on the ground, grinding it with the ball of my foot in an exaggeratedly sexy fashion, as if I were wearing stilettos. I was Olivia Newton-John in *Grease* when we were younger – and still now today. I would always be the lead. I studied her closely for signs of wanting to be number one, but she didn't seem to mind. She made the old familiar gesture of bowing to my grace, beauty and undeniable talent. I was momentarily re-instated to the pinnacle of us.

'Come on, girlfriend. Let's see you in that swimsuit you were telling me about. I bet you look drop dead,' she said, her colour high.

I blew her a kiss, took her by the hand and led her to the vintage store, a tiny saloon-style place decked out in velveteen on every surface; even the floor had the ragged, fake red-velvet carpet treatment. The whole vibe was indulgent and slightly seedy, the dimly lit changing rooms reminiscent of an old-fashioned brothel. Linda wolf-whistled (I didn't know she could), as I wriggled my body into the Monroe-style swimsuit.

'There should be a licence against a girl like you wearing something like that!'

I grinned. 'Meaning? Too slutty?'

'No, too damned gorgeous. You make the rest of us mere mortals look like trolls.'

I quite liked that idea even as I knew it wasn't true; the advent of Honor had toppled me off my perch. I turned around in front of the mirror as Linda slapped my bottom. The swimsuit had been an inspired idea, I had to admit: the bottom half fitted like hot pants, the ruched top made me look like I had boobs, and the halter neck straps accentuated my gymnast's shoulders and toned arms. I flexed my biceps as Linda squeezed them. 'Nice guns!'

I turned around and wiggled my behind in the mirror, starting to get high on the attention.

'The best buns on campus!' she said, clapping wildly.

I was doing an approximation of what would now be called 'twerking' – though at the time there was no such language for a white Irish girl shaking her stuff.

'You need a coat of some kind,' she said standing back to assess me.

'Do I, though, really?' I was still warm from the exertion and liking the look of my bare shoulders.

'Yes, you do. It'll be freezing outside at four in the morning,' she said, sounding more like her old cautious self. She shouted out to the assistant, 'Do you have any faux furs?'

The girl handed us a bolero-style, dark brown glossy number. 'You sure this isn't real?' Linda asked. The girl looked baffled, said, 'Too cheap to be otherwise.' I was sure it was factory-farmed mink and, though I didn't like the idea, I wasn't going to say anything; the thing was long dead now anyway, and it was perfectly slinky and sybaritic. I liked that it smelled of must.

'Fishnet tights and platforms, to complete the look … what do you think?' I said as I went out into the main shop and pulled the shoes and tights off the shelf.

Linda blew me a kiss. 'I think you're a genius! Put on the whole outfit,' she said. 'I'll join you.' We went back into the changing room as she fished her satin dress out of the bag and stepped into it. I pulled on the fishnet tights.

'Dress rehearsal!' I said, delighted. The part of me that loved to be on-stage understood the transformative nature of a costume, but as this was real life, it intensified the charge. I suddenly got what each image change did for my friend's expanding sense of identity.

She removed my bra. 'Don't need one with those perfect Kate Moss buds. Sexier without.' She was right. We stared at each other's reflections in the looking glass and were mesmerised. By our own beauty, youth, the currency of it.

We skipped out of there on a retail high, having spent fifty quid of Mark's money on my outfit, a small fortune back then.

'Tell Mark I'll pay him back,' I said.

'Oh no, you don't have to do that. He'd like the idea of being responsible for dressing us both.'

A thrill coursed through me. Of course he would.

'Fancy another sociological experiment?' she said once we were outside.

I looked sideways at her, adrenaline building.

'Let's go find somewhere we can cause some trouble!' she continued.

'Yasss,' I shouted, a full shot of cortisol now coursing through my veins.

'I know just the place!' That dangerous edge to her voice propelled us along the city streets, through the doors of a dreadful anodyne bar, all white and antiseptic, a recent addition to the Dublin scene, a sanitised import peopled by young stockbroker, lawyer, trader types. 'Perfect,' I said, as she pushed open the door. As we made our grand entrance, many heads turned. Were we *actresses*? We headed straight to the bar and perched on high stools, our hands touching each other's bodies, which seemed to whip the men around us into a state of hormonal agitation. You could feel the tension. The power of it.

Mark's scholarship money paid for four rounds of G&Ts.

'I think I'd better stay at yours tonight,' she said, giggling, flushed and electric.

'Won't Mark mind?'

'No. He's encouraging me to spread my wings a bit.'

'In what way?' I asked her.

'Just. To be free, you know…'

'Does he want you to be sexual with other people?' I went on, almost blurting out a confession, half believing that she might be on board with it, but even in my loose, loquacious drunken state, I knew that could never be spoken aloud.

She cocked her head to one side. 'Do you think Jacques would like this dress?'

I batted back: 'Do you think Mark would like me in my swimsuit?'

'I think both our men would approve of each other's girls.' She caught my eye, then ran her finger over the rim of the glass and ducked it in the gin before placing it in my mouth. 'Now suck,' she said. She had been instructed well. A ripple ran through the bar.

'Hey, not to upset you or anything,' she said. 'But what's going on with Honor and Jacques?'

'Nothing,' I said, too quickly. 'Why?'

'I think she likes him.'

'Well, that's her problem,' I said. 'I'm secure in our relationship and she can fuck right off.'

'Have you ever heard of the concept "compersion"?'

'No. What the hell is that?'

'Being happy for your loved one's sexual freedom, or something…' she said, biting down on her cuticles.

'Linda, feck's sake.' I rounded on her. 'That's not you.'

'I wish I could be less possessive.'

'That is bullshit. And you know it.' I went on, incensed: 'Look, the duchess could have anyone on campus and she's gunning for my man. She's a megalomaniac egomaniac.' My anger rendered me inarticulate.

'She genuinely likes him,' Linda said, now tearing at the cuticle on her right index finger with her teeth.

Did she believe this, really? 'And do you?' I asked, removing her hand from her mouth. She let me.

'What? Like Jacques? No, don't be ridiculous. That's *paranoid*.'

'No, I mean, do you like her?'

'She's a good friend to me. But I don't like that she's moving on your man – though I also see that's quite parochial of me.'

I smarted. *Parochial*. The fucker. 'How is she a good friend?'

'We have a lot of fun. She doesn't judge me. She likes me for who I am.'

Which version? I almost asked but stopped myself.

'I do feel like I'm expanding, as a person, you know. I feel free recently. Like I'm me for the first time in my life, you know?'

Those words were becoming an anthem for our group.

She went on: 'I don't hear my mother's vicious voice in my ear everywhere I go. I don't feel her accusing eyes on me…'

'And I'm happy for you, Lindy, I really am. But –'

'Always a "but" where my happiness is concerned.' She looked sharply at me.

'No, I mean, are you sure those drugs are good for you? Your moods are all over the place.'

'Look who's talking! *Ms Moody Myrtle!*' – Sue's term of endearment for me when I'd stomp through the house in one of my hormonal rages.

I smiled. 'I'd hope I'm a little less chaotic now.'

'Maybe a little…' Linda winked at me.

Two guys in suits took this as their cue and they approached us. 'What are you having?' one or the other asked.

'Each other,' Linda said, as she leaned forward and French-kissed me.

I wasn't sure if it was all for show. One of the guys clapped, the other silently observed. His gaze was the most attentive. He ordered a bottle of champagne – 'the best' – and we drank and we drank and we drank and I bombarded Linda with questions: Is she making a move on my man? Is she? Is she? Who does she think she is? Fuck aversion, or conversion, or compersion, or whatever the fuck… He's mine, mine, mine… I remember the men laughing and one of them saying what a possessive, feisty little thing I was, and how he would like to be all mine. He said I was *intense* and that was beyond sexy.

Here, my memory fails me. Nothing… Except Linda and I woke up naked together in a bed in some empty corporate apartment high above the cityscape. 'Creepy,' Linda said, looking around her as we both shivered our way back into our clothes. At least whatever had happened involved the both of us. To this day I don't remember any of it: I don't recall leaving the bar, or how we got to the apartment, or what they did to us, or whether we did things to each other, or their faces, or how I got the bruise on my underarm. I have never asked Linda what happened that night. I might have, but it seemed so trivial in comparison with what subsequently played out. And anyway, no harm done: no one was seriously hurt, no need for stitches, and as it turned out, no one was pregnant.

'Mark will be proud,' Linda said as we walked home in the cold grey light of the dawn. I doubled over and vomited, thankfully all over my pedestrian clothes, as one of the men had carefully folded our dress-up outfits into a tote bag and laid it on the bed with a note attached: 'Thanks for a ball, Racy Bitches.' That bit I do remember.

48

'Wilkommen… Bienvenue… Welcome!' Mark was a cabaret act, dressed in a smoking jacket, pinstripe trousers and rust-coloured dickie bow, his hair mussed, sporting impressive stubble I hadn't known he was capable of. '*Mr Conscious Contrivance of Disorientation*' – though, it had to be said, he wore it well this evening, with an even more poised arrogance than usual. He was holding a silver tray aloft with a bowl full of pick-and-mix sweeties, which he offered to everyone who passed through the threshold of his door. 'Close your eyes… Lucky dip.' Jacques and I had agreed that tonight we'd go for it. We'd look out for each other, we said.

I had barely been able to look him in the eye since that morning when I came home covered in vomit two weeks previously, rambling that I had stayed out all night to mind my friend, who was so pissed she couldn't walk, and wouldn't get in a taxi because of the recent scares involving drunk female students, so we got a hotel room, to stay safe. (Linda was a sport, happily taking all the blame, before she crashed out on my bed.) He bought the story, no questions asked. Before – before what? Honor had begun to drown him in attention, and Mark and he had become *close*? – he had been attuned to the tiniest shift in my mood, but recently he didn't seem to notice or care that I had withdrawn. We continued to have sex, I went through the motions, sometimes even enjoyed it, but was there any intimacy any more? And where did I go to in myself?

'*C'est-le-moment-il-est-temps*!' Jacques said, putting his hand in the bowl, just as I did. We locked eyes, nodded at each other and ceremoniously popped our pills at the same time. Linda appeared just at that moment, with two goblets of red wine.

'I thought we weren't meant to mix with alcohol,' Jacques said.

'No rules tonight,' Mark said.

'It's the Wilde Ball!' Linda said, stating the obvious. She was amped up to the extreme, elated and gorgeous, her lips defined in a new wine-red lipstick and her hair wavy and tonged à la Clara Bow.

'Looking lovely tonight, Linda,' Jacques said, in an entirely appropriate manner, which didn't lessen its impact on me.

She blushed a pretty deep pink. 'Looking good yourself. Love the suit.' Jacques was effortlessly delicious in a dark maroon velvet suit. I didn't know where he had bought it, or with whom. I was too scared to ask.

'Not so bad yourself, either, Jess,' Mark said to me, sounding amused. His eyes took in all of me, resting on my inner thighs, clad in my fishnets. A rush of warmth and wet spread between my legs.

Linda came close to me and breathed in my ear. 'She's stunning, as ever.'

I caught her eye and curtsied. 'Why, thank you, girlfriend!' Neither of us had spoken about the drunken night since it happened.

'Thank my generous man,' she said. I threw a warning look at her, and she caught it.

Jacques appeared confused, but no one enlightened him that Mark had bought our outfits, even though Mark was regarding us both with customary possessive delight. I had no intention of starting this night off on the wrong foot.

'Hello, beautiful people!' Jonathan said, coming through the door, looking like an old-fashioned movie star in a tailored midnight-blue suit. Linda wolf-whistled, again, this time with even more vigour and lasciviousness. Was this another trick Mark had taught her? Jonathan smiled delightedly. 'A gift from Phil,' he said. More accurately, from Phil's *daddy*, I thought.

Jonathan took his pill and the goblet of wine, kissed Linda on the cheek, told her she looked dazzling. As he passed me by, he reached out for my hand and squeezed it tight. 'You ride!' Tonight was going to be a good night.

Inside, candles danced on every surface, flickering to the agonisingly soulful voice of Sinéad O'Connor, her voice modulating from a soft whisper to an agonising growl in a heartbeat. Mark had chosen her album *I Do Not Want What I Haven't Got* to set the tone: hip, transgressive, transcendent, raw, something to get the heart going – the perfect score for the psychosexual melodrama he was orchestrating.

People milled about, more than I had expected: floppy-haired boys in suits and bow ties, shiny black formal shoes or scuffed leather slip-ons, girls in the expected crinoline debs' dresses, shaggy, layered hair, and neat 'mammy' heels paired with black tights. There were others, the outliers, who sported bra tops and tight trousers and loose, tangled hair, teamed with Doc Martens. Though these girls were somewhat racier than I had envisaged, Linda and I still outshone them all. Our originality was without doubt. Sinéad's hypnotic voice rang out: 'Nothing compares to you.'

I had thought we were to be a select gathering but it seemed that Mark was feeling magnanimous. He was offering a free gateway. Had he supplied drugs to everyone here?

'Hey, slow down,' Jacques said. I was on my second glass of wine. 'We need to pace ourselves, see the effect this has on us. I'd rather you drank water.' His fingers crept underneath my fur stole and stroked my bruise. He whispered, 'Are you ever going to tell me where you got that?' I thought he hadn't noticed.

The drug worked fast on me. The world suddenly snapped into sharp focus, organising itself into straight lines: this life, its external chaos, this room, the messy people in it, my internal tumbleweed all aligned in a horizontal and vertical criss-cross direction – coded, ordered, contained. A similar experience to that one time I tried cocaine, where it felt as if Dublin had transformed into the gridded streets of New York, which I navigated sure-footedly, a rock star, in the highest dagger heels. Then just as suddenly as this feeling came over me, it changed into something softer, flowing: I was barefoot in a field, in soft sunshine in the west of Ireland, and I was assailed by such beauty – the wide-open skies, the bleating lambs, the green, green grass –that I wept, openly.

Mark walked in our direction. 'Hit you already, I see, Jessica?'

I smiled. My eyes were portals to heavenly realms.

'How about you, Jacques?'

'Nothing yet. Do I need some more? Seeing as I'm such a big brute?'

'No,' Mark said. 'Trust me. It'll hit.'

Scattergun memories assailed me: the scent of honeysuckle, which I hadn't smelled since my childhood, Sue's baking, the soap she used to wash me with – 'Pears' *so soft and smooth and kind*; the feel of her hands gently brushing my hair and tying it with a pink satin ribbon; and oh! my ballet shoes, and the two of us dancing, me *en pointe*, her hand on my lower back, holding me steady. Light, tinkling piano music wafted and soared, so delicate and aching I fell to the floor – I had to. I lay there for a moment on my back, staring at floating dust particles, tiny dancing fairies. Jacques sat down beside me, laughing. 'I hope I have even the tiniest bit of what you're having!' I sat up and cuddled him, as a vision of my father floated before my eyes. He was tickling me, telling me to 'stop the crying now, no need for tears' – laughing, always laughing, everything was a joke, but it wasn't, was it, Dad? Then the tears became about grief, but still pure, still cleansing. A light filled me, sparkling white. I was in it, I was of it, I *was* the light.

'You look so radiant,' Jacques said.

Mark was standing over us. 'You two are so fucking beautiful. You've no idea…'

Jacques started to laugh so hard that his body shook, and tears streamed down his face.

Mark was studying him. 'There now, Jacques, I told you!'

Jacques turned to me and engulfed me in a bear hug as the two of us lay down on the bare floorboards and were entranced by life and each other, our fingertips alive with prickling sensations and almost unbearable ecstasy.

This first rush spiked fast, then receded, only to build again at various points in the night, each crescendo perfectly orchestrated by the maestro – or so it felt. Mark was everywhere that night, planting whispers, setting things alight, pushing his 'subjects' as far as they could go.

Jacques and I managed to sit up, using each other to lean against, and we swayed back-to-back in beautiful harmony. Then, sometime later (time had no meaning) we stood, before we separated briefly, before coming back to each other, before separating and coming back again, flowing like a river, away from and towards the source. I was one with it all, free of all conditioning, all ego, all jealousy, all envy, all insecurity as I walked, nay, danced! around the room. There in the corner, was my darling, dazzling friend Jonathan with his new lover, who made him so happy. Who was I to want anything less for him? I threw my arms around my friend and told him that I loved him, then said to Phil that anyone who made Jonathan happy made me happy. My heart was open and expansive and full of a powerful love that surged against my ribcage. Phil laughed, and I didn't construe it as mean or condescending. We both loved Jonathan. *C'était tout.*

Jacques came behind me and put his arms around my waist, squeezing tightly. '*Je t'adore*,' he said softly into my ear. The most beautiful words in the most delectable language I had ever heard: fresh and delicate and erotic all at once. I turned to him and we kissed, eyes closed, the sensation like edible velvet.

In that first phase of the night there were no challenges to my happiness, my equilibrium. In other words, I didn't see Honor at all.

We stayed in Mark's rooms until night fell, so that we could slip outside into the melee of the ball under cover of darkness. I couldn't believe he'd gotten away with getting so many people in for free. (Of course nothing was without an agenda with him: they were sure to be indebted to him after, especially since he was so generous with his goodies.)

'*Perpetuis futuris temporibus duraturam*.' Mark spoke our college's motto, as he opened his front door into the magically transformed grounds. *It will last into endless future times…*

Flashes: a giant spinning disco ball underneath the campanile, exploding into fire, sparks flying, pinwheels, Catherine wheels, pink helium balloons, roving lights, neon pink and green spots on statues of monolithic men, past provosts, writers, philosophers, spotlights calling out their maleness, scaffolding still at half mast, marquees, circus troops, fire-breathing stilt-walkers, dry smoke, strobe lights, techno tents, rave gigs, ska band, dance tents, the Prodigy, baggy trousers, people milling, spilling, passed out, a giant stage set, a stranded car installation, flashing screens, litter strewn, Carlsberg cans, flashlights chasing, noise, insane decibels, smoking, dope and cigarettes, acid-dropping, ecstasy, love, food stalls boasting 'Victorian hog roast', feather boas, suits, dickie bows, screens, sweat, sex in public places, and dancing, dancing, dancing.

The fresh air, when it hit, propelled me into a sort of ecstatic frenzy. My body started to cartwheel, on the cobblestones, in my platform heels. So much of what I recall of this stage of the night is a sensation of tumbling, of feeling like I was Topsy-Turvy (is there such a Blytonland? There should be).

In a heaving, sweating dance tent, the Cure's frisky 'The Lovecats' was playing. How I LOVED this eighties absurdly theatrical jazzy number, and I started to prance, like the kitty cat I was. Miaaaoooowwww. Jacques was hovering beside me, laughing. Jonathan and Phil were openly making out on the dance floor, and I felt buzzed. Finally, my friend was being true to himself. Linda, my bestie, was drawn to me from the opposite side of the marquee by our shining golden umbilical cord of love, which tonight flowed unimpeded between us. The world was one big open-handed place filled with beauty and magic and music and dance and song and soul and '*la lumière et l'amour*'. The heat and the sweat, the bodies moving, the euphoric tingles, and oh how Sue would love this! My heart suddenly ached for my darling Sue. How I had neglected her. No more. Tomorrow we would go visit her in our finery in the cold light of day and she would feed us home-made scones and hot tea and she'd light up in the radiance of my love. In a startling flash of clarity, I saw the truth for what it was: Sue standing in our shitty kitchen on the eve of our departure for college, saying, 'Fuck your father, the narrcccisssisttt…' and I thought, yes, Sue, yes, you were right. He left. You didn't. You could have.

'Let's go see Sue tomorrow,' I whispered in my best friend's ear, and she beamed and said, 'Yes let's', then twisted my wrist so hard that it burned. Then, she leaned her lips against the pulse in my wrist and kissed me there.

'Your heart is beating so wildly,' she said.

'Yes,' I said, pumped up on my young, rushing blood and an insatiable thirst and appetite for the new. I undid the clasp of my tiger eye pendant and hung it around her neck. 'Looks beautiful on you.' I had never felt so generous, so expansive. The amber winking light offset her shining hair and the luminescence of her skin. She placed her hand over it and closed her eyes, said nothing, just swayed as if in rapture.

Moving inside the Dungeon now: packed, hot, heaving, stoned, humming, its walls wet and sozzled, no windows, no ventilation and the Prodigy were playing, and it was where everyone wanted to be. There was electricity in the air and heat in our bodies and I wanted to rip everyone's clothes off, craving skin-to-skin contact and the sound of hearts walloping against each other and the taste of sweat and the bliss and sweet agony of prolonged orgasm and the delicious darkness of oblivion and the feeling of recklessness and love and belonging and *holy holy holy*. So many mouths to taste, so many bodies to explore. Jacques was on high alert, aware of my porous boundaries. I found him irritating and constraining, protective and perfect, my knight, my captor. The tempo on the dance floor went up a notch and the crowd became even more energised, crazed.

That's when I saw her: my nemesis in an emerald green 1950s swimsuit, a replica of mine, although hers looked prohibitively expensive and in an eye-catching colour and she looked fucking mind-blowingly gorgeous with her thick, mussy, dirty-blonde hair thrown up into a loose chignon with naughty curls cascading down her neck. Had Linda told her about my outfit? How else could she have known? Static started building up inside my head. I stared at her, as she stood at the edge of the dance floor, sucking on a straw, surveying the plebs who almost fell at her feet in wonder at her beauty. Then her perfect face lit up as she waved at us: me and

Jacques. Jacques waved back, his eyes glittering dangerously. Just at that moment someone swept her up from behind, lifted her off her feet, twirled her in a circle. Patrick. Of course. He planted her down on the ground and turned her to him and the two of them French-kissed theatrically before he swaggered off, and she continued her siren's journey towards us. Jacques was entranced as she swayed in our direction. If she thought she was going to do a repeat performance… Linda seemed to appear out of nowhere then, a sprite, a dangerous little minx, as she whispered in my ear, 'Compersion…' A pounding in my head: the beat of the music, the rage, the rage, the rage, the rage. Honor was in front of us, her eyes shining, light emanating out of her. Her radiance was blinding. She held her hands out for my man, said to me, 'Do you mind?'

'Of course she doesn't.' Linda placed her hand on my forearm. She poured into my ear: 'Let him have his freedom.'

Jacques looked at me, smiled widely, shrugged. 'Just a dance, baby.'

The two of them moved into the centre of the floor, and there was much jostling of bodies, and someone blocked my view and I tried to swallow, but it was as if I had chewed on shards of glass.

Linda pulled me close, cheek to cheek. She was crooning nonsense. 'If you let him go, he'll come back if he's yours… But then, *yours* and *mine*. What are these but petty concepts designed by insecure people?'

I broke away from her, stared directly into her eyes. It seemed that this was the part where the truth serum kicked in. 'Right well, then, in that case you won't be surprised to know that Mark and me…'

'Shhhhhhhhhh,' she silenced me by putting a finger to my lips. 'What I don't know won't hurt me.'

It was as if someone had thrown a bucket of ice over me; a cold clarity hit momentarily. 'That's fucking bullshit and you know it…'

She looked at me, her eyes brimming with light and tears, and said, 'No. I will not have you ruin this beautiful moment.'

'How's this for a beautiful moment?' I shouted as I ran into the centre of the dance floor to find the duchess undulating in front of my man. He was transfixed, staring at her, as she oozed sex. If looks could slay, mortify, burn, I would have pinioned Honor with my stare, then lifted her and thrown her on a pyre. The *witch*. The drug granted me no such supernatural power, only an ability to fixate.

A breath in my ear. 'You OK, sweet-cheeks?' Linda's voice from behind me. 'There's enough of Jacques to go around. Don't worry...'

Did she not see what I saw? The sorceress – with a plan afoot to steal him, the love of my life, and her, my best friend in the whole universe, without whom this life held no meaning, or so it felt in that moment. My whole body was jangling, a discordant screeching noise, a sound like foxes mating in the night filled my ears. *La Jalousie* saw her opportunity and she seized it. She climbed inside me and occupied all of me spectacularly.

Mark was watching me from the other side of the room. I could see his eyes glinting in the dark, his mouth twitching. *O beware ... the green-eyed monster which doth mock the meat it feeds on...*

Linda squeezed my hand before she moved away from me towards the enchantress, who turned to her with an open smile and open arms. They dissolved into each other and began to dance slinkily, my man still staring, bewitched. The two girls were vibrating with wanton energy, two exhibitionists unleashing super-ninja sexual vibes. Had we started the same year, there's no doubt the duchess would have been Top Filly and not me. I was about as in control of myself as a two-year-old in the throes of a tantrum when I flung myself into the centre of the dance floor and pushed my boyfriend out of the way with so much force he almost toppled over. My arms outstretched towards the girls, ostensibly in a gesture of female camaraderie, *Come, my beautiful goddesses*. I grabbed hold of both their hands, and we spun in circles, then as the music intensified, the crowd started to jump, head-bang, and the dance floor became a mosh pit, inviting wildness – and carnage. Not my fault. It was my forehead that made contact with the delicate cartilage of her perfect nose. A clean break, apparently. Only an accident, a silly, unfortunate accident. Honor seemed fascinated by the flood of blood coming from her nose, which others attributed to the drugs. She wasn't in the least distressed; there was that.

Linda was shocked into momentary sobriety as she grabbed me forcefully by my arm and steered me off the dance floor towards the ladies. 'What was that, you loon?' She seemed on the brink of exploding, whether with anger or laughter, I couldn't tell. The duchess even looked fucking gorgeous with blood pumping onto her lips and chin and, of course, as soon as it happened, she was surrounded by her minions. It didn't matter; none of that mattered. I had reinstated m'anam cara, ma meilleure amie, my *sister blister* by my side – by whatever means necessary. Jacques was following close behind us, trotting after me, where he belonged.

In the mirror in the toilets, we were witnessed: the rush and charge of seeing the reflection of our young, lithe bodies, intensified by the drug running through our veins. A sudden snap: the blue lights made us look ghoulish and I felt nauseous. A cluster of girls gathered. 'You look like a clown,' I said to one of them, who had way too much rouge on her cheeks and lips. She was pouting pathetically and studying her stupid face at all angles. 'Oh, look who it is,' one of her friends said, about me. 'And just who the fuck is it?' I said, way too loudly. 'Who, may I ask, am I?' I looked at Linda, who was doing that colluding bullshit thing with these other girls, shrugging at them apologetically. I wanted to smash her stupid face against the mirror – Linda's and the clown's and then all the rest of them. The shifts in mood were swift and acute.

'Jacques better not be anywhere near that witch,' I said as Linda escorted me out of the ladies. He wasn't, he was still waiting outside the loos, concerned for me, not for her. 'Baby,' he said as he wrapped me in his arms. I grabbed onto Linda who was trying to skip away, having delivered me safely. I wouldn't let either of them go. I clung on to my dearly beloveds as if without them I would collapse and crumble and nothing would be left of me but dust. After some time, Linda and Jacques managed to extricate themselves from my tentacles, and they stood apart from me but still close enough so that I could touch them. Mark and Jonathan wandered over to us and Jonathan asked if I was OK, the concern on his face real. 'Are you hurt?' I felt the beginning of a bruise on my forehead as Mark said, 'That's going to be quite the shiner tomorrow.'

How I revelled in the attention, the fact of the five of us being together again, with me at the centre.

Memories come and go, flickering impressions: the intermittent shock of the cold damp air as we moved between sweaty interiors and the cool outdoors; the trees, glorious giantesses, whispering invocations in the wind; the artificial lights in the darkness, strobing, stroking, shocking; the clouds whipping – there *were* lands beyond this realm.

'What is dem stars?' Linda said dreamily when we were out of range of the thumping beats.

'Those twinkling things in the bright sky?' I asked, playing along.

'There are no stars, Linda. It's too cloudy,' Mark said.

'I see them too,' I said.

Mark said something about twinkling hallucinations and seeing only what we wanted to see.

'Pretty intense back there,' he said, slyly.

'The Prodigy does something to a person,' I said.

'Whips them up into a frenzy, you mean?' He went on. 'I hope Honor's injuries don't threaten her future as a model.'

'What injuries?' Jacques asked.

'It looked like her nose was broken when your mad girlfriend banged against her!' Mark was gearing up.

'You make it sound like it was deliberate!' Jacques said, affronted for me.

Mark turned to me. 'Was it?'

'Was it what?' I said.

'Deliberate? Did you mean to break her nose?'

'I should fucking hope so!' I said, as Linda sniggered. We caught each other's eyes, and she poked her tongue at me narrowing its tip. I did the same back, rolling the two sides so they touched.

'That's amazing!' she said. 'I didn't know you could do that ...'

'There are many things about me that you don't know!' I said, echoing her earlier words to me.

'Don't be ridiculous, baby, it was only an accident,' Jacques said, unwilling or unable to conceive of the possibility that I might be psychopathically jealous. And capable of such violence. I went to him and hugged him tight. 'Of course it was only an accident,' I whispered in his ear.

I turned to Jonathan. 'Where's Phil?' I asked, needing to flip the attention away from me.

'I'm not his keeper,' Jonathan said, having been schooled well.

I blew him a kiss. 'You two are so good together.'

Mark smiled. 'My, we are expansive this evening!' He pushed his glasses up on the ridge of his nose.

I had to stop myself from guiding his hand to my inner thigh.

He looked at his watch, then smiled at us. 'I think it's time for a top-up, don't you?'

Jacques furrowed his brow as he looked at me and Linda, asked was it necessary. Jonathan told him not to worry, this was the best bit.

'I have the dose perfectly titrated,' Mark said.

For what, exactly, I remember thinking even as I swallowed the pill. We all did.

Who knows how much volition we had at this stage anyway?

Immediately I felt a rush of warmth. 'It's such a beautiful night!'

'Actually, it's unseasonably fucking cold,' Mark said.

'Well, I'm hot, hot, hot…' I felt as if I had a fever.

Linda laughed. 'What part are you playing now?'

I put on my best absurdist French maid's accent. 'Ze fire is burning within me…'

'Oooh la la!' Linda said.

I started to run, propelled by a restless energy, an unquenchable heat, the others following, whooping and hollering, through the playing fields, clouds scudding across the night sky, a glimpse of the moon illuminating body parts, white buttocks for the most part, bobbing up and down. The cricket pitch was the scene of orgiastic abandon.

'Wow!' Mark said in wonder. Was he thinking he was responsible?

'Phil better not be one of those butts!' Jonathan said.

'You don't own him,' Mark said.

Jonathan went silent, his eyes glassy. I started cartwheeling, someone was cat whistling, I wanted to experience every extreme state I could, I wanted to be on a different plane, high, higher. Out of the darkness loomed the silhouette of the Wise One. There was bewitchment afoot, and her branches were bony fingers beckoning me.

I looked at Linda. '…It's a really enormous tree… Its top goes right up to the clouds – and, oh Rick, at the top of it is always some strange land…'

'Oh Rick,' Linda said, sighing dramatically, as we walked closer. I placed my hand on the giantess's trunk.

'What are you two going on about?' Mark said and I could see that it irked him, our private world that he had no access to, which filled me with power.

'What is the Wise One saying?' Linda said, leaning her ear against its bark.

'Adventures await!' I said, climbing up to its lowest branches.

Linda hitched the hem of her long dress into her knickers. The boys watched, clapping and laughing. I reached down for her hand and pulled her up beside me.

Linda shouted down: 'Truth or Dare?'

'Dare,' Mark shouted back.

'Well?'

'Climb to the top! Push your limits.'

(Had he orchestrated that we get here, to this tallest of trees?)

The two of us climbed up effortlessly to a high branch, where we hunkered down in a nook, like woodland creatures. Voices were shouting below. Linda looked down, shivered.

'Are you scared?'

'Terrified!' she said, grabbing on to me, laughing wildly.

'Time to conquer your fear of heights,' I said, playing a part whose lines had been written for me.

Both of us were crouched on the same sturdy bough, which transformed beneath us into a silvery, golden, coppery moving thing, a broomstick, a magic carpet, a rocket, transporting us to far-off places. The sensation of the fire inside whipped and seared through me, gathering in my throat and splitting my vision, so that what I saw next was not imagined but as real as anything I had ever seen.

'See that ladder there?' I said, pointing into the pulsating sky above the tops of the kaleidoscopic trees.

'Not sure I do,' she said.

'You do, you do, it's golden and glowing.'

'You are so high!' she said.

I put on Sue's best storytelling voice: 'At the very top of the tree they discover a ladder which leads them to a magical land…'

'The Land of Goodies,' she said, looking up.

'I think we entered that place many hours ago!' I hollered. I stood, letting go of the branch I had been holding on to, and simulated flying, my arms outstretched to their widest span. Linda grabbed on to my ankle and squeal-giggled, a sound that was equal parts fear and excitement. I continued, 'We can go anywhere … the Land of Take-What-You-Want, the Land of Do-As-You-Please…'

She shouted at the top of her voice, 'The Land of Freedom.'

A challenge, a threat, a blowing me open.

I bellowed out a bugle sound (more in Golding territory than Blyton-land). A rustling in the leaves far below us, a warning.

'I dare you to climb the ladder,' I said.

'I still can't see it,' she said.

'It's only visible to those who believe in magic.'

Linda's face was pure enchantment, her pupils huge and dilated, as when Sue first read *The Faraway Tree* to her, and she stood shakily on the bough, holding on to the trunk for balance, determination in every bunched muscle.

'Climb, climb, climb,' a chant erupted out of me. I was channelling some force bigger than me, possessed by a need to wrest back control, to be her number one.

She reached up to grab hold of a higher branch and tried pulling herself up. I was flitting in and out of extreme spaces of lucidity and spaciness, but my memory never fails me on what happened next: I cupped my hands together and I gave her a leg-up.

Jacques's and Jonathan's voices rang out from far away, shouting as if underwater, instructing us to come back down now. Mark's voice pierced through, or was it my own? 'To dare is to lose one's footing momentarily.'

Linda and I were in our own private gilded world of childhood, and she was fully mine again. 'Do you see the ladder yet?'

'I think so.' Linda stopped where the branches became perilously thin, where the sky met the tops of the tree, and looked down at me from the precipice, in terror and bliss. She held her hand out for me to join her. I shook my head at her and smiled in encouragement. 'You have to go alone.' I would be the final link in her bid for liberation; I would be the defining voice in her ear. I reiterated the vow that I made to myself the first time I had witnessed her in her terrible home: to forever be her protector, her saviour. I wanted her to be free of her past, free of her mother, free of that man. *Breaking free requires a sort of severing* – in that moment, Mark's seductive logic was fully my own.

She turned back, looked up at the shimmering sky, and took a deep breath. I watched, filled with love, in awe at her bravery. She climbed and she climbed even when it appeared there was no more tree, and then I saw my Silky Fairy step onto the ladder, her wings poised for flight.

I made no move to stop her as she walked up those golden steps into thin air.

The End

49

I blacked out then, a sensation of falling: can guilt make you do that? Shock can. Cowardice can. Horror can. Shame can.

Still today, I imagine I saw her tumbling, crashing to the ground; I imagine I heard a sickening thud, a crack; I imagine I saw her twisted at the base of the tree, unconscious; I imagine I heard the sirens, saw her being carried on a stretcher; I imagine we were all together in the ambulance; I imagine (most impossibly of all) that Mark proved himself to be a loyal boyfriend, apologising for his part, for the dare, for supplying the drugs that were responsible for the whole wild ride; I imagine Linda woke as I stroked her brow, that she walked on crutches for a few months, then she recovered; I imagine we all remained friends.

In reality the last thing I remember was her on the ladder, which was as tangible as anything else from that night. Then I was on the ground. I must have climbed down that tree unscathed, for I recall standing at its base, looking up, as the dawn crept in and cast everything in a cold, harsh light. The tree was bathed in blood. I vomited. No one moved to touch me or comfort me. Between us, only silence and chill.

The comedown that followed was everything I deserved. The isolation, the not knowing what had happened to her – there is no memory of an ambulance, or her body on a stretcher, though these things happened. I desperately craved Jacques's arms around me, but his body was rigid, arms by his sides. He couldn't look at me, let alone touch me. He must have heard me, seen me egging her on. There was no denying any more who I was, what I was capable of.

I rack my brain for a picture of Mark in the immediate aftermath. He was there, I know he was, but he was so detached it was as if he were a stranger observing a collision on a motorway. And then, if I hold the image, burrow down into it, I can see his mind ticking over, his generative mind, that would in time reap creative rewards from this calamity. Was there any remorse? Or ownership?

No, he had set me up perfectly. He had steered his creations on the road to wilful destruction. He had unleashed the forces of chaos. And in the final analysis I was his star.

Jonathan and I tried to keep in touch for a while, meeting on campus, attempting to talk about it, then trying not to talk about it, trying to keep things casual, to keep our connection, or even the appearance of one, but it was as if we were allergic to each other, physically making each other sick. I never saw him with Phil, or anyone else, in the months that followed. Mark managed to complete his scholarship and sometimes in the year that followed I thought I saw him, but he always disappeared. He perfected the knack of vanishing just as perfectly as he had of materialising: out of the ether, back into it.

Jacques never spent another night beside me, and then I *was that sink-hole*. Still am. I finished out my remaining three years, but they remain a blur. Jacques must have graduated later that year, but I have no recollection of it. I spent the remaining time at Wilde, scuttling about in the shadows where I belonged. I was no longer anyone's number one. *HUP!* replaced me at the top of the list the following year. I managed to just about hold on to my bursary – and my life. There was no sex, or none that I can remember, none sober, anyway. (But this stinks of self-pity, and it won't go into the novel.)

*

'What happened immediately after the accident?' Dr Collins steers me back to the sequence of events.

I wince, imagining hearing the crack of Linda's spine.

'Linda was in hospital for weeks, then months in rehab, then she moved in with Sue.'

I think of that strange portent of a nightmare, me hubble-bubbling in a dark corner, excluded, unloved, rejected, by my own hand.

'A very generous thing for her to do.'

'A very Sue thing to do.'

I think of how she kitted out our home so that it was wheelchair accessible, and no longer my home, but a place that would forever confront me with what I had done.

'Linda broke her back at eighteen. Imagine the pain, the trauma of that?'

'There's no denying the impact of such an injury on such a young life, but it sounds as if she adapted well with a lot of support.'

I think of how she embarked on a PhD in psychology in the last few years, in her mid-forties. I think about the care Sue has provided and how close the two have become; how much they rely on, and love, each other. And how much of an intruder I have become.

'But her life could have been, *should* have been, a lot easier.'

'And your life, Jessica?'

I think of my doomed marriage, my failed career. And my self-inflicted isolation from the only family I ever knew. The last time I visited six months ago was excruciating, the polite pretence we were enacting choking us all.

I am uncontrollably struck by grief, and for once I let my tears fall unchecked.

Dr Collins pushes a box of tissues in my direction.

I almost roll my eyes but there's not a trace of the actress left in me.

'I miss them.'

The unbearable weight of this guilt is moving through my body, making me shudder and convulse.

Dr Collins leans in ever so slightly; she holds the silence, the space, beautifully.

'Have you decided on your ending?'

'I finished college, somehow, and the five of us never spoke again.'

'I don't believe that's the end of the story…'

‘You mean it needs a coda?’

‘There is room for something else, yes.’

I look out the window: an unlikely shaft of light illuminates the wall, and the mould is transformed into a soft bed of bright green moss, and I see a teeming otherworld, peopled by tiny creatures. There are lives, realities, beyond my own.

I turn back to Dr Collins for the last time. ‘I have a title,’ I say. ‘For the novel.’

‘Yes?’ she says.

‘*TRUTH GAME*.’

‘I like it.’

‘The final note is still undecided.’

‘All my favourite books end on a question… Space for a new beginning.’

I realise that she is much better than I ever gave her credit for.

‘Finish it and send it out.’

‘But I don’t fully remember.’

‘No one fully remembers,’ she says.

I look at my hands, notice that the veins are protruding even more. Time is passing.

‘It’s your version, your truth, your story. Own it.’

‘Thank you – for everything,’ I say. I mean it.

‘Pay heed to your life, Jessica. Be kind, stay present, pay attention…’

Her voice trails me as I leave for the last time.

Outside it is a gentle day in May and I notice. The scent of freshly mown grass, the play of light. This theatre called life.

CODA

I stand outside my childhood home. *C'est-le-moment-il-est-temps* – I woke up this morning to Jacques's voice in my head – the first time I'd heard it since that night. I try to calm myself, to pay attention, to notice. Two scrawny tabbies are stretched out in patches of sunshine – stray cats are still drawn here. I see bowls by the front door, one for water, one for food. The door has been painted over, no longer fuchsia, but a lacquered black. Looks smart. Not like Sue.

I walk up to the front door, my finger hovers over the bell. I feel Dr Collins's hand on my lower back, guiding me forward. It is over two years since I last saw her. The book is out in the world; it sold well. The narrator is too unlikeable, the reviews say, too self-absorbed, and then expecting the reader to give a shit, or some version of this. At least I didn't completely let myself off the hook.

I press on the bell. I swallow and wait. No one comes. I imagine I see curtains twitching at the upstairs window. But then I notice that the car is not in the driveway – they are not hiding from me. I almost faint with relief. I place my hand on the door, close my eyes. Am I praying?

One of the cats comes to me and rubs her mangy body against my shins. I bend towards her, my fingers automatically rub under her chin, and she stretches her neck, inviting more. I lean in and kiss her on the top of her head. Too much. She hisses, swipes the air, withdraws.

The light fades, the sun cools. I find the last patch of sunshine, sit in it on the doorstep. Almost thirty years have passed since that night. I think about the concept of legitimacy, of ownership, of memories. Was it ever my place to write about it?

The cat comes back to me and sniffs. I let her take her time, make no move to startle her. She climbs up onto my lap, her paws kneading me, as a deep purring starts. The sun disappears; I think I hear the car chugging up the street. I hold my breath, the cat stops her thrumming, mirroring my unease. Every part of me wants to bolt.

The car is in the driveway now, the glare of the headlights startles the cat, so it digs its claws into me before running away. I steel myself to stand slowly, to smile, to face up to my past.

Sue rolls down her window, 'Hello, stranger … What are you doing standing there in the dark?'

I can make out the outline of Linda in the back seat. I imagine she is eight again, and she is sticking her tongue out at me, its narrow tip an arrow. My God, how I missed my strange little alien.

'I came to see you both,' I say.

Sue climbs out of the car, leans against it, as if to steady herself.

'Sorry it's been so long.' *Lame.*

'You're here now. That's the main thing.' She stays where she is, at a safe distance.

My body wants to fold into hers.

I am that girl whose father left. I see her standing on the doorstep, clinging to Sue, sobbing, wailing, then kicking, hitting out, and I want to hit her back, but Sue is cuddling her, comforting her. I smell the freshly baked fairy cakes, hear Abba's 'Waterloo' blasting, his swan-song, our battle cry. (Ever the drama – not my fault.)

Sue goes to the back door of the car, opens it, attaches a ramp so that Linda can wheel herself out. *Hello my sister blister.*

'Hey,' she says.

'Hey,' I say back.

'I read your book.'

I inhale sharply, hold the air in my expanded ribcage.

Sue walks to the boot, busies herself with shopping bags.

'I'm sorry,' I say. 'I should've told you.'

She shrugs. The air between us fills with everything that has been left unsaid.

'It was honest.'

I allow myself to breathe out a little.

'Much better than the Whitman version.'

'Oh, you saw *The Jealousies*?' I say, exhaling fully.

'I did. I hated it. Overblown, theatrical nonsense.'

'The critics liked it,' I say.

'Of course they did,' she says. 'They remain as seduced and bamboozled as we were.'

My voice is small as I ask, 'What did you think of his ending?'

'I preferred yours,' she says.

'I agree,' Sue says as she joins us, her arms weighed down with Tesco bags. 'No way was it all that girl's fault. Your version allowed for more nuance, complexity.'

'Oh you read it too?' My throat constricts. I had thought I was prepared for this.

'You were both drugged, groomed…' Sue plonks the bags down on the driveway.

'I didn't completely absolve that girl though. I didn't mean to anyway.'

We all fall silent, the years unspooling between us.

After some moments Sue speaks. 'I'm so proud of you … I've wanted to say that for a long time: how proud I am of both of you.'

I go to press on my sore spot but I stop myself, breathe, swallow.

'You know Linda graduated last week?'

'Finally,' Linda says. 'The oldest grad in town!'

'Congratulations, that's incredible,' I say. 'You're incredible. Are you "Dr" now?'

Linda nods briskly. *None of that fawning, patronising stuff.* She wraps her coat around her and wheels herself towards the front door.

'I liked your title,' she throws over her shoulder.

I look at her in her wheelchair and think, *some fucking game.*

'Well, are you coming inside?' Linda says from the doorway. Sue falls in step beside me, her arms now laden with the groceries. I reach out and help her, carry some of the bags. She turns her head and smiles, the edges of her eyes crinkling. *This.* My heart – it dances.

I cross the threshold.

ACKNOWLEDGEMENTS

Thank you to my tireless agent, Clare Alexander, for your patience, guidance, and insight. To my powerhouse editors, Allegra Le Fanu at Bloomsbury and Tara Parsons at HarperVia for your brilliant, sparkling input. I am indebted to you both

To the whole team at Bloomsbury, it is my honour to be published by you again. Special thanks to Fabrice Wilmann, Akua Boateng and Thea Hirsi for all your hard work and belief in the book. To Charlotte Norman, for your copy-editing skills. To Carmen Balit for the inspired cover design. To the publicity wonder team: Ben McCluskey, Cormac Kinsella, and the book's greatest advocate, Allegra Le Fanu. I can't thank you enough for your energy and support.

Huge gratitude to my fellow writers and friends Joanne Hayden and Elizabeth McSkeane, who read many, many drafts and gave generous and incisive feedback along the way. To Tom Farrelly for his vision and friendship. To Linda Walsh, Hugh O'Conor, Emer Conlon, Michelle Moran, and Michele Forbes for their kind reading, input and encouragement. To Paschal Gannon for his kindness. To Gillian Stern for her early reading and perceptiveness. To Anne O'Neill for her dynamism and cheer-leading.

Thank you to the Irish Arts Council for the opportunity to be Writer in Residence at University College Cork. To my colleagues, Liz Quirke and Danny Denton for the inspiring chats. Eibhear Walshe, we miss you dearly. You were a guiding light for so many.

To my students at UCC and everywhere I have taught, including at The Irish Writers Centre and Arvon. Your curiosity and passion are inspirational.

To the Tyrone Guthrie Centre, Cill Rialaig, and Arvon for providing beautiful spaces in which to write.

To Trinity College where I went in the early 90's and again in 2013. To my tutors on the M.Phil. in Creative Writing at TCD: Deirdre Madden, Carlo Gebler, Mary Morrissy and Eoin McNamee.

To my parents, sister, brother, uncles, and all my family and friends who supported me along the way. Special shout-out to my four-legged buddies. RIP little Faye, you were quite the warrior; you're sorely missed curled up at my feet.

To you, the reader.

To F. For bringing the light and love.

A NOTE ON THE AUTHOR

LISA HARDING is a writer, actress, playwright and the author of two novels. Her previous book *Bright Burning Things* was shortlisted for the Kerry Group Irish Novel of the Year and The Dalkey Group Prize. It was a *New York Times* editor's choice, a Today Show Book Club pick, a *People* Magazine pick and was named as a book of the year by the *Observer*, *Grazia*, the *Irish Times* and the *Irish Independent*. She lives in Dublin.

A NOTE ON THE TYPE

The text of this book is set in Minion, a digital typeface designed by Robert Slimbach in 1990 for Adobe Systems. The name comes from the traditional naming system for type sizes, in which minion is between nonpareil and brevier. It is inspired by late Renaissance-era type.